I0822742

# EMBRACE THE MAYHEM

**Wonderlust Book Two**

Maddison Cole

Dirty Talk Publishing

*Embrace the Mayhem* by Maddison Cole

First published in Great Britain in 2023 by Maddison Cole



Editor: Jo Preston

Cover Designer: Megan J Parker-Squiers

Illustrator: Nautilus Visuals

Print ISBN: 978-1-916521-03-2

*Best friends are like perfectly-brewed cups of tea.*
*Difficult to find, but once discovered, there's no going back.*

*For my bestie Jo, without whom I'd perish in a pit of despair.*

# CONTENTS

# TWEED'S PROPHECY

This world hangs on a precipice, the outcome still unknown.
The Knave is the deciding factor on what happens to your home.
Should he choose correctly, no more blood needs to be shed.
A soul intended to be a pair will fuse to the one he weds.
Heed this final warning, should you remain to stand.
For one queen to thrive, the other must fall, by her descendant's hand.
Find the final Caterpillar's cocoon, keep it hidden until the day,
That marks the twentieth anniversary, of when Alice went away.

# MALICE'S PROPHECY

Two women stand on a hill, high above a sea of carnage below. Dismembered beings, human and animals alike. Thick rivets of blood carving a stream back towards the town I fled from. More specifically, right up to the front door of the abandoned Hattery. Movement on the hill draws my attention, a shadow stepping out from either side of the women. I notice their crowns now, tall against the sunset. Regal dresses burst from their tiny waists, dwarfing their similar heights. The shadow's outlines betray who they are, but not once do their features come into the light. The Queens lean into the side of their designated Tweedle, staking their claim as a voice booms from the sky.

*One is your destiny, the other your demise. Revive the world that once was before twin blood moons rise.*

# CHAPTER 1

Up. Down. Shining crimson. Purest blood. Blood that smears. Blood that stains.

I refocus, throwing the apple again. Up. Down, fitting snugly into my palm before departing once more. My eyes track the movement, back and forth. Away from my face, then close enough to cross my eyes. The stone floor is cold against my back, though it has long since lost its icy edge. Goosebumps prickle at my legs beneath netted stockings, the only reminder I'm still grounded. Still capable of feeling, which I wish to avoid. The entirety of my focus is captivated by the apple leaving and returning to my hand. Up. Down. To and fro. A solid weight. A concrete form.

There are worse ways to spend the rest of my life. I've traded one cell for another, but I sure do have a new story to tell. One of deceit and duplicity. Two betrayals, one I welcomed and one which blindsided me. I don't know which is worse.

Glinting by lantern light, the apple continues to gravitate back to me, much like the fleeting memories I hold at bay. My mind is mush, sloshing around my skull like the waves of a restless sea. Somewhere in the undertow, voices whisper, urging me to dip my toes in the water. But no. There is no sense anymore. No rhyme or reason. Only the sphere of red thumping against my palm, drawing me back to the realness of this room. This prison.

Movement shuffles in my peripheral. Muttering prickles my ears, but I bat the words away. Muffle their concern, avoid their all-knowing eyes. Eyes similar to the other apples amongst the fruit bowl. Shining green granny smiths, wrapped in twine and trickery. I purposely took the red one to remind me what's at stake. My insanity, my life, the very tainted blood in my veins. A memory niggles at the edge of my subconscious, a flash of fang. Hint of a smirk. Images I cannot entertain. Switching hands, I catch and throw the apple before words written along the length of my left thumb catch my attention.

*Read me.*

The hesitation is minor, but enough. Slipping through my fingers, the weight of the apple crashes into the center of my face. I cry out, holding the bridge of my nose as my eyes water. A fresh wash of red blossoms against my skin, the tang of copper so deep within my senses, it's all I can smell and taste. As I turn onto my side, both forced and real tears drip into a nest of vibrant, orange curls. Leather binds constricting my body creak as I push myself upright, shaking the pain from my skull. *Fucking apple.* You had one job – to keep the doctor away. Seems we all fail in our duties sometimes.

Spotting the scrawled writing on my thumb once more, I open my hand to see more scribbles covering my palm, a list stretching along the length of black veins which now web across my wrist and forearm.

*What I know:*

*Gloopy egg head vision.*

*Destiny and downfall.*

*No men left.*

*Cash is a cunt.*

~~*Tweed's dick is huge.*~~

*Stan is safe.*

*My name is Malice.*

*I'm the Mal Hatter.*

Yolky ash lingers in my throat. I try to claw my tongue free of it with chipped nails when a small murmur comes again. "Did you say something?" I tilt my head, ears twitching and tongue still scraping around my teeth. Hatter pauses crocheting another coaster, brightly colored wool trailing between the mess of cups and plates across the littered table. When he doesn't answer, I blink a frown into myself. I'm sure I was doing something. Maybe...thinking something.

Shrugging, I place the fallen top hat back on my head. It shrinks to size, nestling between the curls as if now part of my appearance. Spotting a stick of charcoal beside my thickly soled boot, I smile and let my consciousness withdraw, base instinct taking over. There's happiness to be found in detachment, contentment within distancing from the plague of thoughts which quickly overwhelm. If only I could remember what I was supposed to be avoiding...

***

As the last nub of charcoal between my finger and thumb crumbles its final mark onto the wall, I sit back on my heels. At some point, I lost concentration and started doodling a man with a spade on his chest being eaten by the Bandersnatch. Do I know him?

A tug of foreign emotion tightens in my chest with a vice-like grip, claiming my next breath and sealing it inside my lungs. He's familiar, despite the jagged spikes of his hair being the wrong color. Curious that I decided he should deserve such a fate. I don't even know him. I raise my fingers to scrub the Bandersnatch's jagged teeth away as a teacup smashes against the wall. A waste of perfectly good tea seeps across my drawing, washing away all evidence I was here at all.

I glare over my shoulder. Hatter whistles through the gap in his front teeth, avoiding my gaze as his eyes wander in opposite directions. Dormouse isn't so shy though, full on scowling at me from beneath the teapot lid. No wonder all of our tea tastes like fur and ass.

"The twin to win is to smother his brother," Dormouse growls through her tiny teeth, sinking from view. My brow twitches. Twins. *Tweedles.* Clarity spears my mind like sunlight on a frosted morning. A rush of betrayal and lust captures my heart, mirages flashing behind my eyes faster than I can track. Maneuvering myself into the nearest chair, I sway off balance. Cash's devilish smirk is front and center, framed by Lillianna's laughter. The longer I envision his glistening green eyes, visualize his razor-sharp fangs, the harsher my heart beats.

I know better than to submit to clichés, being a walking one myself, but still...I was desperate for Tweed to be the bad guy. My bad guy. I always fall for the villain, and I wanted to screw him to kingdom-cum. But it was Cash I should have been guarding myself from. I should have seen his motives from miles away. Perhaps I did. Maybe that's why I fell for him so hard. And look where that got me...trapped.

I glance around the narrow room, large enough for our six-seater table. Clocks cover the wall, all out of tune with one another amongst the empty picture frames. Once I've latched on, those tick, tick, tickings bury into my skull, my eye wincing of its own accord. Sometimes, Hatter wills the back wall to open up into a forest for a leisurely stroll, Fantasy Walk accommodating his every whim. All, except the one which would see us escape.

Time is unobtainable in here. It flees as quickly as it lingers, filling the air with the stale stench of regret. Each drawn-out second causes my anger to fester, my grip on the chair beneath me causing the wood to crack. Another teacup hurtles through the air, flying towards my face as I barely react to swipe it aside. Keeping my hand raised, I turn my wrist to flash a middle finger in Hatter's direction.

"Stop doing that!"

"Stop thinking. The past stays so, for the future to flourish."

"We're not flourishing much in here," I grumble, standing and kicking the chair away. The legs splinter, groaning wood collapsing in a heap where I recently sat. "We're wilting in body odor. Spiraling into boredom. What's the point of having this power to believe anything into reality, if I can't believe the damn door to open?" It's my turn to throw things, anything which comes to hand. Plates, knives, scones. Hurtling the teapot with Dormouse inside, she yelps at the wall's impact and floats on a mini parachute to sit on Hatter's shoulder.

"Ancient magic courses beneath our very feet. For where the castle of Clubs once stood, a Club of new has taken its place." Hatter swirls the fingerless glove of his hand around in the air. A rare moment of lucidity centers both of his differently colored eyes, their keen focus eerie. "The Shadowlands consume innocence. Their rivers run with the ink of a raven's quill. Only Red Kingdom can overpower such malevolence, consuming the very blood of their enemies to feed their crimson intentions." I shudder under the weight of his gaze, his grip on me like bands of steel. Then he blinks, and it's gone. "But, nothing a cup of tea can't fix."

Sighing, I move to sit in my chair, forgetting it is a heap of splintered wood on the floor, and join it in a tangle of limbs and screams. My butt hits the stone so hard, it will surely bruise. Scowling at myself, then my companion, I ponder what my life has become as I scoot over to the wall. The only one clean of drawings or clocks. The one which would provide my freedom, should the asshole on the other side deem it possible. Folding my arms, I huff, burying my head in my knees. Nothing a good cup of tea, and a nap can't fix. If only because I have nothing else to do.

# CHAPTER 2

A faint click causes my world to spin as I fly backward and crack my skull against a carpeted floor. Pain blossoms deep underneath my orange curls. My breasts, strained in the leather corset, heave for clarity. A pair of black combat boots are planted either side of my head, the curious head tilt of their owner staring down at me.

"It's been eighty-four years," I rasp, my eyes searching his emerald ones for a hint of recognition. Strong hands whip me upright and spin me into a tight embrace.

"It's hardly been two hours, you crazy loon," the male growls, at odds with how he snuggles into my neck. He inhales deeply, once, twice, and I do the same. A woodsy scent, similar to the one I've been ignoring, floods my system. The one I've been desperately trying to erase from my memory. Then an undercurrent of fresh mushrooms and raw pine seeps through the fog, circling with an equally solid embrace as his arms. *Tweed.*

I don't allow myself to collapse into his hold, my senses remaining on high alert for his mirror-image. The one I'm going to flog, skin alive, screw one last time, and spear a diamond dagger into his heart while I climax–in that order. I'd better write it down before I forget.

Pulling back an inch, Tweed searches my face. A fight happens between his features before he relents, licking the dried blood from my face. His soft moans of pleasure are hard to deny, as is the rough pad of his tongue. Energy pulses through my body, awakening me from the avoidance coma I'd allowed myself to slip into.

Deeming me clean, there's a brightened spark to his eyes, a rippling happening within his muscles. Despite the strange clucking sound he makes, scraping his tongue against his teeth, his thumbs absentmindedly stroke my biceps, the icy burn of his touch searing me into reality. In my mind, his hair wasn't as sun-kissed, his skin not chilled into such flawless alabaster. But his frown is exactly how I remember. Lips purse in my peripheral as my eyes wander toward the club's lobby.

"Cash isn't here, if that's who you're looking for. I remained hidden until he and Lillanna left for her castle. We need to get back to the Red Kingdom before they return."

Then he's gone. Distancing himself to the other side of the hallway. It's only when I feel the cold sweep of Tweed's walls crashing down between us that I realize I should have hugged him back. Given him the reassurance I too feel the insatiable need to grasp onto something concrete, and hold on for dear life. Green eyes skate over my shoulder, Tweed lowering in a bow.

"Good to see you again, Hatter. You've been sorely missed." At Tweed's announcement, a gloved hand slides over my shoulder, Hatter's face coming into the artificial light.

"Absence is the greatest form of presence." Hatter glances at the crocodile skin wallpaper. I half look his way, admiring the similar shades of our orange hair, but my attention is elsewhere. Adrift on the various shaped doors lining the walls on either side of the hallway, on the sentinel statues at the far end, each metal body representing a different card suit. Like the men locked in Arabelle's dungeon, awaiting their freedom. Those bearing red symbols, the heart of a blood ruby and diamonds of crushed cherries, hold spears in their frozen hands, glinting with retribution. Exact replicas of those I killed in Diamond Maze.

Memories flutter past, seeping from the walls to play out and disappear once more. Even seeing myself, blonde and full of hope, feels like another lifetime. Then, when a flying seahorse appears and I know what, who, is coming next, I drag my eyes back to Tweed. He avoids looking at me directly, his mouth thin now instead of pressed with concern as it previously had been. It's been merely two hours for him, but much longer for me. Weeks, perhaps a month, stuck in a confined space with my thoughts. An extremely dangerous situation to be in.

"We must hurry," Tweed has already turned away. "Arabelle is waiting."

"Ughhhh," I groan. "Screw Arabelle, I'm ready to return to your cottage and never see anyone again except you, Hatter." Tweed looks through me blankly like I'm a fucking idiot.

"Hatter has pledged his allegiance to the Hearts. It's where he must return to." Returning to address Hatter, Tweed dismisses any follow-up arguments I may have had. "I've arranged transport from the Hattery. It is the quickest and safest option." Removing yellow bottles from his tweed jacket, I spy the small hat-shaped door by his feet. Hatter rounds my front, humming a tune as he wanders towards the entrance of Fantasy Walk.

"'Fraid not," he wags a finger in the air. Tweed frowns over his shoulder but doesn't argue. Pocketing the bottles, he crosses his hands in front of his cargo crotch, every bit the Knave he was always meant to be.

"Portal through a painting?" Tweed queries further. Hatter continues to stride away.

"Not possible," is mumbled with a shake of orange curls. Dormouse slips out from the hair at Hatter's nape to perch on his shoulder, looking back and also shaking her head. I miss when Stan would do that.

"You're Hatters," Tweed states with a bite to his tone. He has yet to compliment my new attire or appearance, but he's no fool. It's likely Tweed knew what I was to become since the very beginning. "You can believe us to be in Arabelle's bedchamber for all I care. We need to go as quickly and undetected as we can."

"Look closer, young Tweedle. The hike ahead won't only be a physical one." Hatter turns one way, then swivels on his heel and disappears from view in the opposite direction. I groan, shrinking my shoulders inwards and draping my arms. *Hike*, after Cheshire knows how long lazing around. A yawn forms at my mouth and as I attempt to cover it, Tweed snatches my wrist mid-air.

"What the fuck is this?" he growls. Those emeralds in his head burst with a glow of fury, jaw clenching hard at the writing marring my skin. I merely sigh, failing to tug my arm back.

"Look, I know some people have an issue with the c-word, but it was all I could fit in such a small space," I attempt to twist myself free once more. Tweed holds me to the point of breaking my wrist. "Oh, this is about striking out your huge dick. It's great and all, but I've had better." I twist my mouth, shrugging in a way that says '*I'm really not that sorry*' about it either.

"Stop deflecting with your lies," Tweed grinds through his fangs, dragging me a step forward. I snort. "This," he points at the black webbing creeping from my palm towards my elbow. I tilt my head. Huh, perhaps there are more spindly lines than the last time I looked. "What is this?"

"You really should learn to be more specific, *young Tweedle*," I mock Hatter's tone and bop Tweed on the nose. "Yeah, that. I was stabbed by Lillana's thorn and now black magic is attacking my magic so we need to be boring mortals and walk everywhere. Sucks, huh?"

This time, Tweed does release me, his grip going slack like his jaw. Not one to dwell for too long, and not allowing the poison of doubt to spread further, I follow the way Hatter left, swishing from one side of the hallway to the other. After being cooped up, I want all the space at my disposal. The boots behind me don't make a sound, stationary where I can hear the cogs turning in Tweed's mind as if the words were tumbling from his full lips.

*Plagued. Plagued. Plagued.*

I figured that would be the end of it. Tweed can't save a dying girl, neither can the prophecies be fulfilled. As I locate Hatter rifling through Cash's old bedroom for fresh clothes, I also presume Tweed's stomping boots are him making a grand exit. But I was wrong. Whipping me around, his solid chest crushes me against the wall.

"I shouldn't have left you in the trial," Tweed pinches the bridge of his nose and steadies himself. "Any use of magic will only accelerate the flow of poison, and I can no longer feed on you, lest I would become infected too." I scoff, rolling my eyes. Trust Tweed to be looking out for himself at a time like this. "I mean it, Malice. *Do not*, under any circumstances, use your magic."

Unlike last time, there's no familiarity in his hold on my arms. No relief at my wellbeing. Only rage as if he were scolding a child. "No chicken fried fingers, no believing yourself to have wings or scales or to glow in the dark. Do you understand?"

My eyes widen and my mouth pops open. *Holy shit, I can do that?* Tweed seems to read my mind, a growl only he can achieve tearing from his throat. The length of his body presses against me in what I'm sure is supposed to be a threat, but does nothing to intimidate me.

"How long have you known exactly who and what I am?" I query, lifting his head to meet his gaze. Our lips are a breath apart. I feel his conflict, the uncertain twitching of his fingers. It's Tweed who looks away first.

"There's a treaty dating back centuries. Red kingdom requires a Hatter to reside on its grounds in order to keep the balance. It's my duty to return you to safety." Tweed pushes away from me and I slowly clap my hands together.

"Incredible job avoiding the question. What a diplomat you could be." My claps echo around the archway I've found myself in, adjoining the rooms of Cash's apartment together. Each one is louder than the last, like the claxon of a cannon firing. Must be twice as loud and annoying to vampire ears. Within seconds, Tweed is thrusting a backpack at me with the order to pack supplies.

"As you wish, dear Knave," I smile sweetly and curtsey. If Tweed wants to pull rank on me, reminding me that he is acting out of his duty to Arabelle, then I'll assume the role of unhelpful prisoner, starting with the bag in my hand.

# CHAPTER 3

"Did you pack *anything* other than alcohol?!" Tweed shouts as we stop for our first hydration break. He helpfully holds the backpack open, gaping inside, so I can lift a bottle of rum out for Hatter and a pink gin for myself, dragging the cork out with my teeth.

"Of course I did. I'm not a total idiot." I take the bag from his hands and lower onto a fallen tree trunk. Digging around in the bottom, I drag out the bowl of honey-roasted nuts I snatched from the bar. Most have spilled all over the bottom of the bag, but a few have remained cozy in the glass bowl which fits snuggly in my palm.

"A couple of nuts for two adults," Tweed stares at me. Just stares, as if he expected a full camper's inventory and med kit.

"Why didn't you just pack yourself if you're going to keep judging me about it?"

"I don't know what humans like to eat," Tweed grumbles and paces away. I call bullshit. He wasn't always a vampire and even if he has forgotten, he's cared for Arabelle long enough. When a spike of jealousy slithers through me at the thought, I drink harder.

Hatter hums to himself, circling the dirt around my log. The woods are becoming dark, the trunks around the clearing seeming to grow taller against a dying sunset. Finding his preferred spot, Hatter crosses his ankles and lowers to sit. Just before his ass touches the ground, a picnic blanket appears. Three flasks filled with steaming tea, sandwiches wrapped in wax paper, and an open bag of oranges so plump they look like they've been freshly picked from an orchard litter the blanket before him. Okay, maybe having real supplies on hand isn't the worst idea.

I casually slump down to join his side, taking my gin with me. Hatter untwists the cap of a flask, lifting it to his lips as Dormouse dives from his shoulder and enters the tea with minimal splash. He either doesn't notice, or prefers her fermented taste. Each to their own, I suppose. Tweed doesn't wander too far, returning every so often and adding to his firewood pile. I pointedly ignore him, mostly because of the way my heart double-flutters with each appearance.

Firstly, because my mind keeps falling for the trap it may be Cash returning to kiss me senseless with apologies. Then I remind myself I hate Cash's traitorous guts, and the second flutter comes at remembering how Tweed held me. How relieved he seemed to have me back in his arms. It's a dangerous path to trek, wondering if someone as dead inside as Tweed might actually feel an inkling of emotion other than hatred for me. We work better as captor and annoying tagalong.

Luckily, my focus is shifted beyond that and the squelching of the orange in my hand to a shadow of movement nearby. Followed by the snuffle of a whisker-framed nose, a small bunny edges closer toward the blanket.

"Hey, little fluffy," I muse, offering out a segment of orange. He hops over, sniffling further before taking a bite. Instantly, his eyes bulge and roll back in his head, just before his head twists around in several full circles. I hastily drop the orange and gin, grabbing hold of his two floppy ears. This only causes his body to spin instead, a horrendous high-pitched squeal escaping him. Without knowing what else to do, I throw him as far as I can. His little body sails through the air, screaming the entire way until he lands and scampers away with erratic movements. Hatter just watches me scrape my hands down my leather corset, trying to rub the rabies off.

"Do rabbits have a citrus allergy I don't know about?!" I try to calm myself. Lifting the discarded orange, Hatter carefully twists it around to reveal where my teeth have pierced the skin. Like a virus caused by my saliva, black ebbs into the center, bleeding through until the orange is rotted from the inside out.

"Oh," my shoulders sag. "I have the plague." Silence settles. The heavy type. The wind shifting through the trees tries to soothe me with a lullaby, as does Hatter by pressing his shoulder against mine. I force a smile up at him. My chosen father. The man who believed in me and would never cast me aside for not being what he expected. I reckon I could tell Hatter I'm leaving for the real world to become a nun and he'd wish me a safe journey. He knows I'd return. With him is where I belong, and for that reason alone, I will see through the prophecies. The curses and betrayals, and whatever else is coming my way.

Something flickers in the distance. Directly ahead through an opening amongst tree trunks. At first, it's faint. So much so, I passed it off as my imagination, but then it glows brighter. Flickers against the horizon.

"Um, Hatter?" I say softly, pointing towards the light. "The fuck is that?" He nudges me aside to get a better angle, needing to put extra effort into centering both of his eyes. Instead of answering, I get a quizzical hum and suddenly Hater has shot to his feet. Dormouse is quick to clamber from the tea flask to climb his patchwork trouser leg, as Hatter clicks his fingers and the picnic around me disappears.

“Do you think...” I stand, and then I feel it. A tug. Falling into step with my predecessor, we clear the woodland with even, long strides. Everything else tumbles away into the falling night, the canopy of branches barring us from what could be a beautiful, starry night. Nothing is as beautiful as the light ahead though, shifting from the deepest purples, through palest pinks and onwards to the brightest yellows.

“Malice!” someone shouts, but it’s too distant. Muffled by the space in-between. The air is dense, while the wind seems to be blowing stronger as if trying to guide us toward the mysterious light. Approaching its steady pulsing, two giant wooden doors like that of an abandoned barn become highlighted. The closer we get, the more the light ebbs, as if it’s waiting for us. Drawing us to step inside and behold whatever treasures are hidden there.

The wood is rough under my fingertips as I push the huge door open, the creaking of untouched hinges almost deafening in the silence. Inside, the space is vast, stretching out before us in what appears to be a Gothic cathedral. Carved stone walls hold delicate tapestries depicting of old and new, whispered secrets etched in every arch. Stained glass windows dance with kaleidoscopic illusions, painting the interior in hues of forgotten dreams.

Amidst shadows and light, the cathedral itself seems to be breathing, expanding and collapsing around Hatter, Dormouse and I as we creep down the central aisle. The light pulses steadily at the altar, casting eerie shadows on the dusty pews. I shiver involuntarily, wary of the thousands of eyes staring down from above.

"Hello?" I call out, my voice echoing around the room. There is no answer, and the light hastily goes out. My heart is pounding, the adrenaline rush making me dizzy. Instead, my hand hunts for Hatter's, my voice betraying the truest fear I've felt in a long time. "What is this place?"

"You already have the answer you seek," is Hatter's response. I expected similar, and he's right. I feel it as surely as I know Tweed's dick really is the largest I've ever seen. It's instinctual.

This is the Cathedral of Time Passed and Yet To Pass. Against my peripheral, the characters displayed are shifting, accommodating the will of their current company. It's that fear which has my gaze refusing to move above my usual eye level. I don't want to know. I refuse to see what may become of my life, or relive the past events which have brought me here. There is only the present where I'm concerned.

"This way," I urge Hatter to cut through the pews where a door awaits, ajar and eager. It's simple compared to the grandeur in which it resides, an aged slate of wood and simple brass handle. Hatter doesn't hesitate, permitting himself entry without looking back. Once again, I follow his lead and step onto the candle lit staircase descending within.

Magic thrums through this building, the intense kind which would only present itself to those who require it. There's a reason the cathedral appeared to us, why the light coaxed us at this precise time and place. I can only hope it has something to do with curing the poison in my veins. Finding out I have an unlimited amount of power at my fingertips, only to not be able to use it, is a cruel trick. But not one I can't handle.

The temperature plummets. Cold skitters through my netted stockings, slipping through my corset as if it's not bound with thick leather. Regardless of the solid stone floor beneath our boots, we were descending into a rabbit hole, falling into a dark abyss with no way out. I know this, but there's no going back now. If only I had a fierce protector who would pull me out before I fall too far.

Blowing out a shuddered breath, a thick, fur-lined coat drapes across my shoulders, reaching the back of my knees. I wrap it around myself, smiling at the back of Hatter's orange curls. He doesn't pause until he reaches the bottom level, pressing a kiss to my forehead before continuing. Lighted by similar floating candles, a long hallway stretches out before us, devoid of sound and life. The air is thick with the scent of dirt and decay, making the recently ingested orange churn in my stomach.

Suddenly, there's a soft whisper, as if someone is calling out to us. "Wanderers," comes the choked murmurs again. We freeze, unsure of what to do. Any sense of calm reassurance the pulsing light had given is quickly snatched away. As my eyes adjust to the darkness, the shape of an old woman silently shuffles towards us. She's hunched over, with a gnarled cane in one hand and a flickering candle in the other. Her eyes are pure white without irises, her long wispy hair the same color.

"It's been too long since I've had Wanderers," her voice is crackled like a fire dying in a pit. Gooseflesh lines my skin as the last of ember of that fire is snuffed out, and I drag the fur coat tighter around my body. "Ask what you seek. I shall answer."

What I seek? What *do* I seek? The longer it takes to come up with an answer, the more I shift uncomfortably on my feet. It shouldn't be so hard to know what I'm looking for, but the answer is as obvious as the old woman's need for a facelift. I have no idea. No purpose. I'm flittering around, doing as I'm told, going where I'm asked. But I'm not in control of my life anymore. I don't have a say in what becomes of my fate.

"What am I even doing here?" I ask, hating the vulnerability she steals from me so easily. Her answer is instant.

"This is the tale of a lost, desperate child." Immediately, my heckles rise. "She surrounds herself with those loyal, but they do not provide what she needs."

"What does she need?" I breathe tentatively. Hatter remains frozen in place, not so much as humming to break the tension.

"No one came to call in her cell. No one questioned the men who came to steal her in the night." Each word scrapes against my ears uncomfortably. "Devoid of love, drained of compassion. Now she strives for power. Yet power cannot fill the empty void within, and this makes her relentless." A thud sounds from beyond the walls, a gentle tremor beating beneath my boots. I ignore it, pressing on.

"Power? I don't care for power." Another thud, this one louder. Small rocks tumble from the walls. *Thud.* Accompanied by a roar. *Thud.* A crack skims over the ceiling. But I can't listen to the small voice in my head which tells me to run. The old woman smiles knowingly.

Twisting her gnarled wrist around the top of the cane, her long nails scrape against the wood. Beneath her palm, the light reappears. Softly pulsing, tempering my anxiety once more. I lose myself within the glow, not caring how the stone vessel around us shakes and cracks. Within the light, a figure takes form. Small at first, until she unfurls. The bars around her become visible, those of a cage. As she throws herself against them, her huge, pleading eyes of icy blue stare out from a curtain of limp, black hair. The air is knocked from my lungs. The old woman knows it too.

"This is not your tale." She smiles, and smiles, and smiles, with teeth that grow into sharpened points. Her skin falls away, melting from her skeleton in gruesome globules. Free from her human form, the creature elongates on a strangled cry, the cane becoming merely an extension of its arm. Shadows rush forward, draping the bones in a black cloak which is only speared by those shining white eyes. Okay, *now* I'm scared.

Opening its jaws, wide enough to swallow me whole, a final thud precedes the wall exploding. I scream from both the gigantic teeth and raining rocks, raising my arms to cover my head. In a blur of movement, I'm wiped off my feet and swept away. Chunks of brick slam into my body, leaving welts of agony where they're not cushioned by the fur coat. Braving a look through my fingers, I spy Hatter on the shoulder opposite to one jabbing into my stomach, Dormouse hanging onto a strand of his hair. The creature is taking chase right behind.

"Spritely for an old lady," I mutter to myself. Bashing against the tunnel created in the undergrowth, the black cloak stretches out clawed fingers. I take the nearest and give it a little shake. "How do you do?"

"Stop interacting with it!" the Tweedle beneath me roars. Sharply turning, he jumps high into the air like a worm springing out of the Earth. Gravity takes me from his hold, tossing my body high into the air, only to thump me down on the woodland floor. No sooner has the 'oomph' left me, do I see my savior leaping upon the creature as it climbs from the tunnel. Ripping its caned arm free, he stabs its jagged end through the cloaked skull and sends it screeching back into the hole. Then, silence.

"Is it dead?" I push myself up on fur-clad forearms. Hatter rolls across the ground until he pops up at my side, handing me the hat which must have fallen off during my unplanned flight.

"It can't die. It's a Verax." Hatter supplies the answer, although my question was directed to the silhouette carefully watching the hole, its biceps bunched in anticipation for another attack.

"What's a Verax?" I whisper back. Hatter instantly bops me on the head for being curious, but it's difficult to shed a vital piece of my personality just because I'm deemed Hatter-ish enough. Pulling ourselves up onto our knees, we take turns dusting each other off as Hatter's eyes wonder, his voice deepening.

"A fusion of nightmare and scale which prowls the desolate wastelands. Its eyes gleam like malevolent stars, its wings span the length of the horizon. Razor sharp fangs drip venom, and its thunderous roar shatters sanity. They call it the omen of doom, since its very presence chills hearts and stains lands with eternal darkness." In a rare moment of seriousness, Hatter's brows furrow and his mouth tightens.

"Wow. That sounds awesome. How do I befriend one?" I quirk my head. Hatter breaks out in a wide grin, his tumbling laughter spilling around us. I laugh with him, waiting out the hysterics before raising to my full height. It's truly dark now, the trees around the clearing only evident by their leaves rustling in a gentle breeze. Any trace of moonlight is at their discretion, faint spears trickling through the canopy sporadically.

"Something is lost," Hatter decides, scuffing his shoes through the dirt as he paces away. I'm inclined to agree. Hunting for Tweed, I walk forward blindly until arms suddenly wrap around my waist, whipping me away from what I imagine is the gaping hole in the ground just before I fall in. I await his grumble, a rough shove and order to be more careful. But none of that comes.

Instead, he holds me. His skin is cold, his chest firm at my back, yet a warmth blossoms from within myself. I don't want to be the kind of girl who depends on a male to make her feel safe, but time and again, Tweed continues to save me. To tease me with glimpses of tenderness. And in this moment of weakness, I accept it.

"Every truth the Verax tells comes at a price, and it does not possess the ability to lie." He mutters beside my ear. Fangs scrape just beneath, a deep inhale and soft moan following as if he can't help himself. "Tell me, how many truths did it tell you, Crazy One?"

I opt for a lie. "It didn't say anything before it went all 'rawr'," I make claws with my fingers, and then my brain trips over itself at the term of endearment. *Crazy One...crazy one, crazy one*. The words roll around my mind like a tumbleweed until I can place it. Or rather, until I can place *him*. The voice crooning beside my ear isn't full of irritation or laced with impatience. It's lighter, softer, as if delivered with a smile.

"I think you're full of shit Malice, but I sure did miss you." Rubble crunches under boots across the clearing, a strip of moonlight announcing the real Tweed's arrival. Hands flecked with crimson are filled with firewood. His green eyes catch on the hole in the ground, then raise to me.

"What the fuck happened?!" he drops the logs and rushes to peer down the hole. I twist to grab a hold of Cash, but there's no one there. Just the whisper of a chuckle slipping away in the breeze, taking with it all traces of his scent and the moment of comfort he provided. For what reason, I couldn't even begin to guess. We're enemies now.

"Malice!" Tweed yells. "What in the bloody hell did you do?!" On second thought, I'm not sure who my enemies are anymore.

"A darn sight more than foraging around for firewood," I stomp over to kick his pile into the open hole. A distant scream sounds from deep within, but I ignore it, bashing my shoulder into Tweed's and striding past. I find Hatter on the way, inspecting an acorn with a magnifying glass in the dark. Any tiredness I may have felt prior to entering the cathedral has fled. I'm too wired to settle, too annoyed to stand still. Once again, Cash has screwed with my head, but it's the Verax's fuckery which has me questioning what I thought I knew.

Lilliana was imprisoned once, utterly alone. Just like me. She was trapped, scared, desperate. No wonder she went stir shit and decided to dominate an entire kingdom–I've had similar notions myself, but I'm far too lazy. Still, I shouldn't be able to compare myself to the bitch who poisoned me and stole my other Tweedle. I shouldn't be able to sympathize with her. So why does each step I take toward Red Castle feel like a betrayal?

# CHAPTER 4

"Well?" Lillianna snaps. I've barely stepped foot through the portal, spiraling from a whorled tree trunk in the Spade Castle lobby. It's not supposed to be here, but in Lillianna's absence, nature has taken back control of the desecrated land. Careful not to step on the vines snaking through cracked tiles, I pluck a peach from the branches and toss it back and forth between my hands.

"Well, what?" I quirk a brow. Lillianna's eyes are molten pools of gold, ones I used to drown in, but lately, they don't seem to have the same effect.

"Did you see them? Are they headed straight back to Arabelle like good little soldiers?" I take a moment to formulate my answer, drifting my gaze over the plumes of underskirts enlarging Lillianna's already imposing dress. Rivets of gold netting and black satin float an inch above the floor, shifting in small waves as she walks. Tightened into a corset at her bust with the same gold shimmering down her arms she's every bit the ethereal queen I once thought. Now? I'm not so sure.

"No," I state, tossing the peach for her to catch. Turning, I seek the solace of my bedchamber. Lillianna ordered me to hunt down my brother's little gang and discover what their next move is, and I'd agreed for the sole reason I would get to see Malice again. Smell her again, hear her laughter once more, if only from a distance. It's all I think about. All I crave when my fangs are deep in Lillianna's wrist.

What I hadn't expected to see was her wandering into a Manifestation Cathedral. They appear when one is lost. Truly lost. In place, time and mind. Inside, Malice would have seen exactly how her story will play out, and I'd have sold my soul all over again to know those answers. Whether it's by my hand, Tweed's, or if she'll be the destruction of us both. Alas, vampires can't enter places of worship, but we can pummel our way into the Verax's lair underneath. Scratch that, I don't need to see Malice's future to know her curiosity will get her killed.

I'm about to turn the corner for the grand central staircase, shrouded in flowering weeds, when I slam into an invisible brick wall. A groan is torn from my throat, my senses hit with the undeniable smell of copper. It overrides my thoughts, stalls my actions.

Suddenly, I'm turning, my eyes zeroing in on the slow steam of stark crimson circling Lillianna's wrist, caused by the dagger in her other hand. A single droplet parts from her alabaster skin, plunging to the ground. An audible splash against the tile causes me to clench my middle and groan again, a pained and powerless sound.

"Did it sound like I was finished talking to you?" Lillianna asks, her voice low and a single brow raised. I can't respond more than a strained head shake, the veins in my neck as taut as my jaw. I didn't realize how hungry I was until being presented with the substance which has both freed me from mortal life, yet doomed me to be its slave. Skidding my foot forward, Lillianna smiles and meets me halfway. Her wrist is pushed against my mouth, her fingers slipping in my hair.

"Let's try that again. Did you see Tweed, Hatter and Malice in the Tulgey Wood?" I nod against her skin. "Are they headed to Arabelle?" Again, my body betrays me and I nod. The blood against my tongue, as intoxicating as it is, is tainted with a bitterness of my own creation.

I start to pull away, to question what the fuck I'm doing here, when Lillianna's grip on my blond hair tightens. She forces me to drink more, to drive my fangs into her flesh and take more. Lavender and sage creep into my senses, calming my overactive mind.

"We can't let them reach her, Cash. The Red Kingdom is at its strongest with a Hatter, and now they have two." I'm a fool to fight, her essence taking hold of my mind. My bite slackens, my shoulders sagging before Lillianna will permit me to pull away from her wrist. It's an effort to stand upright, my body dredging through the sluggish after effects of feeding. It only happens this way with Lillianna, as if I need more time to recover before my senses snap back with keen sharpness.

Out of nowhere, a hand cracks against the side of my face. Stinging sharply, I wince down at the small woman who dared to strike me. Only one with the confidence of my allegiance would do so, and fortunately for her, I have nowhere else to go. No one else who cares for me the way she does. "Snap out of it." Her fingers click in front of my hazy eyes. "I need you to focus on saving what we've worked so hard to build."

"And what is that, exactly?" My fangs throb. Lillianna only smiles. Turning on her heel, she strolls away with an exaggerated sway to her hips. All part of the foreplay, encouraging me to follow. I can no longer remember a single reason not to.

"Do what it takes to bring me a Hatter, kill the rest, and you will be rewarded tremendously." Peering over her shoulder, Lillianna's smile is nothing short of cruel and calculated, yet who am I to argue? The lost orphaned boy trapped inside of me is still hunting for a home, searching for a purpose. It's only fitting that it has come in the form of killing my own brother and all who side with him.

# CHAPTER 5

I sense, rather than see, the moment I step across the boundary line into the Red Kingdom. Like a trickle of magic patting me down, followed by an invasive anal cavity search. The sharp sting of rejection comes swiftly after. Lillianna's poison isn't welcome here, but that's not what stops my feet from shuffling forward.

Peering back, as the first few rays of light kiss an otherwise inky sky, I chew on my lip. Out there, across grassy panes and rolling hills we've spent all night hiking, Cash is lurking. Somewhere, everywhere. Prowling like a lion stalking his prey, and somehow the magical barrier doesn't provide any solace.

Rather, it's just another obstacle between us. Another hurdle separating me from the vampire who saved my life in the woods, huskily spoke my name and disappeared without a trace. Why does he toy with me, and why am I praying he might do so again? I love the game, and crave the chase–that's why.

"Is there something wrong?" Tweed asks from a little way down the borderline. Even with his arm buried in a hollow tree trunk, digging out supplies, he's tuned into the erratic beat of my heart. The way my heart has sunk and breathing has hitched for all the wrong reasons.

"No, just...Lillianna's black magic." I lift my arms. I'd ditched the fur coat a few miles back. Its heavy weight, another burden I couldn't be bothered to carry. "These lands don't seem to like it." Walking over, Tweed and Hatter assess the black veins creeping far beyond my elbows now. Neither comment, but their frowns match. A clunky object in Tweed's hand knocks against my leg. "What's that?"

"You might want to put this on. We've entered from the south where the border divides us from the Black Kingdom. Certain...precautions have been taken to keep just anyone from walking through," Tweed says, dropping the deceptively heavy gas mask on my forearm. Worn leather straps are marked with evidence from many battles, the smeared glass eyepieces speaking of a haunted history. Tweed secures his own, as do

Hatter and Dormouse, peeking out of his breast pocket and breathing heavily. Very well then.

I stretch the tight mechanism over my face as Tweed instantly appears to tighten the straps. I can't help myself from leaning back into his chest. My body betrays me, my need for a hint of comfort taking over. Of course, Tweed's stubbornness isn't inclined to humor me for a single second.

"Erm, what the fuck are you doing?" His voice is muffled and heavy within the mask. Jolting back to my senses, I stomp away, glad the mask is covering my blush. I'm fucking embarrassed–me?! The queen of nonchalance. Something is happening in my mind, and I don't bloody like it.

Somehow, through the marred goggles, I manage to plant one foot in front of the other and make it a considerable distance while remaining upright. A smile graces my lips, muttering insults back to the pussies lingering behind when the first heavy weight collides with my face.

*Thwack.*

I stumble sideways and another comes. Then another, as I ricochet around like a ping-pong ball. My foot slips, knocking me flat on my back. The ground is warm, slippier, but that doesn't stop my head from slamming against the solid woodland floor.

My thoughts are sluggish, and I blink, the dirty goggles clouding my vision. No, not the usual smears, but a fresh smattering I can't clear away well enough. Shadows of trees stretch high into an endless sunrise, reaching out above me like the arms of needy orphans.

Hands grip my upper arms, dragging me up with a grumbled curse which belongs to Tweed. Something about slowing him down, but I'm too distracted to care.

Wiping at the red splatter on my goggles, I manage to catch a glimpse of what knocked me from my feet. At first, I think I'm hallucinating. My mind has always been able to conjure up horrors which others would consider their wildest nightmares. But nope, this isn't a trick of my imagination. A gruesome tapestry of bodies litter the view as far as I can vaguely see. Secured to outcropped branches by huge metal hooks, humans, animals, and everything in between are rendered upside down with slashes across their necks, their faces coated in thick rivets of blood. What little skin, feathers, or scales are visible, are drained of color and life. Somewhere close by, the cackle of a crow rings out.

"We need to keep moving." Tweed growls. His continued cursing becomes muffled and further away as I continue to wipe the stains on my glasses. If only to clear them enough not to be caught unawares by the swaying bodies, their limbs twisted and broken at unnatural angles. The maze becomes denser as I'm ducking and weaving, trying to navigate my way through. My boot skids numerous times, and I can imagine how thick the air is with the stench of rotting flesh.

Focusing on the rhythmic wheezing of my breath through the mask, I narrowly avoid a headless duck strung up by its webbed feet. The wind seems to do a U-turn, whisking one way and boomeranging back, whipping up a tornado of torsos. Friction brushes at my shoulder before I can twist around, the stubby end of an amputated arm scraping at my skin. Whatever stole it from the man bobbing around had vicious teeth judging by the marks around the exposed bone. A wave of nausea washes over me and I double over, retching into my own mask.

"Oh, for fuck's sake," Tweed shouts at the sky and retraces his boot prints in the blooded path. "I thought you, of all people, would be able to walk through a field of bodies without being affected. You clearly don't care what happens to your own." I disregard that last comment as I'm struggling to keep the contents of my stomach on the inside.

"You don't understand," I hold up a hand. The air in the mask is beyond stuffy, musked with the sweat of whoever wore it previously, but somehow I manage to keep it together.

"I had a–a roommate first semester in college. She had this boyfriend who was an amputee." I smack my forearm when words fail me. "One time, I walked in on them getting dirty. None of us cared; I'm pretty sure a threesome was on the cards anyway. But then I saw...I saw... his little elbow nubbin rubbing all over her clit, and she was all, 'stump me!' 'stump me!' Since then, I just can't do it. I can't be stumped."

A shudder rolls through my spine as the wind once more blows the body in my direction. Tweed yanks it down to the ground with a sharp tug, his eyes narrowed through his mask. Grabbing a fistful of my orange hair, he yanks me along. A moan escapes me, which sounds too much like 'oh daddy' for either of us to deny. Regardless, Tweed doesn't release me until we've reached the other end of the bloody field, his patience truly run out.

"What's his problem?" I scoff, finally able to drag the mask from my face. The air isn't any more pleasant with it off. Hatter tilts his head, watching Tweed scuff his boots clean on a shrub and continue moving onwards.

"Blue balls," Hatter nods once. I turn to him, my lips parted.

"I think that's the smartest thing you've ever said." Unphased by our entire night of walking, Hatter blindly follows Tweed, whistling through his gapped teeth with a slight skip in his step. I'm not so quick to move on, taking a breather whilst looking over the field we've left behind.

Now the sun has fully risen and my view is unhindered, I'm not sure what to make of the sight. There must be hundreds of them, all hung up like ornaments. But for what reason? Do whatever you want behind closed doors - as that whore Holly did with her nightly stumping - but for someone to air out their kills like laundry on a washing line? That's personal. Wait...

I sprint as quickly as my tired legs can carry me, misjudging a step and slamming into Tweed's side.

"For the love of fuck, can you not go two minutes without falling over?" Tweed snarls. I ignore him.

"You know what this seems like to me," I jerk my thumb back to the field, my voice more breathy than wordy. "A vampire trap." Tweed doesn't acknowledge me clinging onto him, the blood smeared all over my body now staining his tattooed bicep. "You knew Cash was following us." He grunts now.

"He's my twin. I can sense him a mile off. No surprise when I returned from setting this up, his scent was all over you." And there it is, ladies and gentlemen. Jealousy.

"And those people you've killed. Did they happen to be in the wrong place at the wrong time?"

"I needed to feed," he shrugs. I call bullshit. Beneath his layers of I-don't-give-a-fuck, Tweed has a righteous streak. He's the Knave of Red Kingdom for a reason. No, I'd bet the victims we've left swaying in the gentle morning breeze were already convicted of horrible crimes.

"Don't tell me you have a conscience all of a sudden," Tweed laughs bitterly. He side-eyes me, pretending he's not watching my every move. "If you care about those strangers so much, perhaps you could have cared how I felt watching you pine for Cash. After everything he's done, you still look for him. All that blood, all those deaths down there, they are on your hands."

I stop walking. Pursing my lips, I stand still until Tweed can't resist turning back to argue with me further. Hatter cleverly keeps walking.

"Firstly, get fucked by a porcupine dick." Holding up a finger, I opt to start with my middle one. "Secondly, I'm not the one who went all Hannibal Lecter because I'm too much of a pussy to fight my twin for what I really want." I use my thumbs then, to point at myself. Yeah, this bitch went there. Tweed scoffs, folding his arms and drawing my attention to his huge biceps. Bastard.

"What's there to fight for? You chose him. You entered the Nightshade Trial for him, got yourself poisoned and now we have at least another two day's walk before we reach the closest guard station. And after all of that, you walked straight back into his arms the first chance I'm out of sight. So yeah, I'm pissed."

My eyes narrow into slits when he turns his back on me. Hunting for the first object which comes to hand, I happen upon a hedgehog shuffling through the grass. Not quite a porcupine. but the sentiment is the same. I hurl it through the air, knocking Tweed in the back of the head.

"And thirdly," I shout at the top of my lungs, knowing it'll hurt his ears. "You and Cash have the same fucking face! Clearly, the attraction is there, so you can take the blame straight back for having such a shitty personality!"

I rush past, making sure to stomp on his foot on the way. Tweed grabs my throat and yanks me hard enough to toss me aside into a pile of cow crap. "Oh-ho-ho. You slimy, cheap shot motherfu–" I dive for his shins and attempt to drag him down with me. And so the brawling and squabbling continues until Hatter pushes a pair of brandy snaps into his ears.

# CHAPTER 6

Tweed wasn't exaggerating. Elevenses, lunchtime, teatime, and any other excuse for cake passed before we reached the first guard's station. He steps aside as I shove my weight into his side, making me topple over myself. A few inches from the ground, Tweed grabs the back of my nape, spinning and setting me back on my feet.

"Arrogant asshole," I grumble. It's true I ran out of energy several miles back, not that I would admit defeat in trying to irritate him. About two hours ago, it occurred to me he could have simply carried and ran us all here in a fraction of the time, but stubbornness kept my mouth zipped shut. Story of my life. Speaking of stories, Hatter is hopefully bringing his current one to a close as we approach our transportation back to Red Castle.

The carriage is a simple wooden structure no one would suspect was any less or more–other than the bison attached to the reins. With a rumble and a stretch, he shakes his mane in a proud manner. The coachman gives a whistle from his bench up front, causing the bison to begin moving forward and the wooden wheels to creak. My eyelids droop at the slowness of the beast, my lengthy patience almost at an end. Regardless, Tweed takes a spot upon the bench, while Hatter and I hop into the open door.

"Woah," I breathe, my interest instantly piqued again. Defying the exterior, inside the carriage is a huge room, lavishly decorated in the deepest purples and golden accents. Walls adorned with intricate tapestries and paintings create a hexagonal shape around plush velvet furniture. The ceiling is high, arched, and painted blue to look like the sky, with clouds that seem to move as if alive. On a small table in the center, a decanter of wine is classically labeled 'drink me' with two and a half glasses set aside.

Hatter settles into one of the huge armchairs, gesturing for me to take the one opposite. My mind drifts and I'm wondering if Tweed has opted to sit out front because the air in here is overpowered with scents of sandalwood and sweet jasmine, or if he's avoiding me. I was rather enjoying our games of fuckery.

As I settle into the plush armchair, Hatter continues to speak in a low voice, as if he's telling a secret. "The story I have been telling you, Malice, is not just any story. It is a tale of magic and intrigue, of darkness and light. And, most importantly, it has a moral." Hatter holds up one finger in his tatted gloves, seeming awfully proud of himself. Dormouse abseils down his waistcoat, leaping towards the half-cup of wine awaiting her. "Can you guess what the moral is?"

"Don't accept hats made of cheese from strangers?"

"Curiosity is the key to every mystery." Hatter's slanted smile is at odds with the razor sharpness of his gaze for a chance. Rolling my eyes, I set my sights on the small window within the carriage door. Rolling fields, distant woodlands, and not much else meets my gaze. We're moving terribly slowly. Not that I was worried Cash might struggle to keep up. Would he make it through Tweed's blood trap? Will he follow me all the way to Red Castle, and if so, what does that mean for us? I mean us as in...fuck, I don't even know anymore. Hatter clears his throat and sips his wine.

"Do you miss him?" My cheeks instantly flame, as if feeling anything except indifference is something to be embarrassed about.

"Yeah. Fuck, I know I shouldn't, but yeah, I really do," I admit. Accepting my own glass, I toss back the stark red liquid. It's smooth, aged in oak, with a timeless allure which has me reaching for a refill. This is the answer I seek. To get blind fucking drunk and cry about my feelings. Come tomorrow morning, I'll be emotionally spent and back to the carefree version I prefer of myself. "It's like he's burrowed in my mind and created a little nest for himself. Every time I try to scratch him out, he tunnels deeper."

Flipping my hair upside down, I shake my orange curls erratically. All I manage to do is make myself dizzy. Easing myself back into the armchair, I sigh and pinch the bridge of my nose.

"And yes, I know exactly what you're thinking. '*Just fuck Tweed, they're practically the same person.*' Except they're not. Their personalities are polar opposites, it's like they don't even look the same to me anymore. But sure, I could cancel out all of my problems by just sitting on Tweed's face, cause it's not like I even have to look at him anyway, right? But I'll know it's not Cash, and I know the three of us won't get to be naked and freaky together ever again. A girl has needs!"

Throwing my arms up in the air, I catch sight of Hatter's evident confusion. I narrow my gaze at his widened eyes and even paler face than usual. "Wait, who were you talking about?"

"I meant your father...do you miss your father?" Oh shit. My back straightens and my mouth runs dry. Time for more wine. If I thought speaking about Cash and Tweed made me vulnerable, this is a totally different ball game.

"Fuck no," I scowl, refilling my glass. Silence falls around the spacious room, pressing in on my sides tight enough to make me feel claustrophobic. Hatter taps his heels on the carpet in tune with whatever song is playing in his head.

"I kept track of you," he hums. Nothing about his demeanor would suggest we're discussing my turbulent past. "I read about his death in the newspapers White Rabbit retrieved for me. Nasty business–stabbings. Rather hasty and incredibly messy."

"I'll ensure to pre-meditate my next kill better," I drawl, giving him a look which would suggest he's adding himself to that list. In actual fact, I'd never harm a single wiry hair on Hatter's head, and his wide smile suggests he knows it.

"So much anger. To be a Hatter, we need to release the emotions that hold back our muchness. Anger, rage, guilt, shame. You'd better get to work on that, Malice." In an effort to ignore him, I reach out for the decanter and pause when my eyes snag on my arm. The veins, black as ink, are thicker now. Pulsating, as they stretch towards my shoulder. Poison of Lillianna's creation, which Cash did nothing to stop. He knowingly walked me into his queen's trap.

I slap myself across the face, much to Hatter's and Dormouse's surprise. Cash isn't following me; he's hunting me. Checking that Lillianna's poison is working, and if it isn't, perhaps he'll finish the job himself. I was a fool to his touch, an idiot to swim in the playful lightness of his voice. Slipping from the armchair to the floor, I curl myself around Hatter's legs like a sad koala.

"What if I don't live long enough to become the Hatter you wanted me to be?" I whimper, squeezing as tightly as I can. I need to remind myself what's real, and who's real. And amongst my internal screaming, I glance to the wall of the carriage which Tweed is sitting on the other side of. "Oh, I've really fucked up, haven't I? I'm sorry. So sorry," I babble, feeling the wine take hold. Dammit, I forgot I'm a teary drunk. Hatter pats my wild hair, shushing gently.

"Hush, my dear. You couldn't be my daughter if you were perfect." Somehow, through my sobbing, a trickle of laughter breaks through. There's a backward compliment if I ever heard one, but it's exactly what I needed.

When we arrive at Red Castle, I'm stepping out of this carriage as the Hatter I'm supposed to be. After some seriously reckless drinking, slutty dancing and pouring my heart out through karaoke and crying. That's how normal people deal with their problems, right?

***

*"Alice," a loud snap sounds beside my ear. "Focus." I jerk awake, my head heavy against the mountain of pillows. Groaning, I turn onto my side, but the voice follows. "What happened next?"*

*"Next?" I mumble. My bedside lamp is switched on, irritating my tired eyes. A figure moves to sit at the edge of my mattress, his outline blocking the light. "I'm too tired, Dad. I'll tell you more tomorrow." I yawn, but his pen prods my shoulder.*

*"You got to the Jubjub bird. The tweedle boys dived in front of its claws to protect you. What happened next?"*

*"Ahh, yes, the tweedles," I smile to myself. "Dee makes me laugh. He always has a joke to brighten the worst situations. But Dum," I snuggle into the cover, "Dum has a protective streak. No matter the danger, he always jumps to save me first."*

*"I sense someone has a crush," my father singsongs. My gasp overpowers the sound of his pen scratching against his notepad.*

*"Daddy! I couldn't possibly choose between them. They're two of the same. There isn't one without the other. I would never let myself divide them." Cracking an eyelid, I frown at his rushed scribbles, my name linked with Dum's in a heart.*

*"Someone is going to one day. If not you, then who?" my father half-shrugs. Rolling onto my back, I shrink into my nightgown.*

*"Why do we need to think of such things? It's not like I'll ever go back."*

*"You must go back!" my father shouts so suddenly, I flinch. "We need to know what happens next."*

*What happens next? There is no 'next'. I've wandered the woods within my family's estate a thousand times, all of them with my father hiding behind a nearby tree to watch on. The White Rabbit is nowhere to be seen. Whether I did something wrong or my time is simply up, it's clear there is no going back for me. I wasn't right. I wasn't good enough.*

*"Please let me sleep, Dad. At least in my dreams, I can pretend I'm with those I consider my closest friends." At last, my father relents. Kissing my forehead, he tucks the covers into my sides and switches off the light. My breathing deepens as he reaches the doorway, stopping halfway out.*

*"Dream hard, Alice. The publishers won't wait much longer, but perhaps a romantic sequel could be exactly what I need." Sleep drags me under before I can figure out what on earth he's talking about.*

# CHAPTER 7

The carriage lurches, tossing me from my nap into an impending hangover. Luckily, enough wine is still in my system to give me a blissful buzz and the ice cream Hatter gifted me magically remains frozen. I lift out the spoon, sucking on a huge chunk of cookie dough when Tweed whips the door open. His green eyes are striking, like endless fields glinting in the midday sun, despite the lack of light behind him. Those eyes track the spoon between my lips, to the tub, and back again, my tongue slowly licking and flirting.

"You better not have conjured that ice cream for yourself," he grumbles. My grin widens.

"What are you going to do to me if I did?" It must be a trick of the light, but I'm sure I saw the hint of a smile tease the corners of his mouth. It's gone by the time I've blinked, his features set in full control-freak mode once more.

"We must pass through this town to reach the castle," Tweed directs his words towards Hatter. "And it seems we're not alone." Unlike before, my heart doesn't lurch at the prospect it could be Cash causing the hold-up. Seems my drinking and ice-cream binge worked perfectly to freeze my heart over once more. "We'll have to take a detour, avoid whoever is blocking the path."

"Nope on a rope!" I shoot upright, only swaying slightly. "I am not prolonging this trip any longer. I want a bubble bath, a proper bed, and a date night with a monster tentacle vibrator. Enough of the hold-ups." The hold-ups, and the turmoil between my head and my heart. Tweed's hands fly to my waist to help me down from the carriage as I try to push my way past him. I linger in his hold, expecting him to fight me–not steady me. Frowning, I nod and step out of his touch. These boys sure love screwing with my head.

We've stopped upon a hilltop, peering down at the town below. As Tweed stated, there is a visible presence of fiery torches around the outside, their holders standing shoulder to shoulder to create a man-made wall. If I peer straight ahead and tilt my head a little, turrets are just visible, with the iconic hearts at their peak. Red Castle. I nod to myself, swinging my arms in time with my large strides. Tweed helps Hatter from the carriage as I take a moment to pause by the Bison's twitchy ear.

"I can crawl quicker than you," I seethe. He jerks his giant head, a low rumble emanating from his chest.

"Fuck off, I had to come out of retirement for this." Holding my stare with the singular eye on the side of his head, I decide on a truce and leave him to grumble to his coachman about manners.

My companions catch up to me halfway down the hill, Dormouse balancing in Hatter's hand. She's dressed in a full karate gi, complete with a black belt at her tiny waist and wraps twisted around her clawed hands. Giving me a wink, her stance is sturdy and ready to fight. I admire her courage. Syncing our steps, we create a wall of our own, nearing our latest enemy with a rhythmic stomp, stomp, stomp of boots.

"Who goes there?" A booming woman's voice stops us in our tracks. The echo would indicate she has a megaphone pressed to her lips. "State your business!" I wince at the assault on my fragile mind, a headache quickly blossoming. Stepping ahead of the others, I hold up a hand to block out the flames.

"We're just passing through. Close your eyes and count to ten. You won't even realize we were here." I call back, relying on this mellowed-out version of Tweed to speed us all the way back to his home.

Through the haze the wine still has me under, I squint at those who draw their swords. At first, I see so many legs I think my tentacle fantasy is coming true sooner than I'd expected, until my mind catches up with my eyes. They aren't tentacles or even human legs, but horses'. The clink of armor follows and my breath saws out of my parted lips. "Humpty Dainty?!"

"Malice!" her reply comes instantly. I tell Dormouse to stand down, although it's Tweed who looks wholly prepared to fight. Before I get too distracted by the traps on his bunched shoulders, I head over to the giant egg running in my direction. She stumbles and wobbles with each hazardous step before leaping into my arms. Jeez, I forgot how heavy she is. "You've returned! We've been awaiting your direction. You left so quickly before, but I knew you'd be back. I told my horse-women to wait right here, not to move a single muscle."

I swallow thickly, placing her back on her stumpy feet. They've been standing here the entire time, waiting for *me*? It's only a fluke we chose to travel this way. Reaching beneath her wig, Humpty Dainty pulls out a whistle and blows hard. My ears ring in time with the shaking of my eyes, a whoosh of dizziness knocking me off balance. A strong arm bands around my middle, the other being raised to present a stained wrist at my mouth. Tweed stands firm, uncaring of our audience as I latch onto his congealed, orange blood and suck. Both of us manage to restrain our moans, although he instantly hardens at my back. Humpty Dainty watches the scene with keen interest.

"Is he the one?" She asks when I push Tweed's arm away, all of my hungover ailments disappearing on cue. Ahh shit, I forgot about the gloopy vision she gave me. "The hero we are to follow?" Stepping free of the vampire's hold, I clear my throat. All eyes are on me, but none hold as much intrigue as Tweed's.

The prophecy wasn't wrong, one Tweedle would be my destiny, and the other was to be my downfall. No guesses needed as to which is which, but it doesn't make sense to separate the two. From where I stand, if I accept Tweed as mine, my destiny and downfall will be one of the same. I'm too erratic to belong to only one being. Tweed is stunning, stoic, secure. I don't need a safety net. I need a lifebuoy lingering on the edge for when I swim too far and need to be pulled back. I need the intrigue, the rush of danger, the spontaneity.

Yet I can't deny that he's the one standing here. Still protecting me, still putting up with my bullshit, no matter how much I push him away. And let's be honest, this isn't even about me. This is about providing Humpty Dainty's army hope, about getting through this damn town unscathed, about giving Tweed the validation he's been searching for his entire life–knowing that he's wanted.

"Yep–Tweed is your hero." Humpty Dainty gaps and clicks her chubby fingers. In one slow movement, the zombie army slips from their horses and kneels in the dirt. Humpty Dainty lowers with a wobble, and when I turn, I see Hatter also on the ground. All that's left is me, and I kneel for no man. "As such, the Knave requires safe passage back to Red Castle. Would you be able to assist us?"

"Naturally," Humpty Dainty hastily agrees. "The hero of Wonderlust is to be a key ally to the Diamond King. Once he hears of our valiant efforts to help you, he'll drop to his knees and beg me to be his wife." Two soldiers aid the egg in standing before interlinking their arms in a makeshift throne to carry her away on. Tweed gives me a cocked eyebrow. Too many questions in his expression to answer right now.

"Doesn't she know–"

"Shh," I interrupt him. Now isn't the time to admit I beheaded the Diamond King weeks ago. Hooking my arm through Hatter's, I signal for Tweed to walk on first. "Take the lead, hero. We've got a castle to get to." There's no denying how Tweed's chest puffs out on instinct, his mouth definitely slated as he does just that. We make it three steps beyond the wall of soldiers when a familiar siren bleeds through the air. Ahh fuck, I remember this town now.

The Step-herd wives pour into the streets, their heels clicking. Frilly petticoats blind me with their offensive patterns and colors. Rushing forward on stalks and hooves, I brace myself for their attack. The wailing starts first, high-pitched screams encased with the fluttering of feathers and chattering of teeth.

Releasing Hatter's arm, I pull up my fists, my sights set on the flamingo leading the stampede, when a word comes clear amongst the masses. 'Hatter!' Whooshing past me, they dive onto Hatter, knocking him clean off his feet. I panic, losing sight of his jazzy waistcoat but he quickly resurfaces above the crowd. They hold him high, chanting and parading him through the high street towards his Hattery.

"That'll be you one day," Tweed comments.

"Hell no," I grumble in response. He chuckles–actually chuckles. The sound hits me deep in my core, reminding me of the mysterious male I hardly understand. How can I hate him one moment and yearn for his laughter the next? I want to crack open his skull, delve into his psyche, and understand what makes him tick.

By the time we've raced to meet the back of the parade, Hatter is placing his hand on the gnarled front door of his shop. The entire building breathes a sigh of relief, a groan of wood accompanied by the shuddering of brick dust. Everyone and everything is glad to have Hatter back and I have to remind myself I played a part. If I hadn't gone searching and made my mistakes, he'd still be locked in Fantasy Walk by the twin who smiled all too easily and joined me on my search. *Fucking traitor.*

“Hey,” Tweed touches my shoulder tentatively. Jerking his head towards the abandoned shop, I follow him away from the crowd towards an unoccupied shop across the street. The door is wide open, beckoning us into the rails of clothing on display. “It appears we might not be in and out of this town as quickly as I hoped.”

I share Tweed’s watery smile, spotting party lanterns being erected on lampposts. Music begins playing from a gaggle of geese with fiddles and ukuleles.

“It’s okay,” I lie through the lump forming in my throat. Hatter is at the heart of it all, smiling and laughing. Twiddling his fingers in the air like a conductor and singing a merry tune. He’s a figurehead for these creatures. That’s a huge mantle to be passed when I struggle to be social with my own reflection.

“If you’re not in the mood to party, we could hide out in the carriage. Pretend we don’t exist until morning.” Tempting, trust me. Tweed plucks at a fraying hem on a glittery blue dress, avoiding my gaze.

“Perhaps,” I half-shrug, picking out the first outfit to come to hand. “But first, even I can’t resist the urge of some retail therapy.” Leaving Tweed wondering, I slip into the back of the shop where a row of dressing rooms await. I’m all for exposing my sexuality, but I’m still human. There’s only so long I can wear a corset and not feel like it’s literally holding my organs in place.

Stripping free of the leather, netting, and suspenders, I pull on a simple t-shirt and a pair of light blue jeans. They get tight around my knees, but I don’t give in. Tugging the denim over my thighs, I wriggle them up most of the way. It’s just my ass left, as I jump several times with pained grunts. *You will go on, you fuckers.*

Jumping one last time, I misjudge my footing and stumble into the mirrored wall. Tweed is flinging back the curtain within half a second, hunting for an invisible assailant. All he finds is me and a suspicious amount of cool air circling my ass cheeks. Braving a look into the cracked mirror, my eyes lower in time with his. The denim has torn in a perfect circle, from the waistband to the thighs.

"I–I should," Tweed tries to shuffle away, but his feet barely move. His lips are forced apart by the lengthening of his fangs, his gaze consuming me in an emerald fire. I inhale sharply, suddenly remembering the last ingredient normal people use to get over an ex. A rebound.

"Do us both a favor and don't leave me hanging. A girl has needs," I brazenly reach up to grab the coat hooks on the wall and stick my ass out further. I expect him to reject me, to come to his senses, scoff and walk away. But he steps forward. The roughness of his cargos scrapes against me roughly, his arms coming to rest on the wall on either side of mine.

"And what do you need, Malice?" he asks seductively. Until that moment, until his husky voice caressed my ear, I could have sworn I was kidding myself that Tweed would ever touch me again. I hurt him–I know that. I hurt myself much more in the process; I just refuse to admit it.

"I need to *feel* something. Anything," is my desperate reply. He stalls, creeping through my psyche again. I'm in the process of swallowing when his hand cramps around my neck.

"Feel me then, and afterward, I want a straight fucking answer." Giving my throat a squeeze, his thumb lingers on my pulse. The beating of it thrums in my ears, my ass pushing further back. He retracts his hand as quickly as he raised it, and before I can turn my head, his tongue is between my ass cheeks. I moan loudly, unable to catch myself. No more playing cat and mouse, I'm his to lick, tease, and seduce. As long as I'm coming by the end of it.

Gripping my cheeks hard, Tweed parts me for his greedy tongue. It roams over my ass, dipping down towards my pussy. He's cold, like a freaking icicle sliding back and forth. To and fro. Enticing me to arch back further, exposing all of myself to his wanton desire. Seeking out my clit, Tweed sucks hard. Hard enough to make me scream in shock.

"Oh yes," I groan. There's a clatter somewhere within the shop, but neither of us cares enough to pay it any mind. Leaving an icy trail from my clit, Tweed returns to my pussy. He inhales me like a vampire possessed, his tongue nudging at my entrance. "Please," I whine, pushing back further. My knuckles have turned white on the hooks, but I don't care. I need him to finish what he's started.

"Do it," I try again. The more I urge, the slower he moves, toying with my sanity. I feel the tip of him push between my lips, his breath cold against me as he stills, and I'm certain he's about to pull away. But then his tongue moves roughly upwards. I gasp into the wallpaper. No, scratch that. My face becomes one with the wall, smearing away days of sexual frustration like a leopard print exfoliator. Tweed fucks me with his tongue relentlessly, pushing into me deeper with each thrust. My legs are shaking from the effort of holding me up.

I barely register as his hands push deeper into the denim, and without much effort, the jeans are torn open further. My entire crotch is at his disposal now, his hands not leaving anywhere untouched. Moving his tongue back to strum my clit like an instrument, his fingers seek me out. Two in my cunt, one in my ass, and I'm lost. Drowning in the sensations claiming my body, building the inferno within.

"Just like this," I hiss. Even if Tweed were to change his mind about pleasuring me now, there's no stopping the climax beginning to tremor in my core. Luckily for both of us, he doesn't. Tweed steams ahead, all fingers and tongue, thrusts and moans until I shatter for him. I convulse around his fingers, wave after wave of pleasure crashing through me. His name tumbles from my lips, my body taut with release.

"Fuck, you're incredible," I mutter out of nowhere. I don't pay the words any notice as Tweed pulls out of me and causes my legs to give way. He catches me in those strong, muscled arms, the hands delicately holding me laced with the scent of my arousal. I avoid his gaze, almost as if looking into glimmering greens will trigger a phase of our relationship I'm not ready for. Oh god, even the word *relationship* makes me twitchy.

A crash slams through the shop, the trickle of a bell preceding the front door from slamming closed. Then, silence. Tweed attempts to place me down, his protective nature arising, but whoever it was, and I bet we all don't need three guesses as to whom, has gone.

"Stay," I ask, wrapping my arms around Tweed's neck. He pauses, and somehow, it's even more awkward now than before. Licking my lips, I lower my head onto his shoulder. "We could keep going," I say shyly like a frigid virgin.

"Malice," he growls my name as a warning shot. Sitting upright, I stare him down; sharp jawline, full lips, protruding fangs and all. "We both know what just happened here was about base instinct and didn't really have anything to do with me. I could have been anyone, or an eel with a monocle for all you care."

“They are slippery fuckers,” I muse over his shoulder. Tweed tries to place me down once more and I cling on tighter. “Wait, wait. You really think that I don’t care about you?” I frown. Fuck, who even am I?

“Do you?” Tweed challenges. I chew on the inside of my cheek as words fail me. This time, I have no fight left when Tweed sets me aside and raises to his full height. Brushing his blond hair back from tormented eyes, he’s the image of lethal beauty. “When you decide, I’d like to be the first to know –if you don’t mind.” Bowing in mockery, he walks away, leaving bitterness behind in the air.

# CHAPTER 8

I stand back from the pulsating energy of the street party, which hit full swing when the moon reached its peak in the sky. Streamers hang from bunting, spelling out Hatter's birth name. It contains more letters than the alphabet, stretching further than one would have the patience to track.

Under the moon's soft glow, the city street has been transformed into a vibrant carnival. Neon lights and music fill the air, laughter and cheers echoing off the topsy-turvy buildings. Food vendors have set up stalls, the aromas all blending into an intoxicating mix, which makes me wish I could still digest food. Revelers dance, their silhouettes framed by flickering street lamps, and right in the center, is Malice.

Her curls seem to have a life of their own, bouncing and twirling in harmony with her movements. It's as if the sun itself decided to take residence in her hair, casting a fiery glow that illuminates the entire street. I thought I preferred her blonde but no - those vibrant orange curls cascading down her back suit her wild demeanor far better. I can't look away, her curvaceous body dominating my every thought.

Never, in a million years, did I think the skinny, annoying girl from my childhood would return as a woman. Although, 'Temptress' may be a more accurate description. After discarding most of the clothing Wonderlust has to offer, she's settled on a black tank top and fraying jean shorts, no shoes.

My cock hardens at the sight of her back in denim, the memory of how I found her in that dressing room playing on repeat in my mind. Her sweet scent, her large doe eyes, and smooth, bubbled ass sticking in my direction. There was no denying her after that.

She moves with an unrestrained grace, a solo dancer in the heart of the euphoric crowd. Swaying to the rhythm of the music, her every step is a testament to the captivating allure she possesses. It's impossible not to be drawn to her, now I've found my walls have lowered enough to do so. Just like seeing her skin flushed and her screaming with release, I'm captivated by the mesmerizing spectacle before me.

"Care to dance?" a voice asks from beside my foot. I peer down at Dormouse in her sparkly evening gown, her tiny hand outstretched. My lips stretch across my fangs awkwardly, as if it's been years since I last had a reason to smile.

"I prefer to observe." I tilt my flat cap. Malice's orders, when she finally ventured into the party. Placing the hat on my head was as far as her familiarity with me went. After that, she was a mistress to the music. Dormouse quickly moves on to her next conquest, finding a rat much more suited to her tastes. His three-piece suit would put some of the finest noblemen to shame. Speaking of rodents...

"I don't believe you were invited to this party," I twist my head, speaking into the darkened alley at my back. A soft chuckle answers.

"There was a time when no party was complete without my presence. I was the main attraction after all." Using my heightened vision, I see the outline of my mirror image brazenly walk forward. Remaining in the shadows, he leans against the brick wall near my side and crosses his ankles.

"Those times have passed," my voice is low, my gaze seeking out the party once more. Cash will not rile me tonight. He may be at the top of my shit list, but Malice currently has my full attention. I'll kill him tomorrow.

She's right where I left her. Entranced by the music, though her twerking and slut drops are completely off beat. On closer inspection, she's singing a completely different song about windows, walls, and sweaty balls. I smirk to myself, expecting nothing less.

A stolen diamond necklace sparkles from her neck, hiding the bruises deepening underneath. I take full responsibility for those. I marked her. A sense of pride builds within my chest. The stones catch on the neon lights of the surrounding buildings, creating a kaleidoscope of colors that dance alongside her. The curls framing her face accentuate her delicate features, and her radiant smile is infectious.

"Do you really think she could be satisfied with only you?" Cash dares to interrupt my thoughts. I ignore him, which somehow is confused with a request to step closer. "She's made no secret of her desire to have us both. A few indiscretions on my part won't change that. Instead, I think it'll make her crave me even more."

My jaw twitches. I refuse to pay him any notice. It's what my brother wants. For me to make a scene, to start a fight with him and ruin the Hatter's party. The guest of honor is currently doing the futterwacken on stage amongst his friends and supporters. He deserves this night after being locked up, even if it is my own flesh and blood who put him there. The longer I don't react, the braver Cash becomes. He nears, resting his folded arms against my upper back.

"Our roles have switched, brother. I'm the bad boy now and you're the one sporting love-sick eyes. I planned on a daring kidnapping, but this seems far more amusing. Let's see how long you can keep her entertained." His laughter echoes in my ears as he shoves me forward. I rush to catch myself, stumbling as I almost step on Dormouse and her companion. Twisting, I come to a halt before the biggest pair of glistening blue eyes, their purity as deep as the ocean.

"Hey," Malice smiles. I open my mouth to respond when she takes my hands, pulling them around her lower back.

"Oh no, no. I don't dance," I grumble. But any protest dies on my lips as she presses her body into mine, her hips swaying to the melody that thrums through the air. A shiver runs down my spine as I feel her breath hot against my neck.

"Just relax," she whispers, trailing a finger down my arm. "Let go of your inhibitions and follow my lead." That's all I've been doing since I entered the dressing rooms earlier. Or if I'm being truthful, since I overheard her pouring her heart out to Hatter in the carriage. I didn't mean to eavesdrop, but I literally couldn't help it. And even if I'd wanted to, it's rare to gain an insight into Malice's inner workings. She licks my neck, causing my chest to rumble.

"To dance is to feel alive. Two things you need to embrace more often," she says, squeezing my shoulders before twirling away from me. I want to tell her that's the most Hatterish thing she's yet to say, but now's not the time.

I should leave. I should push her as far away from myself as physically possible. With all of the events yet to come, it would be so much easier to hate her. But Malice has other ideas.

She's like a magnet, pulling me in with every flirtatious wink and nibble of her bottom lip. Time slows. Malice consumes my focus. From this close, I watch in awe as she spins, twirls, and sways to the music, her body exuding an irresistible magnetism that is impossible to resist. The world around us fades into obscurity as I am completely ensnared by her presence. I'm vaguely aware Cash is still nearby, watching on. I can sense his gaze, both curious and envious.

Good. Let him suffer. As I've had to on so many occasions, witnessing her choose him over me. Not anymore; I'll see to that. My twin has unknowingly issued me with a challenge and there is yet a trial I am to fail.

I was always meant to walk as a pair. My soul was always supposed to have two halves. Malice left me once, pushed me away second, but I'm not going anywhere. Someday, I'll be the one she dances with, the one who gets to share in the joy that radiates from her every move. For now, however, I'll stand back. Watching on as the woman with the huge, orange, curly hair continues to dance her way into my heart, leaving a permanent mark I couldn't remove even if I wanted to.

# CHAPTER 9

I only retreat to the carriage when I'm sure my feet are bleeding against the cobblestones. Hatter is still going strong, the life of the party seeping from his veins. His smile is a mile wide, as it should be. Seeking solace, I approach the bison released from his reins.

"Hey, is Tweed in there?" I jerk my thumb toward the carriage. The bison pauses chewing on the grass, and gives me a bored expression. One which says 'I'm not your personal Tweedle tracker', but he huffs and nods anyway. My heart flutters as I skip towards the door.

Tweed disappeared some time between the fireworks and the pinata. It was wheeled through the streets and the only batons we had were our fists. One minute I'm leaping into the air, pummeling the cardboard version of my childhood self, the next he was gone. It was a decent form of therapy to be honest, something I wish my shrink had thought of years ago.

Bracing my palm on the handle, I exhale low beneath my breath. Something strange is happening between Tweed and I. After days of essentially beating him up, he went down on me, insulted me, danced with me, and disappeared. Although, I could summarize most of my adult relationships similarly.

Tugging the door open, the plush lounge from before is nowhere to be seen. A golf course, stretching all the way to the eighteenth hole in the distance, rolls over hills and grassy banks. No sign of Tweed. Only a lone giraffe dressed in plaid, using his own head as a club. Catching his eye, I quickly slam the door closed. Opening it again, an art gallery awaits. Every painting is a different type of fruit being appreciated by bats in spectacles. Nope again.

This continues for a while. Open, greenhouse, close. Open, bear board meeting, close. After interrupting fuck knows how many beings, I whip the door open for a cloud of steam to billow out. My vision is obscured, my nose tingling with aromatic oils. Wafting a hand before my face, Tweed's outline becomes visible within the sauna.

"Shut the door. You're letting all the heat out," he grumbles. I do as he asks, just with me on the inside when I do. Four tiers of wood-clad benches rise high into a glittering black ceiling. Droplets of hot water drip onto my face when I peer up at the dimmed lights, my skin instantly too warm for the clothes upon my body. Padding across the mosaic tile floor, I stop before Tweed on the second tier. He doesn't look at me. Doesn't shift from where his chin is resting on his fist.

Very well. Taking his lead, since the towel circling his waist is all he's wearing, I strip. Tossing my clothes aside, I move to sit by his side. A towel appears just before my butt touches the heated wood. I cross my legs and lean back on my hands so my chest juts out, more than comfortable in my own skin. My breasts lift and fall in time with my calm breathing, the mist circulating the room soothing the conflict I previously thought. It isn't so awkward between Tweed and I. Just a battle of egos and overthinking, which needs to be put aside.

"Can I say something?" I speak into the nothingness, with the steam floating by to create a sense of anonymity. "You're angry the path I chose didn't involve you, but you left me first." Tweed instantly stiffens, his back shooting straighter than an arrow. I hold up a hand to silence him, allowing me to finish. I've had hours of movement therapy to dance through my thoughts. "I was chased out of Wonderlust when I was eight years old, and for years, I searched for a way back. No matter what anyone said, how they ridiculed or labeled me, I never gave up hope. But you did."

"I apologize. I was busy being imprisoned and forced to fight against my will," Tweed growls through gritted teeth. I shake my head.

"Not the entire time. You became a Knave, what, ten years ago? About the same time I was thrown into a mental institution with metal bars on the windows. Yes, you were a prisoner for a while, but afterward, you made the active choice not to look for me. And you have the audacity to say I'm the one who doesn't care."

Slumping his posture, Tweed remains quiet. He's thinking, I know, but I'm not quite done yet.

"Since the moment I've returned, all I've received is the blame. For the men disappearing, for your hardships with Cash, for not becoming Hatter's heir sooner, for freeing Lillianna...but none of it hurts as much as when you look me in the eye and blame me for your heartbreak. For your decision not to take a chance and come find me. I needed a hero as much as Humpty Dainty did. As much as Wonderlust still does."

Tweed looks in the opposite direction, muttering that he's not the guy everyone thinks he is. Perhaps the opposite is true–everyone else can see exactly who Tweed could be, if he were ready to accept it.

"I'm sorry I hurt you," I swallow my pride and reach out to hold his hand. Yes, me–the master of all stubbornness and refuser of all apologies. Somewhere along the way, my ego battle with Tweed lost its appeal. Probably every time I looked into his sunken eyes and had to re-face the fact I fucked up. I did the one thing I promised never to–I chose between the Tweeds. Had my father been alive to tell the tale, I'm sure his publishers would have been thrilled. I, however, am not.

"I used to be gleefully happy. All the time, as if no other emotion existed." Tweed sighs, squeezing my hand tightly. He refuses to look at me, but that's fine. His voice travels amongst the oil-infused mist and low whale song leaking from hidden speakers.

"We were imprisoned the day you left. Two travesties which plunged me into darkness. That was the first time I'd felt sadness, and it was a bitter bottomless hole which was easier to hide within than climb out." I feel the despair transferring through our touch. The image of them both curled up in the dark is something I wish I could rid from my mind. "The longer you didn't return, the easier it became to see you as a symbol of selfishness, childishness. A reminder that there is no use having hope because one day, it'll abandon you."

Tugging my hand into his lap, I nudge over. The entire length of our arms, his pasty white, and mine littered with black veins, are pressed together. Desperation claws at my chest to comfort him. To make the pain go away. To finally allow the Tweedle he was always meant to be, to shine.

"You were just a child, Tweed. If it's forgiveness you want, it's yours." My words fall on deaf ears, Tweed spiraling down the rabbit hole of his memories.

"I had to be the strong one. I had to look after Cash, never having a day off. Never even having a second where I could let down my guard and shed a few tears. You didn't hurt me, Malice. I just...needed a hero, too." His eyes meet mine amongst the steam. Two pools of endless emeralds, swirling with torment. I shudder, despite the sweat pebbling all over my skin. A bead runs the length of my cleavage, reminding me of my nakedness. When he's this close, when he's this raw, all I want to do is heal his pain. Help him to forget the hardships he's been forced into.

"Why didn't you just say that in the first place? Why continue being an asshole if you wanted my affection?" I plead, craving more than just his body. I want Tweed's mind, his warped rationale, his suffering. Unload it onto me. Cheshire knows I can take it. Tweed ducks his head, his eyes scraping over my nipples as if it were his knuckles.

"I can handle your hatred, but not your rejection."

"I'm not going to reject you again. I've learned my lesson," I cross my heart and offer a weak smile. As far as apologies go, it's not the best, but I'm new to this remorse stuff. By the time Tweed's eyes return to mine, they're glazed. His jaw is set firm and I'm sure he's about to tell me to get fucked and leave. His hands move faster than I can track, grabbing my face as his mouth crushes onto mine. I gasp into his kiss, his lips laced with the icy burn of a fever I don't want to break. *Tweed's kiss.* I've wondered for so long, ached for so long.

Relaying what his words can't express into the press of his lips, every inch of my body tingles with awareness. The surprise quickly fades, churning into something much more toxic. I kiss Tweed with the same ferocity, knocking him off-kilter. My arms instinctively wrap around his neck to pull him closer, seeking out whatever lies between us. Is it real or fabricated by two beings who need to feel something more?

Our tongues become intertwined in feverish passion, each movement urging him to lean further over me. My back touches the heated bench, at odds with the coldness of immortal muscle caging me beneath his biceps. My body trembles with desire.

A storm festers within my core. Dull at first, but quickly escalates into more. I can't get enough. I need him closer, my nails dragging down the length of his back. Reaching his waistband, I try to tug the towel free but Tweed pulls away from our kiss. His features are taut, wild with desire and uncertainty.

Pushing himself upright to lord over me, Tweed's fangs protrude from his lips, panting with undisguised hunger. In the dim light, his eyes glow, filled with a feral yearning I recognize instinctively. I've seen that look before. It's the same look that hunters give to their prey. Well, string me up and show me your weapon, because this doe is ready to be pursued.

"Leave me again and I'll kill you," Tweed delivers with almost perfect conviction. The glint of mischief in his eyes gives him away. Romantic passion isn't our comfort zone–unadulterated resentment is. Shoving him off me, he tumbles onto the next bench down, his towel falling away of its own accord now. I pounce, straddling his hips.

"Let me leave and I'll kill myself," I smirk until I hear myself. Wait, that's not sexy. It doesn't matter either way as Tweed's hand finds my hair, tugging me lower to meet his mouth. Just as our lips brush, the entire room lurches forward and we both go flying.

"Party's over, lovebirds!" Hatter shouts from outside. "Time to go home!" I try to stand until the carriage lurches once more, the bison's gruff laughter sounding all around. Tweed catches me, easing a satin robe over my shoulders. Tying the belt around my waist, I pout at him, my libido not at all happy with the change in circumstances. Tweed smiles–actually smiles, causing my chest to flutter.

"You heard the man–we're going home," he grins. And damn myself, I melt into a puddle right there on the sauna floor.

# CHAPTER 10

If a toddler were to use chess pieces as building blocks, bunching and staking them together in a haphazard combination–that's how I would describe the Red Castle. Turrets of rooks, horizontal hallways of bishops, and pawns scattered wherever they felt like at the time of construction. At the center, a singular queen piece stands tall and proud, ringed with stained-glass windows and balconies. The structure's only saving grace is its white marble coating, glimmering in an endless summer.

The closer we traveled, the warmer the weather became. Now, standing on the castle's footsteps, a steady coating of heat beats down but is in no way overly humid. The perfect blend of sun-bathing temperature without my lacey bralette and harem pants stroking my skin. Magic hums along the breeze like sea horse flies, fluttering by on shimmering wings.

"The air," I wheeze, "is so fresh, it's burning my lungs." Only Dormouse chuckles as the grand doors are opened inwards. A pair of heart play cards standing either side, their gaze fixed on each other. "Aww, I remember my first gay crush," I muse as I enter, patting the large 'Two' printed where his shoulder should be. "Emily Scrupps, fifth grade. She used to twizzle her gum around her finger. All very suggestive," I bob my eyebrows. Hands at my back push me forward into the entrance lobby.

"They're desperately trying not to look at you," Tweed mutters in my ear, rushing me along into the lobby. A grand affair of chandeliers and polished tile, no other colors than white, black, and red used within the decor. "They're human men, remember?"

"Not really, T-Dick," I return to his old nickname. No matter what impasse we've reached, where the teasing seems lighter and the quick glances appear more heated, my frustration bleeds through. "Since nothing has been explained to me, I don't remember anything at all."

"A travesty which will be rectified at once," a sweet voice chimes from the top of the stairs. She's exactly as I remember, not a hair out of place beneath her jeweled crown. A wispy, scarlet gown flows perfectly around her, just barely brushing her ankles upon descending the steps as if her slight feet have no need to touch the floor at all. Her vibrant red hair is fixed in cascades of curls that highlight her delicate features. The image of authority and grace, and I hate her for it.

"Hatter, it's so wonderful to have you back." Arabelle inclines her head toward my distracted friend. He's too busy grinning at the ostentatious decor. Shifting her focus to Tweed, the queen rushes in for a brief hug before stepping back, fully composed. "You've had quite the journey, valiant Knave. Take the time to rest and center yourself." *Weird*. Then, last and certainly least, she turns to me.

"And Malice. At last, I can formally welcome you to my castle." Offering me her hand, I raise one eyebrow. This must be some secret form of handshake which I give my best shot. Slapping her palm, I trickle my fingers across hers and click them a moment later. *Nailed it*. Arabelle clears her throat, brushing down her skirt. "Please, join me. I have already set up the dining room for high tea."

Swishing her skirt, the queen leads the way while I hang back. Both playing card statues step forward, spears in their hand vibrating through the tiled floor. Seems I don't have much of a choice. At least Tweed hangs back, giving me a half shrug.

"She's not so bad if you give her a chance. Once you see past her title, she's like the little sister I never had." He smiles easily here, as if the weight of the realm can't find him in this castle. After all, this is the only home he's ever known.

"Must be a big moment for you. Bringing a girl home to meet the family," I wink. Dangerous territory I'm entering, feeling all too comfortable declaring myself as Tweed's girl. Playing into the sweet fantasy which no doubt won't last, his fingers link with mine.

"It's no different from the added pressure of making a good impression on Hatter, as your Wonderlust father figure."

I stumble over myself. Tweed's chest rumbles in what I'm sure should be laughter, his grip on my hand tightening. Of all the things he could have said, that was the one to catch me off guard the most.

Stepping into the dining room, the dainty woman now seated at the far end of the table immediately shoots a glance at our joined hands. I shake mine free first. The heart painted over her lips tilts knowingly as Tweed pulls out my chair, at the furthest point away from her as possible.

Other guests flock through the doors to join us. Apparently, this tea was an invitation to all who reside here; the white rabbit who still can't walk in a straight line, a few oxen dressed as guards, a gryphon whose gaze lingers on Tweed until the vampire has found his seat, all the way down the table at Arabelle's side. The place of a Knave, obediently waiting for his Queen's next order. A click of her fingers, and it's deemed time to eat.

Irony is a bitter bitch at the best of times. All I've craved, since I became a Hatter, is tea and cake. Yet now, with the most magnificent display stretching across the dining table, I've undoubtedly lost my appetite. Whether from the lack of trust I have in Arabelle's intentions, or the way she and Tweed are having a hushed conversation between themselves, which happens to repeatedly mention my name, who can be sure?

"Hatter," I interrupt him, half making-out with a Victoria sponge. He has no such qualms about the food. "I'm not quite aware of Wonderlust's customs. Is it usual to be summoned for high tea, but not invited to partake in the general gossip?" Unhelpfully, Hatter shrugs and goes back to eating. Across the other end of the table, however, two pairs of startled eyes are now fixed on me.

"Forgive us. There's much to be discussed. Tweed and I aren't used to sharing our thoughts with outsiders," Arabelle smiles politely. Turning her attention to piling up her plate with jam tarts, I'm not so easily placated.

"Share away," I gesture with a flick of my hand. "I'll just be here, dying in the meantime." At the sight of my arm, the gryphon chokes on his cranberry juice and spits the straw out of his beak. Reaching across Dormouse's mini tea party on a table mat and taking my wrist in his claw, he turns it back and forth. The word 'plagued' is muttered up and down the table before I snatch my arm back. Now I have everyone's attention...

"Is there a king around, or is he hiding in the dungeon with the others deemed unsuitable for freedom?" My eyes narrow at the Queen. Tweed may be giving me a warning shake of his head, but I don't know Arabelle. Least of all, I definitely don't trust her. Despite it all, she smiles sweetly and speaks with years of self-control.

"I've been told men don't hold the same social standing in this realm as the one you are used to. In Wonderlust, the strength of the monarch is down to the individual, not their gender. The strong will rule and the weak will follow. That's logic," Arabelle tips her head to Tweed, relaying the phrase he would commonly use as a tubby, carefree boy. How times change.

"Indeed," I purse my lips. I have yet to see the strength Arabelle claims to hold. Maybe I should take her into the back garden with a pair of rusty pipes and see who fairs better.

To break the tension, small bouts of chitchat break out amongst the oxen. Some try to engage Hatter but he's occupied, filling my plate with finger sandwiches, scones, and slices of cake, before pouring me a cup of tea. There's a distinct lack of mouse-butt hairs in this tea, which is the only reason I accept it. Slumping back in my throne-like seat, all red velvet and thick cushion, I sigh contentedly and sip loudly.

"Is the food not to your satisfaction?" Arabelle breaks through the chatter. She seems wholly concerned with my actions, rather than the gecko creeping between the plates towards her jam tarts.

"The food is fine, the company is debatable," I shrug. There's a sharp intake of breath from the other guests. I pay them no heed, swirling a bright orange curl around my forefinger. Like a true Karen, I'm taking my grievances right to the top–-the big boss who refuses to falter in her perfect smile and delicate mannerisms. In fact, Arabelle lightly laughs.

"I suppose you'll have to give me time. I'm familiar with the ways and words of the only Hatter I've known. It'll take some adjusting to get to know your quirks." My eyebrows shoot to my hairline. I'm one-thousand percent sure she intended to insult me. Continuing to slurp my tea, Arabelle holds me in a stare-off until her fist snaps out, slamming the gecko into the tablecloth. Yet still, *still*, her smile doesn't falter.

"It's just occurred to me, you haven't had a formal tour. Please, allow me to show you around." Arabelle pushes up from her seat, dabbing at the corners of her mouth with a handkerchief, and tosses it over the gecko splat. Tweed rushes to join her, but she eases him back into his seat with a gentle touch on his arm. What a basic whore.

"At ease, Knave. I can manage from here. You should feed and rest, there is much you need to decide upon." *As cryptic as ever*, I roll my eyes. I wait until Arabelle has rounded the entire table before I sigh and stand. Gesturing to the doorway, I mutter to get this thing over with when a rush of wind whips my hair aside.

"You cannot kill her," Tweed feels the need to warn me. I pout, but huff in agreement as I follow Arabelle into the next room. Despite how disjointed the structure appears from the outside, each hallway and room flows flawlessly from one into the next. I even hunt for a disjointed crack in the striped wallpaper, imprinted with gold-framed hearts, but there are none.

In her shimmering gown, Arabelle leads me through the castle with a mischievous twinkle in her eye. Maybe it should be me who's worried about her going on a murdering spree. The corridors twist and turn like a labyrinth, while chandeliers swing from the ceiling to a violin's tune, seeping from the very walls. Encountering talking portraits along the way, we pass another version of the dining room where tables serve themselves and chairs pirouette in circles. With each step, I gain more of an understanding as to why Hatter pledged his loyalty here.

Along the labyrinth of corridors, each room unveils an enchanted spectacle. The hall of mirrors distorts reality, while the library of talking books whispers forgotten tales. In the kitchen, bespelled pots and pans dance merrily, whipping up a concoction of foreign smells which aren't completely unpleasant. The garden, a riot of colors, blooms with upside-down trees and floating flowers. In itself, Red Castle is a hive for madness and mayhem–a Hatter's preferred state.

"This way," Arabelle has yet to pause for half a second. I've placed us at the rear of the main lobby, directly underneath the largest Queen chess piece. A discreet staircase mirrors the grand one on the other side of the wall, spiraling upwards. My calves start to burn halfway up, my thighs screaming three-quarters of the way, until I'm crawling over the final step, panting.

“You–,” I gasp for air, “You do that every day?” Arabelle peers over her shoulder, her golden eyes confused at my struggling. Using a brass statue to pull myself upright, I approach Arabelle in the spot where she’s finally stopped. There’s no need to guess whose room we’re standing outside of, the wooden door vast and curved with a thousand hearts in all sizes.

“I hope this will give you some clarity on how things work around here,” the young queen breathes. Wrapping her slim fingers around the handle, the lock yawns and clicks open for her. I mimic her stance, ramrod straight as the door swings inwards. I blink once, twice, and many more times until my mind catches up with my eyes.

“What...the fuck am I looking at?” At first, all I see is red, as expected. My brain automatically warped the shapes around the extensive boudoir into hearts, but on closer inspection, they’re...vulvas. Thick, juicy lips set with a round clit at the hilt. And they’re everywhere - cushions, bedding, curtains, the rug with an extra mound of fraying threads which resemble public hair. Arabelle tries to follow me inside, but I duck aside. This isn’t a murder mission; it’s a tribade trap.

“I sensed some concern pertaining to my relationship with the Knave. I wanted to reassure you, my relationship with him is strictly platonic. He holds nothing of use to me, and I pose no threat to you.” There’s nowhere I can look in this room, which doesn’t shove a pussy in my face. Somehow, even the flames on vaginal candles flicker in the same suggestive shape. Fine, Arabelle is a lesbian–that’s all she had to say. I’m a carnivore and I don’t feel the need to hang meat kebabs all over my walls.

“At most, I was hopeful we could be friends.” I twist around to face her so sharply, Arabelle jolts back a step. All of my instincts scream this is a trap, a clever way to drop my guard. I’ve been betrayed, harshly and recently.

But if I turn off the millions of voices in my head, Arabelle merely waits for my response. Perfectly poised, but her years of etiquette training shouldn't automatically make her a pretentious asshole.

"No one has ever really wanted to be my friend," I tilt my head. "I suppose it makes sense to pop my friend cherry in your vulva vault. But don't get any idea–I'm all about the dick."

"Noted," Arabelle chuckles. "But admit it. If I hadn't shown you my bedchamber, you'd never have believed I didn't hold any romantic interest in the Knave." I nod in agreement, whilst backing out and closing the door. There are some things I'd happily never see twice.

"Speaking of bedchambers," a lop-sided smile takes residence on my face. Arabelle inclines her head, preparing to dismiss me.

"Choose whichever you would prefer. Perhaps one with a lonely vampire moping inside wouldn't go a miss," her smile grows and cheeks pinken. Okay, Miss Minx, I see you playing matchmaker. Unluckily for Tweed, I run on a strict treat-'em-mean, keep-'em-keen program and dicking where I doze is a strict no-no. Being a Hatter requires chaotic freedom, and being Malice...well, that's just a damn shitshow in itself.

# CHAPTER 11

I've paced these halls for longer than I care to acknowledge, hunting for a free space I can occupy while I'm visiting. During my lonesome stroll, I've come to the conclusion that having my very own bedchamber holds more sentiment than I originally thought. Sure, I could crash in Tweed's room, invading his personal space, and that would entertain me for a short time. But I've been trapped in a psych ward with the door wide open for years, and before that, I rarely stayed in one place long enough to feel like I belonged.

Rounding a corner, a pair of swans watch me from inside of a painting.

"Look Abigail, there goes a strange one." I flip my middle finger towards the birds in bonnets and keep walking. I've heard worse. Hell, I call myself worse.

An endless hallway stretches ahead, its checkered floor tiles making me dizzy. The same striped wallpaper adorned with whimsical hearts lines the walls, creating an illusion of perpetual motion. As I walk, the distant echo of my footsteps plays tricks on my mind until I'm sure someone is following me.

Twisting back, there's no one. Not even a shadow. I shrug and continue on. A door embedded into the wall has appeared to my right, which absolutely wasn't there before. I ignore it, figuring I wouldn't want to listen to those nosey swans every time I entered and exited. Eventually, I reach the end of the hallway and turn left.

"Look Abigail, it's back again," the swan comments. I still, staring down the same hallway.

"Oh, it is rather strange, Amelia," the second one agrees. "What an odd little beak." I gasp and touch my nose. How rude. "And it's hair. Perhaps they don't understand grooming back where it came from." Opening my mouth, I clamp it back shut again. Nope, I'm not entering into an argument with a painting. I'll just return later and slash it to shreds.

Looking back, the hallway behind appears to be the exact same. Fuck my life, why's it always me? This time, I stomp, preferring the slapping of my feet against the tile. Maybe if the castle knows I'm angry, it'll back off. Again, that lone door is awaiting. Tiredness wins. Shoving the door open, the hinges groan in time with my own grumbling. Seems neither of us are happy to be here.

The room is huge, evenly coated in a thick layer of dust. The four-poster bed has a slumped canopy hanging over aged bedsheets, an ottoman placed at the foot of the kingsize mattress. Across the Persian rug, two high-backed armchairs tilt inwards to face a stone fireplace, separated by a low coffee table. And above, a huge mirror glints through the cobwebs. None of that matters as I spy an additional room, the door ajar to reveal a claw-foot bathtub. Well, I'm sold.

Slipping into the bathroom, I close myself inside. It's oddly clean in here, and pristinely white. Discovering there's hot water running through the taps, I smile in relief. A bath is drawn in no time, steaming amongst the mass of bubbles spilling over the sides of the tub. Sinking down into the water, I smooth out my hair. I'll show those swans 'grooming', I tell myself, rubbing the bubbles into my matted orange curls. In fact, I'll show them all. In the mortal realm, I may be considered strange, but here, I'm just another resident of Wonderlust. Here, I fit in.

***

Thoroughly scrubbed, exfoliated, shaved, and plucked, I exit the bathroom as a new woman. Apparently, the room has decided to welcome me as one too. Lit by flickering candles along the fireplace, coffee table, and windowsills, not a scrap of dust can be found. The bed sheets are fresh; black satin with a set of folded pajamas on the end. On the bedside table, a box complete with a red bow awaits. Fixing my towel around my breasts, I pad across the room and spy my name on the gift tag.

*'In case I'm not enough. T-Dick.'*

Briefly, my eyes flutter closed. Emotions I'm unfamiliar with war inside my chest. I swoon, gripping the gift box to my chest. He did this–the room, the gift. My nose tingles, pre-empting the tears which well in my eyes. I'm generally not a crier but fuck. How dare Tweed make me tingle without even being present. When I've got a hold of myself, I pull the bow apart and lift the lid. A mixture of surprise and laughter bubbles from me, ending with a snort.

"A tentacle vibrator, huh?" A smooth voice travels through my chosen bedchamber. Wait one fucking minute...I whip around, dropping the box on the floor. "Is that a new kink I should be worried about?" Standing tall, fighting leathers clinging to his body, Cash's green eyes sparkle through the mirror. Behind him is a room that matched this one prior to Tweed's adjustments.

"I'm something you should be worried about," I point the vibrator at him. Its base must be a decent five inches wide, the shaft twisting upwards into a slender point. Large suckers decorate the mauve silicone, adding extra depth and texture. I'm getting hot and bothered just holding it, but I can't fall into bed and get to work with Cash staring at me. I mean, I could...but that's beside the point.

"What the fuck are you doing in my room?!" I shout. Cash pushes away from the armchair he was leaning against, sliding his hands into his pockets.

"I think you'll find you're in my room. This is where I lived back when I was welcome at Red Castle." He peers around from the inside of the mirror, taking his time to assess the changes. I stand tall, silently cursing the castle for bringing me here.

"Well, it's not yours anymore. You've made sure you're no longer welcome in Red Kingdom, or my sexual endeavors. So if you wouldn't mind fucking off, I've got multiple orgasms to see to before I start plotting how to separate your head from your body."

"Another tool you'd use to masturbate, I'm sure," Cash smirks knowingly. The image of his severed head between my legs shouldn't arouse me, but now it's stuck in my mind. As if Cash can scent my arousal through the glass, he chuckles. "Unfortunately, this mirror backs onto my room at Spade Castle, and you're far too entertaining to ignore. Please, continue with your evening plans. I won't say a word."

Zipping his lips, Cash turns the armchair and sits, one leg resting over the other. Even from across the room, there's no denying the bulge within his leather pants. He's dressed for battle, all in black, with daggers strapped to his chest, waist, and ankle. Devoid of all other colors, his blond hair pops more vibrantly than usual. Like the sun has taken residence behind his head, creating a halo effect. And those eyes, they spear me with an intensity I struggle to resist. Still, after everything I've endured, every promise I've made to Tweed, his twin makes me weak.

Lowering the vibrator, its weight corresponds with the dull ache growing in my core. I can't deny I'm aroused by the prospect of Cash watching me come, and Tweed did suggest I should use the sex toy when he hasn't pleasured me enough.

"Okay," I nod, flicking open my towel. It drops to my feet. "Enjoy the show." Lowering onto the bed, I lean against the headboard. My hair, straight with the weight of water, drips around the curves of my breasts, pooling in my belly button. My arm stretches aside, the vibrator tumbling from my fingers and hitting the floor as I speak. "Tweed! I need you!" I knew he'd hear me, and the door bursts open barely two seconds later. Faster than Cash can tear his gaze away.

My chest heaves beneath Tweed's glacial stare. His fangs grow past his lip, another burst of speed putting him naked on top of me. He enters me in one, slick moment. No pleasantries. No foreplay. As if his next breath only existed to pleasure me, he slams through my wetness, sheathing himself fully.

"I was hoping you'd call," he groans into my ear. Pulling out just enough to tease us both, he thrusts back in even more forcefully this time. "I've been aching to be back inside of you." I daren't mention it was only last night, because I agree. The longer Tweed isn't inside me, the more I feel the growing ache of emptiness. My mouth presses against his shoulder to conceal my grunts, my hands braced on his torso as I become accustomed to his punishing rhythm. The corded muscles of his six-pack shift beneath my palms, his skin icy cold to the touch. A perfect remedy for the inferno he's building within me.

"Didn't you like my gift?" Tweed mutters into my neck. I nudge his head with my chin, forcing him to look into my eyes.

"I don't need it. You'll always be enough." I don't know where the declaration came from. The tiny voice in the back of my head, which refused to be silenced, whispers I won't be able to keep such a huge promise. But I know Tweed needed to hear it. He needs to feel like he's worthy.

Pressing my lips against his, our kiss is short, disrupted by my cries. Pushing his hands beneath my ass, Tweed tilts me upwards and forces me to take him another inch deeper. I'm unbelievably wet, the water droplets streaming south on my body acting as added lubricant.

Digging my nails into his ass, relishing the dimples which appear with each thrust, our bodies move together as if they were crafted for this sole purpose. With each thrust, I feel the intensity of his desire fill me, pushing my own further toward a place I've not even pictured before in my fantasies. Somewhere I'm content with one person, one dick, and the endless orgasms he'll provide. Tweed's pace quickens further until he is pounding mercilessly into me, driving me higher and deeper towards the point of no return.

I tense just before screaming his name, my ankles locked behind his back, with my toes curled to the point of pain. Slipping from reality, I become a mess of pleasure, writhing beneath him, my hands lost in his blond hair. He's my anchor, my calling back to reality when I'm adrift. And Tweed gives me no reprieve, his movements equally as insistent as he speeds towards his own release. This is his pattern. The first time is about base needs, but he won't be satisfied until I'm beyond sated, my limbs limp. And then he'll still take one more from me.

Waves of heat course through me–all the way from my toes to the top of my head until it's overflowing outwards into the atmosphere all around. My hands slide over my sex-drenched skin, tugging at my nipples in an effort to acclimate my senses. The heavy scent of sweat and arousal burns through the air, the pulsing line within my neck capturing Tweed's attention. How I wish he could puncture through my skin, to drink from me, and own me in ways no one has before. But I'm sick–poisoned. I won't let him risk it.

"I need to taste you," Tweed groans. The rumble comes from deep within his chest, a basic instinct. I almost falter, debating tearing my own lip open if that will appease him. Just a small lick to ignite his own desire further, but Tweed has other plans. Jerking himself free, I gasp at the loss of contact, but in an instant, it's replaced with his tongue. Tweed moves at a rate I can't track, and I've never been so thankful for it. His tongue enters me, cleaning my cum from the inside and, in turn, creating more.

Tugging at Tweed's hair, I peer across the room to lock eyes with Cash. He hasn't moved from his chair, although his fingers are tearing into the upholstery. A smile lifts the corner of my mouth, my moans filling his bedchamber. I watch him track the flush on my chest, the sharp points of my pebbled nipples, the shifting and clenching of my abdomen. All the way down to my fingers threaded through his twin's hair. And it's the least he deserves.

Cash betrayed me. Well, here's my payback, and it tastes sweeter than any amount of violence ever could.

# CHAPTER 12

The low beat of drumming rouses me from the most blissful sleep. I stir in the darkness, rolling into a cold dip in the mattress. Stretching out, I vaguely wonder if it was the side Cash preferred when this was his bed. It sure is comfortable, and the same size as his large body. His thickly muscled, solid body…I shoot upright, halting that particular thought process. The room is silent, no sign of the vampire I can't forget lurking within the mirror, nor the one responsible for my intense wet dreams. Even in sleep, I can't get enough.

My feet touch the floor, that gentle drumming beating distantly. I refuse to be rushed, opening the curtains on a fresh morning. Having the time to sit at a vanity and prepare myself for the day is a rarity. The white pine drawers are filled with all kinds of lotions and gadgets I plan to take full advantage of. Early rays of a beautiful dawn leak through the windows while I primp and preen myself, pointedly ignoring the mirror behind. This is my room now, my space to re-discover myself.

Finding the wardrobe filled with clothing for me, I pick out something I would have scoffed at a few weeks ago. A white mini dress, dotted with daisies. Slung around the neck of the hanger, a pair of white cork wedges have been set to match. It's cute, and hell, I can be cute.

After I finish dressing and smoothing down my hair, I head into the bathroom to brush my teeth. The girl who stares back at me over the basin is foreign, her large blue eyes framed by long, thick lashes and my best attempt at make-up. My orange hair has been straightened into a sleek curtain which tickles my waist. But it's the healthy pinch of color and the confident smile which strike me the most. I walk without a single wobble in my step, assuming the 'new me' as I reach the main bedroom door. A scoff sounds just before I pull it open.

"Is there a problem?" I tut without bothering to look back. I can sense Cash lingering within his Spade Castle bedchamber.

"You look ridiculous," he growls. "A few nights with my brother and you're inclined to change everything which makes you special? I thought you were better than that." A bitter laugh escapes me as I release the handle. Like a fish on a hook, Cash knows exactly how to reel me in.

"I'm the one who looks ridiculous? You're so shrouded in your own bullshit, I can only just make out the jealousy in your glare." Placing my hands on my hips, I look Cash up and down. He appears as if he hasn't slept, his eyes tormented with dark rings and his skin is ashy. If I cared enough, I'd also note his cracked lips are thin and muscles appear slimmer, but I'm not going to do that. Equally, Cash ignores anything I have to say, steamrolling ahead with his mission to make me doubt myself. Good luck with that.

"I'd have had you exactly as you were. At least then I know I'm getting the real you, not some imitation of any other girl in any realm." Fury explodes through my veins, but I manage to keep it locked within, a mask of indifference fixed upon my face.

"Except you're not getting any of me," I roll my eyes. "You ruined your chances, and trust me, I gave you enough. If you don't like what you see, stop looking. But you're not going to drag me down into your self-destructive pit where no one loves you. I'm on a different path now, to discover exactly who I was supposed to be." This time, I grab the handle and yank the door open. Striding into the hallway, the door begins closing of its own accord when Cash's last quip slips free.

"I sincerely hope you live long enough to see that through." I stop still. A shudder rolls the length of my spine, an outburst of anger seeing my fist smashing through the nearest vase. Blood drips from my knuckles as I continue to stride away, leaving Cash's bullshit far behind.

"Fuck that guy," I growl to myself. The hallway doesn't appear half as long today, the corner with the swan painting quickly approaching. They're asleep, snuggled together and snoring softly. I pause, wondering if the old or new Malice will prevail. Reaching out, I grab the frame and shake it vigorously. Old Malice it is. The swans honk, their necks becoming tangled as I walk away snickering.

It's not hard to find my way. I merely follow the beat of the drums to the top of the grand staircase. At the base, the pair of playing card guards are patiently waiting, their stubby arms beating the instruments slung over their bodies. They break their stare-off to eye me suspiciously.

"The Queen requests your presence," Number Eight says. Both turn sharply, leading the way. I expected them to take me towards the dining room, hoping breakfast would already be served. That will teach me for skipping out on yesterday's cake-fest. Instead, the guards march towards the rear of the lobby where an exit takes us into the gardens.

Color blares from every direction, the flowers being tended to by gardeners. Moles in weeding gloves and sun hats, to be specific. They pay careful attention, using their sense of smell and touch to sniff out the dead blooms and pluck them free. The air is perfumed with sweetness, an undercurrent of rich soil just beneath. Beyond the rose bushes, it occurs to me, there are no walls. The royal gardens flow effortlessly into the rolling, green hills, open to anyone who may decide to wander in. A bold, potentially naive, move.

Around the next bend, I'm led into a commotion. A deep snarl causes everyone else in the gardens to freeze, except for me. My core tightens deliciously, my teeth sinking into my lower lip to hold back a moan. Pushing past the card guards, I find Tweed. The sight of him is my undoing.

Blond hair pushed back from his scowl, his jaw set in the hardest of lines. There's a tick beating there, one I am seconds away from feeling out with my tongue. At the collar of his knave uniform, his Adam's apple, a particular weakness of mine, bobs before he smells the air. I clench my thighs together harder. Glowing green eyes, swirling with fury, snap to my face.

"Woah," he breathes low. I caught it though, a faint blush coating my cheeks. At the end of his raised forearm, a six-foot piglet is writhing for breath.

"I-I didn't mean any off-ffence, Sir," the piglet squeals. He's extremely well dressed, in a suit of checkers and hearts, brass buttons and golden cufflinks. Tweed seems to remember he's pinning the creature up against the bush and snarls in his face once more. "I only meant to suggest–"

"Don't suggest. You're either serving or you'll be served–to the queen with an apple in your snout. Now leave. Everybody, leave!" Tweed whips his arm away. Another harsh reminder of the monster he is, another whimper lodging itself in my throat. The card guards, the moles and the piglet all rush to obey. I would too if I thought my legs could carry me.

Tweed waits for there to be no sounds of movement, not even the sway of leaves in the wind before he joins me beneath the floral archway. I lift a hand to the rough leather covering his chest, admiring the swarm of thick veins rippling from the short sleeves, from biceps to wrists.

"For someone who has a hard time accepting authority, your Knave act tickled my pickle there."

Tweed's scowl eases, his lips twitching with the hint of a smirk.

"How do you know it's an act, and this isn't just everyday me?" A few weeks ago, I'd have easily been convinced there was nothing more to Tweed than the asshole he lets the world see. I should have known better.

"I have fantastic intuition," I shrug. Tweed throws his head back, barking a sharp laugh which others would mistake for a sound of irritation.

When he returns to look at me, the icy edge to his eyes has melted. In fact, I could swear those emerald pools are heating as they travel the length of my body.

"What's the occasion?" he asks, slipping his fingers into the straightened length of my hair. It falls through his hand like a waterfall, leaving those cold knuckles to brush the base of my throat instead.

"A pair of swans in the painting down the hall commented on my grooming," I opt for. It's not a lie, but the rest I'm withholding is as blatant as the pink tinge to my cheeks. Fuck, who even am I right now? "And I woke up this morning feeling like it's time for a change." That part is undeniably true. I've made the firm decision to put Cash behind me and keep pushing onward. With Tweed, at Red Castle. I can have a stable home here and I refuse to let myself fuck it up this time.

There is no reply. Not a verbal one, anyway. Dragging me aside into an alcove, hidden within the white vines of a willow tree, Tweed's hands explore my body. My hair to my nape, his thumbs brush over my pulse. My throat to my breasts, his fingers dipping inside the bra cups. I arch against the summer dress, desperate for connection with my nipples, but he evades me. Traveling south, he strokes the top of my thighs, dipping inwards to find me bare and soaking wet.

"Do you like it?" I breathe, eagerly awaiting his response. Tweed dips his head, his lips an inch from mine.

"I like you," he admits. My eyes flutter closed. "No matter how you package yourself up." Claiming my mouth, I lean into him, savoring the taste of his lips. I will never tire of this feeling. An explosion of lust, tongues clashing with unrestrained passion. He refused me for so long, unknowingly making me yearn for the impossible. Those fingers, cold as ice, remain between my legs. Toying with me, circling in my wetness but never going deeper. I groan in frustration.

"Surely Arabelle won't mind waiting while we–"

"Arabelle is waiting for you?" Tweed snaps upright as if I've slapped him. Despite the warmth of my skin, a bitter coldness shuts down between us as he steps away.

"Seriously?! Can't we just...fool around for a bit?" I plead like a virgin pining for the quarterback. Apparently, while I was busy scrubbing the frizz from my hair, I accidentally washed away my undeniable appeal. Pulling back the vines, Tweed snaps his fingers and the card guards come running.

"I'll see you at dinner tonight," Tweed offers me a small smile, ushering me back through the archway. The guards start marching, not even looking back to check I'm following. Well, I suppose I don't have a choice if Tweed won't mess around with me while I'm under Arabelle's summons. Whatever the female equivalent to blue balls is, that's what I'm currently sporting. While I chew on the inside of my cheek, silently fuming, we travel far from the castle until the canopy of trees hides it from sight. Rose bushes line the thin walkway I've found myself on, approaching what seems to be a dead end.

"We shall wait here," Number Two announces, coming to a swift stop. I look past them at the raised bank of green grass. I know better than to ask questions which won't be answered. Sucking in and slipping between them, I squint through a twisted thicket of towering mushrooms. Hidden behind, lies a cave. I shift at the iridescent flora, discovering its entrance is a whimsical archway of entwined vines and opalescent crystals, beckoning the curious to enter. Cue me.

I need to use the walls for support as my wedges teether on uneven ground, tree trunks creeping through the stone. Diamond icicles drip with morning dew, casting a soft, ethereal glow further within. Cash told me once, only a diamond stake from the Cave of Wonders could kill him. He also mentioned Arabelle gifted this cave and its contents to her darling Knave.

Outstretching a hand, my fingers hover over one of the spears hanging low. It's razor-sharp, sure to slice my skin if I were to take a hold. Withdrawing, I clench my hand to my chest in fear instinct might take over and I try to tug it free anyway. Moving onwards, I make a mental note to ask Tweed to retrieve one for me. It's only logical to be prepared for Cash's next attack because after this morning, I'm sure it's closer than ever.

I continue on, steering further through the darkened tunnel. Luminescent moss carpets the floor, guiding the way to the cave's centerpiece: a crystalline pool of magic. The water shimmers with hues of every color imaginable, and it pulses with otherworldly energy. At the edge of the pool, seated regally upon a throne of rose petals, is Arabelle. Her red hair cascades behind her back like molten rubies, and her eyes sparkle with an enigmatic allure. Wearing a gown of midnight blue satin, the material reflects in the pool's glow, appearing as if the fabric is shifting like liquid moonlight. Her gaze is focused on the water, entranced by it, until I wobble on my wedges and cause a trickle of rocks to fall loose.

"Malice," Arabelle beams at me. Her eyes lower to the ground, where I'm struggling to stand upright. "Oh, forgive me. Can we make our guest more comfortable, please?" Her question is directed at the stone around my feet. The ground instantly smooths out, allowing me to join her side. High above, a skylight, which has packed the chamber with morning light, fills with autumn leaves, all falling in a choreographed motion to fluster around my legs and back. A throne similar to Arabelle's is fashioned from the leaves, sturdy enough for me to settle onto.

"Thank you," I say to no one or nothing in particular. This place is writhing with magic, and Arabelle's presence is infused in the midst of it all. I could easily imagine I'm standing at the heart of Wonderland itself, where the boundaries of reality and fantasy blur. For a short while, I'm happy to sit in the comfortable silence Arabelle was enjoying previously. But soon enough, my leg begins to shake and I fiddle with the hem of my dress.

"Are we...is there a reason you've summoned me here?" I struggle to say without sounding short. "I mean, because it's breakfast time. Most important meal of the day and all." Arabelle slowly drags her eyes away from the pool to meet mine, her smile growing impossibly more. Unlike usual, she isn't wearing a scrap of makeup. Her face appears even more youthful, her skin flawless without the need for cosmetics. Bitch.

"I thought we could have a bit of girl bonding time." I swallow thickly, and as if the leaves can sense my discomfort, they shift me an inch away from the queen.

"I've fallen for this trap before. One minute, it's girl bonding time. The next, there's a double-ended dildo hanging out of my ass." Arabelle's eyes widen, her cheeks turning pink.

"Erm, no." She states quickly. A bit too quickly. Now hang on, what's the matter with me? Am I not hot enough for her? "What I meant was, as two important people in the Knave's life, we should get to know each other." I nod, figuring that makes sense. Although I can't shake the feeling they've been speaking about me.

"Okay, sure. What do you want to know?" I exhale loudly. My past isn't something I like to discuss, but seems to be all anyone wishes to know. "How I killed my dad? Why I didn't escape the mental institution sooner? Or is this more of a," I finger quote in the air, "'*What are your intentions with my Knave,*' sort of conversation?"

To her credit, Arabelle doesn't seem put off by me in the slightest. My defense mechanism to scare people away before they get too close is not working in any sense.

"Why has no one ever asked to be your friend before?" she raises one slim eyebrow. I sigh. Oh god, we're starting here.

"I don't really know..." I stare into the pool of shimmering magic, hoping I'll find any answer amongst the shifting colors. "I mean, before I first visited this realm, I was the weirdo who lived in her daydreams and wandered the woods of her family's estate alone. I reckon if I hadn't been so distracted by an argument my parents had been having that day, I wouldn't have fallen down the white rabbit's hole." I kick at some stones by my feet.

"But then I came here, and although it was new and strange and scary, I loved it. I don't know why I was so intent on returning to my boring life. Yet I did, and then I became the weirdo who spouted nonsense stories. The only person who I thought believed me was my father. He would come to my room every night and listen to my tales. Our little secret, he said, until he re-wrote and published them for the world to see. It was like having everyone read my private diary. I felt so betrayed and angry I lashed out, and now he's gone."

"I'm truly sorry," Arabelle breathes, not looking my way. I suddenly remember she also was responsible for her parent's death. If there's anyone in Wonderlust who might understand the emotional turmoil of doing such a thing, it would be her. I reach across, giving her hand a gentle squeeze.

"It's not your fault. Where I come from, people are driven by greed."

"Hmmm, yes, that too. But what I'm sorry for is that you were able to leave Wonderlust in the first place. You were supposed to stay here, but you always manage to find a way to do the impossible. That's why Hatter–" Arabelle suddenly catches herself. Tugging her hand away, she stands to pace around the far side of the pool.

"Arabelle," I say in a low tone, pushing to my feet. "That's why Hatter, what?" I ask with no room for argument. She presses her lips together, regret filling her features. Time for a different tactic. "I thought you wanted to be friends. I'm opening up to you, now it's your turn." Nodding to herself, Arabelle reaches out, swirling her finger through the magic. It responds to her touch. An ink spill of midnight blue, a perfect match to her dress, blooms in the center and spreads, consuming all color in its path. Once an even coating of shimmering navy covers the surface, images appear.

Hatter stands in front of his house, and he's crying. I gasp, gripping the edge to lean forward. I've never seen him look so sad before. Dropping to his knees, his fingerless gloves push into the dirt. He's speaking, although I can't hear the words.

"Hatters are gifted with the magic to believe whatever they wish for into existence," Arabelle tells me. "The Hatter we know and love only ever wanted one thing. To have a child, an heir to his legacy. Yet what he wished for, wasn't of this world. You took so long to get here, Malice, that he tried replacing you with another. But, finally, you arrived. Our land was to be saved the turmoil of being Hatter-less."

"Why are Hatters so important?" I look up to ask. So much hinges on her next words.

"Your realm has Gods, we have Hatters. They are central beings who keep the balance of chaos and calamity in check. They are the Heart of Wonderlust. Without them...well, you've seen a fraction of what had become of our world while he was missing. And now we have two." Arabelle's eyes sparkle, her face the picture of awe as she stares at me. I'm to be a central being to these people. Turning my gaze back to the image floating below, I swallow past the lump in my throat. The Hatter in the vision is still babbling silent words, his fingertips glowing beneath the soil. Except he's not babbling. He's chanting.

"What did he do?" I ask gravely. Arabelle wrings her hands in front of her.

"You managed to find a pocket in our realm," she babbles more to herself. "Like a tear, which should have been sealed after you entered. The Hatter was beyond distraught, and his misery was what started the black magic. It seeped from him, into the very earth on which we stand. What you're witnessing here is a recollection spell, designed to pull you straight back. But it didn't work that way. Hatter accidentally created what we've been calling, 'The Allure'. Instead of tugging you back towards us, it caused the males of our land to seek you out. Most of them were never seen again."

"Figures," I mutter, my heart sinking. Arabelle walks to my side, trying to take the hand I've curled into a fist. "I should have known there was a reason Tweed kept coming back to me." My voice, although low, rings around the cavern with deflated certainty. For the first time in too long, I don't feel as invincible, and that scares the shit out of me.

"Malice, you misunderstand." I allow Arabelle to hold my hand to her breast. "The Knave isn't a living being. Such magic doesn't work on his kind." Her words are careful, not wanting to state the obvious. The Allure doesn't work on Tweed or Cash. Their pull to me is purposeful, as is mine in response. "What he feels for you is real. And trust me when I say, he doesn't offer his affections freely." This, I'm well aware of.

Nodding slowly, I retract my hand. Now is not the time for fuzzy wuzzies in my tummy. In the pool of magic, Hatter's hair has dimmed, his fingers sprawled in the soil. The spell he chants must be powerful, as it drains the color from his very being. Such sacrifice, yet he never said a word. Not once has Hatter mentioned how much he gave to get me back, but I suppose a humble father wouldn't. He's just happy I'm here.

"Thank you," I incline my head to the Queen. "For telling me the truth. And for being the truest friend I've yet to have." Despite sharing a polite smile, Arabelle's unease is evident. She didn't expect our bonding session to take this turn, for so much information to be divulged.

Once upon a time, I may have consumed this knowledge and acted irrationally. As it stands, all I see in the magic is a broken man who yearns to love and be loved. How different our lives would have been if I'd stayed. Something I will regret for the rest of my life.

# CHAPTER 13

I haven't seen Cash for days. Not that I'm looking, but even his presence beyond the mirror has been non-existent. I keep expecting him to burst through the portal, declaring war. But there's nothing. I suppose he really does despise my new look.

Smoothing down my perfectly straightened hair, I pace out onto the balcony and lean on the curved stone wall. The drop below is not one I would survive. Although, I'm not looking down today. In fact, I haven't even thought about escaping since I arrived at Red Castle. For someone who's sent her life running away from herself, it's at odds with my psyche to be so still. My feet are itching to take off, the little voice in the back of my head telling me to jump. Not this time.

Instead, I look up. The sky is a clear shade of blue, too perfect to be real. Birds soar high above, their wings spread wide as they dance through the summer's breeze. I watch them for a while, jealous of their freedom. I may be content, but I still can't fly. To glide over Wonderlust, learn and understand all of its chaotic beauty, and still return to this bedchamber by choice. That's true freedom.

A stifled groan sounds. So low, I almost miss it. The hairs on the back of my neck prickle, an ornate awareness arising. He's returned. I inhale deeply, steeling myself against whatever sarcastic taunt is about to come. But when it doesn't, I look over my shoulder, peering into the darkness beyond the mirror. No sign, other than distant shuffles accompanied by pained groans. Wherever he's been, probably battle planning with his Queen like Tweed currently is, it's depleted his usual jokey energy.

I take a step towards the mirror, his hidden outline slinking over to the bed. His movements are hindered and slow. My hand lifts, a question ready at my parted lips. Then I remember, I don't give a fuck and stride from the room before I do something stupid.

An off-the-shoulder gray sweater sways in time with my hushed steps, as if I can power walk my way back to good sense. Black PVC leggings cling to my legs, knee high boots putting me four inches taller. If Cash had looked up, I wonder what he'd have thought of today's look. No doubt, he'd eagerly insult me again, but would it have been with a glint of hunger in his eyes? And why the shit do I even care?

The swans are ready for me this time, glaring with beady eyes as I pass. "Oh, good goose, Amelia. It's on stilts today."

"Now there's more of it to look at, Abigail." The swan in a blue bonnet gobbles, flailing her head around as if her eyes are burning. The other quickly joins in. I don't pay them any notice, waiting until I'm out of their range before lifting a crossbow from the nearest suit of armor. The arrow sails directly into Abigail, spearing the canvas. Their squawks accompany me all the way to the stairs, bringing a smile to my lips. A valid punishment for insulting my appearance.

One step down the grand staircase, a snorting mass rushing upwards barges me off my feet. The stack of bedsheets piled on his trotters fly in all directions, many of which landing on me.

"Oh no," he snorts, scrambling to knock them aside. His attempts to help only aid smacking me in the head several times. "Oh, h-heavens! I'm so sorry, so so sorry. Please d-d-don't tell m-my master about this." Bundling up the bedsheets into a heaped pile, I set them aside, too intrigued to care.

"Hey, I know you." I push myself upright, brushing down his embroidered suit. "I saw you in a nasty kerfuffle with Tweed the other day." The piglet winces at the Knave's given name.

"I can't t-talk to you," he whimpers, attempting to rush past. I refuse to let him.

"Of course you can't. It's not safe to talk to strangers. I'm Malice," I shove my hand forward. The piglet tries to evade me once more, slipping on the mound of bedsheets. He tumbles a few steps down in a fantastic display of floppy ears over ringed tail. I follow straight after, grabbing his trotter to pull him upright and give it a firm shake. "Now we've shook hands, you must give me your name. Them's the rules." The piglet stops struggling, his snout twitching.

"I m-m-must obey the rules," he mutters. I nod with a serious, slightly crazed, look in my eyes. Hanging his head, he finally relents. "I'm PB."

"Like peanut butter?" I raise a brow. He scoffs.

"Like p-pork belly. A constant rem-minder that I'm only useful as food if I can't s-serve my m-master." I nod in understanding. To be fair, it sounds like the sort of thing I would do if I had a pig for a servant. And smear apple sauce on his ass when he was asleep. That would really scare the shit out of him.

"Well, PB, today is your lucky day. I'm bored, so you've just gained yourself an assistant," I beam. PB looks like he's about to shit out his colon.

"No, no, n-no, no," he shakes his head. While he plays out the rest of his fit, I re-fold the bedsheets and pile them up in my hands.

"Lead the way. We've got business to attend to." Juggling the tower on one arm, I manage to smack his ass and send him bolting down the hallway with a squeal. Oh, today is going to be a fun day after all.

The hallways are forever changing, but somehow PB knows the way. From one bedchamber to the next, we knock, enter, change the sheets, and leave. It's a wonder how PB ever manages alone, when his rounded hands and the fitted sheet corners seem like mortal enemies.

Once we've finished the human rooms, we move on to the more exotic. A circular bed with a feline-like imprint dipping in the center of the mattress. A cupboard which resembles the inside of a cage, wood chippings, and torn newspaper all over the floor. I flick my finger against the bell hanging from a perch and PB squeaks, ushering me outside. He remains closer after that, his beady eyes flicking back to me every few seconds to anticipate my next move. Good luck, I rarely know myself.

"So, what did you do?" I ask when the curiosity bubbles over. PB tilts his head, continuing to lead me down an endless hallway. "The issue in the garden. What was Tweed so upset about?" At this back, PB's tail shoots out straight in alarm.

"I shouldn't tell you," he ducks around the nearest turning. I sigh, slapping my hands against my leggings now I have no bedsheets left to carry.

"And here, I was hoping we'd smoothly jump from acquaintances to friends." PB stops so suddenly, I crash into his back.

"Fr, fr," the pig shakes his head, the tag in his ear flapping as he struggles to compute. With a relenting nod, I quickly wipe the smirk off my face. That was much easier than expected. "I was informing my Master the honeymoon suite was still prepared should he have use for it." Now it's my turn to freeze, the color draining from my face.

"Honeymoon?" I breathe, feeling all kinds of sweaty in the wrong places. PB jolts, trying to stroke my arms.

"N-no forgive me!" The pig becomes even more flustered. "It's n-not like that. It's not intended f-f-for you, I mean."

"Then who the fuck is it intended for?!" Forget sweaty shock. Cue all-consuming envy. On the shitty end of my death stare, PB makes a high-pitched whining sound. I clamp my hands over my ears, in fear they might bleed. Tugging at his jacket, he bucks, struggling to remove the material. This is getting us nowhere, I think, and grab a hold of his shoulders.

"Okay, stop. Breathe, in for three, out for seven." Mimicking the rising and falling of my chest, PB slowly copies. He really doesn't have much puff for a piggy, but I suppose that's what wolves are for. Turning extra pink in the face, his body sags in my hold. "There we go. I always find the quickest route to the end is to start from the beginning."

"It all began with a mission," PB's nose twitches. He leads me into a room which is undeniably, Hatter's. The air is pungent, smelling of tea, sweat, and old clothing. There are clocks on every wall, and bookshelves running the length of the room, lined with teacups of every shape, size, and color. Two large windows hang over a huge bed, where hues of scarlet and gold catch on the four-poster canopy. The bedspread is covered in patchwork blankets. I make a mental note to return and explore the embroidery properly later.

Showing me to a dainty table fit with four rickety stools, PB explains to me the secrets Tweed seems to have been hiding. The mission to retrieve a mysterious object, how that object unleashed a prophecy over Tweed and Arabelle, and that the prophecy centered around Tweed taking a wife.

"Once the new Queen was crowned, she saw to it that her Knave received frequent female visitors of all species. He was ordered to lay with and feed on them, in the hopes one would present herself as a suitable bride. These exercises were always held in the honeymoon suite." Now we're alone and settled, PB speaks with a wiseness beyond his years without a single stutter in sight.

"So you were asking Tweed if he still had the need for such a space?" I clarify. PB's black eyes shoot to mine.

"I-I didn't mean to cause offense. The Knave has been my master since he rescued me from the woods, but he's never been forthcoming. I only meant to be prepared."

"Trust me, I'm almost impossible to offend." I reach across to take hold of his trotter and ignore the voice laughing in the back of my head. *Unless your name is Cash and you say I look ridiculous for giving a shit about my appearance for a change.* Yes, apparently, my offendibility depends on who is speaking.

Sitting back on the creaky stool, I rest my chin on my fist. So Tweed has been sleeping with every available female since Arabelle was crowned. And here I was thinking the fuckboy of the Tweedles was sitting in Spade Castle. A bitter feeling curls within, much more potent than the poison polluting my veins. I feel it bubbling like acid, creeping up the back of my throat as if I might be able to spit venom or just scream '*Vampire Whorebag*' really fucking loud.

The piglet opposite leans back in his seat, eyeing me with caution. I blink free of the impulse to find this honeymoon suite and shred the mattress open, and focus. PB is a male, yet he isn't drawn to me by the Allure. He also is the first one around here to give me a straight and honest answer. I want to press him, verbally gut him open, and make him squeal, but another thought takes hold.

All of those females. Those lonely, isolated females without enough men to distract them. No wonder being Tweed's mistress was their best option at companionship, regardless of how cold I can imagine he was towards them. So many factors, so many issues I can't solve. But I can do something minor today which might just assuage some guilt. Even if it's only mine.

"PB, there's somewhere I'd like you to take me."

Somehow, I've begun to make sense of the maze inside of this castle. With PB trying to guide me wrong on numerous occasions, I manage to stay on track and eventually approach the dungeon Cash once brought me to. The pig's teeth chatter the entire way. As I heave the heavy door open and it clangs against the stone wall, PB pees himself a little.

"I c-c-can't let you g-go in there," he stutters, shaking like a lone leaf in a gale-force wind. I raise a brow, daring PB to try and stop me. Instead, he squeals a lasting high-pitched cry, turns and runs in the opposite direction. Smart pig, he knew he wouldn't be able to change my mind. Inhaling so deeply my chest is puffed out, I step over the threshold.

Below, a series of flames flicker to life where torches are fixed into the walls. I've only been here briefly before, but I don't recall the eerie weight of desperation lingering in the air. I walk down the stairs, my fingers trailing the damp stone as the ceiling lowers.

Once at the base, I step into the cavern, which holds rows of cages. Thick metal bars separate the towered stacks of playing cards trapped within. Once, I believed Arabelle to be cruel, but now I have context. This was the only way she could save those loyal to the other Suits from flocking to Lillianna's castle, never to be seen again.

Shuffling in the end cell grabs my full attention. Playing cards wander forward, their miniature sizes allowing these ones to move around more freely within their confines. The children.

"Hello," I approach. The children's eyes widen in surprise as they see me approaching. I can sense their fear and apprehension, but also a glimmer of hope in their tentative gazes. They've been trapped in here for far too long, with nothing to do but play poker with themselves to forget their predicament. I smile gently, crouching down to their level.

"How are you all doing?" I ask softly.

One of the younger boys, who can't be any more than six years old, steps forward and takes my hand through the bars. It's tiny and cold, despite the white glove he wears. "We're scared," he whispers. "We don't know if we'll ever get out of here."

A spike of sadness pierces my heart, knowing I cannot guarantee their release from this prison. I've only just become aware of the Allure which has been placed on me and am yet to discover if there is a way to break it. Perhaps I should do them all a favor and speed up the poison traveling through my veins, reuniting these boys and men with their families in an instant. But that won't stop Lillianna, and if Wonderlust falls to ruin, they'll all be dead anyway.

Sighing, I squeeze that tiny hand tighter. It seems I'm as trapped as they are, but I'm not without my uses. I can at least offer them all a moment of respite, a brief escape from reality through the power of my storytelling. After all, I've always been good at stories.

"Well then," I say, with a twinkle in my eye. "How about I tell you all a story? A small tale to take your minds off of things?" The children's eyes light up at the suggestion, and they gather around me eagerly.

I take a deep breath and begin my story, weaving a fanciful tale of a humorous and daring knight on an adventure to save the deranged girl from her padded cell. They encounter many strange, wondrous creatures, becoming lost in an enchanted wood with no apparent escape. But they have each other. As the story takes shape, the hero becomes convoluted, a mix of the twins until I can't tell which one I'm describing.

My words free us all from the constraints of this musty dungeon and the fate that awaits. I may be the one walking freely, but my body contains a ticking time bomb. The least I can do is bring a small measure of peace to those I've unknowingly imprisoned.

The children's fears began to fade away, replaced by a sense of wonder and excitement. More hands slip through the bars, reaching for any free part of my arms. I let them pull me close, hoping the small amount of comfort I can provide is enough to see them through. The knight in my story holds his damsel similarly, making promises to destroy the invisible binds weighing her down. For the playing cards' sake, and mine, I hope it's not all just a story.

# CHAPTER 14

I toss and turn in bed that night. In a way, I feel relief. I was able to provide a moment of distraction to those who needed it most. On the other hand, the prison those cards must endure to avoid me while I lay in a plush, snug bed seems wrong. If anything, I should be the one caged. Kept hidden so Wonderlust can thrive. It seems no matter where I go or what I do, I'm always the problem.

"Can't sleep either, Crazy One?" Cash's voice fills the bedchamber. There's a pained croak to his tone, one which instantly tugs on my heartstrings. I flop onto my side, jamming the pillow over my ear. In doing so, a shot of pain bursts along the length of black webbing slithering further up my body. I don't need to see it in the dark to know of the spread. I can feel it sinking over my shoulder blades and downwards across my chest.

Despite my efforts, Cash's voice manages to slip through the cracks. "Maybe we can tire each other out." His chuckling quickly turns to a hacking cough which pulls the corners of my mouth into a frown. Slowly, I sit upright and spy him in his bed across the other side of the mirror. A simple lamp glows, highlighting his exposed back as he curls onto his side and tries to get his coughing under control.

"I figured vampires couldn't get sick," I comment. Damn, my curiosity is always getting the better of me. He doesn't answer, which is even more disconcerting. Cash wheezes, rolling onto his back. I watch as he continues, straining to pull himself upright to slouch against the headboard. I catch the peculiar hollowness to his face, the concave dips of his cheeks falling into shadow. Lifting a hand to push his hair back, his fingers refuse to extend from their gnarled, curled position. I'd expect such a sight from someone starved, but surely Lillianna is taking perfect care of her prized possession.

I beg myself to turn away. *Please don't fall for his bullshit. It's just another trap. Remember how fiercely the last one burned*. But when my mouth opens, my own voice betrays all of those voices ringing in my head.

"What the hell is she doing to you over there?" I breathe. Perhaps if no one hears me, it doesn't count. But, of course, he does.

"When the twin blood moons clash," he rasps, "and the sky begins to fall..." Phasing out, Cash's head lolls against the headboard. Staring directly into the lamp, I grow cold from the lack of green in his eyes. Only endless pits of darkness, void of humor or interest.

"Cash, you're scaring me."

"When tomorrow isn't set to arrive," he continues, tied up in his own thoughts, "and the man I've become doesn't matter anymore, will you come to me?"

I exhale too quickly. My chest tightens, a shiver claiming my spine. My mind both reels with too many responses yet goes blank all at once. I can't trust Cash. Not again, but when he sounds so helpless...I really wish I could. Lifting my gaze back to the being in the opposite bed, I find his focus is squarely on me.

"If nothing was promised, would you let me hold you through the night and fall into the abyss with you, Crazy One?"

I can't breathe. The poison in my chest seeps deeper into my system. A much-needed spike of pain and awareness clears my mind, but for some reason, I can't find the venom I so regularly depend on. When Cash is staring at me so intently, I can't bring myself to tell him to get fucked. Whether he's being truthful, or very cleverly exposing my weaker parts so the poison is taking a quicker hold, he's doing a fantastic job.

So instead, I snuggle into my pillow and say, "I'm tired, Cash. Let me sleep." And then proceed to lie awake overthinking in the darkness.

# CHAPTER 15

I've seen a lot of shit in my life, but watching Malice from a distance is one of the hardest I've had to witness. Especially when *he's* there. The door cracks open in the early hours of the morning, long after Malice has slipped into a fitful sleep. He wanders around, wasting time as if he's not going to slip beneath the covers and hold her tight. It's what I would do.

Eventually, he strips down and does just that, soothing her soft moans and jittering with his cold touch.

My jealousy for Tweed runs deep, intertwined with a deep-seated hatred for the life he forged for himself. A Knave, respected by his Queen, revered by those around him. And now, he has Malice. The one thing we used to share, or at least the memories of her we shared.

On this side of the portal, my own door flies open. Lillianna saunters into the room, her ever-present smirk twisted into a mischievous grin.

"Oh, Cash," she mutters, mockery and disappointment lacing her tone. "You're weak. Why aren't you allowing yourself to heal?" Her eyes gleam with a wicked satisfaction as she leans in close. "Do you think it will spare you further?" I glance at the mirror one last time, checking both Tweed and Malice are asleep to spare myself any further embarrassment. They can hate me all they like, but I will not be seen without my dignity.

Lillianna lowers on the edge of the mattress, strapping my wrists into iron cast manacles attached to the bed frame. I don't fight her, reserving my energy. She hums gently, placing a leather pouch onto the bed. Rolling it open, a range of instruments glint in the moonlight breaking through tears in the curtains. Scalpels, jagged knives, syringes, and the likes. I swallow against the lump which has formed in my throat.

I don't know what she wants from me, but every time I fail to provide it, the torture becomes worse. As Lillianna chooses her weapon, I prepare myself for the inevitable pain. The first cut is always the deepest, they say. But I know from experience that each cut is just as bad as the last. Running a finger along one of the scalpels, admiring its sharp edge, she looks back at me with a coy smile.

"What do you say, Cash? Shall we play?" I bite my inner cheek, closing my eyes as she traces the cold metal along my cheekbone. Too late, I realize that the blade is made of diamond. Slicing the skin on my face, Lillianna continues south, steering clear of my pulse. It wouldn't do her any good to kill me. I'm the only one she has left. I grit my teeth, clenching my fists as she continues to make her way down my chest and stops in the middle of my sternum. I know what's coming before she digs in deeper, cutting open my chest cavity.

Lillianna moves with precision, each move deliberate and calculated. She doesn't take her eyes off me, relishing in the agony she's inflicting. Her fingers are cold and cruel, twisting and turning as she searches for something. Extracting pieces of flesh, organs, and bone I'm sure I should need. She then turns to withdrawing blood with the syringe directly from my heart. I don't know what she's looking for, but by fuck, I wish she'd find it already. Even if it's the last ingredient she needs to complete whatever she's planning, I'd happily give it to her in exchange for my freedom.

The little boy inside of me wants to go home. Wants to find a home, where he won't be ogled or misused. I'd take a box room without light if that's what it takes. Anywhere I might find a slither of happiness with myself.

I should've known Lillianna wasn't going to wait too long before visiting me again. She's ruthless in her methods, and I am at her mercy. But I won't ever give her the satisfaction of seeing me break. Twisting and turning the sharp tools in her hand, I close my eyes and focus on my breathing, refusing to make a single sound. Not with Malice sleeping within earshot, Tweed breathing softly beside her ear.

Better than any vice, I concentrate on the bitter rage which sees me through Lillianna's next weapon of choice. A chisel to break my ribs individually. That same rage has kept me in its grip, growing increasingly tighter since I locked Malice in Fantasy Walk and left her behind. I was under orders from when I believed I had a choice of which side I was on. It's clearer than ever, that I never did. Lillianna enjoys watching me suffer, relishes in my pain and agony. And in that moment, just like her, I wanted to inflict a modicum of that pain onto someone else.

Despite my best efforts, the pain is unbearable. With each slice, saw, or break, my body tenses up, and I feel as though I might pass out. Lillianna is enjoying this too much. She delights in my suffering, her eyes glowing with a sickening pleasure as she continues her torture for what feels like hours. Making cuts and bruises all over my body, she whispers cruel things into my ear to keep me present. Somehow, probably from practice, I manage to make myself slip away into a world of my own. A world where Tweed isn't with Malice, where he is tortured just as I am.

Lillianna's hand moves with precision as she carves into my flesh, creating intricate patterns that only she can appreciate. She leans in close and whispers in my ear, her hot breath on my neck sending shivers down my spine. "You know why you're weak, right?"

I don't respond, gritting my teeth even harder as another wave of pain racks through my body.

"Because you live in the past with your memories," she continues. "Malice is back in Wonderlust, here in the flesh, and she still doesn't want you. She'll never want you, Cash. You might as well give up that glimmer of hope I still see in you and fully submit to me." The smell of burning flesh fills the air as she cauterizes each wound for the sheer fun of burning me. "After all, she looks rather cozy with Tweed. They make a cute couple, don't you think?"

Lillianna looks to the mirror and more than anything else tonight, this makes the breath lock in my lungs. I was hoping she hadn't seen them, but I know better than to underestimate the Queen of Spades. She hasn't assumed that position by luck.

Clearing my throat to bring her gaze back to me, I grapple for something to say. I want to tell her she's wrong, that Malice has nothing to do with me refusing to heal. It's about everything she's taken from me. My freedom, my humanity, my sanity. But I know it will only make things worse. Instead, I lie still, preferring to hold Lillianna's attention if the alternative is her interest becoming piqued by Malice. Poisoning her is an act I've already vowed to make sure the queen pays for in the end.

As the night wears on, I start to lose track of time. The room is dark and silent except for the sound of my own ragged breathing and Lillianna's soft humming. It's not until hours later, when the first light of dawn begins to filter through the window, that Lillianna finally stops. She removes the manacles from my wrists with a pout and stands up from the bed.

"It's not half as much fun when you don't scream," she says as she gathers her instruments. One last slice, this one along her own palm, Lillianna squeezes droplets of her blood into my mouth. I wish I could spit it back in her face, but I'll be no good to anyone as a corpse. My tongue darts out, soaking up the sweetened droplets as Lillianna chuckles and leaves the room. I struggle to inhale a full breath, my limbs shaking.

I just lay there, my mind racing with thoughts of escape and revenge. The room is silent except for the soft creaking of the bed as I shift my weight, catching my breath and trying to gather enough energy to move. Slowly, I push myself up onto my elbows, wincing as my muscles protest and ache. With the fresh, magically enhanced blood in my system, my bones reset and my skin knits back together. I'm left sitting, staring into the opposite bedroom with not half as much fury as before.

Perhaps I should turn my anger where it's deserved. Back at myself. I've made these decisions. I decided my own fate. I've acted out of spite of my twin at every turn. I took Malice into the Nightshade Trial, effectively signing her death warrant. If anything, I should be thankful she has someone who can soothe her through the nightmares and comfort her through the hard days to come.

I will also be doing those things from a distance. I'll be waiting for her in the shadows, loving her through the void which separates us. That's the only capacity I deserve to have any claim over her. We will have our time, even if Malice never knows it.

# CHAPTER 16

A waffle flies over my head. A currant bun joins just after.

"Be still, Rabbit," Arabelle chastises. The hippity hopper bounces in his seat, his white fur on end as if he's been electrocuted. Whether he heard or not, he continues throwing food around the room. An ox standing guard has a jammy bagel stuck to his shoulder and hasn't been permitted by his queen to remove it. I scoff beneath my breath. If

I were queen, I'd allow my subjects to run riot, do whatever they want. Suppose it's best for all I'm not, especially since I'm being fueled by no sleep and a double espresso this morning.

Crunching loudly on a breadstick, I watch Tweed flinch with each clash of my teeth. Every meal we have at this damn dining table, the other end seems to stretch further away. I'm on my own down here, left with only my bad attitude to keep me company. That doesn't stop his conversation with Arabelle, though.

"Bitterness lingers longer than the repercussions of resentment." Hatter muses. I give him a heavy dose of evil side eye.

"Well," Arabelle stands and brushes down her dress. A gothic take on a ballgown, black with red accents around the heart-shaped bust. A thick crimson ribbon cinches her waist, the hint of an oversized bow at her back. "We'd best return to the battle room. One can never be too prepared." With a nod, we're all dismissed. Unfortunately, the growl in my chest didn't get the memo. Pushing myself upright, I stalk after the Queen and her dearest Knave. Right until my slow reactions cause me to crash into his back.

"Was there something you needed?" Tweed asks, frowning over his shoulder. The growl ripples tenfold, a slice of bitterness slicing me in half.

"Yeah, attention," I shove Tweed's shoulder. The battle room is fifth on the right, one I've stalked past multiple times a day. There's a stark contrast between being confined inside a room and being shut out of it. Upon entering, a pair of uniformed oxen holding machetes step into my way. Arrabelle is quick to disband them, gesturing towards a seat on one side of the huge table holding a replica model of what I imagine Spade Castle looks like.

Shrouded in shadow, encased in enmity. The spokes are sharpened into dagger-like points, ready to spear the moon should it come too close. Twin blood moons, like the ones which appeared to me in the restless fits of half-sleep I managed to catch, flash before my eyes. Nope, no thanks.

Rounding the table, I take the seat at Arabelle's side. The one clearly intended for Tweed. He raises a brow at me, seemingly far too amused. Of all the reactions I wanted, that wasn't it. My hackles are raised, my need for a fight simmering on the edge.

"I don't know if our talks will be of any interest to you," Arabelle flashes a kind smile. I wave her words away.

"Considering I'm the one with poison leaking further into my system, I'd say I hold much interest." The queen frowns at Tweed, who takes the chair on my other side. We're joined by a few beings I recognize; Gryphon, Dormouse, Playing Card number Two. The rest are made up of the ox army, and a lone female who slithers in just before the door is closed. Now her, I do not recognize.

Blue iridescent scales cover her skin. Her large green eyes are tipped upwards at the corners, two slits in the center of her face instead of a nose, similar to the gills on her neck. It's impossible to ignore the tightness of her seaweed dress, her figure that of a supermodel on lengthy, toned legs. Waving a webbed hand at Tweed, he ducks his head and gives Arabelle his full attention. Wait a minute...

"Have you fucked her?!" I blurt, much to everyone's surprise. Clearing her throat, Arabelle commands the attention of all those present.

"The ravens have reported back. There are indeed wards around Spade Castle which would need considerable time to break down before an attack can be launched."

"There's a herd of guinea pigs in the study, working on their wizardry skills," one of the army members says with more grunts than words.

"I can swim them upstream undetected. The beavers are almost finished building trenches and can safely house them until the wards have been lowered." The scaley woman looks all too proud of herself, constantly fluttering her lashes at Tweed. As if sensing I'm about to throw myself over the replica castle and strangle her to death, he reaches out and takes my hand. His movements are tracked by everyone.

"The longer we wait, the more powerful Lillianna could become," Tweed's shoulders bunch. "It unnerves me that she's been quiet this long." His statement is joined by multiple hums of agreement.

"We know she doesn't have an army to speak of," Dormouse chimes in.

"Or any followers," Gryphon scoffs. I drown out the conversation. All this discussion of Lillianna is making me acutely aware of the ink creeping through my veins. It curdles, drawing my limbs closer into my body to resist gagging. In the center of it all, a light turns on in the mini castle. A figure walks past the window and my eyes widen. It is just a replica, right? I know my answer when he retraces a few steps, pauses, and then nears the window.

Even in a miniature version, the outline of broad shoulders and haphazard hair are undeniable. I blink rapidly, my heart picking up its pace. Through the mirror, it's almost possible to convince me he's just a mirage. A figment I've conjured to keep me company when the darkness creeps in. It wouldn't be the first time. But seeing him within the castle, studying him so high up in a single tower...it appears I might not be the only one feeling isolated. I push out my next breath through pure necessity, suddenly reminded of the huge distance between us. And not just in miles.

"Hey," Tweed whispers. "Are you okay?" Dragging my gaze away, the prickle of sweat on my brow becomes apparent. As does the sea of eyes staring at me. Opening my mouth to answer, no sound comes out. The poison within me surges upward, closing around my vocal cords. Seeing the castle, feeling the corruption seeping from it, steals the little energy I had left. My head sways, and suddenly, strong arms are banded around me.

“Let me return you to your bedchamber,” Tweed whispers. I’m not fully lucid at this point, but the hissed words from across the room seem to seek me out.

“The Knave surely knows his way around all of our bedchambers,” the Siren Slut snickers. I jerk in Tweed’s embrace, glaring through blurred eyes. Not even the castle’s clutch can contain my responding outburst.

“You’ve totally fucked her!” I point a finger in her direction. Tweed moves in a flash, whipping me up against his body and rushing the pair of us out of the room. Planting me on my feet, his hands hold my shoulders. This is it, the fight I need. The excuse to burn off some of the rage fuelling my veins. What I’m angry about is anyone’s guess. But when Tweed’s eyes catch sight of mine, there’s no anger there. Only compassion.

“Is everything okay?” His fingers tuck my hair behind my ear, his knuckles lingering on my cheek. Freed from whatever forces were at work inside the battle room, I whimper, swaying on my feet.

“How can I compete with that?” I whisper, blaming the tears which cloud my vision on the poison. Something has my emotions in extra bipolar mode, and that’s as good an excuse as any. Lifting my face to his, a chilled thumb strokes my bottom lip.

“Who said you’re competing with anyone?” Tweed frowns, lowering his mouth to hover over mine. “Malice, I only have eyes for you.” His kiss is short, yet filled with everything we struggle to say. That thumb presses on my chin, opening my mouth and soul up to him. Fire pools in my core, crackling into a swift tornado which spirals toward my heart. I grip Tweed's biceps, holding on for dear life when nothing else seems to make sense. Breaking away, a soft press of lips touches my forehead before I'm drawn into his solid hold.

"I'm just...tired," I sigh, refusing to look down. In my peripheral, thick spiderwebs splay beneath my skin, disappearing into the vest. I didn't realize just how tired I was until the words left my mouth, and not just mentally. I'm bone tired, as if the life is being sucked out of me from inside. An unfamiliar weakness shudders through my legs, and Tweed quickly catches me before I fall. "You're right. I should go back to bed."

"Let me take you," his lips brush against my forehead.

"No!" I shout. "I mean, it's fine. You stay. Plot how you're going to kill Cash. I'll be fine." I stumble away with the use of the wall, bitterness coating my tongue like ash. I wish my tone held more conviction, but he's already suffering as it is. Maybe that's punishment enough.

"For the record," Tweed says as I reach the corner. I pull to a stop, figuring he'd already gone back inside. "The reason these talks are taking so long is because I'm looking for any way possible to save Cash. Not kill him. He is my brother, after all, when he's not under the influence."

"The influence of what?" I ask but Tweed tips his head and re-enters the room. My mind reels, making its own conclusions as I retrace the steps up the grand staircase. The swan painting is more crowded than usual, rows of birds in all shapes and sizes squeezed into tiny chairs. I half glance at the menagerie, spotting Amelia wailing over a casket at the front. A pink bonnet sits on top of the mahogany, Abigail's name spelled in blush-colored roses. I can't even find the energy to laugh. The rest of the walk back to the bedchamber is a slow, resigned one.

"How did it go?" Cash asks as soon as I slump against the door. I flinch, my arms seizing painfully. I really should remember my cell here isn't so padded and definitely isn't as private.

"How did what go?" I indulge him.

"The spying session." The confident swagger in his tone has returned. "Normally, I don't pay any notice, or on occasion, I run around the castle, lighting up every room to give the oxen a fierce headache, but I was particularly aware of your presence watching me today." Pushing myself up on my throbbing feet, I pointedly ignore looking at him.

"You seem awfully chipper considering last night, it was all doom and gloom. The world is about to end." Something I visualized in every which way possible, and in all scenarios, I couldn't convince myself it would happen with only one Tweedle by my side.

"I've recovered."

I huff, shaking my head to myself. Am I a fool, a moron, or both?

"Good for you," I sneer, holding up the middle finger, which is entirely black now. My shins grace the Egyptian cotton bedsheets when Cash calls out again.

"Play with me."

I hold myself entirely still, imagining his head as a football to do keepy uppies with. That's the only way to indulge both Cash and my frustrations. Tossing the vampire a hard stare, I find him closer than I anticipated, sitting on the armchair and angled towards me. There's a chessboard of sorts on his coffee table, and a matching one sits on mine.

The fireplace gently crackles beyond, alluring me closer with the illusion of comfort.

"You've been in my room," I comment dryly.

"My room," Cash corrects, that mischievousness back in full swing. Signaling towards the chair, I drink in his cocky posture once more, his tattoos beckoning me to take a closer look. I shouldn't. I should deny this pull which continues to tug me back to him like a bungee cord I can't sever, but there's only so many times I have it in me to deny Cash. And now isn't one of them.

Dropping into the armchair, a footstool shuffles forward. At the same time, a fluffy blanket sneaks around the armrests and tucks into my sides. I recline, reaching out to lift the game board, but my hand wraps around a cup of steamy hot tea instead. I sigh contentedly, much to Cash's satisfaction. Leaning forward in his chair, he grins as if he's won a great prize.I can't let him live on that pedestal for long.

"I'd ask if it was poisoned, but it's a bit late for that," I state as the cup slowly rises to my lips. Cash's smirk dims, soothing a conflicted knot in my chest. Cash may have apologized, but I can't let him forget what he's caused so easily. Not just yet, anyway, although the thought of him doesn't fill me with quite as much anger anymore. Seeing him doesn't make me wish for my hatter's ability to fry him alive in a giant saucepan anymore. But worst of all, there's the persistent niggling to apologize for my harshness, to put that smile back in its rightful place.

Sipping my tea and finding it the perfect blend of caffeine and sweetness, I offer a small smile as a thank you.

"Teach me how the game works then." The light which floods Cash's face is an instant reward.

"Simple," he nods to the board of black and red diamond spaces. Three rows of figures sit on either side, all some marvelously craved creature I've never seen or even imagined before. "It's Swindler's Chess. You can only move forward, except when you need to go back. To take a piece, you balance yours on top and call out its name. If you say the secret word at any time, the board scrambles and resets. The winner is the one who takes the other's flibbertigibbet first."

Indeed, there's a figure in the middle of the back rows, the only one I can recognize. I squint at the young girl, how her hand is raised to her mouth and head turned slightly as if she's whispering a juicy bit of gossip.

"What's the secret word?" I ask. Cash shrugs.

"No idea. It changes every time."

"Is there a dice?" I raise a brow. He shakes his head. Very well. "I'll make you a deal. For each piece of yours I take, you have to tell me the origin and meaning behind one of your tattoos."

"And for every piece I take?" Cash's eyes darken a fraction. Heat prickles at my coreness which have nothing to do with my sickness. Don't say remove a piece of clothing, don't say remove a piece of clothing. Regardless of the false sense of security a game and tea can provide, ignoring all Cash has done to push those closest to him away, I'm intertwined with Tweed. I'm opening myself up to new possibilities, allowing myself and him to be vulnerable. I owe him my loyalty, if nothing else.

"For every piece you take, I'll forgive one of your misgivings." His back shoots straighter, a low breath sawing through his fangs and lips as I watch him over the rim of my mug.

"Ladies first," Cash says all too seriously. I've raised the stakes, given him a way to play for my absolution. Let's hope I don't regret it.

# CHAPTER 17

"Again," I growl, ready to smack the game board onto the floor. Cash chuckles, waving his hand in the air for the pieces to reset. Holding my sixth cup of magically refilling tea, my eyebrows tense as I focus.

"Pixie forward six," I start, hoping my boldness will knock Cash off kilt. This small wooden piece, a young boy with hugely pointed ears and a spiky tail escaping his loincloth, moves of its own accord. Stopping just short of his gnome, the pixie dances on his tiptoes before settling cross-legged on his space. None of the theatrics matter at this point. Cash's smirk has become permanent.

"Oh, I forgot to say, the mystic can leapfrog over any gnome of her choosing." On his command, the robed woman hurdles over the gnome's pointed hat, revealing some killer carved calves. Balancing on my pixie's head, I glare at Cash with the sharpness of a thousand daggers.

"Don't you d–"

"Pixie," he beams. The mystic is brutally fast, tugging a hammer free of her sleeve to smash my pixie into pieces. My jaw drops.

"Fully forgiven me yet?" Cash raises a brow. I grumble into the blanket, tilting my body away from him. Let this day be recorded as the first time Malice has admitted defeat.

"Oh, don't do me like that, Crazy One," Cash gives undeniable puppy dog eyes. I scowl at him. The fucker didn't go easy on me for one single move, but I suppose half of the blame is on me. I set the stakes too high. Relenting with a laugh, Cash holds up his hands.

"Okay, fine, I'll give you a freebie. Pick a tattoo and I'll tell you what it means." It's on the tip of my tongue to tell him I don't take handouts, but it's a day for exceptions. As Cash relaxes back in his armchair, my eyes roam his torso.

Ignoring the glaringly obvious spade symbol etched onto his right peck, a small rabbit in mid-hop sits at the ridge of his waistband. From shoulder to wrist, flowers span his sleeves, an adder slithering amongst the leaves. One love key is hidden within, but where Tweed's is on his finger, Cash's has been marked on the inside of his wrist. My interest would be piqued if

I was a novice to being trapped myself. Keys symbolize freedom, and the fact both of them hold one is a link they can't break. Not deep down.

"I'm not taken with any I see. What else have you got?" A yawn pulls at my mouth. Cash's smirk deepens, turning dangerously intriguing. I've seen Cash naked before, although I was too distracted to track and explore his ink previously.

Standing, Cash's hands tease his belt. Unlooping the leather from a brass buckle, he strokes it suggestively. Through one hand, then the other, and repeat. My mind scrambles, my mouth going dry. Whatever force has been moving my game pieces, removes the mug from my grip and places it on the table. Pulling the length of his belt free, Cash drops it on the floor. His pants quickly join.

Unlike the monochrome ink covering his top half, color bursts across Cash's thighs. So vibrant, I know they weren't there before. A mass of characters merge into each other, intertwined by winding dark smoke. Fitting, considering Lillianna is that black tendril trying to tear us all apart. It's only natural I seek myself out, figuring I wouldn't have made the cut. I'm not from here–I'm not an original.

"You've been busy," I comment dryly, still hunting with my eyes. Twisting his leg to flex the thigh, there I am. Set apart from the rest.

"I've had a lot of time and space to fill," his eyes twinkle knowingly. I wish I could say I was honored to have a patch of his skin, but my brows pinch. A small girl in a flamboyant dress, completely drained of color slams her fist against the inside of a glass bottle. It swallows me in its entirety, a look of pain imprinted on my face. I feel the walls of the bedchamber close in around me, the air stolen from my lungs.

Suddenly, I am that small child. Confused, imprisoned in my fantasies. A label hangs from the neck of the bottle, but instead of the typical 'Drink Me' sign, it says something else. Something which drags a whimper from my throat.

*Help Me.*

Why would he show this to me? Why would he put me back in the bottle I've long since shattered? Every instinct I'd let slide snaps back with acute awareness. I can't trust Cash's intentions, and I can't let him blindside me into falling for another trap.

"Do you like what you see?" Cash asks, his hand lowering to his shaft. Usually, my eyes would track the movements, how his cock jerks for my attention, but I can't rid myself of the sinking feeling. That I'm still the girl in the bottle, clawing to get out.

"Not really," I force myself to sigh. "I've always been more of a piercing kind of girl." A bald-faced lie I can't maintain, so instead, I push to stand. "If you'll excuse me, I'm going to entertain myself instead."

"Wait," Cash frowns, stepping forward as if he might come through the mirror. "We were having fun."

"As per usual, you were having fun, Cash. I'm just like that pixie, waiting to be destroyed the next time you're bored. There's more to life than fun and sex," I scowl at myself. Fuck, who the hell am I? My mother, that's who.

"But..." Cash's voice drops, becoming filled with an emotion I can't decipher. "Fun and sex are all I know how to do." I walk away, refusing to let myself drown in his pity. I'm having a hard time trying to manage my own. Pushing open the bathroom door, my nails embed in the wood.

No sooner have I stepped onto the tile, does a body collide with mine. I'm thrown into the nearest wall, an explosion of poison slamming against my chest from the inside. It doesn't matter though.

"I can't wait one more moment to have you." Pine and wild mushrooms flood my senses. Cornered in the darkness, cold lips skate across mine. The hint of an invitation awaits. One I eagerly accept without a second thought. Our bodies merge together like missing, forgotten pieces of a jigsaw puzzle. Encouraged by a passion which cannot be tamed, the darkness around us intensifies. I dive into the offered kiss, seeking an escape from my thoughts.

Each stroke of tongue and caress of lips calls for the fire raging within. The heat radiating from my body is enough to warm us both, his arms wrapping around me in a flame-fuelled embrace. Briefly, I forget where I am and who I am, lost in the heat of the moment. Panting with unrestrained desire, those lips are torn from mine with a ragged growl.

"I've been trying to get away for hours, desperate to check on you. How are you feeling, my love?" I choke on my own breath. Whatever I thought, wished, I'm not even sure. I blink my eyes open to stare at Tweed. Sweet, stable Tweed, staring at me with a mix of concern and barely controlled lust. His words echo around my head. 'My love.' An off-handed comment or a term of endearment? I already know the answer.

"I'm confuzzled. And I'm overthinking everything." I pout. "Nothing makes sense sometimes, and as a Hatter, I shouldn't need it too. I just don't think I have enough muchness to see this through," I sigh. Tweed's green eyes ground me, and soon enough, my concerns become apparent. I'm not equipped to move on from the confusing asshole on the other side of the mirror when he's always around and refusing to let me hate him.

"Speak openly," Tweed encourages, switching on the soft spotlights and easing me towards the bathtub. The facet switches on of its own accord as we sit on the lip, steam immediately spilling through the room.

"I was wrong, Tweed. I was wrong about Cash and Lillianna, even about myself. And I was so, so wrong about you." My shoulders sag with relief. The turmoil of keeping it locked up was killing me faster than any poison in my veins. Taking my fingers in his, Tweed's eyes remain downcast.

"You once told me I had no Tweedle left inside. That I'm just an emotionless shell." I feel his pain as if it were my own. A warped cloud festering in my chest, a bottomless pit of rage and self-doubt twisting around my vital organs. Since we've arrived at Heart Castle, Tweed has been worrying about my feelings so much, he's forgotten about his own. Those old wounds are still festering beneath the surface. Lifting his chin, I force him to look at me.

"I made a mistake. I've made thousands of mistakes, but none I regret more than hurting you. I thought you were distant from me because you preferred being an asshole." Tweed rolls his eyes, but I jerk his chin, regaining his focus once more. "But even after everything I said, after I pushed you away and did the exact opposite of what you told me–you were there. You're still here, looking out for me. Humpty Dainty's prophecy told me to choose a Tweedle, and I'm choosing you."

"Because Cash screwed up his chance. You wouldn't be with me now if he didn't." The dejection in his tone, the soul-sucking abyss I feel inside, it's too much to bear. I don't do romance, I can barely string a sentence together without doing so in rhyme. I squeeze Tweed's fingers tight as a single tear springs from my eye. In an instant, I sense the heaviness in Tweed's chest lighten.

"It's okay, Malice," Tweed whispers, wiping away the moisture from my cheek. "I feel what you're struggling to say." Blinking up, his smile is waiting for me. A stunning show of full lips and fang that makes me quiver with anticipation. As soon as I'm cured, I want those fangs skating over every inch of my skin and sinking into every available vein. Tweed groans as if he shares that thought. "Tell me what you need," he asks. I quickly decide to give him the real answer he deserves.

"I want you to fuck me, Tweed. Up against the wall, on the floor," I breathe. Touching his forehead to mine, a low hum of electricity passes between us like the spark of a lightbulb. One I should have seen coming a mile off. "Erase the chaos and strip me down until I make some sort of sense. Until somewhere, between the mix of silent cues and hidden thoughts, our vulnerability merges together and we can be one." Tweed hesitates, his hands smoothing up my arms to rest on my shoulders, thumbs absentmindedly stroking my pulse.

"I've been missing half of my soul for so long," he mutters. Embarrassment and uncertainty leak through this newfound bond we share, and I know what I need to do. What must be said to start fixing the cracks in both of our hearts and make us whole again.

"Then let me complete it." Our faces, now inches apart, finally collide in a passionate kiss. Tweed wraps his arms around my body and tugs me closer, becoming the anchor to this world which I've been missing.

His lips are soft and tender but entwine in a turbulent embrace as our tongues dance together in movements as old as time. I can't get enough. He tastes like danger, a direct contrast to the blossoming within. Like sugar and spice, sweet and sour. On a muffled growl, his fangs tear into my bottom lip, and I jerk back as far as the cage of his arms will allow.

"Tweed, the poison," I say breathlessly. His responding smile is all beast and no man.

"I don't care." My lips part as his tongue slides back inside, delving deeper into the recesses of our connection. Further into my psyche. I always was a sucker for a good kisser. When our lips clash with need, our tongues becoming too feverish, Tweed ducks his head and seeks out my neck. He licks at my pulse, yearning and just barely resisting taking everything I could possibly give. And I would, willingly.

Lost in this moment of craving, I stand between his legs so we are matched in height as I begin to strip us both. I want to be his equal, his everything in this moment. Nothing is promised once we leave this room, but right now is ours. Tonight belongs to us.

Pulling away, Tweed eases me a step back and assesses the curves of my body. It doesn't take more than a flick of his wrist to rip the remaining clothing into pieces, falling free of my body. Popping his pants button, his erection stands between us like a mast, waving a flag with a capital M on it. M for Malice, M for mine.

I race to drag his t-shirt over his head, needing his inked flesh bared to me more than I need my next breath. I've missed how full Tweed can make me feel, how deep he can go. When he refuses to let me climb him like a tree, I find his glimmering eyes staring directly into mine.

"Malice?" Tweed wraps his arms around my back, holding me too softly.

"Mmmhmm," I reply, fisting his shaft. The sheer girth of his cock is the perfect distraction from my internal woes, but Tweed will never let me forget about them so easily.

"For the record, you make complete sense to me." Tweed's thumbs chase the black webbing beneath my skin. A visible barrier between what is and what could be. We sigh in unison, preferring to stare into the rising bubbles. Honey and coconut fill my senses, soothing the war taking place within. "And nothing out there exists in here." Tweed reiterates. I side-glance at the door when he bends over to test the bath water. Did he see Cash in the mirror, butt naked and flexing for me? I quickly suppress that image as Tweed sits back. His smile refreshes my mind, like pressing the reset. So rare, yet pure. "I won't rest until I've freed you from this poison. I refuse to lose you again."

"I know," I smile back, resting my head against his shoulder. Somewhere along the way, I've come to depend on Tweed. Cash is many things, a naughty tease being one of them, but Tweed is good for me. The stability a girl so at odds with herself needs.

Cold fingers stroke the length of my arms, creating a path down to my sides. Every touch is controlled with the gentleness a vampire shouldn't possess. I lean into his touch, savoring how his chill chases away the confusion. Freezes over my brain until there's only silence.

I remain to stand between his parted legs, allowing him to stroke and savor the feel of my skin until his lips find me. Tender kisses are placed across every inch of my body. Tweed worships me. Each blemish I've gained through my own stupidity. Each scar I've caused in my own need to feel *something*. It seems like lifetimes ago. Now, I feel so much.

"Tweed," I groan, stroking his blond hair. Pressing a soft touch of lips against my hips, I can't resist pushing his head south. My leg raises of its own accord, balancing on the tub. If I thought he'd hesitate or deny me, I'm immediately proven wrong. Tweed dives into my center, into my scent and taste. His tongue laps at the wetness I have waiting, his lips close around my clit. The tugging sensation forces me to cry out, a blissful smile spreads across my face. I want him to consume me, devour me.

"More," I groan, attending to my own pebbled nipples. I chase the release as fast as Tweed causes it. Two icy fingers push into my cunt, circling upwards against that spot I relish. The deep pooling in my core expands within seconds, a desperate need soaring through me. The vibrations from between my thighs echo those leaving my throat. "Fuck yes. Just like that." His fangs scrape at the inside of my thighs, making my toes curl.

"Do you want to come?" Tweed groans, headywith his own desire.

"Yes." I'm too breathy, my head light, and skin flushed.

"Say it," Tweed urges, pausing the assault of his fingers. Pulling back an inch, he sinks those sinful fingers into his mouth, his pupils dilating at my taste. I whimper, gripping his hair once more and tugging hard at the roots.

"Make me come, Tweed," I demand. He immediately obeys. Thrusting his fingers into me harder and faster, pulling my clit into his mouth, I lean back against the tub. My chest thrusts out into the air, being caressed by steam. It's more than I can take, and I fall apart, clenching around his fingers. My body spasms, tingling from top to bottom. I break for Tweed, as I have many times before, but this holds a weight to it. One which goes deeper than a basic finger fuck.

"Holy shit," I shudder. He's over me in an instant, pushing his tongue and my own taste into my mouth. I suck him clean, clawing at him to get closer. I need his skin against mine. Sinking into the hot water, I pull Tweed in with me. As his arms close around my back, his cock slides inside of me without effort. The water sloshing over the side of the tub is canceled out by my screams, and I hope to hell Cash is listening to every sound.

# CHAPTER 18

I'm fucking it up.

I know this, but stopping the pattern seems impossible. Spending time with Malice and attending to her mental health seems detrimental at this point. I can't love her if she's dead and buried, but on the flip side, saving her at the risk of pushing her away...well, I might as well package her up in a bow and ship her off to Spade Castle. I saw her reaction to Cash's silhouette in the battle room. There's no hiding her draw to him or how the tether we have is becoming strained. Fuck, falling in love is complicated.

From the armchair I've repositioned, I have a perfect view of the slip of moonlight leaking through the curtains to spill across her face. Its pink hue is yet another reminder I'm running out of time. The Blood Moons are fast approaching. Arabelle has informed me of their power; that at the time they clash, the magic in the realm will be raw and untamed. Worst of all, it will be freed, and accessible by any who should wish to consume it. I have no doubt who is at the top of that list.

Honey and coconut seep from Malice's skin, coating me in their embrace. We remained in the tub, fucking and re-washing each other until the water ran cold. I watched her break several times over until she had to beg for a reprieve. Her orange curls are back in full force from where they were bundled into a dripping wet messy bun and left to dry against her pillow. I half-smile, adoration creeping into my deadened heart.

"Strangely peaceful watching her sleep, isn't it, brother?" The whisper comes not much more than five minutes after Malice began softly snoring. Cleverly, he keeps his voice low, not wanting to alert her to his presence. For the same reason, I ignore him.

"Suspicious she would choose my old bedroom," he continues. The humor in his tone sours my mood in an instant. Also fucking joking, even now.

"Fuck off, Cash," I grumble, falling for the bait. His responding chuckle grates my ears. Leaning forward, I brace my elbows on my knees. At times like this, it's hard to remember he's not himself. He's being influenced, and it only speaks to his own weakness that he can't seem to pull himself through. Shuffling around beyond the mirror, I try to drown him out.

It's hard, as my heightened hearing picks up on the sound of him pacing around.

"She doesn't have much longer, you know."

My foot twitches. He says it so casually, so matter-of-fact. Clenching my jaw, I try to find solace in her beautiful face. Except the black lines creeping towards her jaw break the illusion, the truth staring me in the face.

"I can see that."

"You should let me help. Maybe I could–" I twist in my seat, glaring at him through the dark.

"You've done enough."

Halting his pacing, Cash leans across the back of his matching armchair. At damn last, he frowns as if something in this world might affect his impassive exterior. Too bad it's far too late to matter.

"This isn't just another one of our squabbles, Dum."

Anger flares through me at the mention of my old name. Always living in the past, always reflecting on what once was. What has been lost. I shoot across the room in a flash, standing before the one I used to rely on to keep me sane. Now he fuels my hatred.

"If you cared for her, you never would have taken her to the Nightshade Trial. Now I have to clean up your mess once again. I hope the loyalty you have for your precious queen was worth it." My fangs extend with deadly intent.

"As much as yours was, when you chose Arabelle over me," Cash shoves the armchair aside. It crashes to the ground, causing Malice to stir. She frowns, rolls onto her side, and drifts back to sleep. One of these days, I'll dive through the mirror and throttle some sense into my twin. As it stands, such an action would be as good as declaring war on Lillianna's turf, and we're not prepared yet. First, we cure Malice. Then we invade.

"I don't want you here when she wakes up," I growl, folding my arms over my chest. Only a pair of boxers cover my decency, the rest of my muscles bunched and on full show. Cash copies the action in his pajama pants, chuckling once more with his teeth glinting in the lantern light.

"Why, brother? Are you worried she might realize there's no need to settle?" I scoff, widening my stance.

"If settling for me means I don't try to get her killed, then color me selfish. At least I'm man enough to be true to myself."

"Don't make me laugh," Cash barks, copying my every action like a true reflection. "You're not capable of feeling anymore. You ditched that part of your soul when you left me behind to survive on my own."

"I was shielding you from the pain I had to suffer every single day!" I growl, my voice growing louder of its own accord.

"You know nothing of suffering–"

"Enough!" Malice shouts. I whip around, noting she's crying in her sleep. Black, gloopy tears stream from her eyes and stain the pillow. I race to her side, slipping beneath the covers. At the touch of my body, Malice throws herself into me. Her hold is tight, her face damp on my chest.

"Shh, my love. It's okay, I'm here," I soothe, stroking her wild hair. I keep whispering those words, trying to calm her. Angling her face upwards, my heart breaks at her torment. How the poison claiming her reprieve of sleep smears across her cheeks as I attempt to wipe her tears away. Guilt racks me.

I shouldn't have left her in the Nightshade Trial. I let her words drive a wedge between us, and I knew she wouldn't make it out unscathed. Then and there, I should have thrown her over my shoulder and dragged her back to Red Castle, kicking and screaming. Even at the cost of her hating me for all eternity, anything would have been better than this. Watching her suffer, noticing the thinning of muscle on her frame. She's been weakening before my very eyes, and I've been too consumed with revenge to see it.

"I'll always be here from now on," I vow. My own words knock me off kilter. It's been too long since I made such a promise, and such has only been offered once before. To my own flesh and blood, no less.

I cradle Malice until the sobbing passes and her breathing evens out. Sleep calms her once more, not a nightmare in sight. Speaking of which, when I look back, my twin is nowhere to be seen.

# CHAPTER 19

I stir from a lengthy, fitful sleep. Straightening my limbs one at a time, I stretch out before rolling within the sheets. I relish everywhere my heated skin touches a cool body, finding a new position where my ass nestles a girthy cock. What a way to awaken.

"How are you feeling today, Beautiful?" a calm, male voice seeps to me. I smile, recognizing Tweed by his tone, his smell, his feel.

"Like I've been hit by a train," I mutter, rotating my shoulder. Stiffness claims me, like a skinsuit which has been shrunk in the wash. "How long was I out?

"Two days," Tweed hums, placing a kiss on my head.

"Two days?!" I jerk upwards, hit by a sudden onslaught of pain. Tweed encourages me to lie back down, to *relax.* I wish I had the vigor to deny him, that I could fulfill the restlessness in my legs. But it's no use. As soon as my head touches back on the pillow, I feel the energy ooze out of my pores.

"I'm going to get you some food," He says, withdrawing his arm from beneath my head. I instantly ache for him. Without his closeness, his coldness, the voices sink back in. The thoughts which whirl around my mind, making me even more dizzy. The door clicks shut and I shiver, tugging the covers closer. I shouldn't be so dependent, but when Tweed is offering me constant comfort, I'd be a fool to resist.

"Psssst." I duck my head further under the cover. "Psssst." I push my palms against my ears. I swear he's taking great pleasure in invading every moment of peace I manage to find.

"Fuck off, Cash." I swat my hand in the air, freeing up one of my ears. He laughs.

"Why does everyone keep saying that?"

Holding the cover over my face, I count to myself. *One, two, three, four. Hold off until Tweed comes back through that door. Five, six, seven, eight. Don't engage with the twin you're supposed to hate.*

"Don't worry, I'm not going to bother you for long," Cash calls over my hushed chanting. "I just wanted to show you something. A surprise, if you will." Pulling the cover down just past my eyes, I wish I never looked. Holy moly, I really wish I never looked. "Do you prefer what you see now?"

Cash's green eyes are glowing with mischief. Sitting back in his armchair once more, he's completely naked. His thighs are spread wide, his weighty balls hanging in between. Slowly, ever-so-teasingly, he pumps his hand up and down his cock. It's rigid, a solid vein trailing from base to plump purple head. A glint of metal catches the light.

"You didn't," I breathe, unable to form any other words.

"I did," Cash nods. Silver balls sit on either end of three wide bars, creating the rung effect of a ladder up the underside of his shaft. My thighs clench. Eyes locked on mine, he strokes his cock with more power. The veins in his arm tense, his knuckles are white from the crushing grip.

Following the curve from bottom to top, he leans forward to spit on himself and I'm lost, watching through a haze of desire as his moments are slickened. Much like the wetness seeping between my legs. Every ascent causes those metal bars to pull tighter, shifting just beneath the skin. Thank the moons for rapid vampire healing.

I merely lie there. Unable to look away. Consumed by the sweet torture he provides. My lips pry open, unweaving breaths sawing in and out in time with his pumping. My tongue skates across my bottom lip as a bead of precum glistens at this tip. Cash tracks it all.

A soft moan escapes him as his hips rock into the rhythm he sets. Drowning in his intense green eyes, my own become dilated with lust. Cash slides his other hand south to cup his balls. Kneading them in his palm, widening his thighs further. I have a full, unrestricted view.

His growl pierces me. A sound of pleasure mixed with agony that has my pussy clenching in response. He may as well be right before me, not in another kingdom, for the effect he's having over my clammy skin. My fingers drift towards my nipple, scraping my nails over the tight bud. For all the reasons I shouldn't encourage him, I can't stop. He's an enigma.

His pupils become blown out with anticipation, tattoos dancing wildly across his flesh. Like an animal on the crest of a satisfying kill, his fangs protrude from his lips. I can’t stop tracking the thrusts of his hand, squeezed tight enough to turn his cock a deep shade of purple. Cash’s hips buck as he prepares to explode. I'm right there with him when the door to my bedchamber opens.

I shoot upright, my hair as wild as my eyes. Tweed enters backward, steering a tea trolley of plates over the threshold. In my peripheral, a string of cum escapes Cash, his hand clamped over his mouth as he jerks and writhes. Then he's gone, leaving my cheeks pink and muscles tense.

"You look perkier," Tweed comments with a smile. Pausing by my bed, he kisses my temple and I scramble for an excuse.

"I, um, fell back asleep for a second. Must have done me good."

Scenting the air, Tweed's brow raises knowingly.

"Indeed." Wheeling the trolley around the bed, he pauses to yank the curtains back. I hiss, covering my eyes. "It's such a beautiful day. I thought we could sit on the terrace. Get you some fresh air?"

"Yes, fresh air would be preferable," I scramble to get out of bed. Anything to shake off the desire I tumbled into. Each movement comes with a tightened sense of pain but I force myself upright. Tweed provides a satin bathrobe, blood red with a heart embroiled over the breast pocket. I slip it on while Tweed ties the rope around my hips.

"Better?" He grins devilishly. With a nod, I let him lead me into the sunny outdoors. Coming to a swift halt, I blink rapidly. Where the balcony used to end at a curved wall, it is now open to a wooden bridge. The walkway is even, sanded to perfection, and not a splinter in sight as I step onto it. Holding both railings, Tweed follows right behind with his trolley rolling smoothly.

Winding sideways, we walk amongst the leafy canopies until a treehouse becomes visible. A pleasant balcony wraps around the exterior, set with a small yet chic white table and wicker sofas. Overlooking a glimmering pond–the same blue hue as my eyes–frogs jump between lily pads. Birds with watery wings skate amongst the reeds, singing sweet tunes.

"What is this place?" I ask, reaching the front door. Peering inside the glass, the interior has been decorated to integrate with its surroundings. Large leaf prints on the walls mimic a rainforest. The curtains match, framing the space with serenity. Between scattered potted plants, a huge wooden bed in the center is bathed in golden sunlight. Banana leaves stretch high to scrape the ceiling, creating tropical tranquility throughout.

"I thought you might like another option, in case your room feels too...crowded at times." Looking over my shoulder, I narrow my eyes knowingly. It would be stupid to think anything gets past Tweed, but instead of accusing me, instead of blaming me, he's given me another option. I sink onto the sofa, my heart feeling lighter than it has in a long time.

“You deserve better, Tweed,” I look away. The trolley is filled with a vision of delights. Sweet cinnamon buns, dark coffee, and a selection of fruits spread across two levels. Another indulgence my newfound conscience feels I should push away. Lowering at my side, Tweed tilts my face to meet his.

"Believe me when I say, I didn't think I would feel this way about anyone. Arabelle's been trying to get me to pick a wife for the longest time." Panic flares within my eyes. Tweed laughs, a raw, unused sound. "I'm not proposing. If this is all we ever are, it's enough for me. I want you. Only you, in whatever form I can get." I inhale sharply.

Maybe my overactive brain is at work, but I'm sure that was a hint at the foolishness I've been indulging in with Cash. I wish I could say it's over, but I don't feel in control of that decision. I once vowed to never choose between them. Even now, it's ingrained so deeply within, I can't ignore it.

Releasing my face, Tweed transfers the plates onto the table, humming a tune to himself. He's so carefree, at odds with the battle scars marking his back and the bunched tension in his arms. I stroke his shoulder around the loose vest he's wearing, moving up to play with his hair. He shudders and smiles.

"There's some hard times ahead. Let's share this one brunch as if nothing else matters." The silence that follows is a peaceful one as he feeds me bites of fruit between kisses. Pouring and handing over a coffee, I snuggle beneath Tweed's arm, gazing out at the scenery. The Red Kingdom truly is beautiful. A place where vegetation thrives and people long to live. Where one can settle and be happy, without ever needing to leave.

It's just my luck that half of my heart is aching to run the length of rolling hills in the distance, hurtle over the boundary line and see what other adventures await. Or rather, to see who may be waiting, regardless of all his sins. I wasn't lying when I said Tweed deserves better.

"Do you know why I've been trying to save Cash?" Tweed catches me off guard. I frown, playing with his fingers against my thigh.

"An incomprehensible sense of duty?"

He grunts, exhaling into my hair.

"Because it's what you want," Tweed replies amongst the birdsong. The serenity of our surroundings keeps Tweed's voice soft and my heart at peace. "Deep down. You don't want to see him dead, and I reckon you'd never forgive me if it was by my hand." Biting my bottom lip, I press my cheek over his chest. Surely, Tweed knows nothing I do is out of spite against him. Where Cash is concerned, I just can't seem to help myself. Opening my mouth to say...anything, I'm interrupted from the ground below.

"Malice!" I lean out of Tweed's hold, my eyes heavy as laziness once again takes over. The queen is wearing a catsuit of sorts, black down one side and red on the other. All four card suits are stitched into the PVC fabric, her vibrant red hair thrown up into a haphazard ponytail. Killer boots put her several inches taller, the curves of her body on full show. Arabelle waves her croquet stick in the air.

"Come, have a game with me!" I'm already shaking my head when Tweed stands us both and leads me to the railing.

"She'll be right down," he answers. I grumble, slumping into his side. His chest vibrates with laughter and for that reason only, I force myself to agree. "I have some business I need to attend to. Thank you for this moment of calm. I will see you this afternoon." Kissing my hand, Tweed retreats along the bridge, leaving me as curious as ever.

# CHAPTER 20

"He was the only guy I knew in the entire nudist colony who could carry two coffee mugs and a dozen donuts at the same time."

Arabelle's cackle is raw as if her throat isn't used to creating such a sound. It spurs on my own laughter as we breach the treeline. The sound of chatter within the castle sharply halts, followed by the shuffle of feet. A procession of statuesque beings forms two lines, welcoming their queen through the entrance. I'm not wholly sure such a display is necessary. She's only been gone a few hours at most and didn't even leave the gardens.

Passing her subjects with a regal stiffness to her spine, I rush to stay at Arabelle's side, refusing to follow her around like a lost lamb. Those present incline their heads as I pass, oblivious to the anguish each step causes me. Apparently, Hatters are hot shit. It's time I assumed such a role. No one moves, not even Tweed. It's a good look on the Knave, all hard muscles and stoic obedience. I wonder if I could convince him to replicate it for me in the bedroom. Who am I kidding–of course I can.

Reaching the end of the lobby, an audience of relieved sighs sounds behind. Arabelle whips her head around, the sternest look I've ever seen upon her face. Every being, Tweed included, shoots bolt upright, not a sagged shoulder or deflated chest in sight. The queen holds her narrowed stare until a lone, upright fish in a suit can't hold his breath anymore. Bubbles frizzle from his moist mouth like a round of fanny farts. Catching my eye, Arabelle winks and continues on. Now that's the kind of girl I can be friends with.

An additional set of steps fall into pace, Tweed's presence pressing against my back. I don't need his body warmth to set off mine. His aura alone sparks a heat within my veins and a yearning between my legs. The three of us find Hatter in one of the many lounges, talking to a suit of armor. It raises an arm, holding up White Rabbit by the ears.

"I recommend a twenty-four-seven suicide watch," the Suit of Armor groans, his mouthpiece in desperate need of oiling. Hatter accepts Rabbit into the cradle of his arms and joins our gang of fuck ups. I don't need to ask where we're going, because one hallway later, I'm being ushered into an infirmary. A crowd of four-foot canaries rushes forward, flipping their wings and chittering instructions. Bone necklaces clink around their chubby necks, each wearing a different style of black hat, cape, and war paint over their beaks.

"What's all this?" I query, unnerved that not even Tweed will look at me. Instead, he takes my hand to lead me towards a leather bench which looks suspiciously like a surgeon's table.

"I hope you don't mind," Arabelle says tentatively. "I took the liberty of calling on the best witch doctors Wonderlust has to offer." Her frown at the network of black webbing which trickles over my shoulders is brief, but mimicked by all others watching on. Their gazes snap back up as Arabelle clicks her tongue. I merely shrug.

"I'd have minded a whole lot more if you hadn't fed me powanger fruits the entire walk back. You've learned quickly–a sated Malice is a tolerant one." Arabelle inclines her head in agreement, her hidden agenda unraveling. Befriend me, feed me, and now she'll attempt to fix me. Hopping up onto the table, I take a moment amongst the chaos to pull Tweed close and whisper in his ear.

"Just in case they spoil my dress, I wanted you to know - this was all for you." I chew on my bottom lip as his fingers slip into the smoothness of my hair.

"I promise the next time you dress up for me," his voice is deliciously deep, "it'll be for a proper date. Perhaps we'll still end up here so I can bend you over this table and try out a little Frankenstein roleplay."

"Sounds sexy," I scoff sarcastically. Tweed's eyes hold a glimmer of humor.

"Shattering you into a million pieces and piecing you back together in a way only my dick can sounds rather sexy to me."

My mouth drops open, a naughty shudder rolling through my spine.

"Well, we're here right now. We could kill two birds with one stone," I bob my eyebrows. A canary nearby flaps his wing against my back, twittering I should be more careful with my metaphors. Tweed's rare playfulness shuts down, his brows pinching.

"Curing you of this poison is more pressing than my desires." Another yellow canary, with zebra stripes across his chest, approaches with a pair of metal shackles which Tweed hastily snatches and growls for him to back off. Such a mix of emotions is at work within his psyche, and the strained smile he tries to give me fails.

"I won't let you be restrained against your will again," he mutters, referring to how he found me tied to the table in Charmsfield Mental Institution. He rescued me that night, and I gave him nothing but shit for it. Dumping the chains on the floor, I feel the loudness of their clanging in the pit of my soul.

Across the infirmary, Hatter places White Rabbit in a hospital-style bed. He unravels a ribbon from his hat, carefully wrapping it around Rabbit's bloodied wrists. What the hell happened to cause him to be the most erratic one in this room? I don't have time to think about it as a pair of wings slip over my shoulders and tug me to lie back. Tweed's hand slips into mine, as Arabelle takes the other. Smiling reassuringly, she tells the witch doctors to begin their treatments. I just didn't think she meant all at once.

One releases a cloud of overly-perfumed smoke in my face. I cough and splutter as another pushes needles into the crooks of my elbows. A third unleashes a jar of snakes on my stomach, the slimy reptiles slithering all over and up me. Going inside my mouth, down my throat, and deep into my stomach where they continue to wriggle. I can't breathe, can't settle the writhing of my body. Gagging on the dirty taste lingering in my throat, I'm about ready to pass out when the fourth witch doctor uses his own feathers to tickle my feet.

"Settle, Malice," Tweed begs. "It won't seem so bad if you settle."

I shake my head.

"I'm trying," I wretch and whimper. "It's not working."

"It will," Tweed assures me. "Just a little longer." The needles in my arms dig deeper before a tugging sensation makes me want to crawl out of my skin and die. Like a siphon, he's trying to suck the poison free, and it doesn't like it. The feathers move up to my knees, pushing the snakes further into my system. Quickly becoming drained of all the strength in my body, I can only hold out for a few seconds before giving in to a hair-raising scream. One which sounds foreign leaving me, the girl who has been experimented on by numerous doctors at my therapist's request. But this is different. This is utterly insane in the worst possible way.

"It doesn't seem to be working," Arabelle sounds distant yet distressed.

"It will," Tweed insists. "It takes time."

"I don't have that sort of patience," I pitch in, my neck taut as my head twists off the top of the bed.

"We do," Tweed pleads, gripping my hand tighter. "Please."

Clamping my eyes closed, I pull the shadows of my soul around me like a shield, using every tool in my arsenal to survive this. The tugging, the wriggling, the tickling. Another puff of perfume dominates my face, pulling me from my efforts. I thrash, crying to them to stop.

"Give it more time," Tweed whispers beside my ear, stroking my cheek. Wetness smears over my skin and it's only then I realize I'm crying. "A little more. A lot more."

"Tweed," Arabelle barks this time, her tone leaking authority. "That's enough." Instantly, the witch doctors release me. A short whistle calls from the snakes to wriggle up my esophagus and evacuate my body. They feel worse coming back up but at least I can finally slump back on the bed, panting.

My bravado has also seeped from my body and when I brave a look, the black webbing has spread further. Coating my arms and upper chest, they directly contrast the white femininity of my summer dress. More than that, I couldn't feel them before. They were a cosmetic inconvenience. Now, as if the poison has created a defense mechanism for itself, a dull ache weighs down my veins, pulsing with the low hum of pain.

"I can't go through that again," I shake my head.

"I'm afraid you must," Arabelle sighs. "It's imperative for all, that you're freed from the binds Lillianna has trapped you in." My mind seeks more information, but I can't get my mouth to correspond. Shame coats my cheeks. I'm supposed to be stronger than this, but perhaps the poison has been secretly at work beneath the surface. Releasing my hand, Arabelle drifts her fingers over my forearm, her perfectly delicate face pinched. "I think it may be time we call in the specialist."

"Why didn't we start with that?!" I cry out, hissing at the responding shot of pain. Tweed's head is hanging low, his blond hair pitching forward to brush my neck. Around us, there's a whole bunch of flutters and chitters but I couldn't care less. Arabelle ushers the witch doctors out and welcomes in a new bird of prey. A macaw, easily seven feet as he towers over me, his red and blue vibrant coloring broken up by the white surgical coat he wears. There's a stethoscope hanging around his neck.

"Hello, Malice. I'm Dr. Squawkington. I understand we have a black magic problem." I barely respond, tears still freely leaking from my eyes. "I'm going to conduct something called the Arcane Antidote Extraction Ritual. In a peanut shell, it involves removing a sample of the poison from you, in order to devise a counteracting antidote." Shuffling his huge, clawed feet around on the stone floor, the doc tries to nudge Tweed aside. I grip his hand as hard as I possibly can.

"Don't you dare let me go," I growl. Tweed pries his fingers from mine to move up the bed, leaning his hip beside my hair. His hands cup my cheeks, cleverly blocking the parrot from my vision.

"I'm not going anywhere," Tweed assures me, his thumbs stroking in smooth circles. "I'll be right here when you wake up." I frown, unable to respond before Arabelle hastily places a mask over my nose and mouth, and everything goes dark.

# CHAPTER 21

Sliding my arms beneath Malice's limp body, I carry her from the infirmary. It hadn't been my intention to withhold information from her, but it's easier this way. The quicker we can have her back to full health, the sooner I can give into the emotions plaguing me night after night. Vampires are perceived to be monsters, yet since Malice gave me a glimmer of hope I could be meant for more, I've felt nothing but an intense craving only she can satisfy. My mind is centered on her - her wellbeing, her needs, her happiness. Which is dangerous because I'm distracted from my duties.

Squawkington mimics my strides, his claws grating on the tiles of the hallway. "Nice costume," I comment dryly. Shedding his coat, he dumps it on the ground for PB to rush forward from the shadows and pick it up.

"I figured it would put your human friend at ease. Give her something she can associate with. In a sense, I am a doctor of sorts." I snort. It's a short walk to the chapel, where Arabelle has already trotted ahead and tugged the door open. For this brief instance, we aren't queen, knave, and royal alchemist, but three beings striving to repair the escalating pressure Lillianna is putting on our realm.

The chapel sits at the base of thirteen steps, a room dimly lit by candles and mystical sigils inscribed on the walls. Squawkington has been down here all night, working to create a controlled environment. I was desperately hoping we wouldn't need to use it, but his prediction was correct.

Placing Malice on an altar-like table at the center of the chamber, I'm careful not to smudge any of the protective runes etched into the soil beneath my feet. The shimmer of a transparent magical barrier encases the table, preventing any potential outbursts of dark energy from hitting the rest of us. By the time I turn back, Squawkington has donned his usual enchanted robe and ruby red amulet.

"I know we've spoken of Lillianna's curses before," he steps aside to speak to me privately, "and the hold she seems to have over your twin. I wish to prepare you, young Tweedle, this is something far more potent and incredibly more dangerous. The best course of action would have been to cut the poison out of her at the time of infection. As it stands, I fear that is not an option anymore." I swallow thickly, keeping my eye on Arabelle and stroking Malice's hair aside. At this stage, not even the queen is safe from my possessiveness.

"Take your sample, make the antidote." I growl, itching to return to her side. Arabelle watches me closely, seeing too much with her wide, amber eyes.

"We'll save her," the queen promises, although we both know nothing within this magically enhanced chamber is in our control. I'm merely a spectator now, as I silently vow to repay every pinch of Malice's suffering back onto Lillianna tenfold. Squawkington starts the incantation which will bind us all into this circle until he lowers the barriers he's created with foreign words and spices. Shaking a smoking bell, he places it down and begins to shift his wings over the top of Malice's body.

"Needless to say," I shot Sqwuakington an incredulous look. "If she dies, you die." For the first time, I see the feathery alchemist show a trace of fear. I mean it too. I haven't allowed Malice to worm her way into my vacant soul just to lose her now. Returning to his work, Sqwaukington closes his eyes and waves his wings to and fro. He's searching, testing the reaction of the toxins to his vague touch.

"The witch doctors couldn't touch the poison because it's tethered to her being. I must understand the magic's connection to its source, and evaluate its elemental composition. To do otherwise would ensure our failure." I struggle to focus on the parrot's babbling, even though it was Arabelle who demanded he talk her through the ritual step by step. Unsurprisingly, she has some trust issues.

Malice's face is pale against the black lines creeping up her neck. Slowly but surely, the magic is spreading. Sweat beads her brow and as I attempt to wipe it away, Squawkington slaps my hand.

"Do not disturb the host," he berates me. That host is the woman who's consumed my past and I'm planning to spend my future with. I grind my teeth together so hard my fangs pierce my cheeks. Arabelle had also insisted I fed before joining them today. An order I could not fulfill. Even the thought of it felt like a betrayal. My hunger craves her and her alone. Through my heavy breath and fangs growing long enough to cut my own lip, Arabelle's soft hand eases my fingers out of the fist they'd produced.

"Would you excuse us for a moment?" She smiles politely at Sqwuakington. There's nowhere to go, as the wards are shimmering around us, so Arabelle walks me to the foot of the table and lowers her voice.

"No one wants Malice cured more than I. Wonderlust needs–"

"Forgive me for what I'm about to say," I seethe, struggling to keep my voice low. Arabelle pauses and indicates for me to speak freely. "Fuck Wonderlust. Fuck Lillianna for using Malice's Allure as a way to control the population. Fuck Cash for sexualizing our realm. I don't care about returning our world to what it once was. All I want is...her." That hand still holding mine tightens. Arabelle may be a master at controlling her facial expressions, but she's never been able to fully block me out. A small sigh passes her parted lips.

"Do you truly believe she is the one from the prophecy? The other half of your broken soul?" I withdraw my hand, straightening my shoulders.

"I don't care about that either." I state a little too loudly. Even Malice, unconscious on the table, absentmindedly flinches at my tone. There's nothing but the cold, hard truth guiding me from here on out.

"My life has been miserable since Malice went away, and through it all Cash gave me comfort. He was my reason to keep fighting, my salvation from all the crimes I was forced to commit. And then, out of nowhere, he switches sides." I bite down the emotion that clogs my throat, refusing to feel a damn thing for that asshole. He chose his path, now I'm creating my own. "I've been lost for so long, Arabelle. With Malice, I feel like home is near, regardless of where we are. She's the light within my darkness. I can't lose her so soon after accepting that."

My chest twists painfully. I look up to the ceiling, at the cold curving stone beyond glimmering wards, drawing my focus anywhere other than here. A minute passes where nothing is said. There's nothing to say. I've given my heart to a dying woman. A dying, mortal woman. Regardless of what Sqwuakington does or doesn't manage to do today–the outcome will be the same. I'll eventually have to mourn Malice and live an eternity knowing nothing will ever be right again. But at least I'll have those precious memories to see me through.

Arms wrap around my middle, squeezing tightly and catching me off guard. There's a second where I almost push her away before I remember the time we've spent together. We're more than a Knave and his Queen, akin to siblings. We've trained together and fought alongside each other. I've watched over Arabelle since she was a child. Reason winning over anger, I wrap my arms around her in return and enjoy the embrace of someone who genuinely cares for my well-being and wants nothing in return. Her body, although small and fragile, holds the strength of a warrior and the mind of a fierce ruler. Both aspects I know she'd use to save me whenever needed.

By the time we return to the altar, Squawkington having finished his investigation, produces an ancient device. Much like an urn, created from the deadened remains of a black oak tree and carved into the body of a sloth with the head of a giraffe. Lowering it towards Malice's chest, a spiked needle shoots from its mouth, piercing her skin. A growl is torn from me, yet I dare not touch her. No matter how much hands twitch to steal Malice away and hug her until morning comes, this has to be done. There will be a thousand more sunrises for us.

The needle does its work, alongside Sqwuakington's chants, extracting a strand of the poison from beside Malice's heart. Her body trembles, the weight of pain she's saved from feeling evident in the taut veins seizing within her arms. I've never struggled to follow an order before. Not as a boy, forced to run the maze and complete bullshit trials for the Royals entertainment. I took each challenge in my stride, but there's not enough practice in the world which could prepare me for Malice.

At last, Squawkington rips the needle from her and stumbles back. I catch him just before he triggers the barrier, more focused on the urn wrapped within his feathers. A purple glow glimmers around the edges, highlighting the black mass inside. Alive, volatile, and intent on breaking free. Luckily, Sqwuakington's magical object is managing to contain it.

"I'd hoped to extract more, but I'll do what I can with what I got. I'll work all through the night to bind the sample with protection and containment spells. Only then will I be able to work on identifying and subduing it without risking harm to anyone else."

Arabelle gasps behind me. My gaze shoots back to Malice, and I swear my silent heart thumped an unnerving beat. The veins are growing quicker now, covering every inch of her creamy skin like an ink spill. Dipping beneath the neckline of her dress, appearing again across her thighs and then some.

“I think we might have angered it,” Arabelle says with dread lacing her tone. I rush over, cupping her cheeks but it’s no use. Reaching her eyes, Malice sputters and shoots back to life, her fluttering eyes consumed by poison. Corner to corner, she blinks to adjust to the blackness coating her vision. I already know what she’s going to say before she manages to find her voice.

“Tweed? Tweed, I can’t...I can’t see,” thick gloopy tears spill over. Arabelle is staring at me, but I can’t bring myself to engage in her silent conversation. Tugging Malice into my arms, I hold her head in the crook of my neck.

“This is all part of the process. It’s going to be okay. I’ll make it okay, if it’s the last thing I do.” Sensing the magical barrier lowering, I take Malice from the table, holding her too tightly as I get her the fuck out of that chapel. Sqwuakington had better have an answer for me by morning or I will storm Spade Castle and find a cure myself. This ends tomorrow or so help me, I’ll burn this entire motherfucking realm down and myself with it.

# CHAPTER 22

I pick at my lip for the hundredth time, barely leaving any skin left. I haven't moved from the position Tweed placed me in, the pillow supporting my head and arm. Even if he hadn't tucked me in too tight, I don't have the energy or strength. Instead, I've laid here, occasionally blinking hard just to remind me if my eyes are opened or closed.

Once upon a time, I was fearless. I believed the world was full of misfortune, but if I kept myself detached, none of it would happen to me. And if it did, I wouldn't give a shit. News flash, I'm not invincible and I suddenly give all the shits.

I lay here thinking of all the things I'll never see again. The white rabbit scurrying through the forest, chasing the seconds on his stopwatch. A self-serving teapot supplying Hatter with the most British table spread possible. Bluebells levitating as they sing beautiful melodies through the meadow. Even my twins...In all their endless bickering, I'll never see either one again. Summoned by my thoughts, a shocked curse sounds from nearby.

"Holy fuck, Malice!" Cash hisses. I flinch and then groan at the onslaught of pain such sudden movement brings. "What the hell have they done to you?!" If I could be bothered, I'd laugh.

"They?" I replay, my voice a thin rasp from lack of use. I have no idea how long it's been since Tweed left me here, promising he'd be right back. It feels like an eternity. "This is all on you, asshole." More tears well in my impenetrable eyes. More than I'd shed in years, if ever. I hold them back, but the crackle in my voice betrays the emotion I'd rather ignore. "Tell me why. What did I actually do for you to betray me?"

Silence. For the longest time, no reply comes. I've settled back into the pillow, picking at my lip and trying to remember one of the childhood stories my father would read to me pre-Wonderland, when his quiet answer sounds.

"I had no idea she would poison you," Cash sounds like he's been crying himself. *Pussy*, the old Malice would think. Now–I don't know what to make of his reaction to my ailments. "I thought the Nightshade Trial was created to mock me. By design, they needed two people to complete them. No one in Wonderlust would side with me once Arabelle became queen. I had no one left. Especially someone who would risk everything to help me."

"And what do you think now?" I find myself asking, if only to keep him talking. Hearing his voice does something untold to me, and I can't deny him this chance to come clean.

"Now..." he sighs from behind the mirror. "I'm not sure what it was all for. Tweed chose to serve Arabelle over me, so I picked the opposite side. It was them vs us for the longest time. Not once did I consider they had trapped Lillianna for any other reason than to spite me. Freeing her was my only purpose, until you."

"You might need to start advertising for a new purpose at this rate," I drawl. A cough becomes caught in my throat, rattling agony through my ribs at each forced jerk.

"This is ridiculous. I'm coming over there," Cash states. My hand shoots into the air so fast, I don't have time to consider the consequences. And they fucking suck.

"Don't come near me," I groan.

"I want to help you, Crazy One." His pleading is almost my undoing, but somewhere deep down, I find the resolve to keep my hand firmly in the air.

"No." Pushing my face further into the pillow, I slowly pull myself into a fetal ball.

"Mal, I made a mistake. Let me fix it." Still, I force my head to shake.

"Stay the fuck away from me, Cash." Those tears finally overspill, thick blobs quickly soaking into the pillowcase. "I can't have you near me. I'm too weak to keep pushing you away and...I won't survive you betraying me again when Lillianna calls for you. It's better this way. Just let me go."

Ironically, my death is fast approaching the horizon, but Cash betraying me a second time would be worse. There are only two sides to this coin; Hearts vs Spades. Good vs evil. Why can't he play his role and leave me alone?

"Just stay away," I whisper as the darkness comes calling. It seeps from my soul, offering me a reprieve from the pain taking hold within my chest which has nothing to do with the poison. Allowing it to pull me beneath the veil of sleep, I'm sure I feel the trace of a touch brush my cheek just before I slip into unconsciousness.

# CHAPTER 23

Sleep comes in the form of fitful nightmares and would have, could have, and should have. Many times I think I'm awake, until confronted by the ghosts of my past. They haunt me, judge me. Soon, hopefully, they will mourn me.

The weight of a limb pinning me in place is at the forefront of their assault. Banding me to my bad decisions. I play out scenarios in my head; if

I'd never fallen down the rabbit hole, if I hadn't returned home, if I'd kept my mouth shut and pretended to be normal. I quickly dismiss the last one, figuring that's how psychopaths are created. Troubled, complicated people pretending to be normal until one day, they snap. Perhaps this is my snap occurring right now.

The mattress dips, my body nudged. At first, I believe it to be a figment of my wild imagination, until a hand strokes my cheek. Calloused, from years of fighting, yet gentle with affection. I stir slightly, blinking against the darkness and leaning into the touch until I rouse enough to remember the last person I had a conversation with.

"Cash?!" I try to jerk away. Only my head moves an inch backward. "Get the fuck out of my bed and my life!" In an attempt to sit up, I whimper as two hands cup my cheeks.

"Shhh, Malice, it's me. It's Tweed, I've got you." Relief, and a dash of disappointment I choose to ignore, flood my system. I always did enjoy the fight, and I'd be lying if I said a blind patient and a vampire doctor wasn't one of my fantasies. Relaxing, I lean into Tweed until his cold lips meet my forehead.

"I had a terrible dream," I semi-lie. I wish my conversation with Cash was a dream, because then I wouldn't have to replay the hurt in his voice from my rejection. Following the dip he creates, I sink into Tweed's body until no space separates us. From legs to groin, stomach to chest, we are one entity in the giant king-size bed.

"I won't let anything bad happen to you. Unless you ask me for it," Tweed's lips twitch against my brow. I find myself smiling too, before a thought has my face dropping into horror. If Tweed is attempting to distract me with sexual humor, things must be really bad.

"There is no cure, is there?" A long stretch of silence provides the answer.

"We won't stop looking until one is found." His voice is sure, as steady as the firm press of his chest. I could curl up in his hold for the rest of time, and that's when I realize it doesn't matter if there's a cure or not. I've already admitted defeat. I've lost my fight, so there's really no point in carrying on anyway.

"It's probably for the best," I state. Tweed squeezes me tighter. Pushing back with the little energy I can muscle, I search for his face with my hands, smoothing out the frown between his brows. Each movement sends shooting pains down my arms, but I must see it through.

"We're flames trying to outrun the wind. Our affection burns quickly, and it's best to mourn what we had rather than live long enough for those flames to be snuffed out." I wish I could see his face. The pull of his features are expressions I can't even imagine being on Tweed's stoic face. The indifferent asshole I dismissed as nothing else, now caressing my back and hurting for me. I smile weakly. "It's okay. We're here and together now. It's the ending I would have asked for."

Puckering my lips, Tweed follows my command and kisses me. Slowly, thoroughly. I feel the softness of his careful touch all through the poison which plagues me. Once, he refused to kiss me at all, and now I know why. Tweed doesn't fall easily. He doesn't give willingly. I had to prove I'd choose him, fight for him.

My heart swells, the beat quickening in response to his chilled touch roaming my arms. Wandering upwards, he grips my nape, opening me up to slide his tongue across mine. A groan of pain escapes before I can withhold it and Tweed immediately pulls away from me.

"I'm sorry," he gasps. "I can't touch you gently. It's not in my nature."

"Yes, you can," I disagree. I push myself back into his body, biting on my bottom lip to keep the groaning at bay this time. "Make love to me."

"Malice," Tweed groans in an equal amount of inner turmoil as I, but for different reasons. "I can't bear the thought of hurting you. Not when..." his jaw clenches against my cheek. I don't need him to finish that sentence, and I definitely don't need to be thinking about Cash or how this would have also been my last time to enjoy him as well.

"You ground me, Tweed. Amongst the crazy and the chaos, you're the one who keeps bringing me back to what's real. Now more than ever, I need grounding." I cling onto him as tight as I am able. Of all the times I thought about how my life might end, I knew I didn't want it to be as an elderly delusional woman with no family left to care for her. It was always going to be in my prime, either fighting or fucking my way out. "Consider it my final request."

This time, his kiss is the slowest of burns. Lips move across mine with a tenderness I have only ever dreamed of feeling. My hands come to rest on his neck, thumbs running along its length and over his strong jawline as though memorizing every inch to take with me into the afterlife.

Tweed presses his forehead against mine and sighs. His hands stroke along my back, soothing me with more gentle caresses as our thoughts entwine. His kisses rain down on my face softly at first, coaxing out a longing that has long been suppressed within me. I'm a live fast and screw faster kind of girl, on all other nights except this one.

My lips devour his hungrily as an intensity builds between us both, one we struggle to control. Only the limitations of my body keep me from taking charge, forcing me to lay on my side and accept the sweet torture I pleaded for.

Sliding his hands over my ribs with the lightest touch, his fingers hovering over my skin, Tweed works his way to my heavy breasts. His kneading is subtle, but has the same effect as if I was bound and being whipped. Electricity sparks between his cool fingertips and my pebbling nipples. I strain to push my chest forward, my back arching ever so slightly. I'm a victim to my own body at this stage, yet Tweed is allowing me to suffer at his hands instead.

I feel his smile against my neck as he relentlessly explores every curve of my skin with detailed devotion; tracing memories that will be forever imprinted for him alone should I not survive past morning. One by one, the summer dress and underwear I still wear are peeled from me with aching slowness.

All barriers are removed, Tweed's flawless skin pressing against me in all the right places. I've relied on his coldness before, needing to ease the inferno brewing inside. Now, it's even more delicious. Whatever is at war within my veins tries to resist Tweed's effect on me, but there's no stopping what we've started. His icy touch freezes the poison, allowing the real me to shine through. Nudging his thigh between mine, I gasp at the chill against my center. I bear down, seeking for more. More contact, more *him*.

"I need you," I plead. "I need you so fucking much."

"You have me. More than anyone else." Tweed slides his arm beneath my knee and lifts my leg, slowly hooking it over his hip. His dick is a solid weight against my abdomen, jerking insistently. Vaguely, through the rush of blood in my ears, I hear Tweed spit. The next second, his slickened hand strokes the length of my pussy and eases inside. Once, twice. Just enough to make me moan, before he replaces them with the end of his cock. “I’m yours, Malice.”

His thrust lasts a lifetime. I die, groan myself back to life, and drift back to death’s door again. Without my sight, I swear my other senses have heightened. I feel every ridge of his veiny shaft, feel myself stretch over him like my body is molding itself around his length. Seating himself, Tweed stills, his body tense with the need to dominate. To flip me onto my back and fuck me stupid.

“So. Fucking. Tight,” he grits through clenched teeth. I can only agree by making a strangled sound in the base of my throat. Wrapping both hands around my hips, Tweed tilts me to take every damn inch of his cock, stretching me impossibly wide. The sensory overload sends me into a lightheaded mess, as I clutch his hair and grit my teeth. Tweed doesn’t move a muscle. He doesn’t make a sound. I see stars, digging my fingernails into his scalp.

"Fuck me," I beg for the second time. I no longer care for sweet sentiments and gentle touches. A moan of discomfort passes between my pinched lips, Tweed’s grip on my hips light yet bruising to my tender skin. He holds me steady as his cock begins to tremble, and finally slides back and forth with aching slowness. My entire body jolts from the sensation, his impossibly thick shaft seems to swell and fill me even more each time.

“You feel how fucking right this is? How perfectly we fit together in the most divine way?" Tweed stills again, his mouth pressed to my ear as he pants. “I'm laying claim to your pussy, Malice. This cunt is mine. The scent of your arousal is marked by me, and it's so overwhelming, I can practically taste you."

Every muscle in Tweed's hardened body is taut, the possessiveness in his voice causing me to shiver. "Say it," he growls. He needs this. Tweed needs confirmation that I would have surrendered myself to him regardless of the circumstances. He's still a Tweedle at heart, seeking approval and yearning for love.

"You're the owner of my pussy," I agree. He instantly rewards me by pulling my nipple into his mouth. Swirling, flicking his tongue, I don't feel a trace of guilt at the omission–even though I vowed to never belong to one person. There's no use dealing with fine print now. I'm a dead woman anyway.

Between the shoots of pain, beyond the heaviness of poison dragging me into the abyss, our desire is like blood pouring through my veins. It pumps in sharp waves syncing to our labored breaths, crashing against invisible barriers. In the midst of this building storm, I find myself safe and secure in his hold. Most of all, his steady thrusts cancel out the agony and shift my focus.

There's only one problem.

I'm never going to be able to come like this. The building in my core isn't escalating quickly enough, the desperation in my strangled moans palpable. Between his kisses, Tweed strokes my spine, my cheeks, and hair. It's taking every ounce of his control to go slow, and I melt all the more for it. Unfortunately, my heart is all that's fluttering.

"Tweed," I moan for so many reasons. I have no words to follow. Burying his head into the crook of my neck, Tweed mutters my name back. The pair of us are locked in a loving embrace. If only love was enough.

The trickle of a touch brushes my back. I stiffen, doing a quick hand count. Both of Tweed's are accounted for, knotted in my hair. Even without the ability to see, I try to shift my head, but Tweed holds me in place. His dick continues its slow, steady thrusts, while that extra touch drifts lower. Down, down, until the firm press of a thumb eases between my butt cheeks. I tense.

Pressing against my back passage, Cash doesn't waste time on pleasantries. His thumb pushes inside, adding the exact pressure I needed. My body coils around the invasion as I imagine Cash's smooth, deep voice, if he dared to speak and alert Tweed to his presence.

*"All good things come to those who wait. And you've waited long enough,"* he'd say. I give a trace of a nod, agreeing with my own imagination. Then he'd lean into my ear, his tone a low scrape which bolts directly towards my clit. *"Tweed may own your pussy, but your ass is mine."*

I groan as Cash's speed increases, at odds with Tweed's cock. His thumb intrudes my ass, ramming and twisting with a sense of punishment framing his movements. My breathing picks up, a strange happening taking place within my core. I fight against my own psyche. The betrayal between twins, the conflicting rhythms to their approach. I'm a woman torn between good and evil, on the precipice of damning myself. This is my first real test to show Tweed where my heart lies, but I don't get time to make an active decision.

My body clenches, the flutters building into an untethered storm. Tearing me in half, I break for them both. A stuttered scream, foreign to my own ears, is released into the sniffling air. My thighs clamp as I clench around Tweed, pulsating with the cum leaking from my pussy. Each time I shudder, a bolt of agony shoots through me, but I refuse to come down from the blissful cloud my mind is floating on. There's no pain here, no push and pull of bad decisions. I wanted my world to be rocked one final time, and I've been given exactly that.

By the time my head sinks into the pillow, my body slumping with release, there's no trace of Cash. His intrusive thumb, his grace of a touch. I can sense the emptiness at my back, but I can't dwell on him. Tweed is still here, holding me, stroking me. Slowly, he withdraws his still hardened dick, and I realize too late, he didn't finish along with me.

"Shhh," Tweed hushes me when I open my mouth. "This was about you." Capturing my mouth in a passionate kiss, I settle my mind. It's fine, Tweed is none the wiser to what just happened. My tongue dances with his, a brief moment of neutrality allowing me the freedom to return his enthusiasm. I'm void of pain, finally, which can only mean the end is closing in.

Anchoring myself onto his being, my soul reaches out, connecting our link to life onto one single thread; an exquisite tapestry against a twilight sky. Despite all odds, we lay suspended in this moment together for what feels like an eternity. Simply exploring each other's body through touch alone, stars dancing behind my eyes while mouths whisper words of love forsaken but not forgotten until our paths may meet once again in another distant place, time, or world.

"Rest. I'll be back soon to hold you through the night,' Tweed leans his forehead on mine. My heart returns to a regular beat, my fingers lingering on his chest as he shifts away. I try to not let the space growing between us seem like more than it actually is. Tweed told me he could sense his twin a mile off, but perhaps this time, he was too in tune with me to notice. I wouldn't apologize if confronted. I can't deny the connection I still feel to

Cash, despite everything. I'm afraid I always fall for the bad guy. A dirty habit I can't shake, even now.

# CHAPTER 24

Whether Tweed returned as promised, I couldn't tell when I decided it must be morning. The reprieve of pain is well and truly over, as I force my feet from beneath the sheets. They drop heavily onto the carpet, sending so much force through my legs, I thought my knees might shatter. I cry out, the sound echoing around the bedchamber. I have no doubts, had I remained in bed and given into the crippling need of my bladder, Tweed would have cleaned the sheets and said nothing of it.

"Over my dead body," I grumble. I'm poisoned, not an invalid. The Mighty Malice won't be going out in a patch of piss. Forcing myself upright, I half-hold the bed and hobble to the ottoman before needing a breather. Giving myself a pep-talk, mostly consisting of cursing and a fair amount of self-hatred, I scrape one foot in front of the other, blindly aiming for the bathroom. My fingers grace the high-back armchair, causing me to flinch. I'm sure it was further over but what do I know?

Somehow, guided by a sense of direction I didn't know I had, I make it to the door. Cool tile welcomes my toes, and from there I rush to stumble to the toilet. Oh, the humble throne of smooth porcelain. I've never felt such ecstasy as I relieve myself, my moans similar to those I made last night. And that's before I work my way into the shower and figure out how to turn it on by touch alone.

Scalding heat pours down on my head, heating the aches and pains within my limbs. Once more, I let my imagination take hold, pretending I can feel the thickness of poison washing away, pooling at my feet, and disappearing down the drain. It's brief, but still welcome as I convince myself I'm back to full health. I'm like a walking placebo.

No sooner have I fiddled around to turn off the faucet, do I hear a commotion beyond the closed door. Muffled, angered shouts. The storming of heavy feet. No, not feet–hooves. Reaching out, trying to locate a towel, my fingers brush something soft. I clamp down, dragging it into the cubicle to dry myself.

"Hey! Do you mind?!" a familiar voice hisses in a harsh whisper. The type which would have far too many teeth. I stall, mid-flossing between my ass cheeks and, pluck the softness out.

"Chesh?" Lifting the heavy weight, I feel around for her tummy as a set of tiny claws leap onto my arm. Scampering upwards, something nestles behind my ear, and I gasp. "Stan!" My hand opens on instinct, dropping Chesh in a heap on the floor. She floats back up, reclining across my shoulders.

"We don't have much time to get you out of here. You must do exactly as I say."

"Out of the bathroom? I don't like to brag, but I think I'm a fucking master at this being blind stuff. Got in here just fine." Feeling around the shower cubicle, I forget about the half-step and crash onto the floor. Ow, that hurt like a bitch.

"No, shh. Listen." Chesh demands. I lie there, recovering from the onslaught of tile meeting flesh, forced to obey. Hooves continue to trample through the bedchamber, the vibrations from their stomps reverberating beneath me. There's chatter, harshly barked orders which mention nuclear bombs, the Jabbercocky, and Spade Castle. Wait...

"Chesh, what the fuck is going on?" I whisper. Her tail curls around the front of my face to silence me.

"Tweed led an army into Black Kingdom an hour ago. He's preparing to storm Spade Castle with strict orders to kill any and all beings inside on sight. Something about an unwelcomed butt-fuck?" I sink my head, pressing my forehead on the cold floor. Of course he knew. I was praying my naivety would see me through this once, but I've never been that lucky.

Pressing her paws into my back, Chesh pushes off with more oomph than she needs, returning to drape rough material over me a moment later. I force myself up on shaky arms, threading the flannel bathrobe around myself. Tying the cord around my middle, I feel around for the counter and pull myself up with painstaking slowness. The water weight within my hair drags my head backward.

"There must be a hair tie in here somewhere." I locate a drawer, figuring Cash being a ladies' man has to account for something. A range of objects meet my hand, some small and egg-shaped, others long and beaded. One starts to vibrate, but I manage to find one rogue hair tie and slam the drawer shut. This will do the trick, I think as I pile my hair into a messy bun on top of my head and strain to stretch the tie around the mass.

"That's...a cock ring," Chesh drawls. I shrug as it stays in place. All I care about is using gravity to my advantage and remaining upright.

"So what's the plan? How am I going to get to Cash?"

"Cash?" Chesh stops mid-float behind my face, and I crash into her. Spitting out the furs stuck in my mouth, I feel her stale, fishy breath beating against my face. "There's no saving Cash. Let Tweed take care of him. I just want to get you back to my feather and bone cave so you can scratch my belly for the rest of time."

"Chesh, look at me," I tug up my sleeves despite the pain it causes me. This is more important. Running a hand over my arm, I can feel the shift of black magic beneath my skin. It shifts, wriggling within my veins like another entity. One which can't merge with my own, no matter how hard it's trying. It seems I was wrong - there is some fight left in me yet.

"Soon, I'll be gone, and whether Tweed wants to admit it or not, Cash is all he'll have left. Then there's what happens to Cash when Lillianna decides he's of no use anymore. I need to fix the rift between them." Reaching out, I grab Chesh's round body and jerk her towards the door. "Take me to Spade Castle." Stan snuggles in behind my ear, agreeing with my decision. Look at us, reunited and on the path of fortitude. What a great team we make.

Using Chesh as my navigation system, I walk more steadily towards the door. Stopping in front, I sense Chesh's hesitation before a rumble filters through her body. She's either going to fart or detonate, and I don't want to be at her rear when she does either one. Luckily, she disappears into nothing as I visualize her peering through the door.

"There's a row of Royal Oxes guarding the mirror portal. They'll spot us as soon as we open the door," Chesh reports back, followed by a murmuring about my pathetic mortal body. Tapping my toes on the tile, I rack my brain for a solution. This is Wonderlust, nothing is ever as impossible as it seems.

"What about this mirror?" I swing back, hoping I'm pointing in the right direction. "Cash's room as Spade castle is an exact replica of the bedchamber here. It stands to reason his bathroom should do the same." I gag on my words. I hate being reasonable. Still, I walk forward and flip over the bidet. Fancy, ass-washing bastard. Spinning around, Chesh's tail curls around my neck and leads me towards the basin.

"I commend your courage," she sighs, "but I wouldn't be caught dead in Black Kingdom. Witches and demons congregate in the shadows there to practice their powers. One minute, you're lazing on a branch. The next, you're a frog trying to eat your own eyes." A shudder passes through her body as if she's speaking from experience. I respect her choice, but her warning doesn't stop me from raising my knee to meet the countertop. My thigh screams in discomfort, as if my skin is too tight. Chesh spirals around my body, ending up beneath my other foot to help push me up. I hold the edge of the mirror's frame, its rose-embossed pattern steadying my grip.

"Are you staying with me, Stan?" I ask. "It's probably going to go terribly wrong." Lifting his head, Stan sniffs the back of my ear and nudges me as if to say, '*stop stalling and get on with it.*' I smirk. "That's my boy. See you on the other side, Chesh." Then I summon every ounce of my energy and throw myself through the mirror.

I was right. The bathroom is an exact replica on the other side. A fact I discovered when my foot caught on the tap, my shin smashed against the lip of the basin and I freefall towards the ground. Fortunately, there's the added feminine touch of an extra fluffy bath mat and I don't break every bone in my face as a result. The only thing I'll ever be thanking Lillianna for.

In the room beyond, the splintering of wood mimics a door being kicked inwards. I'm army crawling, dragging the length of me forward by my forearms. One set of lonely boots stomps inside. Opposite to the guards in my previous bedroom, there's no sign of the army Chesh spoke of. Just one pissed off vampire confronting his twin.

"How fucking dare you," Tweed growls on the other side of the door. I quicken my pace.

"I wondered how long it would take," Cash chuckles. I can picture him sitting in the high-back armchair, sipping on a whiskey glass of blood.

"You had no right to interfere! That was possibly my last night with her, and now it's forever tainted with the knowledge you invited yourself to join." Glass smashes against the wall, so close, I have to clasp a hand over my scream. This time, when I army crawl across the floor, it's slower. My fingers touch the wood and instead of using it to stand, I press my ear closer.

"From where I was watching, you needed all the help you could get," Cash laughs again. "It's awfully considerate of you to come all this way to thank me." Another smash, another outburst of Tweed's anger. He's trying to rattle Cash, but he's going about it in all the wrong ways.

"You shouldn't have been watching at all. I hope you stuck around long enough to hear her profess her love to me. She's chosen me, and killing you will be the cherry on top of a perfect Sunday." I snort at Tweed's double entendre. I wonder if he's noticed his Tweedle-ness creeping back in.

"Kill away," I almost hear Cash shrug. "As long as you can handle knowing she only chose you once I was no longer an option." *Oh shit.* I push myself upright now, using my palms on the door to remain steady and locate the handle. "The daring Knave, the favorite twin. How does it feel to be second best for once? Take my leftovers, something else you can thank me for."

I'm not surprised by the telltale thwack of skin on skin. The crunch of knuckle on jaw. Despite his carefree tone, Cash doesn't hold back from the fight Tweed brings. A heavy weight slams before the groan of wood cracks and splits. The coffee table, perhaps? Squeezing the door handle, I try to steady the erratic beat of my heart. Cash's words were meant to taunt Tweed, but they've affected me just as much.

Have I been using Tweed? Is the affection I feel genuine or a consequence of circumstance? I shake my head, almost dislodging Stan. No, there's no faking what I feel. I asked Tweed to make love to me –something I've never experienced, let alone asked for. His arms are a cage I don't feel trapped in, because I know he isn't scared to release me. He knows I'd come back, and here I am. Returning to save what's mine.

Pushing down on the handle, I stumble into the room. They don't notice at first, the sounds of a vicious fistfight taking place at vampire speed around the room. One moment they're to the left of me, next a whip of wind slaps me across the face and they're to the right. Furniture and ribs break, their grunts of excursion making it unclear if one has the upper hand.

I stretch out a hand, hoping to catch them mid-speed-run, when the pain I've been forcing down all morning arises with a vengeance. My chest lurches inwards, like a hammer has been taken to my sternum. Ash, bitter and thick, works its way up the back of my throat, coiling within my nostrils. My limbs numb as my control slips, that internal darkness finally finding its way into my system. The truth is clear now. The poison within me has been spreading yet dormant, and now, something or someone has activated it. A silent scream sounds in my head before I lose all sense of gravity.

"Malice! What the hell?!" The words drift out of my head as if I've been submerged underwater. There's peace to be found down here, but I divert away from it, fearful of what giving in might mean. Following the light to the end of the tunnel would be too easy, clinging onto a false hope it may end my pain. The harder option is to stick around, see this cock fight through to the end.

Multiple hands carefully scoop me up into two sets of solid arms, most of my weight resting on solid muscles I quickly decide are their interlocked thighs. Seems all I had to do was die for them to work together. I'm trembling, unable to control the seizing and contorting of my body. I can hold on, I need to hold on just a while longer. At least until I've seen through what I started. Wonderlust may be at war with itself, but there's no reason for these twins to be.

Reaching out, my fingers graze a firm chest on either side of my body. Two otherworldly beings, ruled by hatred and consumed by jealousy. I may not have done much good in this lifetime, so let this be the first and last.

"I believe..." I croak. "I believe the Tweedle Boys will forever be best friends and loving brothers." If I hadn't already been blind, the onslaught which follows would have seen to it. Every sense of my body is overrun, shutting down in time with the slowing pulse of my organs. My heart echoes in my ears, its beat stubbornly fighting against the webs wrapping around it.

I'm being shaken, the panic rising in Tweed's movements making me smile on the inside. I managed something I never thought possible. I got someone to fall in love with me. On the other side, the softness of hair brushes my cheek, lips touching my ear and when Cash speaks, it's like his words are being beamed directly into my soul.

"Oh, Crazy One. What have you done?"

# CHAPTER 25

"Quickly," I tell Tweed. I can't remember the last time I saw him cry, and the sight is unnerving. "Get her onto the bed." For once, he obeys without question. We carry Malice to the bed, lying her down in the center. Her heartbeat is faint, but still detectable thanks to our enhanced hearing.

Tugging out the restraints Lillianna would use on me, I ignore the curious stare from my brother's teary eyes. Now's not the time to admit the diamond-studded cuffs aren't for kinky shit, but to weaken and starve me. In the few moments of clarity, I know it's to keep me dependent on the gift of her tainted veins, but then the monster takes over and I'm defenseless against my own appetite. Something about Lillianna's unique taste goes beyond addictive. It controls and consumes me.

"Wrap the chains around her wrists and ankles, hard. It might slow or redirect the poison long enough to save her."

"How?" Tweed's defeated voice asks, but he does as I've asked. We strap Malice's wrists so hard, her skin is pinched and breaks in several places. Black liquid seeps from the wounds, spiraling through the air to re-enter through her nose. It's linked to her. "Sqwuakington was working on a cure, but he won't have one in time."

I suck in a breath, feeling the pit of Tweed's despair as if it were my own. I haven't been connected to him like this since...well, since before we were prisoners of Red Kingdom.

Reaching over Malice's twitching form, I take Tweed by the shoulders. His sunken green gaze drifts up to meet mine. "There is no cure," I inform him. A fact I'd overhead Lillianna cackling about in the lab. I'm not sure who she was informing, since I heard no response. I wouldn't put it past her to be gloating to herself, she hasn't been the same since she returned from weed form.

"Well, since I can't hate you anymore," Tweed violently wipes his cheeks dry. "Please tell me you have a way to fix this. I can't lose her again, Cash. I can't, I can't." He's shaking his head so much, it's making me dizzy.

Running through the lists of ideas I've had and dismissed while laying around here bored, I return to the only one I figured may be semi-plausible.

"Maybe. Wait right here. I'll be straight back." Shifting back, Tweed's hand lashes out to grab my wrist, tugging me back.

"Don't betray me on this. It's too important, and I promise, magic bindings or not, it's something I'll never forgive." Nodding, I speed from the room with the same thought tumbling through my mind. If I fuck this up, I'll never forgive myself, either.

Racing down the hallway, it's too easy to avoid the Red Army. Their heavy stomps and labored breathing give them away too easily. Oxen for guards was truly a terrible idea. Instead of fighting against the plants breaking through the floors and walls, I use them to my advantage. Sliding down a thick vine, I stop by the kitchen for a large potato sack and round back to the library.

I still, as I reach out for the handle, only just sensing Lillianna's presence in time. The handle rattles, forcing me to rush around the nearest corner to hide and lose precious time. The Queen exits, still talking to herself with a wicked grin on her face. I duck behind a huge hydrangea. Her shadow draws across the wall, ever so slowly gliding along as the multitude of ruffles in her dress brush the floor. I brace myself to run, my arms poised when Lillianna stops on the other side of the bush.

"Oh, Tweedle," she singsongs. Listening out, Lillianna makes a humming noise in the back of her throat. I know what's coming and I'm powerless to stop her from tugging the dagger out of her belt and slicing open her wrist. The scent slams into me with the force of a wrecking ball, almost knocking me back on my ass. A groan is locked in my throat, stifled by the hand I clamp over my mouth and nose. I can't let her win this time.

My tongue thickens, my inactive organs cramping with hunger. It doesn't matter I forced myself to feed from her merely a few hours ago, I can never get enough. I can't break the habit.

Beginning to stand, an image flashes before my eyes. Malice. Not covered in black webbing, blind and weak, trembling and dying. But the playful woman with hair the color of autumn leaves, her infectious smile brighter than the midday sun. The minx who wears whatever she wants, does whatever she wants and refuses to apologize for being authentically her. In my mind's eye, she turns these baby blues on, filled with so much joy, energy, and...life.

For that Malice, I remain frozen in place. For her, I snap my own nose to resist smelling Lillianna's blood scent, allowing her to move on without luring me from my hiding spot. I zoom to the library, shut myself inside, and barricade the door before my nose heals. I know exactly where it is, I've sought it out a hundred times to check it's still here. Top level, eighth bookcase to the left and halfway down.

Plucking the book from its shelf, I open it on the floor and jump straight in. The fall is short, my boots hitting soil in no time. She's right there, kneeling between the vegetation and utterly oblivious to my presence. Creeping up behind her, I lift the potato sack into the air. A flock of geese flies overhead, distracting me with their strange honks as opposed to elegant chatter of politics. Mary Ann looks up at them too, following their flight pattern backwards to lock eyes with me.

"Cash?" she smiles, her face glowing. In fact, she seems healthy all around, from the pink twinge to her fuller cheeks and defined curves to her figure. Her black hair has grown out, braided down her back. Time moves differently in this realm, I remind myself.

Placing down the thick handled fork, she abandons her gardening and holds out a hand for me to help her stand. I briefly consider skipping the pleasantries, but decide she'll be easier to kidnap standing. Easing her from the knee pad between her carrots and pumpkins, Mary Ann turns to face me. The potato sack falls from my hand.

A huge baby bump protrudes from her midsection. She catches me gaping and rubs over her floral blouse.

"It's a girl," she beams. I grimace before I can catch myself.

"Wow. Um, congratulations," I mutter, glancing up to the quaint farmhouse. Nestled against rolling hills, its white-washed exterior is adorned with ivy, the hatch roof weathered yet charming. I can smell a homemade apple pie drifting through crooked, open windows. A man stands in the doorway, scowling but cleverly doesn't try to approach.

"We're thinking of calling her Alison; Ally for short? Do you think," Mary Ann blinks those huge vulnerable eyes up at me, "Malice will like it? I wanted her to be godmother, after all." Again, my face pinches and Mary Ann's back straightens. "Wait, why are you here? What's wrong?"

"I fucked up," I say in a rush, finally admitting my guilt out loud. There's only so much denial one person can live in, and I've reached the bitter end with mine. "I asked Malice to help me free Lillianna, but I didn't know the queen would poison her. Now she's dying, and there's no amount of magic that can help her so I thought..." My eyes drift to Mary Ann's chest while she takes notice of the potato sack.

"You thought you'd steal my heart and replace it with hers," Mary Ann quirks her brow. I pause, then nod. In reality, I'd planned to kill her and take it without a second thought, but things change.

I anticipate screaming, cursing, scratching, but Mary Ann seems deep in thought as she rubs her belly. "It has merit, I'll give you that. There is no magic in this realm. The poison would linger in me but pose no threat. The only problem being, I'm currently in no state to withstand such a transplant. Would Malice be able to hold on–" I'm already shaking my head, a grave expression on my face. She sighs, chewing on her bottom lip. "How long do we have?"

"We're already on borrowed time as it is," I admit. A spark enters Mary Ann's eye, one I decide is determination. Grabbing up the book I jumped through and taking my hand, she rushes me towards the farmhouse without looking back.

# CHAPTER 26

I hold Malice's limp hand until her skin grows cold enough to rival mine. I should release her. I should be encouraging her to conserve as much body heat as she can until Cash returns. But I'm a selfish bastard at the best of times, and when my girl's breathing is growing weaker by the second? I'm being damn right greedy for every last touch I can get.

That is, if Cash returns. It's now ingrained in me to give him the benefit of the doubt. Surely he wouldn't fail Malice so soon after she saved him from my wrath. She's given everything she is to come here, to reunite us. I just hope we can repay the favor.

The door jingles, my deadened heart lifting in hope. An ox peers around the door, huffing heavily through his nose ring.

"Is he dead yet, Sir?" The beast's beady eyes scan the room. Other than the broken furniture, there's not half enough damage to suggest Cash met his end at my hands tonight.

"There's been a change in circumstances," I reply with not enough growl in my tone. I have appearances to maintain with the royal guards, yet I can't pretend I wish tonight had gone any differently. I wasn't truly prepared to be an orphan and an only child. "Lillianna is our only target until I order otherwise. Have there been any sightings of her?"

"Not yet," the ox grumbles. "We hear her voice, sense her presence, but every time we gain ground, she disappears. It's as if she's walking through the walls."

"Don't let your guard down. She's here somewhere, and our intrusion will not go unnoticed or unpunished. As soon as Malice is fit to be moved, we portal out." Nodding, the ox withdraws and quietly closes the door. A knot of possessiveness within eases with that simple click, giving me back the precious time I need to focus on Malice.

Stroking her forehead with my thumb, I smooth away the bright orange stands which refuse to settle back with the rest of her drying mane. Her hair is one of my favorite attributes, especially now it's as vibrant as her soul and as unruly as her spirit. Or, how it should be anyway. Tugging those strands behind her ear, a sharp sting pierces my fingers. I withdraw them sharply, only now noticing the tiny pink nose sniffing out from the nest in her hair.

"I thought I'd seen the last of you," I narrow my eyes at Stan. He tucks back into his hiding spot, leaving me to focus solely on Malice's unmoving face. Dare I say, beneath the black lines stretching towards her eyes, she appears to be at peace. Although inside, I know her mind will be raging with the unfinished business she has yet to rain down on this earth and the next. Her bullshit bucket list which I'll happily aid her in completing, as long as I get her back.

Leaning in, I press a gentle kiss to her forehead. "We will win, my love. We'll show them all, nothing will stop your chaos." At my words, I hear Malice's heart shudder, and her head sinks further into the pillow. Grabbing her shoulder, I shake hard enough to dislodge the sugar glider from behind her ear. He doesn't try to attack me this time but lifts his tiny paws to shake Malice alongside me. "Hold on for me, beautiful. Just a little longer," I plead. Desperation like I've never felt claws at my insides. I can't lose her. The one precious, pure thing in my life.

As the door creaks open, Cash speeds through the room in a flash of movement to appear at my side.

"You came back!" I leap into his arms. Actually leap, crushing him in an embrace that takes us both by surprise. Even worse, Cash clings onto me just as tight, his face buried in my neck. A small throat-clearing finally wrenches us apart just before things get really awkward. Stepping back, I catch sight of the tented crotch of Cash's cargos. *Too late.*

"Sorry," he rubs the back of his head. "Got a little excited there." I turn around to face our visitor, itching to get back to Malice's side. I don't recognize her at first, the scrawny scared girl who once was is now a fully-fledged woman.

"Mary Ann, you look," my eyes drift lower and widen, "fertile." I couldn't think of another way to say she looks like a damn hippy in a nice way. From the dirt smudged on her cheek, her floral blouse, free-flowing pants, crocs, and the tote bag slung over her shoulder, I can't think of a single reason why someone might dress so.

"Yes well, I have a very angry husband at home, waiting for an explanation as to what we just did on the dining table." I toss a quick glance back at Cash, and he rolls his eyes.

"Not that! Give me some credit, brother. No offense," he winces as she folds her arms and makes a 'humph' sound. I quickly move the conversation along, winding my arm around Cash's shoulders.

"We need to hurry," I urge Cash closer to the bed. "Whatever scheme you have, you need to do it now. I trust you've set your plan in motion rather than gone off on an irrational tangent." Tugging him further, I have the undeniable sense for him to share my precious final moments with Malice. I wouldn't permit anyone else but him to take her hand and kiss her in a similar way. Only because I know it would please her. Deep down, Malice can't extinguish the flame she holds for Cash, and I can't remember why I needed her to. However, Cash holds himself back, looking around as if unsure of himself.

"About that..." he trails off, stepping closer to Mary Ann. "What I'm about to do is going to seem conflicting, but I need you to hold onto that trust for me." Unease ripples through my entire being. I hesitate, shifting my focus to Mary Ann's huge blue eyes for clarity. Then, Cash strikes.

Faster than even I can track, he lunges forward. I don't see his nails extend into sharpened claws until I feel them slicing into my chest, his arm plunging directly towards my heart. I stagger back, dropping onto the mattress. Easing me back, Cash's eyes grow greener, like a siren amongst the agony and calling me home. I don't want to be drawn to it, but my existence is currently being squeezed by his hand. His grip on my heart tightens before he twists and yanks backward. Mary Ann is there all of a sudden, holding out a silver tray. I watch through hazy, unbelieving eyes as my heart is placed onto the ottoman, and from her tote bag, Mary Ann produces a surgeon's knife.

"Stay with me, brother," Cash holds me upright by the hand clamped on my nape. His other is dripping thick, congealed blood all over my cargos. "Hurry, Mary Ann. He's fading much quicker than I anticipated."

"Not helping," Mary Ann clenches her jaw. With the precision of an artist with a paintbrush, she takes care to score repetitive lines across my most vital organ, separating the chambers from each other. My head tries to loll to the side, but Cash refuses to let me. I wish he would, because watching Mary Ann pull out a ziplock bag with another half of a heart inside, and then thread a needle with her mouth sets my mind into overdrive. I try to speak, to shout or even scream, but nothing happens. I'm a host in a corpse, and it's only a matter of minutes before my mind gives up on me too.

"Almost there," Mary Ann fills the tense silence. Placing the hearts together, she pierces my half with the needle, and I phase out. When I come to, I'm lying on the mattress. My chest is exposed, free from the t-shirt I previously wore. Whatever wounds Cash inflicted on me after I passed out have already healed, and the fact I'm alive at all speaks volumes. I stare at the ceiling, taking too long to sharpen my senses to what they should be. Amongst the mental check-over, I realize my hand is pressed against Malice's so I take it in mine.

"Don't move," Mary Ann says sternly. I shift my head ever-so-slightly to see her hunched over Malice's body. My instincts are to jump upright and demand why I can scent so much blood, but Cash knows me too well. His hands are pressed over my shoulders one second, his legs pinning mine in the next, as he straddles and restrains me to the bed.

"Let her finish," he commands. It's been years since Cash has dared to speak to me in such a way, but it's also been too long since I've seen the glint of concern in his eyes. I trust him, I decide without needing to put too much thought into it. Remaining still, I wait for Mary Ann to sigh she's all finished before bolting upright.

We all wait on bated breath. Besides the mass of crimson leaking into the bathroom, there's no change. Malice's skin is still drained of all color beneath the poison, her lashes firmly closed over those once-beautiful blue eyes. I listen out for her breathing, any sign that their plan has worked.

Nothing.

A lone tear slips down my cheek. Mary Ann is many things, including incredibly resourceful, but a surgeon she is not. It was a decent plan, after all, to use a more human approach which didn't involve magic, but Lillianna is no amateur. She knows how to infect and destroy people from the inside out. I just didn't think she'd be able to snuff out Malice's light so easily.

*Bu-bum.* Distracted by the sob rising in my throat, I almost miss it. *Bu-Bum.* Cash grips my arm, squeezing with all of his might. His smile stretches from ear to ear, but I withhold rejoicing just yet. The sound isn't quite what I'd expected. Not a clean beat, but a to and fro, as if the organ is trying to determine how to function properly. Two halves of her heart battling to find an even sync. I frown at the explosive scar left upon my chest, the weakness of trying to stay alive stopping me from healing fully.

Snickering, Cash raises his t-shirt to point at the thin, smooth line to the left of his pec, nestled between his tattoos. How come I got sucker-punched through the chest, while he was eased through a formal procedure? His smug smile says it all. If it wasn't for the sudden gasp which escapes Malice, I would have found the will to punch my twin in the face.

Regardless, Malice splutters, black liquid bubbling from her lips. We're all quick to turn her, mine and Cash's hands circling and patting her back in support.

"That's it, baby," I soothe.

"Cough it up, Crazy One," Cash adds. The webbing covering her body is pulled upwards by an invisible strength, being forced out at last. Mary Ann smooths back Malice's orange curls until all trace of the poison is expelled onto the floor. Cash nudges my shoulder.

"It was Mary Ann's idea to pair our hearts and give Malice a fighting chance with a vampire's trait for healing. The black magic bound is no longer bound to our girl."

*Our girl*, rattles around my head and settles all too smoothly into my psyche. I should be furious Cash would entertain such an idea. We know the tales of Frankenstein's Vampire and how wrong such a procedure can go, but that's exactly why he didn't give me any warning. As it stands, Malice slumps back panting, her crystal blue eyes blinking at the ceiling, and my half-a-heart lifts with elation.

It takes every ounce of my vampire training to withhold my first instinct. To grab and crush her in an embrace and never let go. With a shaky hand, I force myself to brush my knuckles over her cheek, intently watching the steady rise and fall of her chest.

"Welcome back," Mary Ann smiles. Malice's head rolls to the side, roaming her eyes over her old friend.

"I've seen such terrible things," she mutters. I shudder to think what she could mean, but no one gets a chance to ask. No sooner as Cash presses a light kiss to Malice's hand, does a magical pulse explode within the bedchamber. It's heavy, dark, and littered with evil. Dread circulates as thick smoke seeps from beneath the door, permeating our reunion.

"I knew it wouldn't take long," Lillianna's voice sounds, followed by a cackling of laughter. I can't place her whereabouts, the sound coming from the very walls. Both Cash and I shoot to our feet, fangs bared as we shield opposite sides of the bed. The darkness grows thicker, but it's no match for my enhanced eyesight. "The Knave, the Hatter, and the traitor all in one room. Not to mention the bodies of the entire Heart Army are lying dead around my humble home. It must be my lucky day."

The door whips open, cracking free from its hinges, and hurtles towards the bed. Cash holds up one forearm, shattering the wood in half before it can even think about touching Malice.

"This is enough, Lillianna. Whatever you're scheming, I never signed up for this."

"Why, of course, you did." Through the smoke, the Queen materializes. Her dress is one with the shadows, hugging her torso and free flowing into the wickedness she embodies. Her eyes glitter with delight as she regards us all, her lips twisting into a cruel smile. "You promised to free me from an abusive husband and tyrant King. You vowed to help me seek revenge on all of those who have wronged us both."

"What the fuck have I done to you?!" Malice splutters, trying to sit upright. Mary Ann is quick to ease her back down, using her own pregnant body to shield Malice from harm. Lillianna ignores Malice's outburst, floating closer to Cash.

"You were broken when we met," she lifts his chin with one finger to look her in the eye. "A shell of a being who was only good to Red Kingdom for entertainment. Jester, stripper, whatever title you were given was nothing on what I offered. The throne at my side."

"I never asked to be your King." Cash jerks his head away. Lillianna cackles, drifting backward within the darkness.

"Yet you took everything I offered. I gave you immortality. I sacrificed my own so you could infect your twin. You owe me eternal life, and it will be as the sole ruler of Wonderlust." It's my turn to chuckle, bringing Lillianna's sole attention to me. I hope Cash takes the hint to get the rest of them out of here while I keep her distracted.

"There can never be one sole ruler of Wonderlust. The realm is split into four to control the balance. Such power would tear you to shreds." I growl. Lillianna smiles, wider than is natural, causing her eyes to stretch thinner. Spiraling within the shadows, she laughs, the ends of her dress growing larger.

"Don't I look powerful to you, Knave?"

In the corner of my eye, Mary Ann shuffles Malice to the edge of the bed, lowering them both onto the floor and beneath the four-poster structure. I'd hoped Malice would be able to at least walk, but the hearts are taking too long to sync, to pump a fresh blood flow through her tainted veins.

"Turns out," Lillianna continues gloating, "the time you gave me trapped as a dandelion was exactly what I needed. Time. Silence. The reflection of where I was going wrong, how I was so easily captured. I created spells in my mind, worked through the formulas without distraction. I suppose that should be enough to excuse you for tainting my dear Cash," her head whips to the side. Cash steps in front of the bed, shielding the empty outline in the sheets. "But of all the things I am, forgiving is not one of them."

Lashing a hand out, I'm thrown back by an invisible force. Slamming into the wall, my body is pinned there, a slither of a shadow wrapping around my throat. I gasp for air, clawing at the darkness suffocating me. I shouldn't be so easily pinned, but if it's the increase of her power or the lacking half of my heart affecting my strength, I can't tell. Lillianna slithers closer, a twisted smile curling her lips.

"You never learn," she taunts, her voice low and dangerous. "Always underestimating the power of your enemies." She cackles again, turning her back on me. Setting Cash in her sights, Lillianna doesn't attack. Rather, she puts a dagger from the ribbon belt at her waist and slowly slides it across her wrist.

"Drink from me, and all will be as it was," Lillianna offers out her arm. Cash's hands ball at his sides. *Don't do it, don't fucking do it.* My vision blurs as I struggle against the unseen grip of magic tightening around my neck. Lillianna's fluttering eyes at my brother only infuriate me further. She thinks she's won. Summoning all my strength, I push back against the shadow and manage to inhale one full breath. Just as suddenly as they attacked, the shadows release. I slump to the floor, coughing and growling.

Beneath the bed, two pairs of widened eyes catch mine. I place a finger over my lips, warning them to stay quiet. Then I'm on my feet.

My fist meets Lillianna's jaw before she can see me coming. The scent of copper, magically sweetened to be irresistible, meets my nose. It's enticing, but I know better. Shoving Cash to the side, I take Lillianna's responding blow. This time, I'm ready for it.

My feet skid backward, then I'm lunging forward. A push and pull we enter into. My fists meet shadow, binds wrapping around my wrists while Lillianna's heeled boot appears to slam into my sternum. My chest cramps in pain for half a second, enough to make me wince. Both, I decide. Her enhanced strength and my recent organ dissection are both to blame for her gaining the upper hand this easily. In my current state, this isn't a fight I can win single-handedly. Cash's head is twitching back and forth, his eyes glinting from bright green to darkened pits of moss. Confusion tugs his features, his fangs stretching far past his bottom lip.

"Cash," I slap him across the face. His gaze meets mine with a moment of clarity. "Get the women out of here. I'll handle this bitch."

"Tweed–" he starts with no real control over his tongue.

"Just go!" I duck beneath Lillianna's oncoming shadow, pulling Cash into a crouch with me. "Get to safety. I'll catch you up."

"Where are we going to go?" Mary Ann pops her head out from underneath the bed. Malice's poisoned heart lies a few feet from her head, discarded and forgotten. The next blow from Lillianna's darkness knocks me flat on my stomach. Grabbing a hold of an approaching shadow, I use the Queen's own darkness to shield Mary Ann from her vision.

"You're going home. Thank you for everything, but you've got a baby to protect and a husband to placate. I'll never forget this kindness and should you need anything, you only need to ask." Using her tote bag, I find the book Cash used to locate her and open it on the floor. Then, I shove her headfirst inside. She screams, tumbling into the pages and waving. She'll be fine. Probably. Taking Malice's hand, I gently ease her out from beneath the bed.

"Tweed," Malice croaks, her eyes over my shoulder. I roll us both away from a smokey blow which obliterates the book to dust. Catching a glance of Cash, I curse. The fucker is leaning into Lillianna's wrist, his fingers closing around her forearm. Lowering his head, I mutter a quick apology to Malice. I move at the speed of light, lifting the love of my life into my arms, shooting forward, and shoving her wrist beneath Cash's open jaw. His teeth plunge into Malice's flesh, his eyes instantly bursting with emerald green. Lillianna screams, rearing her bloodied arm backward to strike Malice. Over my dead fucking body.

Cash automatically takes Malice from me as I spin us, the lash striking my back with the force of a barbed wire whip. Gritting my teeth, I push my twin towards the mirror portal.

"Take her to Diamond Maze. I'll meet you at the entrance," I order. There's no room for argument in my tone, yet I'm surprised how easily Cash turns and flees. One foot on the armchair gives him enough leverage to vault through the mirror, a whip of shadow smashing the glass a moment later.

"No!" Lillianna roars. Her magic clamps around my neck, lifting me high into the air. I watch through blurred vision as Cash opens a window and disappears through it, Malice's hand outstretched for me over his shoulder. I just have to hope to all hell Cash will make it out of Heart

Kingdom unscathed. He's not safe there, but with Lillianna's wrath building, neither is Malice.

"I knew, from the moment I saw how Cash looked at her, he wouldn't stay loyal to me. Do you really think now he has her to himself, he'll stay loyal to you?" Lillianna speaks into my ear. Her presence at my back is thick, like tar leaking through the cracks of her feeble facade. Spinning me to face her, I grimace and struggle against the invisible binds. I find it in me to smile, either in an effort to try and anger her or fool myself. Malice may have reformed our brotherly relationship, but how far that extends is anyone's guess.

Using all of my strength, I break free of the shadows, only to be trapped in more. They wrap around my limbs like a caterpillar's cocoon, restricting the growl lodged in my throat.

"You've surprised me, Knave," Lillianna hisses, her eyes blazing with fury. "I'm beginning to wonder if I targeted the wrong twin, but it's too late for regrets. Wonderlust belongs to me, and I'll stop at nothing to get it back."

# CHAPTER 27

When faced with another trek through Wonderlust, I take the easy option. Sleep. Clinging onto Cash's neck, I bury my face into his chest, trying to hold onto any ignorance I can for a while longer. Whether I crossed into the afterlife or was merely shown a glimpse of hell at Lillianna's hand, it's enough to convince me I'm in no hurry to return. It wasn't even the demons, the screams, or the excruciating heat; it was the emptiness of my own soul that shook me. As if nothing I've ever done has mattered. As if I'm not worth saving after all.

"Where are we?" I raise my head when I can't bear relieving those images over and over. There's no sight of the sun above the twelve-foot hedges on either side of us. Only the same darkness I'm trying to escape in my mind. I don't get an answer. Cash walks steadily, each footstep made with purposeful silence. Once in a while, he pauses to smell the air, turns, and heads in a different direction.

"I can walk if you prefer."

"Not a chance. I'm not nearly half as ready to let you go yet." His voice is thick with an emotion I can't name. Instead, I settle back into his hold, soaking in his rainforest scent, using it to center myself to this world. As I have done many times with Tweed.

Striding onwards, Cash suddenly halts at the sound of a roar in the distance, retreats, and takes another route. Vines slither along the leafy walls, snapping out every once in a while. Cash punches them away before I've even registered they're trying to attack me. I seek out his face, noting the harsh line of his clenched jaw. So unlike him, so at odds with the jokey vampire I know.

"Malice, I–"

Footsteps rush up behind us. Unlike before, Cash doesn't change direction, relaxing my uneven heartbeat as Tweed catches up to our side.

"Thought I told you to wait at the entrance," he grumbles, stroking a hand through my hair.

"My presence was sensed the moment I stepped into Heart Castle," Cash quips back. Their relationship may not be strained anymore, but they're still brothers. Sibling-like quarrels are to be expected. "The alarm can still be heard if you listen closely enough." I give it a good go, but all my ears are met with is the brush of danger winding through the maze on a low wind. "Did you kill the bitch?" I flinch at the depth of hatred in Cash's tone. A Tweedle should be light, joyful. Especially him.

"She disappeared the moment I got the upper hand," Tweed replies, looking around the maze walls. Cash holds his stare on the back of his brother's head, not wholly convinced. I nudge him with a warning glare. We're all together and not fighting at last. That's all that matters.

Pausing at a fork in the path, a signpost stands beneath a lamppost. I let the twins worry about the route, my focus centered on leaning into Tweed's touch. A small creature hops out of his collar, running along the length of his arm and leaping into the empty alcove in my hair.

"Stan," I smile. "Good to see you boys are starting to get along."

"We're trying to settle our differences. Quite the stubborn asshole, your rodent is," Tweed comments, but I can hear the humor in his voice. I wriggle, forcing Cash to place me on my feet. Brushing down my bloodied and ragged bathrobe, double knotting the tie at my middle, I lean into Tweed, keeping my voice low.

"Are you sure we should be here? After...you know," I communicate through widened eyes. Cash is still blissfully unaware of my familiarity with the late Diamond King, or should I say my accidental familiarity with his head. Well, not accidental, but had I known I was committing high treason...nah, fuck it. I still would have killed that fucker for the trap he tried to lure me into. Tweed smiles, cupping my cheek again as if he's unable to keep his hands to himself.

"I have a hunch," he replies cryptically. My gaze roams his back and I beg to differ, but say nothing as he jerks his head toward the left. Tweed navigates the maze with the confidence only someone who has been in here a thousand times could possess. Before long, we turn a final corner and are presented with a long pathway leading towards the steps of Diamond Castle.

An impressive structure, nothing like the mix-match of the Heart's. Thick columns create its circular form, curving around to the maze which continues beneath. Beautifully constructed from glimmering stone, each fine-tuned peak appears razor sharp, glinting in the lanterns surrounding each tier. Elongated spokes stretch into the starry night, close to piercing the pinkened moons on either side. I gape, unnerved by the harshness of its crystal-like appeal. If I killed the King, who or what could occupy such a vast and ethereal place now?

Following the length of a sleek, black pathway carved from polished obsidian, we pass beneath the pointed archway which resembles a diamond. White flowers hang over the structure, brushing against us. Those which touch the Tweedles shift their petals from the purest snow to an endless darkness. Those which stroke me turn the deepest of blood reds. Oh fuck, the castle knows. I swallow thickly. Tweed squeezes my hand.

That roar from earlier, closer this time, ups our speed. Nearing the castle, I shy away from the giant playing card statues, the spears in their hands sharper than a lumberjack's ax. Am I scared? Pfft, hell no. Just slightly unsure what's happening within my chest, with my magic and between the curious stares being passed over my head. The only one who seems ready is Stan, nudging my ear in a twitchy order to keep walking.

Tweed approaches the door, pushing his weight against the see-through stone. It refuses to budge. Muscles straining, his arms shudder with enough force to crack the door into pieces, but still, nothing. Cash joins in, a curious display of grunting, panting and macho-ness taking place.

"Thought you were meant to be all-powerful vampires," I roll my eyes. Tweed slumps, twisting his lips.

"If you think you're so tough, why don't you give it a go?" he bows low, gesturing to the door. I snort and shrug. It's not like I have anywhere else to go.

I stop just short of the front door, placing my hand against the cold crystal. The door is taller than I can fathom, framed by icicles threatening to release and stab unpermitted visitors. Inhaling deeply, a click sounds beneath my palm, allowing me to ease the door open. For a moment, the castle hesitates, a wash of magic brushing over my skin. Then, a similar relieved inhale sounds from within and the door opens of its own accord.

"I knew it," Tweed grins. Slowly walking into the lobby, a beam of light seems to follow only me. "This is the one place Lillianna can't touch you."

"Why?" I ask, feeling a phantom tap on my shoulder. Spinning, a rolling skirt begins shimmering around my ankles. Raising upwards, I'm powerless to stop it, the ruined robe falling away in patches to be replaced with the finest dress I've ever seen. Glass slippers form around my feet, pushing me three inches higher. From a skyline filling the lobby with moonlight, the material sparkles with the purest of diamonds, but is in no way heavy.

The more I spin, the longer the train becomes, as if the castle itself is gifting me such bespoke splendor. Each curve is being hugged, a boned corset enchanting my breasts. Diamonds create an intricate bust line, a teardrop gap relieving a dangerous amount of underboob and a decent amount of sternum. I feel the weight of a crown being weaved on top of my wild hair, directly in the spot where my Hatter's hat should be. And the transformation doesn't stop there. My skin is luminous, littered with glitter.

"What in the name of haberdashery is happening right now?" Cash is the first one to speak. I catch my reflection in a glass wall, this castle is more like a house of mirrors. I look...royal. Regal. And I hate it.

"Why, she's a Queen," a female voice replies from the open doorway. We all turn abruptly, a low warning sound emanating from Cash. Arabelle waves away this reaction, effortlessly gliding across the marble to take my hands in her filthy ones. There's blood beneath her fingernails, dirt covering every inch of skin around her torn dress.

"What the hell happened to you?" I get distracted by the easiness of her smile amongst the destruction.

"Lillianna launched a strike on Heart Castle while the army was absent. Nothing is left standing." Arabelle maintains her smile while I gasp.

"Oh shit, Arabelle. I'm so sorry." The hint of emotion glistens behind her amber eyes, concealed by her bravado.

"Things come and go. We shall rise again. For now, those of us remaining can stay with our newest ally. The Queen of Diamond Kingdom." Her dirty hands run the length of my arms, mischief evident in her small giggle. "After the court of kookaburras finds you innocent, of course." I frown in confusion, a state I think I'm going to have to get used to. This 'giving a crap' stuff is exhausting.

"Word will spread any moment of your new position," Tweed fills the gaps. For once. "The realm will now know you were the one who killed the Diamond King and have assumed his position. The trial is merely protocol, you'll most likely be cleared of all charges." My eyes fly from him to my reflection and back again.

"And if I'm not cleared of all charges?" I ask, a trace of alarm in my voice.

"Then it's off with your head," Cash growls, his eyes spearing Arabelle's. "Her rules." All hostility between them appears to be one sided, as Arabelle rolls her golden eyes and dismisses him once more.

"Yes, well, inherited rules. Some parts of Wonderlust are too ingrained and a general pain in the ass to re-write history for. Anywho, Malice shall be acquitted, I'm sure of it." Arabelle straightens the glass and diamond crown upon my head, smiling sweetly. "If I know my Hatters, I know it's time for tea." With a final squeeze on my fingers, Arabelle wanders further into the castle, permitting herself as a welcome guest. In my defense, I'd welcome anyone who offers me tea.

"Perhaps we should find the royale suite. You're still adjusting," Cash's eyes drop to my chest. I know what he's listening to, the same uneven beat is thumping in my ears. Now my diaphragm is being crushed in this corset, I can feel the two sides struggling against each other to find regularity. I know this, but I still jump back at his offered hand.

"No! I don't want to lie around on my back anymore!" I shout, an outburst which surprises even me. "I want to run and jump, skid around in socks and pants, ride the railings and dance in the courtyard! I'm supposed to be a Hatter, not a hermit."

"Be a Hatter tomorrow," Tweed chuckles. His eyes drag over my figure in appreciation, a glint of lust in his gleaming green eyes. Okay, maybe I don't *entirely* hate the dress, but I refuse to accept the title. Jerking his head, Tweed signals for Cash to step into my other side and place my arm in his. I sigh in defeat, only because their synchronized smiles are a welcome sight. With a Tweedle on each arm, I enter the dining room, my head held high.

Tea is already served, similarly to the array of cakes, scones, sandwiches, and teapots Arabelle greeted me with to her humble home. As if sensing a party, Hatter is already sitting at the table, licking his sugar-coated fingers.

"Hatter!" I call, flocking to him. He half turns as I wrap my arms around him, awkwardly crushing his face into my breasts. "How did you get here so fast?"

"Fast?" His voice is muffled until I relieve him. "I've been here for three days. Rabbit knew where you'd end up. He has a good sense of direction for these things." True enough, White Rabbit is sitting across the table, sniffing a profiterole. His eyes are dazed, his reactions sloppy, but at least he's able to remain still for a short while. Despite the unnerving way he stares through me, I round the table and wrap my arms around him.

"It's so good to have you with us, Rabbit." Considering the last time I saw him, he was limp and being laid on a bed in the infirmary, I'd say everyone else is relieved he's still with us, too. I know what it's like for the crazy to become overwhelming, for the voices to take over. I debated giving up many times, but there's strength in finding something to live for. I hug him tighter, seeking comfort from his frayed fur. "You are needed, and you are loved, Rabbit." Ducking his head into his flopped ear, Rabbit starts to lick his own ear wax.

"It's gone," he mutters, tilting to look at me. "Where's it gone?"

"What have you lost?" I ask, really not sure what else he could fit inside his ear canal. Rabbit sits upright, sniffing the air.

"Not me. You. The appeal thing, it's gone." I frown, looking at the Tweedles. It's Hatter who beckons me close enough to take my arm. Smelling it, licking it, he seems to come to the same conclusion.

"Malice, your Allure has disappeared!" he grins. I gasp, looking over myself. I don't look any different, a little pale maybe, but now I can walk freely. Holy shit, I'm free.

Arabelle doesn't react, lowering herself at the head of the table, naturally. Cash directs me to take the other, waiting to pull my chair out, a smirk on his face. Tweed scowls at the action, wishing he'd got there first, but opts to pour my tea instead. I scowl at the whole affair. Pick a role and stick to it, guys. These multiple personalities are giving me whiplash.

Lifting the steaming cup to my lips, I feel the intense urge to throw it as far away as possible. Hell no, this is my first tea in days. Forcing a trembling hand closer, I sip and then instantly spit the liquid onto the tablecloth, my gum tingling in a ridiculous fashion. The fuck? Perhaps something is a little different in me after all.

"This is perfect! Absolutely perfect," Arabelle exclaims, clapping her hands. For a split second, I see the child she is as opposed to the mature queen she must pretend to be. Still sucking at my gums, it's Dormouse who answers, popping out of a teapot with her paws clamped over her ears.

"What is?!" she cries. Tweed tries to concentrate on the conversation, but his curious stare keeps returning to me as I suck at my gums.

"That the newest addition to the Diamond throne, happens to side with the reds," Arabelle giggles and taps the corner of her mouth with a handkerchief for no reason, "also holds the heart of the Wonderlust! It couldn't be more perfect if I'd planned it." Another giggle escapes her, a quick glance at Tweed causing mischief to sparkle in her golden gaze.

"The heart of Wonderlust?" I echo back, scraping my tongue across a biscuit. There must be some way I can enjoy this party. Even the Tweedles have the decency to look confused.

"Why, yes! The heart beating inside your chest which has been infused with the gift of Hatter." When she's met with blank stares, Arabelle's smile starts to slip. Her eyes slide to Hatter for clarity. "You know...when one becomes a Hatter...their heart swells to contain the balance of chaos and control. Hatters are the Heart of Wonderlust, remember?" The biscuit falls from my hand, my tongue hanging out of my mouth.

"That wasn't a metaphor?" Tweed's jaw has also gone slack. Arabelle blows a raspberry, another hint at her youth.

"Since when do I talk in m...me...metaphors," she gags on the word. Two sets of green eyes shoot to me with the sharpness of lasers, causing me to flinch and slice my tongue on my teeth.

"Will you excuse us a moment?" Cash asks politely and then whisks me from my seat. Appearing on the staircase in a blur of movement, Tweed is there a moment after. Two firm chests crush me into the railing, their arms propped on the wall by my head.

"You know what comes now," Tweed says in a deep voice which tingles through my core.

"A threesome?" I offer. Both twins lurch backward.

"What?! No," Cash takes my hand. "A grave oversight has been made, potentially losing us this fight before it's even begun." Tweed hums in agreement.

"We need to get your heart back." Hmmm, a threesome sounds like a much better use of my time. Half-shrugging, I watch the twins pace the stairs in a circuit. Up and down, crossing each other on one side and looping back again. Such pensive thoughts pass through their features. Luckily, I'm no longer drowning in poison and confusion. The old me has returned in full force. And as an added bonus, the Tweedles are back together, working out a plan, being a team. Now all I want to do is for them to tag-team me.

"Wait...," I shake my head, grasping the reason no one's tongue is in my mouth yet. "Guys, where exactly is my heart?"

# CHAPTER 28

I drum my nails on the wooden desk. "Stop that," Arabelle slaps my hand. I sigh through my nose, narrowing my eyes at those filling the court before me. If there's one thing in this lifetime I thought I was accustomed to, it's the inside of a courtroom. Turns out, I was wrong.

Preparing to slap Arabelle back, I catch Tweed, Cash, and Hatter smiling at me encouragingly from the front row. They look cute, all suited up for my hearing, whereas I awoke dressed by the castle again. An iridescent, corseted dress with a clear tulle skirt. My underwear is vivid red and I'm not mad about the juxtaposition. Especially when paired with a heavy set of boots and a scowl.

I was irritable last night when the Tweedles disappeared, refusing to give me a straight answer. By sunrise, after waiting for their return all night, I was livid. Now we're creeping into lunchtime and I still have no idea where my real heart is, I'm bordering homicidal. Unfortunately, Arabelle is the closest possible victim, and killing a royal is why I'm sitting in this fake courtroom in the first place.

Whoever was in charge of rearranging the study to squeeze in several pews, a central podium, and a witness stand–failed. No consideration was taken for the sizes and shapes of animals which would cram into the gallery, or the kookaburras creating the jury. Have you ever heard what a riot of kookaburras contained in an oversized birdcage sounds like? I now have, and it's not pleasant on the ears.

"Your honor," Arabelle addresses a giant gummy bear in full monochrome robes. He's a cheery shade of pink considering his eyebrows are thickly fixed into an angry expression. "May we move things along? My client becomes extremely agitated when she's hungry."

"I fucking resent the shit out of that statement. Who told you that?!" I slam my fist on the table. The Queen and Judge share an unreadable look.

"Verra well," the judge replies in a surprisingly heavy Scottish accent. "Malice Liddell, you've been called here today, accused of murder and treason of the highest degree. Your attorney has entered a plea of not guilty on your behalf. Counselor, call your first witness." The suited and booted lizard at the opposite desk clears his throat.

I twist towards the rear doors as they slam open, catching sight of yellow floppy bangs bobbing down the central aisle. I wasn't prepared for what I saw, my cackling laughter setting off the kookaburras, as Humpty Dainty appears in a full widower's outfit. The netted, black material of her dress matches a veil strapped around her humongous head to cover her face. With one zombie knight in tow, she's aided into the witness stand.

"Dainty?" I ask, weeping with hysterics. Fuck, I needed that. "Why the hell are you–"

"Shh!" the Lizard hisses at me. My face immediately falls, all traces of humor disappearing. Stacking his papers neatly, he walks in the figure of eight, formulating his question. "Ms Humpty, you know the accused well. Would that be a correct statement?"

"Objection!" Arabelle shoots to her feet so fast, even I flinch. "Leading the witness." The gummy bear judge is caught off guard, popping gum into his mouth. Waving us off, he chews until the cube becomes malleable. Then smacks his lips together loudly while we continue.

"Well," Dainty's voice wobbles. "I once considered myself the closest friend Malice had. She dunked in my yolk after all." The gallery whisper amongst themselves. I roll my eyes.

"Like I had a choice. Your army basically foot-raped my mouth." Arabelle slaps my hand again. I shudder with the barely contained restrained to punch her back.

"Any more from you and I'll hold you in contempt," the judge finally manages to push some words out. I huff again, slumping back in my chair. If there's one thing I can't stand, it's being silenced. Dainty is given the go-ahead to continue, a white handkerchief now in her gloved hand.

"She told me the Diamond King would return for me. That the Tweedle she chose would lead us all to victory," Dainty sobs. I yawn, catching how Tweed ducks his head from the prying eyes around him. "And this entire time, she knew he was dead! She led me on, dragged me into her strange games. I can only comment on Malice's character, and she's a dirty, whorebag liar!" Dainty points her chubby finger, wobbling on her seat. The courtroom gasps. I smirk, figuring I've just found my next tattoo.

"Look," I sigh, pushing to my feet. I'm bored, horny, and hungry. A toxic combination. "I only met the guy in hare form for like ten minutes, but my instincts are usually on point." Cash rolls his eyes. "And that bastard didn't love you. I'd be surprised if he even knew you existed." Dainty lets out a small shriek, wobbling back in her chair. One kookaburra begins to hiccup, before throwing his head back and roaring with laughter. The rest join in, filling the court with raucous noise. Tweed and Cash are quick to cover each other's ears, hissing at the assault.

"Order! Order!" the judge bangs a giant lollipop on his podium. Eventually, the court settles, leaving Arabelle's hushed berating as the only sound.

"Malice, please. I'm trying to help you here. At the very least, they could strip you of your new title. Queens can't commit treason." My eyes widen at the same time Tweed's do. He heard that, but his head shaking does nothing to stop the words blurting out of my mouth.

"I did it!" I shout. The judge leans forward, angry eyebrows dipping together.

"You did what?" he asks, being cautious while all eyes settle on us.

"I killed the Diamond King. In fact, I completely severed his head and spoke to it for a while. Contemplated wearing it as a hat, but then

Tweed appeared naked, and I understandably got distracted." The gallery becomes a ruckus of screaming and jeers, all except the Hatter's clapping aimed to condemn me.

*Sentence her! A head for a head! She admitted it, kill her!*

Wow, people here sure are bloodthirsty. Crawling onto the table, I stand above everyone else, looking down with as much hatred as my exhausted mind can muster.

"I may not know much about Wonderlust, but if I committed treason, then I was doing you all a service." The room hushes in shock. "The Diamond King came to me disguised, tried to lure me into a trap which I'm now sure was at Lillianna's request. I've saved you all from worshiping, and marrying," I toss a look at Dainty, "a traitor."

"Can anyone confirm your story?" The gummy bear swirls the lollipop around his chubby hand. My jaw clenches, feeling the weight of judgment being targeted my way. No one believes me, they're too eager for bloodshed. To kill the girl they've been falsely blaming for all of their misfortunes. I may be erratic, but I'm the biggest victim here. Yet, even in the face of losing my head, it's failing Hatter which hurts me the most. He trusted me. Chose me. And through my history of reckless decisions, I've lost the Heart of Wonderlust. We're all doomed anyway.

"I can," Tweed stands. My head whips around. "I confirm Malice's story. I was in Diamond Maze, trying to save her from the King. I should have known, she can save herself." There's a twinkle in her green eyes, a small smirk I wasn't expecting. Whatever or whoever's heart beats out of sync in my chest, melts. He's lying of course, but it's the sentiment which matters most. My hidden hero who's been right in front of me the entire time.

"Verra well," the judge comments. He's noticeably bored of the kookaburras squawking in his ear. It's a mystery why they're even here in the first place. "Malice, I find you innocent of treason." Arabelle bumps her fist in the air, celebrating too early. "And guilty of murder. In this event, you may keep your head, but will be stripped of your title. From this day forth, you shall be Malice. Just Malice."

"Not quite," Hatter leaps over the gallery and drags me down from the table. Holding my waist, he swings me around several times before planting me down, placing a kiss on my wild hair. "You'll never be 'just' Malice. You're the Mal Hatter, and my daughter."

Heat fills my chest, all the warm fuzzies I'm used to keeping at bay rising to the surface. They drown out the small voice that wonders, without my heart, if I am a Hatter at all. Clinging onto his neck, Hatter's curls tickle my cheek. I can't hear what else is said around the screams of kookaburra cackles or those in the gallery arguing with my sentence, as Hatter half carries me from the room. An incredible weight has been lifted from my shoulders as if I can finally get back to the real me. The version of Malice I created for myself in Charmsfield. Two seconds out of the room, that very brief fantasy is stolen away.

"How quaint," Lillianna mocks. Her shadow consumes the lobby, her mirage shifting within. Everywhere diamond walls and crystal chandeliers should shine, tendrils of smoke darken. She's not really here, but her presence is suffocating. Ash lines the back of my throat, settling on my skin uncomfortably. I swallow hard, trying to shift the sensation. I've only just rid myself of her poison. Feeling the spores of her essence polluting my lungs which each breath feels like more of a death sentence than the judge could have given. Lillianna's laughter, cold and unsettling, reverberates through the space, echoing from within.

"You have some nerve," Cash growls, trying to push past. I grab his wrist. If Lillianna wanted a fight, she'd be here in person. Whatever figment of magic stands before us, it's here to deliver a message. The ground creaks in protest, as though the very building is resisting the darkness that's settled within.

"Nervous, Malice?" she laughs hauntingly. I grip Cash harder. Nothing gives one a bigger sense of their mortality than being on the brink of death. Am I scared? Pfft, no. Just slipping into a state of panic which could easily be mistaken for terror.

"State your business, Lillianna," I keep my tone level. Lillianna's eyes narrow, her form flickering momentarily as if testing the limits of her illusion.

"I have no business today. Only a friendly reminder," she chuckles. Vines of smoke snake out, shooting for me. Cash doesn't falter, jumping forward to keep me safe. If only I was the target. Closing around Tweed instead, he is lifted into the air and drawn closer to Lillianna. Her teeth shine white, her mirth palpable. "I'll be seeing you soon," she croons, her smoke stroking him seductively. I manage to shove Cash a step aside, to both of our surprise. Must be the adrenaline rush or something. He catches me quickly enough, holding me back when I try to launch myself at Lillianna. She laughs at my feeble attempt.

As quickly as she appeared, a giant swirl of smoke whips through the castle and disappears into itself. Tweed crashes to the ground, scowling at where Lillianna so recently was. Her lasting laughter, twinged with a hint of cruel amusement, trickles away leaving us in stunning silence. Hatter's gloved hand slips into mine, while Cash storms across the crystal floor and yanks Tweed up by the collar.

"You have some serious explaining to do," he growls, dragging his brother up the stairs.

# CHAPTER 29

Dragging me into the nearest room, a small library with a single lamp and armchair by the window, Cash tosses me into a bookcase. "Start talking," he tries to growl, but the sound comes out weak, more of a whimper. Malice's wish for us to be fully fledged brothers again makes it impossible for us to argue anymore.

“I don’t want Malice to know,” I slump to the floor, hanging my head. What would she think, seeing me so defeated? I’m supposed to be her hero.

“Great basis for a new relationship,” Cash tuts. It’s on the tip of my tongue to tell him to go fuck himself, but I can’t force myself to say it. Cash starts to pace around in front of me, so I slide my foot out to trip him up instead. Recovering quickly, Cash lowers down to sit at my side, throwing his head back into a shelf.

“I apologize,” I sigh. Cash murmurs about the fall not hurting but that’s not what I meant. “I’m apologizing for hating you all these years.” My brows furrow while Cash’s shoot to his hairline. “Lillianna is more powerful than I realized. All this time, I thought it was your weakness driving us apart.”

“Tweed...what did you do?” his eyes narrow in concern. I look away.

“I made a bargain with her to let me leave with my head still attached.”

Cash doesn't miss a beat. “You don’t get to shut me out anymore. Brothers, remember?”

I let out a deep breath and tell him everything. How Lillianna had me in her shadowed hold, how I couldn't break free or see a way out, how she intends to use Malice to take over Wonderlust. The more I talk, the more I realize how much danger I’ve put myself and my family in. I should have known better than to make a deal with a witch, but I was desperate. Cash listens in silence, his expression growing darker by the second.

"That's all very well. But what kind of bargain did you make?" he asks, leaning closer to me. This is the bit I was trying to avoid saying.

“When the blood moon’s clash, I will be enslaved to Lillianna’s blood, willingly.”

Cash slams his hand down on the floor, causing a few books to tumble from the bookcase to the floor. “What the fuck were you thinking?”

“That she’d be dead before we get to that point. And that I had to stall while you got Malice to safety.” Cash takes a deep breath, processing my reasoning. I feel the anger radiating from him, but he manages to keep his voice steady.

“You're an idiot,” Cash sighs.

"I know," I agree. I understand the weight of his taut muscles. He has only just been freed of Lillianna's hold, and I've allowed myself to become trapped in his place. I wasn't thinking clearly; only concerned with keeping Malice's newly formed heart beating long enough to build up her strength again.

"I hope you’re right," Cash adds, pinching the bridge of his nose. “About Lillianna being dead before the moons clash. For all of our sakes. I'm not helping Malice to bury you if it all goes to shit.” I know he's speaking out of anger, but his words sting as intended.

"You'd have done the exact same if the roles were reversed. You can't deny the way you look at Malice. She's too important to us." Cash rubs his hand over his face and stands, contemplating lying.

"I'd have found another way." Beginning to walk away, I shoot to my feet and zoom in front of him, my back against the door.

"There is no other way, except to help me kill the witch before she gets too powerful. We need to find Malice's heart, and we need to work together, no matter how much you'd rather avoid me."

"I don't want to avoid you," Cash admits. "But I don't want to lose you either. Watching you live from a distance is easier than potentially screwing up everything you've built, and having you resent me for it. Sometimes I think it's better if we go our own ways." I can feel the pain in his voice and my resolve falters.

"That's all very sweet, but you've also set your sights on the girl I've fallen for," I say softly, rubbing at my chest. The explosive scar underneath reminds me of all I've sacrificed, and that I will not stop until we win this war. "It doesn't have to be so black and red. Malice makes her own rules; so can we."

Tentatively, I touch his arm. Cash doesn't pull away, but he doesn't move closer either. We stand there awkwardly for a moment, trying to rekindle what once was. A brotherly bond nothing or no one could penetrate. Cash stares into my equally green eyes, his hand coming to rest on my shoulder before he finally speaks up again.

"You said Lillianna is going to use Malice to take over Wonderlust?" His tone is grim, and I nod solemnly. Cash figures the rest out within seconds. "She wants to use Malice's heart to break through the barrier that's keeping her out. Once she's in, there will be nothing stopping her."

"There will be us," I reassure him. The strangest notion rises in my chest, one I can't suppress because I know it's been put there by Malice. Slowly stepping forward, I close my arms around the brother I once thought was lost to me forever. Neither of us moves for a few moments, but he eventually allows his body to relax in my embrace. My twin is still here; I just have to find a way to remind him that he's stronger than these invisible chains around his heart. We've both made mistakes at great cost to our lives already, and I hardly deserve more remorse than him. It's time this vicious circle of hatred and blaming ends.

"I'm not going to let anything come between us or Malice again," I whisper into his thick blonde hair. My breath draws in Cash's scent, and I let out a sigh at the feeling of safety it brings me. The other half of my soul clicks into place and finally, in all the deepened crevices Malice's affection can't reach, I don't feel completely alone anymore.

# CHAPTER 30

"You boys finished hashing it out?" I ask, leaning against the wall. Tweed runs a hand through his blond hair, avoiding my gaze as he exits the room. Cash is much more adverse in covering his concern with a smile.

"All sorted. We should prepare for the mission ahead." Holding out his arm, I accept it easily. My boots sound heavy against the crystal floor, a line of glitter leading us towards the armory. I don't need Cash's gentle tug to tell me where we're going, but I pretend to rely on it.

Little do the twins know, as much as I knocked my fists against my ears, I couldn't help but overhear their conversation. I've never wanted to eavesdrop less, preferring not to know how Lillianna snuck her claws into my Tweedle and forced him into a bargain for my sake. No, I'd rather be blissfully kept in the dark because now I'm stuck with an overhaul of emotions I don't understand. If my skin reflected the simmering anger inside, I'd be painted bright red.

"Your m-m-ajesty," a familiar pig bows in his fancy-trim uniform as we enter a grand room of weapons and armor. The hems are no longer embroidered with hearts, but diamonds. I smile, genuinely relieved to see him.

"No need for pleasantries, PB. I'm not the queen anymore." *Thank fuck*, I add in my mind. The servant grunts in confusion, his snout twitching.

"The M-Mal Hatter, then?" he probes, his neck shrinking into his collar when Tweed enters the room. I pause, considering that without my heart, I'm not technically a Hatter right now either.

"Malice," I nod. "Just Malice." Cash tugs me tighter into his side, his mouth dipping beside my sensitive ear.

"There's nothing 'just' about you, Crazy One." His whisper unknowingly makes me flinch, so I quickly turn my head and accept the kiss waiting there. PB squeals in the background, his trotters rushing away as my lips brush Cash's. After everything that's happened, I'm fully aware I need to physically reconnect with both twins. As it stands, this soft touch is the only reminder we have time for.

"My motives may be questionable," Tweed clears his throat, "but we must press on. Another moment the Heart of Wonderlust is in Spade Castle, is another Lillianna could realize she already has all the power she needs to claim this realm for herself." Lingering in Cash's kiss, it's him who breaks away first.

"Tweed is right. There will be time for us afterward." Drawing away, Cash begins to strip down a suit of armor and don the chest plates engraved with diamonds. The surface shimmers with a glittery sheen over the metal. Neither twin needs any more, only their half-hearts requiring protection. PB has Tweed's outfit at the ready, placed along a glass cabinet beside one so tiny, it must be intended for Stan. The sugar glider jumps free of my hair, flying across the room to dress accordingly.

"I have so many questions," I huff, drifting towards the wall of weapons instead. There's a plus side to remaining blissfully unaware of what's going on around me, but there's also only so long I can keep my curiosity at bay. Currently, the question rolling through my mind is of Lillianna's motive. Surely being the sole ruler of a backward and ludacris realm isn't all it's cracked up to be.

This is the first and only wall I've seen in Diamond Castle to be made of stone. Hanging from thick chains, I frown at the array, not knowing where to begin. Axes, hammers, maces, flails, and swords. My fingers itch with a desire to touch them, to feel their weight in my palm and imagine the power they would provide.

My attention is drawn to a particular sword nestled amongst the others, its diamond blade cold beneath my fingertips. Images filter into my mind, memories of battles past. I've faced my own kind of battles. Mostly mental, but each has left a scar. Each is a testament to the dangers I've faced and survived. But none were like these. Bloodshed, hatred, a never-ending rivalry to rule a realm which was never meant to be owned. A familiar heavy weight lowers onto my shoulders, complete with an invisible, fluffy tail stroking my collarbone.

"What do you think it was like before, Chesh?" I asked absentmindedly, not really expecting an answer. "What weird and wonderful entities thrived here before humans and patriarchy took over?" Snuggling into my neck, Chesh's presence isn't as solid as usual. She hugs me silently, the brush of her tail feeling too much like a goodbye for my liking. She's only just arrived, but it's like she's not really here at all. Without saying a word, the weight lifts and spirals away, only to be replaced with another.

Turning, Arabelle's eyes glisten as she guides thick straps up my arms and onto my shoulders. Leaning over me, she works on fastening the contraption to my sternum, but I'm suddenly struck with an overwhelming thumping in my ears. A steady drum working its way through my senses, each one stirring an underlying, primal hunger. My stomach clenches as if it's never been filled before, my mouth salivating.

As Arabelle struggles with the clasp, my eyes zero in on the cause of the drumming. Her pulse flutters like a bird caught in a cage, beating erratically. It's calling to me, I decide, as my head lowers towards her creamy skin. That tingling is back in my gums, my actions being led by instinct.

Opening my mouth, a flurry of movement whisks Arabelle out of sight just before my canines extend and sink into flesh. Cash doesn't miss a beat, strapping me into the contraption as his blood spills across my tongue. My pupils burst, my senses filled with his distinct taste. I've drank vampire blood before, in its sour, congealed form. This time, it's nothing like that.

The blood is fresh, alive, and it's singing to every fiber of my being. I'm lost in it, the world around me fading away into a blur of colors and shapes. Part of him is injected into me, clearing my senses and making each breath a little more intense. Suddenly, I'm aware of everything; the sensation in my skin from Cash's hands on my arms, his half-heart beating beneath the threads of fabric, even feeling the air shifting around us.

Cash remains still as I take more and more of his life force into myself. He's giving himself to me in his entirety, and I greedily take it. Flecks of emotion spark across my skin like little starbursts before coalescing into an intense burning sensation. I'm filled with Cash's essence, his infectious energy. A smirk hitches the corner of my own mouth, but beneath the mirth, there's more. A glow so filled with love and the need to be loved, rational thought can't penetrate it. This is where Cash's instincts rule and no amount of logic can enter.

Suddenly, it's over. I'm pulled back into reality by the sudden ache in my gut, calling for more. Craving more. Gasping away from Cash's neck, I notice Tweed ushering Arabelle and PB from the room. A sharp sting brings me back to my own body, the diamond sword now clasped in my hand slicing my palm in two. Releasing it, my own orange-tainted blood drips to the floor in thick rivets. It heals slowly, but before long, the skin has knitted back together again.

"Now, I have even more questions," I mumble, catching my lip on my teeth. Cash's taste lingers in my mouth, and I can't stop salivating over it.

“I think you already know the answer to this one,” Tweed appears at my other side. His eyes appear greener, flecked with tiny specks of hazel I didn't notice until now. In fact, the entire room seems brighter and more defined. Heaving a breath out between my elongated teeth, I realize now the amount of effort it took. I've been breathing through habit, not necessity. Cash turns me by the shoulders to face a full length mirror, the stirrings of affection and lust in his gaze still present within my psyche.

"Remember when I said you didn't need to change anything to appeal to me?" He looks me up and down like a man starved. "I lied. This is so much more enticing." I shudder, my fangs grazing my bottom lip. Fully fledged fangs, glinting against the outfit I've been magically provided again. The corset I was wearing has risen, cupping my breasts with thick leather and stretching towards my collar bone. The tulle skirt is now molded into metallic spikes, covering chainmail leggings underneath. My skin is deadly pale against it, my hair the only pop of color as the nest of orange curls trickle over my shoulders. Timelessly flawless and undeniably lethal. So much for being 'just Malice'. I'm a freaking vampire.

Cash's grip tightens on my arms, his dick a solid weight against my ass. The connection I've initiated through his blood deepens with lust, coiling around my core and licking deliciously at my g-spot.

"Nope!" Tweed yanks Cash backwards sharply. "We don't have time for this. Save the world, then we fuck." His own voice is graveled with desire as he pulls his twin away. Whether Tweed intended to imply 'then we fuck' all together or not, that's the image now playing on a loop through my mind. I shoot from the room with a burst of vampire speed, hungry to fill the void now growing within. If my pleasure is on hold until Lillianna is dealt with, I've just been given the biggest incentive to kill this bitch.

# CHAPTER 31

The twins have been holding back on me.

As I run from one end of Diamond Kingdom to the other, my boots barely touch the ground. Not even the ever-changing maze can hold me back, because in the event I meet a dead end–I simply burst through the hedges. Vampire speed, senses, sexual appetite, it's all hit me tenfold since being awakened by Cash's blood.

Running beneath the pinkened light of two moons growing ever closer together, I take the time to revel in my newfound power, loving the feeling of being alive with a new intensity I never knew existed. The wind is like silk against my skin, caressing me, soothing out all heartaches and worries so that only pleasure remains. If I'd known it was so easy to rid myself of negativity, overthinking, stressing –basically, everything it means to be human–I'd have done this years ago.

I rush past rose bushes, my keen vision picking up on every dew drop on the scarlet petals as they drop to the ground in slow motion. Their perfume fills my senses, while trees rustle in response to my intrusion. Even those who occupy the forest I'm traveling through, each creature has a unique scent which I can read from afar, accompanied by their body temperatures forming visions inside my head. No wonder vampires are known for being predators. It's almost too easy.

Arriving at the borderline for the seventh time, the twins eye me curiously. "Got it out of your system yet?" Tweed asks, but the hidden smirk behind his mouth shows he already knows the answer. I see it now. His mirth, his similarities to Cash. They're just hidden so deep, the human eye can't find them.

"For now. Race you the rest of the way?" I quirk a brow. Cash is gone in an instant, shouting back that the loser has to watch the others fuck. I purposely slow my instinct to win, tremendously looking forward to the awkwardness of the twins when I arrive at the castle last.

Tweed rolls his eyes before taking off at a sprint, his movements fluid and graceful. I follow closely behind, my newfound vampire speed matching his effortlessly, my senses sharpened and on high alert. Every step feels like I am gliding along the ground, every sound amplified. As we race through the maze, the forest, the realm, and beyond, over rolling hills I spot our destination. Shrouded by thick clouds, the moons aren't visible against black spires and rigged spokes. Just like the replica I've seen. My heart rate increases, a surprising amount of anticipation building inside me.

We near the gates long before sunrise, two giant beasts of iron opening wide of their own accord. Cash slows right down, his hand automatically seeking mine. I bet he thought he'd seen the last of this place. I squeeze his fingers, stealing myself as we climb the stone steps on silent feet. I no longer have the urge to run at top speed. I barely want to take another step–the energy being sucked directly from my damned soul. Against the tar-like door telling me to do the exact opposite, I push against the gnarled handle and permit myself entry.

"Welcome to Spade Castle," Cash mutters bitterly. Whatever hold Lillianna had over him seems to have dissipated. Good riddance.

"I don't feel her presence," Tweed whispers, creeping past. Caution taints his every move. To my surprise, I'm hit by a wave of decadence. The walls are black, but not laced with evil as expected. Adorned with gold and jewels, rich tapestries hang from every available surface. The air is heavy with the scent of incense. If it hadn't been for the vines breaking through the flooring and a gnarled tree protruding through the staircase, I'd have felt a sense of comfort. As it stands, the hallways are eerie. Abandoned.

I feel eyes on me as we make our way through the lower level, each painting and statue on high alert. There's not a trace of the invasion which recently took place here. Not a body or speck of blood on the tiled floor or stairs.

The twins nod in unison and take the stairs two at a time, tracing the way back to a bedroom I vaguely recognize. An explosion has taken place in the center, pinpricks of ash still peppering the air. Whatever furniture I watched Cash use through the mirror, has been destroyed. So have any traces of my heart.

"Well, if it was in here, we're screwed." I state the obvious. Nothing survived what happened in this bedchamber, except for Tweed and the pact he's made to save his twin. He rounds a serious glare on me, his face tight.

"Don't wander off. It must be somewhere." Usually, I would resent his harsh tone, chastising me like a child. This time, I see his concern for the loving notion it is and grab his hand instead.

"I won't leave your side," I promise. Tweed's hard expression melts, his relief palpable on my tongue. Tugging me closer, he places a tender kiss on my mouth. One he's been aching to replace Cash's with. His lips are soft beneath mine, filled with the promise of all to come. The purity of a love which has been lost and found again in one single moment. Cash doesn't miss a beat, stepping in behind to brush his lips over my neck. Two sets of hands roam my body, two solid bodies pressing in to shield me from the evils lurking nearby. I taste what it's like to be loved. I feel what it's like to be adored.

The air around the three of us liquifies as we remain frozen in a moment which could last for the rest of time. Their souls reach into mine, intertwining a bond that can't be easily broken. Not by prophecy, deal or otherwise. We remain entwined, Tweed's kiss deepening, joining with my desperation to exist for more than just the sake of it. Cash applies gentle pressure from behind, his hands clasping around my waist, his chest pressing into my back as if he's worried I'll suddenly disappear.

The world continues spinning outside this bubble we have created, yet the only thing that matters is that we're together–and the passion which, even in the depths of depravity, will keep us forever connected. We let go of each other sometime later, their sighs ghosting across my skin like a blanket of comfort on a lonely night. I no longer feel the chill of their touch, becoming one with their lacking warmth.

"Come on, I don't want to linger any longer than I have to," Cash breaks away first, although his hand remains on my waist. Pulling me into his side, I drag Tweed along while Cash drops his mouth to my ear. "Mark my words, Malice. Once we're out of danger, my brother and I are going to spend eternity worshiping your body. There won't be a single moment you feel dissatisfied."

With that thought in mind, we search the castle for hours. Every room and crevice is checked, even in places my heart wouldn't have been able to up and jump to, whether heavy with poison or not.

"There must be something we're missing," Tweed growls, slamming his fist into a bookcase. The longer Lillianna hasn't shown her face, the braver we're all becoming. I lean against the wall, raising my arm to bathe in the daylight streaming through moth-eaten curtains. Nothing. No searing pain, not even a trace of heat. Cash replaces the books he's been flicking through, desperately hoping one is written by a seer. We have no such luck. I really wish Hatter was here to impart some of his wisdom.

"Perhaps we're not approaching this from the right angle," I try to channel my inner Hatter. The one which responded to his call long before I knew there was anything different or special about me. Cash and Tweed tilt their heads at the same time, waiting for the rest. "We've been under the assumption my heart is lost. But what if it was in fact found?"

"Indeed!" Tweed jolts upright and squares his shoulders. "It's genius."

"What am I missing?" Cash frowns between the two of us. I shrug, only hoping I've managed to trigger some kind of epiphany in Tweed.

"If the heart has already been found, it would have been stored. Cash, where does Lillianna keep her most prized possessions?" Cash smiles a wide, relieved grin and I feel my chest lighten.

"Of course, why didn't I think of it before?! The treasury." I can almost hear the whimsical tune which now accompanies us, a skip in our step all the way down the hall to a winding staircase I'm sure wasn't there before.

Cash takes the lead down a set of winding stairs that I hadn't noticed before. I follow close behind, the dank air feeling heavy across my skin. We pass through halls, open chambers either side filled with dusty desks and empty shelves. No one has been in this part of the castle for generations. Along each wall are gigantic tapestries depicting battle scenes from long ago–men fighting dragons or monsters, kings engaging in jousts with colorful flags waving high.

Stopping abruptly, I peer around Cash to see an arched door, framed by two marble pillars engraved with symbols I don't understand. He looks back at me briefly, an unspoken command to brace myself for whatever is inside. Perhaps this treasury won't be the standard crowns and jewels a queen should hoard, after all. His hand hovers over the metal lock and turns left instead.

Bolts click and rotate, creating a path for a small silver ball to trickle south from the arch. My eyes track the ball, like a cat fixated on a light, until it finally drops into a miniature scale embedded within the carvings, tilting downward until the lock is released with a deafening click. I'm so mesmerized by the intricate beauty of it all, I wasn't prepared for the onslaught which is unloaded on my senses when the door pops free. Tweed is right behind, catching me as I sway on my heels.

Blood. So much fresh blood, my stomach rolls with the richness of it. I'm salivating through a pained groan, the intense bitterness of decay both intriguing and disgusting me. I'm no stranger to death, but never have I been able to feel it like this.

"Take your time, it's a lot for our senses to handle," Tweed mutters, his own voice strained. I use his body as a splint, keeping me upright as Cash steps aside and reveals the horrors hidden within Lillianna's Treasury. She has trophies alright, but not those you peer at through glass cabinets. These ones are hanging by their ankles. Test tubes, boiling potions, and mortified corpses are stretched across tables. Much like science experiments gone wrong.

I take a hesitant step forward, drawn towards the macabre display like a moth to a flame. My eyes scan the room, taking in every detail: decapitated heads on spikes, jars filled with organs, the shelves cluttered with dusty grimoires. This isn't just a place to store valuables; this is a laboratory.

Tweed's hand tightens around my waist, pulling me back from the threshold. He's sensed it before I do, but it's too late. I shake him off, my eyes locked onto a table in the center of the room. A body, much smaller than the rest, has been left, splayed open, and discarded. Tufted brown fur lies in patches, blending into the grains of the wood. Tweed tries again to pull me away, not that my newfound strength can be denied.

"Is that...?" I trail off, not wanting to voice my thoughts aloud. Tears well in my eyes, a familiar scratching behind my ear announcing Stan has awoken and is on high alert. Cash reads my mind, his sigh filled with a thousand regrets.

"Yes. It's Chesh." I whimper at his admission. Shooting free of Tweed's hold, I appear at the table's edge, my throat closing on a sob. Her entrails are splayed open like a grotesque offering to whatever high power Lillianna has been calling to. I shake my head, unable to understand. What could Chesh's death have offered?

Tweed joins my side with an open book, the pages littered with intricate drawings. "Looks like the Queen is trying to find a way to become immortal herself. She's been testing magical creatures, dissecting their abilities and gifting them to herself."

Stan jumps free of my hair, gliding south to land beside Chesh's face. Somehow, her huge toothy grin is frozen in place, as if her light went out laughing. She wouldn't have let Lillianna win, not even in the end. And neither will I.

"I will avenge you, Chesh," I promise. My sadness instantly shifts to a depth of hatred I feel will never lift again. Throughout my loneliest days when I thought Wonderlust had forgotten about me, Chesh was there. She found me, kept me company, gave me a reason to live.

"We must keep moving," Cash says gently. "Especially now." I agree, lifting a weeping Stan from the table. He clings onto Chesh's whiskers, squeaking in a way I've never heard before. It's the cry of heartbreak, the loss of a loved one. I feel the sound resonate within my heart, but I refuse to break now. We will mourn later, at the same time we're rejoicing Lillianna's death. It'll be a public holiday for all.

Treading carefully, the three of us pass into an adjoining chamber. The twins are solid forces at my back, quietly reassuring me I'm no longer that lonely girl clinging onto her imagination for company.

Set apart by a series of steps, the smell of decay down here becomes worse. I hear someone shift within the darkness, my ears on full alert for a trace of the Queen I'm about to kill ten times over. But it's not her I lock eyes with.

"You're-you're not..." the voice is hoarse from screaming. Shuffling forward, bony hands wrap around the bars of a cell. Sunken eyes flood with relief, tears streaming down pale, hollow cheeks. "Saviors. We have saviors!" Suddenly, more bodies rush forward against the bars. Many can't stand, crawling across the cobblestones and using their cages to drag themselves upright. More calls of celebration ring throughout the underground prison.

"Saviors! They're our saviors!"

I gape along the length of the tunneled walls, unable to count how many cells or cowering vampires have been forgotten down here. Each body is exhausted, either malnourished or gaunt from lack of sleep. Each one shivers, reeking of sweat drenched scent. Soft snarls echoing through hallways, stretching from the most distant point, followed closely by muffled pleading.

*'Please! Let us go! We want to go home!'*

"Tweed," Cash steps into his twin's side. "You see what I see, right?" I take a step back into the Tweedle's conversation, planting myself in their embrace. Arms wind around my back, skating away the trepidation I'm battling. Stan scampers up my body and nestles himself back in the safety of my hair when the hollering all around us becomes too loud.

"The missing men. They're all right here," Tweed agrees in disbelief. I force myself to swallow, shaking my head.

"They're not men anymore." Indecision wars within my mind as the twins prepare to step around me and release those now screaming to be freed. My hands snap out, grabbing their wrists. "We need a minute." Shooting them both back towards the treasury, I can't stand smelling Chesh's corpse again so I continue dragging the twins into the room beyond. They frown in confusion as we pause, just far enough away for the prisoners to not overhear my hushed words.

"We can't release an entire army of starving vampires on the realm. The men in them will want to seek out their wives, but what happens if they can't control themselves? We won't need to wait for an apocalypse to wipe out Wonderlust."

"Fuck, you're right," Cash rubs the back of his neck. "I just can't believe they're here. They've been right here the entire time. Lillianna told me they were dead."

"Well, for once she wasn't lying," I sigh, looking back towards the prisons. Tweed clears his throat and squares his shoulders, remembering himself as the Knave he was born to be.

"I'll get word to Arabelle. She'll know what to do." A few weeks ago, I'd have felt a sense of jealousy at his trust in her, but now I'm inclined to agree. Arabelle will have the answers, and if she doesn't–then she can take the blame. She's the rightful queen and one I'll happily put my faith in.

“If it’s any solace for what’s been lost here today, we have a chance to do so much good. The realm will thank you.” Tweed places a kiss on my forehead, and I let him. It’s a perfect chance to hide my disdain. I don’t care what the realm thinks. I don’t need to be thanked. I just want...peace inside my heart. Whatever that is changes day by day. Once, I thought I’d find peace living alone in a cabin. Now, there needs to be space for a pair of broad shouldered, muscled brothers who make me feel unending desire. I have a home with them, and that's what I need to preserve.

"Send word to Arabelle, while we keep searching. Our mission isn't over yet," I state coldly. The room I've brought us to is the rest of Lillianna's laboratory. An overpowering stench of chemicals and magic seeps into my nostrils. More jars of oddities line the shelves, some filled with eyes, others with tongues and fingers. In the center of the room, a giant cauldron bubbles. The liquid inside boils with a sinister energy, spitting out sparks and emitting an eerie green light that casts shadows over us all.

"Careful," Tweed whispers, his hand tight on my shoulder, guiding me away. "We have no idea what effect that potion could have on us." True to his words, as I turn my back on the cauldron, I feel a certain pull towards the roiling mass. As if my soul aches to be near it, I quickly shoot to the other side of the room where Cash carefully steps into what seems almost an altar. Shrouded by darkness and radiating energy, a wooden frame magically stands on the top step. Easily seven feet tall and wide, the painting inside is vaguely familiar. An estate, coated in ivy and surrounded by woodlands.

I creep up the altar myself, squinting as a black cat strolls across the traveled driveway and lies in the midday sun. I recognize her from the white patch on her head–Smudge. She was the replacement my father gave me when I lost Dinah, although we never bonded. In fact, she tried to scratch my eyes out every time I hugged her, and there she is, still ruling over my family's estate.

Cash sighs, pinching the bridge of his nose. Two hands slip into either of mine in unison, shoulders of solidarity bolstering me before I speak words filled with foreboding.

"My heart isn't here, but I have a feeling I know where it, and Lillianna, might be."

# CHAPTER 32

"Is this going to take much longer?" Malice asks from a crystal bench in the courtyard. Halting suddenly, Tweed crashes into my back. My temples throb from where I've been pushing the heels of my palms against them, forcing myself to focus. The first few streams of daylight have begun to blush against Diamond castle, casting golden ribbons over the maze beyond.

Malice has been doing her best to be patient since returning to Diamond Kingdom. Although, 'returning' is a gentle way to describe how Tweed and I had to carry her kicking and screaming away from Chesh's body and the portal to her childhood home. None of her pained curses can compare to the staggering guilt I feel.

I was living above all those men, all of those tortured victims. So consumed by the notion I could only be loved while I had value to Lillianna, I willingly drank from her, knowing she was somehow deceiving me. I didn't care, as long as my presence in Spade Kingdom was hurting Tweed. Now I understand I was hurting many, many others.

"Guys, seriously. We've been out here all night." Malice yawns. The fur shawl we provided is being used as a pillow beneath her head, despite the chill in the air. We're no longer in Heart Kingdom where it's always summer. Although, there might not be any summer left there now the castle is destroyed and their queen has fled. I curse under my breath. The last thing I want to do right now is feel compassion for Arabelle, but I have no doubt she's hiding unknown turmoil beneath her practiced smile. I must ask Malice to check on her later.

"Forgive us, my love," Tweed rushes to her side, pulling her head onto his lap. Malice's mental state visibly lifts. I hang back, watching the display with fascination. "Problem solving doesn't come naturally to us Tweedles." He's not wrong. It's a mystery we've survived this long.

"We were right there, one step away from the portal. We could have been back and dancing victorious by now," Malice squeezes her fists tight. What my brother doesn't want to admit is that he couldn't act with Arabelle's permission. The Knave is a reflection of this Queen, who is currently being praised in Diamond Castle for saving the vampires from their hellhole prison. I heard whispers of a rehabilitation program passing between the budgie witch doctors. The portal was moved here too, for safety reasons.

Tweed strokes the hair around Malice's face, plucking Stan free and placing him on his shoulder. The action releases the tension from Malice's pout as she finds the will to calm herself. "Perhaps if you'd explain what the problem is, maybe I could make a suggestion," she sighs heavily. It's not the first time she's made such a suggestion, but it seems we're out of all other options.

"You're right," I agree. Tweed gives me a quick glance of panic, but Malice deserves to know. She can make her own choices.

Joining the pair on the bench, my instincts scream at me not to lower down, not to pull her upright, wind my arms around her middle, and rest my head on her shoulder. Especially after what I've discovered today, I don't have the right. But the thought of walking away from her is implausible. In a world of bleakness, Malice is the glimmering light of hope guiding me somewhere I might be able to redeem myself. She nudges me.

"Spit it out already. I'm a big girl. Whatever it is, I can take it. Lay it on me." I manage to find a smirk for her, if only to cover my concern.

"Your heart is in the human world. It's...gone. It's over." Tweed looks away, preferring to excuse himself from this conversation. Malice pushes off my touch, standing before us both with her arms crossed.

"Well, it's not gone, gone. It's waiting to be retrieved. If that's the big issue, consider it resolved. We'll be gone and back before lunchtime." Against the rising sun, Malice appears as a goddess. Her flame-fueled hair shines, her face set with decision, her curious body cocked with attitude. I have no doubt, vampire or not, Malice could survive any test life throws her way. That makes denying her all the more difficult.

"I wish it was so easy," I stretch out a hand. After a moment, she accepts it with a huff. "That portal at Spade Castle is most likely the last one to your home world in existence." Tweed lowers his head, grumbling more to himself.

"When so many males left searching for you, Arabelle ordered the gateways to be destroyed. It seems Lillianna used this to her advantage, using the Allure to bring men into her laboratory and experiment on them." I hear the note in his tone and realize, I'm not the only one feeling this guilt.

None of us could have known what Lillianna was planning, but I do know Tweed led the charge in destroying those portals. He turned his back on Malice, knowingly cutting off her chance to return in a bid to protect his own heart. He should have also known, there's no life after Malice. There's no getting over her.

"I still don't understand the problem. We need a portal, we have one. Let's go." Malice tries to pull me to my feet. I yank her into my lap.

"We can't let you go back, Malice. The last time..."

"You were gone for twenty years," Tweed finishes my sentence. That's it. Our concern, our apprehension. We refuse to lose her again. No more words are needed, her understanding dawning.

Cupping Malice's cheek, I lock eyes with her giant blue ones. For once, I let the smirk fall away, revealing the fear I hide underneath. Fear of what I feel, what I'm scared of losing. Our love may be fresh, but it's fierce. A storm not meant to be contained, our desire an inferno which should be yielded with caution unless we're prepared to combust.

Tweed shuffles across the bench and puts his arm around my shoulders for support. Even after all these years apart, we still share the same longing to protect Malice from harm. To love her undoubtedly until the end of time. She's always been our destiny.

“We won’t let you go," I tell Malice, "but we also know you won't be left behind.” Growling with indecision, I scrub a hand down my face. “Maybe it's better if the world falls to ruin. We can start again, just the three of us.” Tweed gasps, undoubtedly imagining all those he would have to sacrifice. I don't have such an issue, as the only people I care for are sitting on this bench.

"Oh yes," Malice drawls. "How about we let the world burn and then it'll just be the three of us, and Lillianna's entire vampire army, left." She rolls her eyes, that spunky girl who captured my interest all those years ago rising to the surface.

“Do you have another answer?” I ask. Malice squishes my cheeks between her hands, staring directly into my eyes.

"Yes. A very simple one. You trust me." Simple perhaps. My trust in her isn’t in doubt; it’s whether I can trust myself to put what is right above my own selfish needs. Malice cocks a brow when I don’t instantly respond. “You should know by now, I’m exactly where I should be. Nothing will keep me from being with the two of you.”

"It could be a trap,” Tweed immediately interjects. He’s the one more adverse in strategic discussions. “Lillianna could be waiting for us to pass through the portal, only to destroy it. We can’t defend Wonderlust if we’re not here.”

"But we'd be together, knowing we did everything we could to save it. I know which option my conscience would prefer."

"You don't have a conscience," I jerk Malice on my lap. We both laugh, the sound cutting through the tension.

"I do when it comes to the two of you," she chuckles, nipping at my neck. My cock responds faster than I have time to react. The playful gesture sends a shiver down my spine, my pulsating erection growing on instinct. Tweed scoffs, but I can sense his amusement too. The three of us have always had a knack for finding solace in each other, even in the bleakest of situations.

The silence which falls upon us is lighter; a comfortable quiet for us to become lost in our thoughts. Malice's head rests upon my shoulder, her weight half-resting on Tweed. How many times has I imagined a moment like this? More than I can count, for as long as I can remember.

"Should we–"

"Shhh," Tweed interrupts me. "Let her rest." I peer down at Malice's somber expression, her lashes pressed against her pale cheeks. Hugging her closer, I rest my head on hers.

The higher the sun rises, the heavier Malice's body becomes as a deeper sleep takes hold. It's been an incredibly long night, and even longer than she's been able to sleep with the knowledge she's protected. I'm to blame for so many things, but Malice has shown me there's always room for redemption. I'll follow where she leads, no matter the risk, just in the hopes I can prove myself worthy. I will be worthy of her love one day.

# CHAPTER 33

Standing in the backyard of my family's estate, I shudder. Never did I think I'd return, even before I was rushed back to Wonderlust. Since the night I was given a police escort to the station, my father's body in the ambulance next door, I'd made my peace with leaving the manor in my past.

"You know what, I'll wait right here in the shade." I sidestep to lean on a tree trunk, trying to look casual as fuck and failing. After all of my big talk of wanting to stay together, I wish the twins would have taken the incentive and dashed through the portal while I was asleep. I could have given them shit for it afterward, while secretly relieved I didn't have to step foot on these grounds again. My heightened hearing picks up on my sister, Edith, shrieking inside about a bouquet not fitting the color scheme.

"You're not backing out, Crazy One," Cash's eyes twinkle. "You wanted to do this together, now get your ass in that house." I reject his challenge, peering at my nails. I'll take on Lillianna any day, but while there is no sign of her, I'll leave my family at the twin's mercy.

"You boys run ahead and retrieve my heart. I'll make it worth your while," I give Cash a long look up and down. His dick jumps on command, ever eager to please.

Tweed rounds on me so fast, I don't see him move. Resting his forearm on the trunk, an inked bicep tenses right in front of my face.

"I thought I'd told you before, we're not boys. We're fully fledged men now."

"I believe Malice needs a reminder, don't you think, brother?" Cash leans over Tweed's shoulder. Seeing them bond, especially over me, makes my hoo-ha tingle. Slipping a hand around my throat like a collar, Tweed forces me a few steps deeper into the forest.

"You get to come once. Then we're back to the reason we're in his strange and backward world," he growls low, ever the Knave with one goal in mind. I gasp as Tweed spins me against the nearest tree. The roughness of the bark scrapes deliciously at my flushed chest, Tweed's weight at my back pinning me in place. His touch is electrifying, weakening my knees. I knew the thrill of a mission together would be too much to resist.

His lips trail my neck, nipping and sucking on the sensitive skin as Cash watches, his gaze dark and hungry. I'm wet long before Tweed's fingers trail down my sides, dipping beneath the hem of my tank top. Trailing a pattern over my sensitive flesh, my thighs clench with need. Cash steps forward and grips the lower half of my face in his giant hand, his predatory stare locking onto mine.

"Let's see, Crazy One," he whispers, the chill of his touch sending shivers down my spine, "whose name you scream first." Cash's hands are rough as they grab my hips, twisting and yanking me closer to him. Tweed doesn't miss a beat, following behind for his hand to slip beneath my plaid skirt, his hands exploring every inch of me. I try to resist the urge to moan as Tweed's fingers find their way inside me, teasing my wetness, and fail miserably.

Cash smirks knowingly, kneeling down and lifting my skirt up fully to reveal my throbbing clit. His head dips lower, licking a long track from where Tweed's fingers are pumping into my pussy, all the way up to that sensitive bud, aching for attention. It's been far too long since we've all given into our desire like this. I whimper in pleasure, unable to form coherent sentences as they both work me in complete unison.

"Fuck, you taste like goddam heaven," Cash growls, kneeing closer and running his hand up the back of my thigh.

I drop my head back against Tweed, a slave to their onslaught. Gripping my chin, Tweed twists my head to capture my lips in a kiss which causes my toes to curl. His tongue invades my mouth as easily as his fingers take me hostage. Our fangs clash, a mixture of copper and lust filling my mouth. I drown in Tweed's taste, reaching behind to grip his thick shaft. Breaking away from our kiss instantly, he pushes my hand away.

"Not this time, beautiful. This is a release for you alone." My hips start to sway against Cash's mouth, riding his tongue as Tweed continues to slide his fingers deeper. Dragging his lips across my jaw, Tweed pauses to tease his fangs against my neck. I arch into him, desperate to feel that slice of my skin, the tug of my vein. If it's anything like when I drank from Cash, I know Tweed will feel the height of my desire and drown in it too. But I should have known Tweed is a man of honor now, and he keeps his word. Moving away from my neck, his head lowers onto my shoulder to shift his focus back to those wicked fingers.

"You're so wet for us, baby." The vibration of Cash's voice against my core sends more tremors through me. Catching me on the edge of a strangled groan, Tweed slides his free hand up my stomach to caress my breasts, taking turns to toy with each of my nipples. My legs weaken, which the twins use as a moment of weakness to hoist me up.

Flipped around, my back is half way up the tree, my thighs resting over Cash's broad shoulders. He eats me out like a monster only just freed from his cage, all the while leaving room for Tweed's fingers to carry out their assault. I whimper, the pressure building inside of me coming to a tipping point. The twins watch in fascination, their green eyes never wavering as I break for them both. Gripping their blond hair in my fists, I can't contain a scream which disperses all the birds in all the trees.

My orgasm slams into me with such force, my back arches from the tree trunk. Never ending waves crash and withdraw, my pussy clenched around Tweed's fingers. Cash won't relent, flicking his tongue over my clit until I'm dizzy, wayward with pleasure. Only when the tremors of my climax ease, does he pull back with a satisfied smirk. Tweed withdraws at the same time, equally as cocky.

"So fucking beautiful," he compliments as I'm lowered back to earth. I wobble on unsteady feet, panting heavily between them both. My knights of pleasure, princes of darkness.

A distant rumbling brings me back down to earth, to reality. All effects of my orgasm vanish, leaving a sickened clench in my stomach as a car nears. Tires on the gravel would have once been my signal to run home, excited to see who our guest was. Who might be able to keep me company for a while.

Peering through the trees, I frown. The approaching vehicle isn't as current as I expected–but a dated Ford with plenty of dents amongst the silver paintwork and dried mud framing the lower half. I watch it near the house, stopping just short of the marble porch. Sunlight bounces off the windows, barring my view until the driver pops his door and exits.

A tall man rounds the vehicle, muscles bulging at his t-shirt sleeves, whereas his middle has more cushioning. Hazelnut hair frames his face, leaking into his trimmed beard. He has the overall appeal of a teddy bear, and I bet he gives the best hugs. Tugging the passenger door open, he offers his hand to a woman half his size. Ink black hair, lithe frame, broad smile. I almost didn't recognize her–again.

"What the hell is Mary Ann doing at your family estate?" Cash growls, suddenly on the defensive. Tweed isn't so quick to react, holding back to assess the full situation. Mary Ann pauses, looking towards the woodlands as if she senses our presence. Her teddy bear leans into the back seat, retrieving a tiny bundle wrapped in a blanket.

"Of course, time moves differently here," Tweed whispers. Pressing my lips together, I storm forward, my boot stepping out of the shade and onto the gravel. Sunlight hits my skin like a thousand diamond daggers spearing my body, the burn knocking me backward. I fall hard, my legs still coated in the sun's glow. Blisters shoot across my pale skin, gnawing an incredulous depth of pain directly into my bones.

Hands drag me backward, into the safety of the shade. Another hand slams over my mouth when I struggle to stifle my screams. Arching my back, I try to relieve the pain. Everywhere I'm touched, where the ground presses against my bubbling flesh, makes me feel as if I'm being branded alive. My eyes burn, the harsh light trying to force its way in through my tightly shut lids. The world starts spinning, and soon enough, it all fades away, drawing the consciousness from my agony-ridden body.

***

My senses return one by one, moments of confusion hovering in the back of my mind. Complete darkness bathes the world until my eyesight catches up with the rest of me. Through the bleakness, two sets of identical emerald green eyes emerge. Their faces glow in the fluorescent light of an ethereal blue hue. The singular moon I've spent many nights wishing on. I choke on a gasp, remembering where I am.

"Wha...what happened?" I twist onto my side, feeling hungover. The thick bed of grass beneath me is dotted with daisies, an undercurrent of energy pulsing from the creatures burrowed within. I hear their heartbeats, moles and badgers scratching at the earth. Two sets of hands ease me upright, my back resting against Cash's shoulder.

"So apparently," he tries to contain a laugh, "vampires are allergic to the UV light in this world." I scowl at the humor in his tone. Next time, I'm pushing him into the daylight and seeing how he likes it. Tweed crouches in front of me, his hands clenched.

"I've done some recon in your absence," he says matter-of-factly. I'd make a quip if his jaw wasn't set tight. Reckless Tweed isn't present right now, this is all Knave. "Seems there's some sort of event happening tonight." Following his gaze across the garden I've been laid in, the house is indeed lit up, guests streaming through the front door and music leaking from every cracked window.

"Nah, Tweed, that's not an event. It's a damn party." My eyes narrow. Pushing to my feet, I recover in an instant. Mostly likely from pure stubbornness. It's not like I expected my family's lives to end when I was incarcerated, but I hadn't spared much thought for the lavish parties and celebrations which would continue in my absence.

Storming across the manicured lawn, the satin of a tight gown hinders my determined legs. Taking stock of myself, I gape at the exquisite dress stretched across my body. The cleavage dips low, folds of satin resting over my breasts and held up by two straps thinner than strands of spaghetti. The heels on my feet sink into the soft ground as I linger, spotting the twins in full tuxes waiting for my reaction.

"I acquired us outfits," Cash shrugs with a boyish smile. Given the extent of their current resources, I can only guess where he acquired the clothes from.

"While I scoured the grounds. No sign of Lillianna or your heart anywhere," Tweed adds gravely. He's a constant at my side, his eyes ever watching, all-seeing.

Cash follows, his hand hovering at my elbow in case I falter. But I don't. My anger propels me forward, fuelled by the memories of what's lost. Christmases, birthdays, the decorations from Halloween and huge buffets of Thanksgiving. Some may say I should miss out, considering I murdered my father in cold blood. But they weren't there. They didn't see how desperate I was for his affection, how he pretended to love me for my words. I may have held the knife, but he backstabbed me first.

The music grows louder as we approach, thumping bass reverberating through the walls. Guests dressed in similar attire are mingling on the terrace, a scattering of faces I vaguely recognize as my father's pompous colleagues from years back, and dozens more that I don't. A mix of aristocrats with hidden sorrows and disdainful associations with money. I feel their stares as we cross the threshold, their whispers like needles in my ears.

"Who is that?" "Where did they come from?" "Is she wearing my dress?" The last one came from Lorina, my other sister. I don't pause long enough for her to recognize me, waltzing directly into the middle of the viper's den–the ballroom.

The glitzy room has been tastefully decorated in pink. Pale blush balloons amongst an arch of rose gold over each doorway, buntings hanging from candelabras. The dance floor glimmers with sparkling confetti, creating a pathway to the pair of thrones at the front. Either side of the couple posing for professional photographers, are huge fluorescent letters spelling out 'M-A-L'. My jaw drops.

"Mary Ann?!" I shriek over the chatter and music. Mary Ann shoots to her feet, dislodging the sleeping baby in her arms. The infant wakes, beginning to cry. Standing from his adjoining throne, the Butch Teddy

Bear eases the baby from Mary Ann's arms, his glare fixated on Cash. I get the impression the two know each other. Rushing through the photographers, Mary Ann takes my hand and whisks me towards the exit.

Even from behind, she's stunning. Her black hair, now shoulder-length, has been half-pinned up into an intricate weaving with miniature flowers around her crown. Her dress is a delicate shade of pale peach, the fabric draped from one side to the other in gentle waves. The corset has detailed lace and beading that glitters like diamonds in the light. The bodice is fitted tightly around the waist, with soft ruffles cascading down the skirt until it fans out into a full-length train. The kind of dress which comes from money. My family's money.

"Ten seconds to explain what the fuck is happening here," I yank my hand from her grip when we're alone. "Go."

"Um, I mean, it's kinda like..."

"Six seconds," I purse my lips. Mary Ann holds up her hands, revealing a delicate, footwork tattoo down her left forearm.

"Okay! Just let me explain. You know when a serial killer returns to the scene of the crime and then helps in the search for a body he knows is simmering in a vat of acid in his basement," Mary Ann's blue eyes are huge, pleading with me to understand her rambling. I'm lost on all counts. "It started like that. There was a nation-wide search happening for you, and your family was offering a huge reward. I didn't want to seem suspicious so I kinda...injected myself into the investigation. I met your sisters and mother, they were good to me. One thing led to another and..." Mary Ann shrugs, her bottom lip wobbling. "I didn't expect to ever see you again. You weren't supposed to come back."

"I wholly don't understand," I mumble, refusing to look away from her worried gaze. It's not too much of a surprise my family was looking for me after my daring escape from Charmsfield. I can only imagine the blood-filled cabin a few miles away was added to my list of crimes. But why Mary Ann felt the need to help, to be close to those who turned their backs on me, is beyond comprehension. Can't she see they're the real monsters in this house?

"Mary Ann, we're about to–" Edith steps into the hallway, halting when she sees me. Her eyes search my face, my body and all the way back up, hunting for that hint of recognition she can't place. On a shrug, she discounts me completely. "We're about to serve the hors d'oeuvres. Mother got the vol-au-vents you adore." Whisking away in her luxurious blue gown with silver trim, I'm left gaping at Mary Ann.

"Okay. Fine, you stalked my family, pretended to care about my disappearance." I scratch my head, realizing I too have intricate braids securing my hair high above my neck. I wonder which twin did that. "But what the fuck is all of this?!" My hands flick erratically at the room beyond the hallway, my voice raising. Confusion is quickly becoming panic, and no one will like me when I'm panicked.

"It's my daughter's christening," Mary Ann ducks her head shyly. "Your family offered to host the after party." The wind is knocked out of me. Leaning back, I peer through the doorway to see Cash is now cradling a blanketed bundle in his arms. The Butch Teddy Bear is leaning over his shoulder, watching his every move.

"You have a daughter?" I whisper, a moment of silence spearing my soul. Cash smiles, stroking the baby's cheek. So natural, as if he isn't a predator holding the easiest type of prey.

"We called her Mallory–Mal for short. To honor you." Mary Ann tentatively takes my hands, drawing me a step closer so I can't see inside the ballroom anymore.

"Honor me?" I mimic back like a parrot. She nods, her cheeks healthily flushed.

"You saved my life. I was a slave, trapped in a realm where no one wanted me. You set me free, and everything I am today is thanks to you. I know you don't speak fondly of your family, but I thought consoling them was a small way to repay the favor. I just didn't expect..."

"That they all hate me?" I huff a laugh, knowing where this is going. Taking my hands back, I smooth down my dress. "Yeah well. Let's say I know something about being trapped where no one wants you." We linger for a moment, unsure where this stand-off is going. Well, that's not exactly true–Mary Ann is waiting to see if I'll make a scene to ruin her daughter's christening or leave quietly. I'll opt to do neither. "Come on then, let's get back to the party. I made my decision to stay at vol-au-vents."

# CHAPTER 34

Mary Ann squeezes my hand, her face soft with relief and gratitude. Leading me back into the ballroom, the guests have begun to take their seats at the elegantly set tables, and I immediately spot my mother sitting at the center table with her back straight and a forced smile on her face. My two sisters are seated next to her, eyeing me with the same curiosity as before.

I take a deep breath and square my shoulders, reminding myself I can handle anything thrown my way. Mary Ann leads me to the table, where an empty chair awaits between the twins. I lower down, actively avoiding Cash's gaze. Don't ask me why, because I'm not fully sure yet.

His hand seeks out my thigh, and I let it settle there, staring at the silver plate placed before me on the table. An array of miniature, warm buttery pastries with savory fillings stir the air, making my mouth water. There's a gigantic flaw to my plan here...I take a vol-au-vent from the plate and bite into it. While I know I won't be able to swallow it, I can at least savor the rich flavors dancing across my tongue like fireworks. My stomach groans in protest. Inhaling deeply, I bask in the final moment before snatching up a handkerchief and spitting it out.

“Mmm, delicious,” I smile in the faces of those staring at me in disgust. My mother arches a perfectly sculpted eyebrow, the gears turning in her head. She glances pointedly at where Cash's arm extends towards my leg, before returning her gaze to me.

"I hope you're feeling well, dear," she says, her tone laced with thinly veiled judgment. I force a smile.

"Yes, thank you. Just a little indigestion." My sisters exchange a look and my mother leans in slightly.

"Speaking of indigestion," Edith sniggers, "I heard that Dr. Thompson's wife is expecting again. Can you believe it? This would be their seventh. I swear, some people have no self-control." Lorina laughs and even my mother cracks a smile, angling her head towards Mary Ann.

"Take it from me, dear, two daughters are more than enough." I inhale sharply as Cash's hand tightens on my thigh.I grit my teeth, knowing exactly what she's implying. But I refuse to let her get to me. In the face of grabbing the steak knife before me and making this family reunion one to really remember, I tug Cash's hand higher. He gets my drift, rubbing his fingers in small circles around the clit he was so recently toying with. I shift my hips forward, needing the distraction. At the same time, Tweed drapes his arm across the back of my chair, fiddling with my shoulder straps. The forbidden nature of our relationship doesn't go unnoticed.

"Excuse me for being abrupt," Edith pops a pinch of pastry into her mouth. "But who are you?" I show my fangs, about to inform Edith I'm her worst fucking nightmare when Mary Ann cuts me off.

"She's Mal's godmother. The woman I was telling you about, who gave me a fresh start." My mouth drops open. Godmother? I look back to the small baby, swaddled in a pink blanket, being passed around the guests at an adjacent table. Each person takes the time to give her a blessing and press a kiss to her forehead in an unspoken ritual. A child so loved by a room of people who so easily shunned me. Should I feel jealous? I'm sure I should feel something.

"Ironic, isn't it?" Lorina smirks around a flute of champagne. She always was a lightweight. "In losing one sister, we gained another." Lifting her glass towards Mary Ann, the rest of the table, bar myself and the twins, do the same.

"This is a celebration," Mary Ann tries to argue. Her voice is lost amongst the clinking. Blushing, her blue eyes slip to mine and I find a small smile for her. This isn't her fault, nor is it her fight. Edith groans loudly.

"You're so right, Mary Ann. I'd also prefer if we didn't discuss Alice tonight. Wherever she's ended up, she no doubt caused her own destruction. I truly believe it's a blessing she wasn't found."

"Edith!" Mary Ann jumps to my defense. I give her a small shake of my head. Let her see my family for who they really are. Not the heartbroken heiress who didn't deserve such a fate. There's a reason I am the way I am, and I'm starting to see it wasn't all down to my father's betrayal. I was an outcast long before I was a convict.

"What?!" Edith giggles, looking to Lorina for backup. "You're all thinking it."

"Alice brings nothing but chaos and misery. Where there is none, she creates it. We're all better off without her." Lorina agrees. The pair clink their glasses again, while my mother's stare is fixated on me. I'd never have described us as close, but surely not even my change in hair color, paled complexion and pointer teeth could fool her.

The music changes now, growing in volume as a slow ballad takes over. Couples at various tables begin to pair up and sway toward the dance floor. I watch from my seat, my mind is too clouded with emotion to even consider joining in.

Between my family's admissions, Mary Ann's declaration, and the twin's hands teasing my taut body, only one thing can draw me out of my thoughts. The small bundle being passed over to Mary Ann's husband. He smiles with such adoration, kissing her tiny button nose. That's how it should be.

Passing baby Mallory to Cash once more, that perplexing feeling swells in my chest again. The one which makes me want to slap him stupid. Tweed, incredibly attuned to my mindset, tugs me to my feet and towards the dancefloor.

"Feel honored," he mutters. "I don't dance." Tweed shoots me a look of unease before raising his head high, forcing confidence across his face.

Placing a hand on my waist, he pulls me close, and we sway to the same rhythm. My eyes search for Cash, who still hasn't looked up from the bundle in his arms. How could he enjoy looking at her that long? It's just a baby. A tiny version of a human, and the one thing in this world I'll never be able to provide for him. Oh shit, there it is.

Even before I became a vampire, I was at ease with the fact I couldn't bear children. The clinical trials at Charmsfield essentially saw me neutered, and I was okay with it–until tonight. Apparently, there's a direct correlation between loving someone, wanting to provide them everything they might desire, and finding fault in one's self for their downfalls.

I attempt to push Tweed away, figuring it's not too late to change my mind about this party. We came here for a reason, and it wasn't to dance and pretend to be social beings.

"I never would have pictured you growing up in a place like this," Tweed comments, refusing to let me budge. He glances between the marble flooring to the diamond chandelier, a pensive look upon his face. "Someone as savvy, eager for adventure, and comfortable without comfort. I'd imagined a wooden shack and a watering can for a shower." Despite myself, a trickle of laughter bubbles from my throat. I stop trying to push away, leaning into the white shirt covering his solid chest.

"I don't know whether I should be offended by that or not." The slow tempo of the music winds around us like a cocoon, blocking out everyone else nearby with their fancy footwork. I don't need any of that from Tweed; just his stability. Clinging onto his back, my heels knock against his dress shoes until the current song ends and the next begins. All the while, Cash is still cuddling that damn baby.

"Do you want to know something?" Tweed asks after a while. I tilt my head up, admiring his handsome face. His clean shaven and sharply angled jaw mirrors the cut of his shirt collar. "I'm glad your family disowned you." I still, my brows shooting to my hairline.

"Excuse me?" I scoff, my hands balling into fists. Smiling one of those rare, heart stopping smiles, Tweed takes my hands in his, clenching them between us.

"You heard me," Tweed nods confidently. "I'd rather they hated you for all eternity, because that means I don't have to share you with anyone except Cash. These lavish parties and fakery over dinner, the in-laws and the stress. No, thank you. I much prefer for no one else to notice how incredible you are, and leave all the more for me." I melt, completely languid in his arms. The words I've unknowingly waited to hear my entire life swirl through my chest. On legs made of feathers, I push myself taller to lean my forehead against his.

"Oh, Tweed," I sigh. Tears prickle the backs of my eyes but in no way am I sad. The opposite, in fact.

"You're not chaos Malice. You're utter pandemonium. You've slammed through the walls I spent my whole life enforcing with the force of a wrecking ball. And I'll love you everyday of eternity for it."

"I want to go home," I whisper.

"Soon, my love."

"As soon as we ensure we have a home to return to," Cash says from behind. He doesn't care for anyone watching; he wraps his arms around my back and joins our gentle swaying, the three of us in perfect timing for a change. One unit. One entity. My eyes close as Tweed sighs against my neck. I may be surrounded by the family I was born into, but the one I chose is right here.

We dance until the music draws to an inevitable end, many of the guests having left in the earlier hours of the evening. The moon is central in the sky now, bouncing off the chandelier and leaving the dance floor in a smattering of light. Tweed takes both my hands in his and kisses them one by one.

"Let's find what we came here for," he urges. It occurs to me then, the twins must have been itching to start searching the manor for my Heart, but stalled for me. I needed tonight to put any undealt with emotions to rest. I smile at the pair of them; the two men who saved me more than once from a life long forgotten. A life I no longer want any part in.

With a groan, Cash retracts his arms from around my waist and steps away. Tweed is right; the sooner we can get back, the quicker the rest of our lives can start. It's the three against the world–human, Wonderlust or otherwise.

"You two start searching. There's something I want to check out first."

"I'll take the upstairs," Cash states as Tweed stakes his claim on the ground floor. After a lingering three-way hand holding session, we separate in opposite directions. It takes every fiber of my being not to shoot off at top speed, just so I can rejoin them quicker. Mary Ann waves me over from the table, breastfeeding little Mal. I decline her gesture with a salute, fleeing to the ballroom on my heels. I'm not a baby person, sue me.

Scaling the stairs, I side step around where my father's blood once stained. Seemed like the respectful thing to do. If only everything was as easily torn up and replaced as the cream carpet beneath my shoes.

Moving on and with bated breath, I ease open my old bedroom door. It comes as a surprise that I'm not standing on the threshold of an impressive gym or a 'we hate Alice' shrine. Instead, my room has been forgotten and is being used as storage. Boxes are piled high, old suitcases propped against the wall my four-poster bed once stood. There's nothing to resemble another Liddel used to live here. Not even the blue pinstriped wallpaper I loved. Stepping inside, I head for the bathroom mirror when a figure steps out of the shadows.

"So, when were you planning on telling us you were alive?" My mother's voice is cold, devoid of any emotion. I stop still, cursing myself for not picking up on her heartbeat sooner. Closing the door softly, I turn to face the woman who should have been my lifeline. Instead, I see a bitter, cold mistress who couldn't love what she struggled to control.

"I wasn't," I reply curtly. "I have my own life to live." I stare down the woman across the room, confused how we're even related. Dark brown hair has been artfully piled on top of her head, her body painfully skinny. A bag of bones in sapphire satin, fixed to her bust by an oversized brooch.

"And yet here you are, crashing a family event," she sneers. "You always did love the attention." A smile pulls at my mouth. It grows, wide enough to make Chesh proud, until my fangs are on full show. Glinting in the moonlight, she notes the threat and wisely swallows down her next words.

"Family event?" I scoff. "Some would say, I'm the truest member of this family. I don't hide behind fakery, putting on an act for the world to see. I've always been myself."

"An insolent child who refused to fit the mold, you mean?"

"Exactly," I nod. Mother flourishes her hand in the air, smiling as if she's won. She should know by now, there is no winning against me. Clenching those fingers into a fist, she snarls, years of hatred shining through.

"All you had to do was be quiet, and receive everything your heart desired. Many would call you spoiled."

"And they can all get fucked," I shrug, leaning against the wall. It doesn't matter what the world thinks, only how I perceive myself. There's two beings in this house who love me exactly the way I am, and that piece of knowledge has done wonders for reinforcing my confidence.

Holding my mother's stare, her face remains squeezed tight like a prune as she assesses me. There's something she wants to say, but is unnerved by the changes in me she doesn't understand. "Speak your mind," I demand. There's no point leaving anything unsaid now.

"You killed my husband," she says quietly. Stepping forward, my mother moves into the gleam of moonlight separating us. For the rarest of moments, a real emotion passes her features. Grief. The truth hits me with a clarity only my vampire mind could commute this fast. My mother did feel devotion and love, just not to me. "He was my everything, and you stole him from me."

I make a decision then. Bracing my hand on the door handle, I exhale a lifetime of bitterness. I could continue to argue. We could go round and round in circles of who stole from who, where the misplaced affection should have been directed, but there's no use. It may have taken me twenty years to find love of my own. I'm good now. Pausing midway out of the room, I look back at the woman I felt no connection to in the slightest.

"I'm not a bad person. I just do bad things. Right injustices no one else wants to. My methods may be erratic, but I didn't inherit the knack to ignore problems and pretend they don't exist. Maybe that makes me crazy, or maybe that makes me the sanest person here."

Leaving the room on steady feet, I shoot to the other side of the manor in a blur, aiming for anywhere my mother isn't. Flying into a room and closing the door behind me, I slump with my head in my hands. Amongst the overwhelming relief, a trickle of anger tries to burn through. At war with myself, my logical brain is in full fight or flight mode, while the vampire in me acts more rationally. What's the point in arguing with no end game?

A small sound meets my ears. Peering up, I catch a glimpse of Mallory stirring in her bassinet. Mary Ann is in a rocking seat nearby, allowing me the time to stand and approach the baby. My goddaughter. She's perfect, wrapped inside the basket like a caterpillar in its cocoon. A yawn pulls at her mouth, her cute button nose twitching until sleep claims her again. The anger trying to invade my soul dissipates.

Mallory doesn't deserve to be caught up in this. If my family will treat her with the love and affection I always craved, then I can take solace that finally, fina-fucking-ly, they're going to do something right. This baby girl will be loved, and she'll never feel the loneliness that tore my soul apart.

"Congratulations," I whisper. "She's beautiful."

"Will you give her a blessing?" Mary Ann responds, her foot on the bassinet's base keeping it swaying gently. I hesitate. If anyone needs a blessing, it's probably me. I rarely wear matching socks and can't locate a hairbrush at the best of times. But looking down at the sleeping infant, I feel a strange connection to her. She's innocent in every way, and I want to protect her from the world's cruelty. Stepping closer to the bassinet, I lay a gentle hand on Mallory's forehead. Closing my eyes, I concentrate on the energy flowing through her. So pure, untainted by evil. I whisper a blessing, wishing her a life full of love, happiness, and prosperity. That wicked will stay away, and her inner crazy will never be dulled. Between my hand and her forehead, a soft glow brightens, filling my chilled palm with warmth. I want to bathe in it longer, but tentatively withdraw before Mary Ann notices. From her seat, she smiles gratefully at me.

"Thank you," Mary Ann murmurs. "It means a lot." I grin back at her, that warmth spreading to my chest before it fizzles out. Reaching into a bag at her side, Mary Ann withdraws a small item and jerks her head for us to move towards the window. "I need to give you something."

Tucked away from the room by the large plumes of velvet curtains, Mary Ann places the small vial in my hand. The content is thick and black, slow in its descent as I tip it up one way and back again. A chain has been attached, which Mary Ann quickly fixes around the back of my neck.

"When I fell through the portal, your heart slipped through with me." She whispers into my ear. I immediately perk up. "I tried to preserve it, but the poison was too deeply ingrained. It was turning to ash, Malice, so I did the only thing I could think of."

"I strained the poison out, hoping one day it might be of use to someone. I'm glad I can return it to you. Do with it what you wish."

I hold the vial, the strength seeping out of me. After everything we've seen and experienced in the name of retrieving this damn heart...and it's been gone the entire time. My mood deflates, wondering how I'm going to break it to the twins. Lillianna already has all the tools in her arsenal to take over Wonderlust, and we'll never get our happy ending.

"But the Hatter's heart...it's the most powerful component of Wonderlust," I almost whimper. Mary Ann closes my fingers around the vial.

"Is it?" she asks, blue eyes full of hope. "I refuse to believe there's any force out there which can stop you." I take a deep breath, feeling the weight of the vial around my neck. It's been so long since I've felt anything close to hope. But Mary Ann is right, there's no point in giving up now. We've come too far, fought too hard, to simply accept defeat. My resolve strengthens as I hug her goodbye.

"Until we meet again," I smile, blowing baby Mal a kiss on my way out the door. Dual heartbeats are waiting for me, hands snaking out to grab me as soon as I enter the hallway. Dragged into their embrace, anyone would think we haven't seen each other in years. I snuggle into their necks, sighing a breath of relief.

"I need to tell you–"

"We heard everything," Cash pulls me back an inch, planting a firm kiss on my lips. "Did you do it?" There's a strange glint in his eye. I frown.

"Do what?"

"Oh, she totally did it," Tweed agrees, taking his turn to kiss me deeply. My protests are muffled, my chest swooning. Without giving me a straight answer, the pair share a grin, before whisking me away from the manor and my childhood estate.

# CHAPTER 35

Whichever world we just portaled back into, I don't recognize it as Wonderlust. The room which housed the frame no longer has a ceiling or walls. Just a barren mound where Diamond Castle is supposed to be. Everywhere I look, destruction and chaos have taken over; each road leading to a place unknown with remnants of past treasures thrown about like mere trinkets forgotten by time. An eerie silence filters throughout the land, dark with powerful magic at play.

"Time moves differently in Wonderlust," Cash breathes. There's a note of panic in his voice which makes me reach out on instinct and take his hand. The sky is a blend of purple and blue, anticipating the rise of two blood moons creeping over the horizon on either side of the panes around us. I sense Tweed's anxiety before he wraps an arm around my waist. He's running out of time.

"We need to find Arabelle," is his indirect order. For once, I agree. Wherever the Queen of Hearts is hiding, she'll have a plan at the ready. One, her Knave is no doubt the star of. We march onwards, through clouds crackling unpredictably and wind howling ferociously beyond rusted gates which hang limply from aged hinges. Vines crawl over heaps of shattered crystal, moss forming amongst the cracks. The grim reminders of what once was continue; a moat now stagnant with deep green water where the maze once stood, pathways of cracked stone where lines of servants no longer march.

Tweed takes the lead, his footsteps slowing as our surroundings become increasingly unfamiliar. A chill in the air preempts the rush of a huge animal breaking free of the clouds. Its body resembles a dragon, while its sharply bared teeth house the Jabbercocky's ferocious roar. I cover my ears, ducking low as it glides overhead, the scrape of scale just skimming my back.

Braving a look at the sky, the beast turns and plummets south once more, a familiar rider clutching the reins on its back. Humpty Dainty has swapped out her wig for black locks which whip around in the wind, her egg-face painted heavily with make-up. It's the dress of shadow which unnerves me the most, as the Lillianna-lookalike angles her new pet for my head. The twins grab my arms, racing me towards a forest in the distance. I jerk myself free of their hold, rushing on ahead at an unfathomable speed.

As if on cue the trees tremble, thick and wild as they tower high above us, grayed bark filled with ancient runes. I don't stop running, my eyes searching for danger in every crevice of this new land. Flame ignites the canopy, bearing us to the Jabberycocky's wrath. I feel a shift in the air; a pull of magic from an unseen source tugging me east.

Without any thought for it being a trap, I dart after it, winding through tree trunks and leaping over the foliage yet to be destroyed. Deep inside my chest, the magic pulls hard, like a beacon of hope guiding us through the gloom. The twins remain behind, shouting about safety being in the opposite direction. Still, I trust my instincts, spying an opening nestled into a grassy mound. It's low, more like a hole covered by brambles.

Skidding onto my side, my satin dress is torn to shreds as I launch myself horizontally into the tunnel. My heels do well to shatter through rocks, my body being battered around until a hole deposits me onto the hard floor. I groan, peering around the underground bunker. Half a second later, my ears twitch, and I roll aside just before Cash, then Tweed, crash to the spot I was just lying in. Flipping onto my back, I regulate my breathing, listening to the Jabbercocky roar and pass the forest overhead, unable to find us.

As the twins catch their breath, I take in my surroundings. The bunker is small, with a low ceiling carved into the packed mud. It's dimly lit by small orbs of light embedded in the walls, flickering slightly as if running out of energy. Despite the cramped space, it's clear that whoever built this had planned for long-term stays. There are shelves stacked with preserved food and water, along with beds, trunks, and a compact bathroom. A lone door stands opposite.

"Hurry," Cash rushes for the trunks. "For someone who's scouted this land a thousand times over, I have no idea whose bunker this is." Pulling out a range of cloaks and clothes in different sizes, we shift through and ditch our finery. I opt for a pair of slacks which happen not to have blood splattered across them, tightening the braces over a grubby t-shirt to stop them from falling down. Tweed passes me a flat cap and the smallest, bland shoes he can find. Dressing, I catch my reflection in a hanging saucepan.

"You know what," I square my cap, "this isn't such a bad look for me." Pinging my braces, Cash growls appreciatively. His hand slips around the back of my neck, preparing to kiss my face off when a noise beyond the door catches my attention. I quickly motion for Cash and Tweed to hide behind the fabric divider separating the toilet from the rest of the bunker. Through the joining slits and with bated breath, we watch as the door is eased open.

"I smell you, strangers." A deep voice rumbles through the bunker. I nudge Cash aside, needing a clearer view of the figure draped in tattered robes, their face obscured by a hood. In their hand, a glowing orb atop of a cane illuminates the room. The creature sniffs at the air, its elongated face tilted upwards as it takes in our scent. "Vampires..." it decides, testing the word on its tongue.

“Hey! I know you!” I jump out of my hiding spot. Tweed grapples to yank me back, but I’m a wriggly fucker at the best of times. The Verax straightens its curved back, a long tongue slipping free to taste the air. Reduced to fit the size of its lair, the creature is a quarter of the size of that which tried to eat me. Spindly fingers grip the glowing orb on top, salvia drips from pointed teeth. Smoke creates a cloak around its skeletal frame while shining white eyes glance me up and down.

“The Malice.” The Verax grins wide enough to be deemed creepy if I wasn’t just so damn happy to see it. Stopping short of rushing forward to give it a hug, I beckon the twins to join me.

“This is perfect timing. We need answers, and here they are.”

“Every truth comes at a price,” Cash reminds me. Both Tweedles flank my sides, hesitant to trust. But I know the Verax, she - I've decided she's a she - will set us back on the right track. The Verax chuckles, the sound echoing throughout the small bunker.

"You always were a brave one, my dear. But do not let that bravery lead you down the path of foolishness." I ignore the warning, too eager for answers.

"We need to find Arabelle, and quickly," I urge. "Name the price you seek." The Verax's smile fades, replaced by a solemn expression. Tapping her cane on the floor, she hobbles a step closer. Reaching out one finger, she strokes the length of my unruly orange hair.

"One strand for each truth," the Verax turns her glowing white eyes on me. Tweed tugs me back in a flash, grabbing the Verax's finger and twisting.

"You will not harm a single hair on Malice's head," he snarls. Cash wraps his arms around my chest to stop me from fighting back.

"Trust us Crazy One. There's no telling what this beast wants to do with your hair. Cast a spell, enslave you to its will." Struggling against Cash, I spy Tweed twisting the Verax's finger too far, cracking the bone in multiple places. She screams at a decibel I can't register. Finally, I manage to tear myself away from Cash's hold, pushing my way between her and Tweed.

"That's enough," I scowl, pushing Tweed's chest away. The Verax shuffles into my back, hiding from the twin's narrowed gazes to whisper her intentions in my ear.

"I just want to be pretty," her voice creaks. I may not know her well, and the only other time I met her, she did try to kill me, but I also know the Verax hasn't been shown kindness. I can sense her loneliness as bitterly as if it were my own.

Pulling my hair over my shoulder, I straighten it as best I can towards my hip. Taking her undamaged fingers in my hand, I flatten the claws into a blade and in a blur of movement, before the twins can tell me otherwise, I slice them through my matted locks. The Verax's nails cut cleanly, removing a decent five inches of split ends. I've been long overdue for a haircut anyway. Placing the clump of curls into her hand, the Verax makes another high-pitched sound which I believe is a squeal of excitement.

"Now will you give us the answers we need?" I plead. She's a giddy mess of bones at the moment, leaning into the saucepan to judge her reflection. Moving over to sit on her cot, barely an inch of mattress beneath a nest of rags, I beckon the twins to join me. "Verax, we really need to know how to beat Lillianna. You showed me a vision of her before," I push. Cash looks at me intently while Tweed doesn't take his eyes off the creature. "Can you show me anything of use?"

"You already have all of the prophecies you need," the Verax clicks her tongue.

"Yeah, yeah. I've heard the riddles," I lean back on my elbows and sigh. "'*One is your destiny, the other your demise. Revive the world that once was, before twin blood moons rise.*' But I refuse to choose between the Tweedles, so give me a new prophecy." I cross my legs. Cash's frown deepens, and the

Verax laughs. A scraped crackle seeping directly from her chest. "What's so funny?"

"I wasn't speaking to you. Our dear Knave has a prophecy of his own to decide upon." She doesn't turn to face us, carefully extracting my hair strand by strand to place upon her head with exact precision. When she speaks again, her voice is distant and hollow.

*'This world hangs on a precipice, the outcome still unknown.*
*The Knave is the deciding factor on what happens to your home.*
*Should he choose correctly, no more blood needs to be shed.*
*A soul intended to be a pair will fuse to the one he weds.'*

"That has nothing to do with Lillianna," Tweed grinds out. "I'll marry Malice once there's a world left to promise her." My focus drops to the floor, the room suddenly feeling much smaller. Tweed spoke without a trickle of indecision. His love wraps around my soul in a dance as old as time. The Verax turns slowly, the hairs she's used worming their way into her skull. Once embedded, more begin to grow. I push to my feet, brushing off Cash's hands when he tries to hold me back.

"In the face of destinies and demises," I whisper, "What happens to Cash?" I know he'll have heard me anyway, but I can't face to speak the words too loud. For my prophecy to coincide with Tweed's, there's no room for a third. I made a promise so long ago, a childish idea that I would never come between them. If saving Wonderlust comes at the price of saying goodbye to Cash forever, then I'm fighting a losing battle against my heart. The Verax leans forward, her mouth wet beside my ear as she matches the volume of my whisper.

"You assume the Tweedle Boys are the only twins in Wonderlust." I gasp, my eyes wide in my head. Two firm chests are bumping against my shoulders in the next second.

"Who are the other twins?!" Cash asks, his hand wrapping around my arm and squeezing tight. The Verax smiles with all of her teeth, the cane extending from her arm.

"Let me show you." Producing the glowing orb in her palm, she strokes it twice for the images inside to come to life. The same as before, I see that young girl gripping the bars, her huge golden eyes pleading to be saved. Staring closer, smoke coils around my body and drags me inward. Cash clings on but there's no stopping the force which whips me into the vision. Into Lillianna's past.

# CHAPTER 36

I stumble forward, transported into the memory of a world consumed by darkness. Shadows creep like tendrils over stone walls, devouring the light and choking the life out of the dungeon. Lillianna is kneeling on the cold, damp ground, her hands shackled to the cage surrounding her. A once beautiful dress clinging to her body is torn and stained with dirt.

She looks up as a pair of guards approach her, their swords unsheathed. One of them swings his blade at the bars, the clang of metal on diamond reverberating through the underground chamber. The other charges forward, intent on doing the same, but the small child raises her hand, creating a burst of energy which knocks him out cold. She turns her attention to the first guard who's now snarling, the grip on his sword tight.

"I have no quarrel with you," Lillianna says in a voice far too confident for a trapped child. "I beg you to let me go."

The guard snarls at her, his sword glinting menacingly under the dim light. "You're a witch! You're responsible for this darkness that's taken over our land."

"I didn't mean to, I promise!" she continues to fight a losing battle. "I can't control the magic when I'm upset."

"You almost killed the princess. Luckily, she remembers nothing. One less person to mourn you." The guard reaches for a handle on the outside of the giant cage, using a rigged mechanism to tighten Lillianna's chains. Her arms stretch to the sides, a scream leaving her. She's so incredibly small, not much more than eight years old.

"That's enough," a deep rumble comes from behind. A pompous woman walks through my mirage, her fur cloak lined with hearts. A tiny crown sits upon her black updo, the leather heart-shaped flogger in her hand making me shudder with recognition. The original Queen of Hearts. "You have a chance to fix the harm you have caused, Lillianna." Dropping the chains, Lillianna hits the ground hard and when her tear-stricken face looks up, she seems to be staring directly at me.

The vision fades in a wisp of smoke, fast forwarding to Lillianna being taken away in a carriage, her small fist pounding on the glass, her hoarse voice screaming for Arabelle. The next, she's deposited on the doorstep of a cottage in the woods as the carriage speeds away. A man opens the door, his fingerless gloves stroking the hair from her face. Hatter.

The visions blur and appear, coming in fast flashes my eyes struggle to track. "You must control the chaos," Hatter urges of an older Lillianna. Beneath the forest's canopy, her thin arms shake under the weight of a black mass between her hands. Just as she manages to curve it into a ball, Hatter's head whips around. I follow his eyeline to see a small blonde girl in a blue dress wandering between the trunks. His smile grows while my chest tightens.

*'You took so long to get here, Malice, that he tried replacing you with another. But finally, you arrived. Our land was to be saved the turmoil of being Hatter-less.'*

Arabelle's words filter through the woodlands on a breeze. I watch the horror fill Lillianna's face, the black mass in her hands becoming volatile. Losing control, she tries to shake it out of existence, and fails. Shooting through the trees, the mass explodes, creating a slice in the air. Barely visible through the slit, on the other side of the portal she unknowingly created, is my family's estate. Then she runs.

I take chase, refusing to lose her. Through time and space, I follow Lillianna from autumn to winter, all the way to the gates of Spade Castle. Her frozen, dying body is picked up by a guard and presented to a King with the head of a bull. I don't need to watch the rest. I feel the burn of her anger as if it were my own. Rejection slithers through my soul, and amongst it all, an unspoken vow for revenge.

The next and final I see Lillianna, she's a fully grown woman. In a gown of jewels and splendor, at the head of a fine dining table. The King of

Spades asks for her to join him beside the fireplace, to address their guests with the news of their marriage.

A flicker of fierce determination crosses her face as she rises to her feet, gold eyes blazing with newfound strength. Her smile is made of steel, her raven hair whipping around her face as she quietly chants an incantation. No one seems to notice as the flames dance around her, nor how she remains untouched by their scorching heat. The shadows of the illusion recede, as if in awe of her power.

I know now, her plan was always to return me to Wonderlust. To use the Hatter's heart she was supposed to have possessed, and rule the realm which turned their back on her. Her goal is revenge, her motivation is abandonment. And I sympathize with her.

"There's an imbalance of chaos in this realm," the Verax whispers, bringing me back to the present. "When the time comes, you'll know what to do. Everyone has their role, and you're playing your part perfectly." I blink, clearing my vision. Both Tweedles are gripping me hard now, trying to shake me back to the present. My head flops lazily, the Verax's smile wide and all-knowing.

"Lillianna is the daughter of the Red Queen. Arabelle's twin." I murmur. The twins halt their assault, hugging me to them.

"Are you sure?" Tweed asks while Cash tuts.

"It doesn't matter. Are you okay, Crazy One?" I nod weakly with absolutely no conviction. My mind is still reeling from the memories of Lillianna's past, of the darkness that consumes her, and the power she possesses. My heart goes out to her, to the pain and rejection which drove her down the path of vengeance and destruction. And yet, I cannot forgive the harm she's caused, the lives she's taken. Color me a hypocrite, but I kill those who have done me wrong. Lillianna kills for personal gain, to fuel her desire for immortality.

"We need to find her," I say, my voice barely above a whisper. "Before she can hurt anyone else who doesn't deserve it." Cash nods in agreement, his grip on my waist tight.

"Where do we start?"

"The cottage in the woods," I say without hesitation. "That's where Hatter took her in." The Verax smiles wryly as she hands me the glowing orb.

"Take it. It will guide your way." Freeing myself of the twin's arms, I step into the Verax's elongated body. Stroking the thick locks of auburn which have now grown past her bony shoulders, I smile.

“Once we’ve won this war, I’ll have Hatter believe you into any version of yourself you’d like. But until then, know that true beauty starts from within.” I touch the empty cavity of her chest, my fingers becoming sticky. “So beautiful,” I nod through tears of ick.

“Don’t,” she smirks knowingly. “That’s a job for the next Mal Hatter.”

“The next?” I frown as I’m guided away from the Verax's lair, clutching the orb tightly between my hands. One step out of the door, a chest collides with my back, arms winding around my middle.

“Thank you,” Cash places a kiss on my cheek. I nuzzle his neck long enough for Stan to abandon ship, flying into Tweed’s offered hand. The pair seem to smirk at us as they pass, best buddies all of a sudden.

“Make it quick,” Tweed mutters, disappearing down the tunnel. Cash doesn’t hesitate, dipping me low to consume me in a heated kiss I might never recover from. Whatever I’m being thanked for, I can’t wait to see what he does when I save the entire realm.

# CHAPTER 37

The sun struggles to shine through thick swirling clouds as we make our way through the abandoned streets of Wonderlust. Keeping a hand firmly wrapped around Malice's braces, I use her confidence to bolster myself. She tugs against my hold, tempted to bolt away and take care of Lillianna herself. Over my dead body.

From shadowed alleys and cracked windows, I feel the heat of eyes on me. Some stare in awe, most in fear of the assassin they believe me to be. *Lillianna's bitch.* A title I'll hold until this generation dies out and the next finds something better to talk about. I push onwards, keeping my sights set on our destination.

Reaching the edge of town and entering the woods beyond, the air becomes cooler. Trees tower above us, their branches blocking out most of the remaining light as Malice follows the orb's light deeper into the forest. The ground beneath my boots is soft and damp with fallen leaves, but I hardly notice as my mind races with thoughts of Lillianna. Malice saw her past, uncovered her secrets, and hasn't said much since. I wish I knew what she was thinking.

We walk until the woods become darker than I ever remember them being. Two moons rise high in the sky, casting an eerie red hue over everything they touch. Unease creeps through my soul, a similar tentativeness emanating from Tweed. He's said nothing since leaving the Verax's lair, his jaw pulsing from being tensed. We both feel it; the intense need to protect what's ours. We lost Malice once, it won't be happening again.

We mimic her every step, our senses on high alert. I shift my focus to her curves, the natural sway of her step. Even in male clothing, Malice is somehow cinched in all the right places, the slacks pulled tight around her ass. Bright orange locks, which have curled at the ends, fall halfway down her back. Soon, so damn soon, I'm going to barricade the three of us in the nearest room and nothing will distract me from drawing out the highest form of Malice's pleasure. I can visualize it now, smell how sweet she'll be, taste her on the end of my tongue.

Suddenly, the orb bursts with light, illuminating a clearing around us. Malice stops in her tracks, peering at the forest wall which seems to have moved into a circle around us. Wind stirs through the trunks, dragging leaves with it as it blows amongst the tall trees. A gray, smokeless haze fills the space as the tainted reddish moonlight hovers over the dead grass like a rancid blanket. The ground is worn smooth, except for a single sapling growing at an angle from the soil.

"What the—"

"Shh," Malice urges, outstretching her hand. Beneath her fingers, a wooden plank appears. "The Hatter's House responds to those most in need."

"Hmmm," Tweed's chest rumbles. Slipping an arm around Malice's waist, she surprisingly lets him lead her a step back. Positioning himself between her and the wall, Tweed raises a fist and bangs once against the wood. The cloak of magic, shielding the cottage from view, suddenly shatters. Malice gasps, stepping back into my protective embrace. This isn't the Hatter's cottage we once knew.

Rotten from the wood itself, blackened with fungus, the shingles old and crumbling, the door torn clean off and lying flat upon the clearing floor. The cottage's roof has sagged, its supports long since worn away by the elements. Peeling paint reveals pale, splintered wooden planks underneath. The shutters hang by a single hinge, their frames black and decayed.

The black-haired woman stands on the threshold, her posture bored yet seductive. Her pale skin is blemish free, her body the perfect mix of muscle and curves. She seemed perfect to me once, but not even the distinct call of her blood can tempt me now. Lillianna stands tall and proud, her black dress flowing behind her like a dark river. Her eyes lock onto mine, a twisted smile playing at her lips.

"I knew you'd come," she says, her voice echoing through the trees. My grip tightens around Malice. Tweed's muscles tense, his shoulders set firm against the woman threatening to take everything we've fought so long to preserve. In our own, separate ways, Tweed and I only wanted a place to call home. Lillianna promised to give me a purpose, but I found it within Malice. A reason to exist.

"You're delusional if you think we'll let you win this war," Tweed speaks, his voice low and dangerous.

Lillianna's smile widens at the challenge. "I already have won, dear Knave. This realm is mine, and there's nothing you can do to stop me."

That is where she is wrong. I lunge forward first, my speed catching her off guard. Leveling a blow to her sternum, Lillianna doesn't budge an inch. I do it again and again, my hand beginning to throb before she shows even a trace of pain. Withdrawing twin blades from her belt, Tweed is by my side in a flash. Not to fight her though, but to drag me a step backwards. Lillianna's smile widens.

Glinting in the moonlight, the small diamond daggers cut through the air as she moves with increased speed. I lurch back, the dagger dangerously close to my half-a-heart, when Lillianna kicks my gut. I fly backward, slamming into the ground. Make that increased strength too. I'm on my feet, rushing for her once more. Blow after blow, Lillianna doesn't falter as anticipated. She moves across the clearing with untraceable speed,the grace of a trained warrior. Fists swinging, fangs on full show, Tweed and I attack from both sides, trying to knock her off balance at least. Lillianna's stance remains set, her arms blocking with ease. We're evenly matched, every move being met by an equally strong countermove. Tweed ducks, attempting to dislodge the dagger when Lillianna grins, slicing it across her own wrist. My senses slam to the forefront, a gasp torn from my throat as I fall to my knees.

But it's not blood that flows from the wound. Thick, blackened liquid pools at her feet, sending tendrils of smoke into the air. The smell of sulfur and decay permeates my nostrils. Lillianna laughs, a twisted sound that sends shivers down my spine.

"Did you really think you could defeat me with brute strength alone?" she sneers. "I have powers beyond your comprehension. Powers bestowed upon me by those who sacrificed themselves to my cause."

"You make it sound like they had a choice," I snarl through the intense tingling pulsing through my gums. I know, somehow from the base of my very soul, if I were to taste a single drop of Lillianna's blood, there's no coming back. The addictive magic she's used to enslave me to her all these years were merely trial runs for whatever is spilling from her veins now. Tweed, whose face is taut, his muscles trembling from fighting the pull of it too, rushes forward blindly. Lillianna is too quick for him, sidestepping his attack and lashing out with her own blades. One catches Tweed across the cheek, leaving a deep gash that drips with blood.

Dragging myself upright, I circle her, trying to find an opening in her defenses. But every time I try to strike, she counters. It's like trying to fight a shadow. Frustration builds within me, and I can feel myself losing control. The shadows leaking from the Queen of Spades wrap around Tweed across the clearing, holding him out of my range.

"That's enough Tweedles," Malice's voice rings out from behind us. Like a switch being flipped inside of me, I fall back. Malice, the image of calm, soothes me as I step into her side, chest heaving from the anger coursing through my system. Her touch is a balm, setting me enough to see sense.

"What do you want, Lillianna?" I growl, my eyes refusing to leave hers. She chuckles, taking a few steps forward. From where he's tied up by smoke, Tweed sizes up the gap she's left between her and the door. He can sense something in there. Or someone.

"Oh, don't you already know, Cash? I want what's mine. This realm, and all its creatures." She pauses for a moment, her gaze shifting to Malice. "And of course, I want your little toy here. Once I've used the blood moon's power to become a vampire, she'll be the first I drain of blood."

Lifting her arm, Lillianna turns Malice's chin this way and that. Malice doesn't resist, or strike as I have every urge to. My fangs elongate in anger. Nobody touched what is mine without an invitation from her personally. In this instance, I will follow the lead of those I love. Take their cues, for they'll be thinking more logically than I can. "Quite the delicacy," Lillianna purrs. Malice slowly raises her own hand to touch Lillianna's arm.

"I understand your anger, Lillianna. And I sympathize with it." Lillianna's gold eyes flash with surprise. "Let's sit and talk things through. We have the same goal here."

"And that is?" Lillianna raises a brow, flourishing her hand through the air. That black liquid seeps towards her elbow, clearly not having the same effect on Malice. I have to sidestep behind her, inhaling the scent of her hair and neck to steady myself. Malice strokes my thigh as if she's not in a face-off with the Queen of Shadows.

"To see you in your rightful place. On the throne of Heart Kingdom." I straighten, snapping back into the setting. Tweed struggles against the binds holding him in place.

"I'm already one step ahead of you," Lillianna smiles again without a trace of warmth. "Everybody knows, Hatters love tea parties." Holding out a hand, Malice accepts it, walking towards the cottage doorway. She halts before entering.

"The Tweedles wait outside," Malice states, avoiding looking at either of us. I scoff.

"Over my dead fucking body." I growl instantly. Lillianna smirks, her eyes lingering on Tweed.

"That can be arranged. I'm supposed to wait to do this, but alas, everyone has a role to play here tonight." Whistling sharply, the liquid about to drip from her arm to the ground lifts in a river of ink's spill. Curving a path through the air, I don't have time to respond, or run. Splitting in half, the rivers shoot in opposite directions, aiming for Tweed and I.

It hits me first, slamming into my nostrils and seeping through my lips. I try to grab it without success. Leaking down my throat, I can merely whimper, pleading with Malice's widened eyes as the blood overtakes my mind. I straighten, void of all emotion as I walk to Lillianna's side.

Serve. That's what I must do. I was born to serve.

# CHAPTER 38

The Tweedles walk woodenly at my back. By distracting Lillianna, I sought to give them time to escape. Clearly, her blood has an effect on them that I don't understand, but she doesn't miss a trick.

Her laughter is hollow as we stroll arm in arm toward Hatter's elongated kitchen and dining room. A billowing fireplace in the corner does little to warm the frigid atmosphere, reflecting against glass cabinets of tea sets and intricately painted china plates. The dining table is a slab of pine, sanded to smoothness on top and varnished. The edges, though, have been left raw, sticking out towards the guests forcefully seated by smoke tendrils tying them to an assortment of odd chairs.

Between PB and Gryphon, Arabelle is the only one conscious, her red hair a mess around her crown. The heart usually painted over her lips has been smudged, her cheeks stricken with tears. Dr Sqwuakington and White Rabbit are either side of the seat intended for me, their heads hanging forward in what I hope is a peaceful sleep.

My stomach tightens. Sitting, I try to keep my composure. But it's difficult with the Tweedles standing stiffly at my back. They weigh me down with their silence.

The table is set with a mismatched assortment of teacups and saucers, and the smell of freshly brewed tea fills the air. "Please sit," Hatter appears smiling from the kitchen, a tray of sandwiches in his hands. "The tea makes you pee and the jam tarts repair hearts. We have apple strudels to give your poodles and baked Alaskas to help you ejaculate faster. Lillianna, would you please pass the sugar?" I frown at his usually erratic presence, his tattered clothes, and whole-hearted smile. But it's his eyes, consumed corner to corner with blackness which causes my heart to seize.

Tweed leans past me, lifting a cage made of breadsticks upon the table, to place a limp Stan inside with Dormouse. *No.* Lillianna won't take anyone else from me.

Focusing on the raven-haired woman who takes the head of the table, I don't betray any notion that Arabelle's foot has snaked out and entangled with mine. I'll get her out of this, get all of us out of this. Lillianna stretches her neck from side to side, bathing in a red night. Above her, a skylight has been blasted through the thatched roof, giving her full access to the twin moons creeping ever closer.

“Can you feel it, Malice?” she breathes as if she’s being pleasured. I force myself to keep a straight face, though I can feel the bile rising in my throat as I try to ignore the way Hatter's eyes seem to glint with madness in the glow of the moons.

"Feel what?" I ask hoarsely. I don't believe Lillianna is aware of the admissions she gave outside, revealing her motives piece by piece. Despite her enhanced strength, she’s not a vampire yet, nor is she aware I am one. As far as Lillianna is concerned, I’m a Hatter with my heart still intact. All I need is a slither of relevant information to bring her down, and to keep her talking.

"The power," Lillianna purrs, running a finger over the edge of her teacup. "The potential. With each passing moment, I feel more alive than ever before."

I glance at Arabelle, who is staring at Lillianna with a look of disgust mixed with fear. Then my attention is drawn back to Lillianna as she continues to speak, her voice growing more and more frenzied.

"I can see everything," she raves, gesturing wildly around the table. "All the possibilities. All the paths. And they all lead to me." Her smile is stunning, one I'd usually be in awe of. Lowering her golden gaze to me, Lillianna exhales loudly.

"It could be us, you know? We could rule this world, Malice. Become its masters." When I give no inkling I want that, Lillianna sighs. As she talks, I feel the weight of her past bearing down on me. The pain is palpable, and I can't shake off the feeling that she's not just a villain but someone who has been wronged too many times.

"I never wanted to walk this path alone. At one point, I thought Cash would be by side," she reaches out a hand. He's quick to move, taking her offering and placing a kiss on the back of it. "But I knew he'd run back to you. Can't fight fate...usually."

Lillianna lifts her cup, taking a sip to hide her grin. Her cheeks must be aching by now. Arabelle watches on, her voice silenced by the smoke clamped over her mouth, but her eyes say as much.

"You haven't told her yet, have you?" I ask, allowing Hatter to fill up my plate. Lillianna's smile slips.

"What difference would it make?" she nibbles on a miniature victoria sponge cake. Not a bad choice for a last meal. Arabelle's amber eyes sink into mine, her foot stroking my ankle desperately. She's burning for answers, and I'm going to give them to her.

"If you were my twin, I'd want to know before you killed me." There's a moment of silence where neither will look at each other. Arabelle shakes her head, her brows furrowed. "It's true, the Verax showed me. Lillianna couldn't control her powers, so your mother had her tortured and outcast. The Hatter tried to take her in, but it didn't work out."

Placing a hand on Hatter's fingerless glove, I smile at him with the hopes he'll recognize it. His features fall, at war with themselves so I pull him in for an awkward hug. The teapot he was holding sits between us, warming my cold skin.

"Enough," Lillianna slams the table. I pull back, giving Hatter a firm nod.

"Your queen needs serving," I tell him. "You must do what Hatters do best." Hatter nods slowly, his eyes not leaving mine. There's a question in his gaze, so I nod my head towards Lillianna. He seems to understand,

and with a slight bow of his head, he gathers a tray of pastries and moves towards where Lillianna is seated. I watch as he places the tray next to her, pouring her a cup of tea with practiced ease.

"Thank you," Lillianna murmurs, her voice unsure. Hatter nods, pouring a cup for all of the guests at the table. He pulls back, his eyes flickering to me before he turns and walks away. I watch him go, then turn my attention back to Lillianna.

"I'm sorry, for what it's worth." I peer at Stan waking within the cage. His huge eyes blink up at me, nose and whiskers twitching. Stan will see sense in the plan I've just thrown together in my head, even if no one else will forgive me for it. "I didn't know, by coming to Wonderlust, I was causing your downfall. I wanted to be as loved and accepted as the next person. But had I known it was at the cost of another, I'd have stayed away."

Twisting to look back at the Tweedles, neither meet my gaze. Stationary like soldiers, awaiting their next order. In time, I'll relive this moment and weep for the loss of connection I feel. Never again did I think this emptiness would consume my heart, the one they gave to me. "I should have stayed away."

"I wish I could accept your apology," Lillianna gives pause. Swirling a finger around her cup, she chews on the inside of her cheek. "Not everyone can move onto new ventures as easily as you can. There's no redemption for me."

"I understand." Beneath the table, I clamp Arabelle's shaking foot between both of mine. "So, what happens now?" I ask, my voice low.

"Now, we wait," Lillianna looks up to the skylight. She mentioned using the blood moon's powers to become a vampire, then she'll be unstoppable. The two lunar orbs have begun to cross one another. In the space where they overlap, a glimpse of luminescent red shines brightly. We're running out of time.

"A toast then," I raise my cup into the air. Both queens glance at me with varying emotions. "To the new Queen of Wonderlust. May your reign be long and prosperous." Lifting the cup to my lips, I pause just short of drinking, turning a curious look on Lillianna. "Shouldn't your sister enjoy a toast at your expense? What's the point of reigning supreme if not all subjects celebrate your achievement?"

"You're right," Lillianna's face twists in a mixture of pride and amusement. She claps her hands twice and the Tweedles come to life, rounding Arabelle's sides. Cash grabs the shadows, tearing them aside enough for Tweed to force Arabelle's wrist toward her cup. She begs with her Knave to stop, whimpering at the clasp he has on her slender arm. Regardless, Tweed forces her fingers around the cup and guides it towards her lips. I tap Arabelle's foot to bring her attention to me one last time.

"I'm sorry," I say silently. Tipping the tea into my mouth, I force myself to swallow against all instincts to spit it out. Seeping to my stomach, I imagine I have about thirty seconds before it spews out of one of my orifices. Which one is anyone's guess. Lillianna and Arabelle both drink at the same time, their throats bobbing in unison.

For the briefest of seconds, I can see the comparison. The shape of their chins, the slight upturn of their noses. I watch as Tweed withdraws the cup from Arabelle's lips, her tongue snaking out to lick the drop which remains there. A bitter aftertaste drenches my throat. In my head, an invisible clock has begun ticking away, counting down the seconds. I don't have to wait long.

Suddenly, Arabelle's face contorts in pain, and she clutches at her throat. Beneath her hand, her skin becomes tainted with black vines which grow and fester at an alarming rate.

"Why me?" she gasps, struggling to push the words out. Stan slips free of his cage, leaping onto my chest and running upward. He gnaws on the chain at my neck, which now holds an empty vial at the end. Widening her amber eyes, Arabelle collapses onto the ground, writhing in pain as the poison takes hold. Lillianna shoots to her feet.

"What have you done?!" she shrieks. All at once, triggered by Lillianna's panicked state, the other guests wake from their comatosed sleep. The room erupts as those around the table struggle to break free from their bonds while Hatter cackles maniacally in the background. The only ones still under Lillianna's spell, it would seem, are the Tweedles who are currently pinning Gryphon and Dr. Squakington into their seats.

“What the...holy fuck, Malice,” Lillianna scrambles. True fear bleeds into her golden eyes, the strength taken from her as she drops to her knees before her sister.

"For once, I've been listening,” I stand and round the table. “There's an imbalance of chaos, but it's not being caused by me. If I'm not mistaken, the realm began falling apart when Arabelle killed your mother. The Queen of Hearts is supposed to be a heartless psychopath. Arabelle is too valiant, too kind-hearted. You, however," I catch Lillianna's eye. "You're perfect. Let your sister die and take back the role you were born for."

Lillianna's breath hitches in her throat as she stares at me, her hands shaking with the weight of her decision. The chaos in the room has escalated to a deafening level, with screams and crashes reverberating around us. The Tweedles can't remain faithful to Lillianna's charm and fight off a room of crazy at the same time. I feel the tendrils of madness creeping in at the edge of my consciousness, but I push them aside. Hatter or not, this is what I was made for. To revel in the insanity. To create it.

Lillianna's eyes dart back and forth between her sister's convulsing body and the room around us. Most have bolted for the door, although Gryphon has decided to pick a fight with Tweed and is being coached from Dormouse on the table. High above, the moons have almost fully crossed paths, about to eclipse one another. Lillianna sees it too.

Her breaths come in short gasps, her mind racing to a decision. Fear and uncertainty fill her eyes, but also the hunger for power. She has always wanted to be the Queen she felt she was owed. Everything Lillianna has done since her exile has been to prove a point. She'd have ruled Heart Kingdom with the same tenacity as her mother.

"I saw it all," I continue smoothly, bending down to look into her eyes. "I know the revenge you seek, and I'd be a hypocrite to stand in your way."

"But..." she stares down at her sister's paling face. "Without Arabelle to taunt every day," Lillianna whispers, her voice barely audible above the cacophony in the room. "She needs to see. I need her to watch me become everything she is not. That I won in the end."

“Well, it’s up to you,” I shrug, scraping my nails on the wood flooring. “But believe me when I say, winning isn’t half as fulfilling when you’re the only one standing at the top.” The realization dawns on Lillianna’s face. With Arabelle gone, she will have no one to compete with, no one to hold her back. This is her chance to take the throne once and for all. And she doesn't really want it. "It's your poison in her bloodstream. You're the only one who truly knows how to cure it."

Lillianna hesitates only for a moment before nodding resolutely. With a flick of her wrist, she sends a bolt of dark magic into her sister. Arabelle writhes in agony, screaming with a thousand foreign curses, as the magic engulfs her. Creamy skin becomes bathed in darkness, and her eyes roll back into her head as the magic takes hold. Lillianna watches with a mixture of horror and fascination, unsure if she's made the right decision. But it's too late to turn back now. I stand back and watch as the eclipsed moons overhead cast everything in a red glow. Around us, the guests still present have fallen into silence, aside from PB's shudders forcing a snout through his nostril every few seconds.

Streams of shadow fight against the ink spilling through Arabelle's veins, painfully withdrawing every drop through Arabelle's mouth and nose. Twisting in the air, the poison I know all too well recedes into a ball of movement, floating towards Lillianna. She takes it between her palms, closing her eyes to concentrate. The ball of poison becomes slithered with silver, glowing in her hands. It pulsates with Lillianna's heartbeat, reverberating throughout the cottage as Arabelle lays deathly still.

"What are you going to do with it?" I breathe. Lillianna's eyes snap open, filled with the darkness she's sold her soul to. The very essence of who she's become.

"Destroy it," Lillianna states heavily. Throwing her arms upwards on a scream, the darkness in her hands, her body, her being, shoots towards the interlinked moons. The silver tendrils follow behind, trailing like a comet's tail, until it collides with the sky. The force of the impact sends tremors through the entire kingdom, shaking walls and dislodging loose objects from their shelves. The light from the eclipsed moons is snuffed out as the orb of poison breaks through the center of them. I brace myself for the deafening boom which echoes throughout the land, a blinding light settling the war I've become swept up in with a flash of finality.

Tucking my head, two bodies collide with mine, their arms protecting me from the sky which rains upon the cottage roof. I duck my head into the cover my Tweedles provide, gripping their t-shirts to hold them close. At odds with the hammering of our joined hearts, they softly stroke any patch of my skin they can hide, letting me know they're back. Lillianna's hold over them has vanished.

When my vision clears, I see that the moons have been replaced by a single, shining star. Save for broken furniture and scattered debris, the cottage remains to stand around Arabelle's limp body on the floor. I clamber over the floor, shaking her desperately.

"Arabelle? You in there, babe?" I try a little sweet talk. Tweed shifts away from holding me to lift Arabelle's head, checking for any signs of life. His grave expression doesn't shift. The air grows still, filled with the weight of grief settling over us like a thick fog. Lillianna, in a dress now torn and limp, lowers onto her side beside Arabelle's body. Through a lack of energy, she manages to reach out and take Arabelle's hand. I watch as Lillianna's features soften, the ticking of her own heart beating in sync with the sister she disowned until recently. Cash holds me close, as if anticipating the sorrow which is about to take hold.

A sudden gust of wind rushes through the cottage, blowing out all the candles and snuffing out the fire. The wind picks up, howling through the broken windows and tossing anything that isn't secured to the ground. I cling onto Cash, seeking comfort from the storm raging outside and the devastation inside. The wind screams like a wounded animal, carrying with it the stench of destruction. The hairs on the back of my neck stand up as I feel a presence in the room, something dark and malevolent.

Through cracked eyelids, I see Arabelle move. She sits upright, her amber eyes devoid of all emotion. Twisting Lillianna's hand in hers, curiosity flickers over her features, before she acts. In one smooth movement, Arabelle drags Lillianna across her lap and steals the diamond blade from her belt. The wind in the room suddenly stills, freezing everyone in place as Arabelle leans close to Lillianna's ear.

"Malice was right. Heart Kingdom needs a ruthless queen, and it's not you." Lifting the dagger high, no one can stop what's about to come. Not even Tweed, forced to sit back on his heels and watch. "Off with your head," Arabelle brings the blade down through Lillianna's neck in one smooth swoop. Blood splatters all over Arabelle's face and dress as Lillianna's head rolls across the ground. Everyone stares, paralyzed with shock. Arabelle watches with a cold detachment until Lillianna's jerking body falls still, her eyes staring lifelessly at the ceiling. The storm that so recently plagued us wilts away, allowing an unusually calm night to fall beyond the broken glass.

Arabelle stands, her gaze still vacant as she looks at the scattered debris around her. I try to scramble up also, but Cash holds me back.

"Hold on, Crazy One. I can't tell which way this is going to go." I don't fight too hard, holding onto Cash's arm around my front. His chest is a firm presence at my back, a solid grip on the world which once again has been turned on its head.

"I do not wish to execute anyone else tonight," Arabelle states coldly. "Knave," she peers to the side. Tweed rushes to her side. "I would like to thank you for your service. You are hereby pardoned from your duty."

"I...but...what am I supposed to do with myself?" Tweed asks, his eyes dancing with confusion. Arabelle simply reaches out and takes the diamond dagger he's holding, sheathing it in her belt.

"This blade will do better in the hands of someone else. You are free to go." She turns away without another word, heading towards the door. This time, Cash lets me break free of his hold, the pair of us rushing to stop Tweed from chasing after his queen.

"It's okay," I soothe, stroking his forearm. "Let her go. She needs to get back to the path she was always supposed to walk." Slightly dazed and still lost as fuck, Tweed lets Cash tug him into the living area which is somehow untouched. Hatter is sitting in his armchair, teacup in hand and little finger sticking out. Gryphon, PB, and Sqwuakington take their leave, flocking from the house and slamming the door behind them.

"Did you say something?" Hatter twists, his oddly colored eyes drifting in different directions. My heart swells. This is what it is to be a Hatter; to find the calm in the storm, the humor in the chaos. Perhaps, with my original heart or not, a part of me will always be a Hatter in that aspect.

"Nothing," I smile. "Everything will soon be as it was, and everything that is not won't be anymore."

"Sounds awfully boring," Hatter whistles between his teeth. Tweed quietly takes a seat across the room as I move to stand beside the man I proudly call my father. We both look out into the night, watching Arabelle disappear into the darkness. The air is heavy, broken only by the sound of the storm restarting in the distance. Bending, I wrap my arms around Hatter's neck.

"I'm sorry I couldn't be the Mal Hatter you were expecting." I whisper for his ears only. Of all the things I wanted to achieve when returning to Wonderlust, appeasing Hatter was at the top of the list. He creates a strange, mysterious giggle, as if he's trying to hold a secret inside.

“Not to worry. The next will arrive sooner or later.” I frown, my mind reeling as Cash intervenes.

"What do we do now?" He asks the question on everyone's mind. I settle into the whistful silence, realizing the opportunity we've all been gifted. A fresh start, a new beginning where the rules of our past don't appear. Stan reads my mind, leaping from my hair and landing on Hatter's hat. I give him a one finger high-five and kiss Hatter's cheek goodbye.

"Now," I raise a brow at both Tweedles. “I believe you owe me a dance." Tweed remains lost in his trance, while Cash's face lights up.

"As you wish, Crazy One," he grins devilishly. Holding out his hand, I move across the room to take it when my stomach rolls. Hot, burning liquid bubbles up my esophagus. Twisting towards the fireplace, I expel the tea which had settled in my system, a disgusting aftertaste of acidic caffeine lining my throat. Well, there it is.

# CHAPTER 39

Malice's laughter trickles through the club, a warming undertone to the music pumping from hidden speakers. Cash rolls his topless body along the length of hers, using his legs to flip Malice across the stage. Sitting with my back to the mass of empty tables, I perch on a bar stool, drinking a cold glass of blood. I offered to give them privacy, but where there's Malice's lust involved, I can't go too far. Now, whenever the pair flop into view in the bar's reflective mirror, either one has one less item of clothing.

Cash started the night in a small pair of leather pants and a tank top, which have now been ripped away to leave him in only black briefs. On his thigh, the tattoo of Malice has been edited for her to break free of the glass bottle she was previously trapped in, shards of glass shattering in all directions. On her face, a look of determination beams out, her hip cocked and arms crossed.

Her giggle cuts through me. In the reflection, Cash's abs ripple with each move, his pale skin highlighted by bright stage lights. He moves around Malice like an exotic animal and she's the prey; strategically moving closer for moments of tenderness, before flipping her over and grinding against her ass. I don't see the appeal myself, but Malice's desire is strong enough for me to smell. Damn, it's sweet as hell.

Cursing myself, I turn in my seat, my back leaning against the bar. Orange hair pools across the glittery stage, a baggy white shirt covering Malice's arched body. Stretching her arms above her head, Cash is given the green light to trail his fingers across her buttons, before ripping them open with a growl which sends Malice into fits of laughter. The large white shirt slides around her torso, her lithe muscles glinting against the shine of the stripper pole by her side.

Malice is here for it too, dancing up against Cash until neither one can deny their urges anymore. Shifting onto all fours, Cash repeats trails of kisses across her back, adding fuel to the inner fire he's been stoking since we arrived back at Club Dee's. Her hair cascades over her shoulders, light reddish hues catching glimpses from every light source inside this sensual playground we've entered.

As the music begins to fade, Cash takes Malice by the hand and pulls her towards him. They share a heated gaze, the electricity between them palpable from across the room. With a quick flick of his wrist, Cash removes his last piece of clothing, leaving him completely naked before Malice. She gasps at the sight of him, her eyes roaming over every inch of his toned body. Jealousy propels me forward.

Finishing my drink while storming forward, I toss the empty glass back over my shoulder and catch a glimpse of myself in the mirror behind the bar. My own tattoos peek out from under my shirt sleeves, reminding me that I'm just as much of an outcast as these two. No longer a Knave, or anyone of importance, except to the two making googly eyes on that stage. With them, I belong.

Spotting my approach, Cash picks Malice up with a wicked grin and tosses her over his shoulder. She squeals in delight as he carries her offstage and towards the private rooms in the back of the club. I follow closely behind, refusing to let Cash have all of the fun.

The private rooms are dimly lit, with purple velvet lining the walls. A large bed dominates the center of the room, draped in silky black sheets. As Cash lays Malice down on the bed, my eyes roam over her body in admiration. I've always found her alluring, with her fiery personality and bold confidence. I can feel the desire radiating off of them as they kiss passionately, their tongues exploring each other's mouths.

"Come here," Malice whispers huskily, reaching out a hand for me while running the other down Cash's chest. Without hesitation, I climb onto the bed and lie next to her. My hands wander over her body, feeling the smoothness of her skin and tracing the curves of her hips. Cash's hands join mine, his fingers trailing over her brasserie while his lips move to her neck.

Watching my twin pleasure my girl shouldn't fill me with satisfaction. Yet, it's like watching the two sides of my soul come together in complete unity. One heart beats between us, one desire to feel alive.

Malice grabs my face and pulls me into a deep kiss. I taste Cash on her lips, the remnants of his blood entwined with her own. While I can't drink from Cash, our blood markers being too similar, Malice has never been one to conform. Her blood is tantalizing, like sparks of fire dancing along my tongue as I lick her split lip.

Sensing my desperation for more, Malice twists my head aside and offers the expanse of her neck. I'm not man or monster enough to resist. My fangs have already elongated as I clamp down on her neck. The taste of her blood fills my mouth, laced with layers of lust and a tenacity only she can provide. I drink her essence deeply, feeding on her life and craving more. I've never craved quite like this before, but like the force of a woman Malice is, she's addictive.

She pulls away from me too soon, a smirk on her lips as she tugs Cash down to meet her lips in a kiss. Watching them connect stirs that lust inside of me with an emerald flame which burns within my eyes. Taking turns, we bite, lick and suck on her neck, her collarbone, her jaw until Malice is gasping for air and grappling for us to touch her.

"I've missed fucking you both," she says breathlessly, reaching for the waistband of my pants. With nimble fingers, she pops the button and tugs them over her hips. My t-shirt goes next. Her hungry eyes travel up and down my body before settling on one of the many scars from my childhood, and the huge explosive scar over my heart. "I hope it was worth it," Malice mutters under her breath.

"What, my love?" I pry, lifting her fingers away from my hip and pressing them to my lips.

"The sacrifices we've made to get to this point." Malice's crystal blue eyes blink with a moment of clarity which takes my breath away. Cash pushes himself up on his elbow, gently turning Malice's face to look at him.

"That's up to us, beautiful. We have to make the hardships worth it, and we've got all of eternity to do it." Her smile is everything, radiating joy and love I could have only wished to feel one day.

Malice sits up, turning to face me while straddling my lap. Her grin turns wicked, slowly making its way down my body before resting between my thighs. My dick jolts beneath the boxers I'm still wearing.

"If you don't mind Cash, I think your brother is in desperate need of cheering up," Malice quirks a brow. She doesn't wait for Cash's reply, shimmying down to kneel between my legs and spring my cock free.

Her soft hand wraps around my shaft, stroking a strangled groan out of me. Malice smirks, running her tongue over the head of my dick, holding it tightly in her fist. My dick throbs in her palm, a bead of precum pooling at the tip. Malice flicks her tongue to catch it. My eyes roll back.

She licks me again, dragging her tongue down my shaft with painful slowness. My breathing hitches as she traces a slow line to the base, her nails drawing patterns over my inner thighs and balls. I'm practically shaking, a thousand images flashing behind my eyelids of how I'm going to make her scream my name.

"I swear, if my dick isn't touching the back of your throat in the next five seconds," I groan, yanking her head up by her hair, "I'm flipping you over and burying it in your sweet cunt."

"Promises, promises," Malice purrs. Liquid fire flows underneath my skin, a jolt of raw pleasure coursing through me as her lips wrap around the head of my cock. Her mouth stretches wide over my dick, soft lips opening to take me deeper into her mouth. I buck my hips wildly, fighting off the urge to cum immediately. Holding me deep in her throat, one delicate hand wrapped around my base, I'm lost in the sensations of it all. Warmth spreads through my deadened body, the thrill of adrenaline racing along my spine. My heart, no longer weighing heavily in my chest, thumps wildly and painfully against my ribs. Silky hair tickles my thighs as I reach down, pulling Malice off my cock.

"Get on your back," I sit upright to growl, my voice thick. Moving at an untraceable speed, Malice twists out of my hold and races up my body. Slamming her hand around my throat, she snarls in my face.

"Get on *your* fucking back," Malice hisses. The glint of her sharpened fangs makes my dick jolt again. I lower down, hands raised in defeat. Inside, I'm beaming with love. Malice can dominate whenever, and wherever she likes. I'm hers in every way possible.

Cash intervenes to grab my ankles, dragging me to the edge of the mattress. I kick him away, previously having warned him not to interact with me when we're pleasuring Malice. I may not mind sharing her happiness, since keeping her placated on my own would be a daily mission, but I don't need the reminder he's in the room.

Malice ignores our rivalry, straddling my waist and lowering herself onto my shaft. She's so wet with barely any foreplay, aroused by the tight hold she maintains around my neck. I lean up enough to grab her ass, pulling Malice down onto me. Grunting in pleasure as she squeezes her thighs, bottoming out onto my hips, we both become hollowed eyed and lost to one another's will. Malice gasps as I buck my hips, needing to feel every inch of myself buried deep inside her.

Moving her hips in a rocking motion, my hands roam over Malice's waist and upwards towards her ample breasts. She leans down, allowing me to latch onto her nipples. My teeth elongate with the urge to bite, but with enough willpower, I suck the pebbled bud gently. The sensation sends shivers down Malice's spine. Lost in unison with each other, we unfortunately stir the primal instinct within Cash.

"Okay, that's enough one-on-one time. It's my turn." The harsh sound of a spank penetrates the air, and Malice hisses against my ear. Nudging my feet to spread wider, Cash doesn't wait for an invitation. No need for pleasantries either, apparently. "Oh, Malice. I know how long your greedy pussy has been hungry for both of us at once."

The invasion of his cock entering Malice alongside mine has us all seeing stars. There should never come a time when one feels his own twin's dick piercings, but I can't bring myself to push him out. And Malice wouldn't let me. She becomes impossibly tight, so blindingly delicious that I barely register Cash slowly pumping his hips in and out. Malice's mouth falls open, letting a shocked, breathy moan escape her. I kiss her, praising how beautifully she takes our combined girth. Swiping away the orange hair plastered to her face, Malice's blue eyes roll to the back of her head. I press her forehead to mine, holding her hips in place and allowing Cash to take over.

"That's it, Crazy One. Be a good girl and stay still. I'll make it hurt so good." Cash works up his pace, waiting for Malice to adjust. Then, all bets are off. Thrusting wildly and gripping her ass in a bruising hold, Malice rocks over me with a flurry of screams leaving her. I jerk my hips from underneath, finding the rhythm we all move to. Each movement of my cock being fully sheathed inside of her brings me closer to ecstasy. Sweet rapture spreads between the three of us, the promise of bliss awaiting as Malice's tight walls begin to flutter.

Collapsing against my chest, held in place by my arms, the orgasm hits her hard. Malice's eyes roll to the back of her head and her mouth hangs open in a silent scream. Her hips jerk and writhe, spasming violently as her core quakes with pleasure. Her body is alight with energy, her movements captivating. Juices cascade onto my shaft and along Cash's dick. He's only spurred on further, pumping into her with reckless abandon.

I can't take my eyes off her. Tightly clenching our cocks, she's the image of desire, her skin tinting with a pinkened flush. Pleasure radiates outward from her core, pulsating around me like an electric current. Tremors run through her body as she succumbs to us, her muscles quivering. I could watch her like this forever, but Cash has other plans.

"Switch with me brother," he pulls out quickly enough to make both Malice and I gasp. "I want to watch the tears stream from Malice's eyes while she chokes on my cum." Malice's muscles tense and eyes widen. Even she can't deny the effect Cash's dominating is having. Her cheeks flush and lips part as her body shakes with pleasure as I withdraw my cock more slowly. Lifting Malice, I maneuver us so she is on all fours on the bed, facing the door. Cash remains by my side, stroking the red handprint on her ass. My eyes trail his fingers, rubbing circles through her sensitized pussy and drawing her juices upwards.

"Take her here, brother," he mutters quietly, pushing two slickened fingers into her tiny ass. Malice stiffens, grabbing a pillow to cry into. Cash doesn't relent, pumping his fingers in a steady rhythm until Malice's arched back relaxes and her cries become desperate moans.

Winking at me, Cash pulls out, excusing himself to the bathroom briefly. I'm left staring at Malice, face down patiently waiting for more and my pulsating cock soaked in her cum. Once upon a time, there wouldn't have been any pause. But Malice isn't just any girl to be fucked and forgotten. She's the love of my life, the one my half-a-heart beats for.

Smoothing my hands over her creamy ass, I nudge the head of my dick against her back entrance. Malice nods her head to my silent question, and I push my hips forward. It's a thick fit, still just as tight as I imagined. Her moans become breathy and desperate. Clenching the pillow, her body yields to me, loving and hating every inch of cock slowly entering her.

Grabbing her by the elbows, I drag Malice upright and slide my tongue along the defined curve of her shoulder blades. Malice groans, clenching around my cock as I bottom out inside her ass. Grunting as I begin thrusting at an agonizingly slow pace, Malice keens loudly. Reaching her neck with my tongue, my fangs grip firmly into soft flesh and hold her in place.

"Don't you dare come," I growl just before sinking them into her. The taste of blood in my mouth is like a drug, blocking out all sound until Malice's screams are no more than an indiscernible whisper. The feel of her fresh liquid coursing through my veins is unlike anything I had ever experienced before, filling every cell in my body which suddenly becomes charged with electricity, causing me to shudder with pleasure.

Adrenaline rushes through each limb. I'm no longer tentative or aware of her pain threshold. The monster within me takes control, fucking Malice as if she's an object solely created for my pleasure. My own cock is being strangled within the vice grip of her ass, contracting and pulsing around me in response to each delicious pump of my hips.

We stay that way for what feels like hours. Malice screaming one minute and twisting, trying to bite me back the next, until she's silent apart from jagged gasps for air. My breaths are stuttering and irregular by the time Cash returns, his brow raised and smirk impressed. I release Malice, letting her flop forward as I grip her hips. Cash takes his position on the other side of the bed.

"Ready for me baby?" he grins, sliding a hand beneath Malice's jaw. She groans her approval, spurring me on. I watch Cash guide her mouth onto his dick, gently easing the length all the way into her throat. "All of it, Malice," he grunts. Nodding, she takes in more and more of Cash's size until he clenches her hair in his fists and begins the slick thrusts into her mouth. She makes a choked sound which will be imprinted in my mind forever.

I still, fully sheathed, just feeling her in his moment. Her skin is incredibly smooth, a canvas to be inked and marked. She writhes and bucks against me, encouraging me to take what she's offering. All of her, body and soul. Reaching around, I rub Malice's clit in quick circles, mesmerized by the show before me. Cash fucks her mouth hard, leaving us all on the brink of ecstasy. Her muffled moans quicken as she tumbles down the rabbit hole of her climax once more. Her full-body trembling is both intense and beautiful, radiating outward from her core, claiming her entirely.

The orgasm spreads through Malice like a wave of electricity, every nerve in her being ignited with bliss. Her muscles spasm and twinge as the sensation builds, becoming overwhelming until it explodes out of her in a blinding rush of pleasure. Each pulse of her walls brings me to the edge of my own release.

Leaning over her and grabbing one of Malice's hands in a tight grip, I bring our writhing fingers together. Grinning at the touch, Cash picks up the pace, determined to finish at the same time. I dig my nails into the fleshy muscles in her ass, causing her to shiver deliciously. Cash and I catch our heated gazes over Malice's back, silently communicating. I bite my cheek and push into Malice's ass until my balls slap against her pussy, falling over the edge and spiraling. I empty myself into her, filling Malice in an intense eruption, white-hot and scalding. Malice screams around Cash's cock as she comes again and again, every muscle in her body tense and shaking.

"That's it, brother," Cash hisses, following straight after. Cum bursts from him and into Malice, the force of it rocking her back onto my jolting cock still seeping inside of her. He buries himself inside her mouth, groaning uncontrollably. Releasing my grip on her ass, I stroke Malice's pussy, wetness dripping down her legs. She screams into Cash, her cunt trembling with pleasure. My cock twitches erratically, the throb painfully intense.

Time stands still as we float above the room in endless ecstasy. Three thundering hearts beat together, three bodies becoming one entity. As soon as the hits begin to dwindle, I let go of Malice's pussy, withdrawing and sinking down onto the bed beside her. Malice's body quivers, her eyes wide and muscles tense. Her skin is flushed with arousal and sweat, pleasure radiating off of her in waves. Cash joins her other side, a tangle of limbs and satisfied urges drifting between us.

"She did you a favor, you know," Malice breathes, staring at the ceiling. I roll onto my side.

"Who?" I frown.

"Arabelle," Malice turns her head to look at me. Cash chuckles while I groan. I'd really rather not be thinking of Arabelle while my dick is still weeping and hard. Malice doesn't care though. "You may not see it yet, but she did you a huge favor. Her last act as the sister figure you knew, before she had to become like her mother, was to set you free."

I blink several times, hit with reality so soon after escaping it. Malice smiles knowingly, winding her arms around my neck and pulling me to rest my head on her chest. I can't deny, Arabelle's dismissal cut me deeply, but perhaps I have been seeing things from the wrong perspective. The Verax warned we all must play the roles we were born into, and truth be told, I wouldn't have wanted to stand by Arabelle while she accepted bitterness into her heart. Her last kindness was to set me free.

"You knew what Arabelle had to become, yet you tricked Lillianna into saving her anyway," I mutter. Malice goes deathly still beneath me. Raising my head, I narrow my eyes as she does everything in her power not to look at me. "You...you did know Lillianna would save her, right?" Malice looks to Cash for backup, which she doesn't find. "Malice?"

"Well, that was some good foreplay. Shall we get onto the real fucking now?" she deflects, running her fingers through my hair. Cash grins widely.

"I'm game." He grabs her face, dragging her in for a passionate kiss. My jaw is slack, disbelief coursing through me. Malice's tongue slips into Cash's mouth, their moaning over exaggerated. I sigh, shaking my nod as a smirk takes root on my face. I suppose I can't be mad about what ifs, when I knowingly fell in love with a woman who exudes chaos. Cash grabs Malice's breast beside my face, drawing a giggle from her at my expense. Well, if that's how she wants to play this, let the real fucking start indeed.

# EPILOGUE

One Year Later

An explosion far overhead is peppered with the crackle of glitter falling towards the earth. No one can see the fireworks in broad daylight, but

White Rabbit is living his best life sparking the fuses. Walking through a balloon arch, I exhale loudly, a huge smile growing on my face.

"What's wrong? You hate it, I knew she would." Tweed pushes his twin's arm. Cash laughs at him.

"Relax, brother. That was a happy sigh." Cash leans into my side, tucking my hair behind my ear to whisper, "Right?" I laugh, pulling the pair into the open field.

"Definitely a happy sigh," I grin. Leaning into his kiss on my cheek, a rush of movement whips in front of me. A man appears, dressed as a sad clown. Huge teardrops are painted into his cartoon style makeup, at complete odds with the wink he gives.

"Welcome, Malice," he hands me a bouquet of oversized daisies. "Happy Shadow Slayer day." I thank him with a curtsy, smelling the pungent perfume infused into the flowers. For better or worse, we all became rather famous after 'Shadow Slayer Day' a year ago–aka, the death of Lillianna.

Tales of all sizes spread through the land at an unstoppable rate, none of which painted the Tweedles and I in a positive light. Only those who were there, like this vampire who saw us in the dungeons, can attest to what's true. He lingers for a moment more, looking over the cute little dress Hatter made for me. Cash growls a warning, Tweed steps forward to attack the guy but he zooms away just in time. I laugh. No one can blame him.

Once upon a time, I would have refused to ever wear this shade of powdered blue again, but I can't deny the gift is beautiful. The sweetheart neckline is streamed with black lace, a soft touch to the tight corset at my waist. In true Hatter fashion, aside from my huge afro of orange curls, I've donned fingerless, white gloves and pulled my stockings up high. Around the hem of the skirt, images have been stitched to mimic the twin's tattoos.

Roses amongst vines, a leaping rabbit, a small key like the one now branded onto my own palm. More back lace peeks out beneath the puffy skirt around my thighs, trickling my sensitive skin.

There hasn't been a single afternoon in the past year in which I haven't been spanked, bitten, and thoroughly fucked by the Tweedles. Now teatime is fast approaching and I'm getting angsty. But this celebration is one the entire kingdom is invited to, and I dare not deny a royal decree.

Rows of stalls direct us to meander through the greenery, the circus theme carried throughout. Colorful buntings connect stalls selling small crafts, food, homemade candles, and the likes. Balloons of Chesh's face float high above, looking down as she would be. She never could miss an event. Dotted in between the stalls, game stands have been prepared, an array of prizes swinging from their rafters. But it's not those which hold my interest.

Couples fill the field, walking arm in arm, hands in back pockets. Humans, animals, and vampires–all back with their soulmates, smiling and exchanging swift kisses. Not a playing card person in sight.

I halt sharply to let Dormouse wander by, a very handsome rat in a fine suit holding up her tail as they cross a particularly dirty patch of ground. She pauses in her floral dress to wave at me, before continuing towards a miniature stand selling marinated breadcrumbs. I link hands with my own vampires, my chest swelling as they give me the same loved-up eyes as the other couples passing by.

Goblins with dreadlocks play flaming toy pianos, a fire spitter on the next stall dancing in translucent lingerie. Creating a gap between stalls, I look down to see my main man Stan, sitting at a kissing booth. He has an impressive line of bugs and small mammals, all waiting to be blessed by his twitching nose and tickly whiskers. What a legend.

I stop at the next stand, drawn in by an otter juggling paintball. She flinches at my approach, quickly placing the paintballs on the counter and wiping her paws on her apron. Pointing to the wall of white roses with a shaky arm, she steps back, lowering her gaze. Cash takes my daisies, acting all chivalrous as if I didn't see him toss the bouquet into the flame-spitter's fire in my peripheral vision. Swinging my arm back, I throw the paintball with deadly aim. It hits the central rose, exploding on impact to splatter every petal in thick, red paint.

"You win!" the Otter cries, relief flooding her furry face. I reckon she would have said that even if I'd thrown the paintball way off target. Reaching behind the counter, she produces a giant teddy version of PB in his heart-trim suit. One of the many heroes from Shadow Slaying Day; none of which are us.

The pig himself hasn't been seen since fleeing Hatter's cottage last year, but rumor has it he's shacked up with a human bachelor with a taste of pork. I'd bet my immortality I'm not the other one with a collection of teeth imprints on my ass. Good for him. I hug the teddy to me, beaming as Tweed rolls his eyes and continues on.

It doesn't take long to spot the Shadow Slayer herself–Arabelle. Sitting upon a throne, her heart painted lips are pursed. Boredom leaks from her amber eyes, her chest heaving a sigh in a stunning gown of red and gold. The queue before her eagerly awaits the flick of her wrist on a fake guillotine, a plastic blade lowering upon the man currently in the booth. The flash of a camera captures his wide smile, while the Queen looks ready to procure a real blade to finish the job. It must be hard being a celebrity.

“Keep moving,” I remind the twins. “You know the rules.”

It took a whole two days for the new Knave, a very serious-looking ox with a machete, to pay us a visit at Club Dee. Or as it’s been renamed–Club Chaos. Arabelle has fully assumed her role as Queen Bitch, starting with our banishment from Heart Kingdom, with the exception of public holidays. In those instances, we may enjoy the festivities if we keep a significant distance from Her Royal Majesty and not allow our gazes to linger. Punishable by beheading.

Tweed hangs his head, his shoulder slumping against mine as we turn away. For the rest of the year, while tucked away in the cottage the twins have built behind the club, Tweed can find purpose in loving and pleasuring me. Although, I suppose when presented with the life he once lived, the sense of purpose he felt, and the lives he served to protect, our banishment really hits home.

Cash, however, is thrilled about being exiled, preferring to dance his nights away in the club and fuck the mornings away with me. I don’t mind. As long as those who come to watch him only do so with their eyes, they’re doing me a favor in bypassing foreplay.

The sound of music leaks through the stalls, drawing me towards a flattened grass circle. I hold Tweed’s hand tight, leading him into the center without room for argument. Cash spots a vendor he’s been trying to stock at the club, and falls into a business conversation I have no interest in.

The music is coming from a small band of pixies, tinkering on their instruments with nimble fingers. Their laughter rings out as they sing an upbeat melody, the kind that makes me want to twirl around the circle and lose myself in the moment. Tweed, however, isn't a natural dancer.

Tugging on my hand, he pulls me into his body, our feet moving to a slower rhythm than those dancing wildly around us. We sway, my head resting on his shoulder as the strength in his arms surrounds me. His breath tickles my neck and, even in broad daylight in a crowd of strangers, I let my eyes drift closed.

"Is it going to be enough?" He breathes beside my ear.

"What's that?" I roll my head on his shoulder, peering at his hardened face. I knew Tweed would struggle today, returning to his old home and seeing those he once considered family. But we can't hide forever.

"The life we have. Hunting prey after dark, reading in front of the fire, throwing parties for three, and becoming lost in our bodies. Is it going to be enough for you fifty years from now, a hundred? Thousand?" My eyes widen, looking to the pale blue sky. I mean, Tweed just described the ideal lifestyle. What more could a girl possibly want?

"My gorgeous Tweedle," I purr, stroking his cheek. "Have I ever been one to struggle with entertaining myself?" Tweed manages to find a smile and presses a kiss against my forehead. Secure in his arms, I can't help but feel like this is all a dream. In the real world, I have never experienced such an overwhelming feeling of joy and comfort in another person's arms. Tweed could always read me like an open book, knowing exactly how to calm my fears and insecurities. And in this moment, his possessive touch just does that. Finding that comfortable spot on his shoulder, I muse at the joy filling my heart and exhale loudly again.

"That was totally a sigh!" He jolts me upright. Green orbs filled with worry look me over, Tweed's features all too tense again.

"I'm not sighing," I smile warmly, placing kisses on his jaw until it slackens. "I'm at peace. Stop worrying. I'm not going anywhere and nothing will hurt us ever again." Tweed's eyes linger on mine, a note of concern still there but we'll work on it.

Within time, Tweed will learn to relax. He's too used to being on high alert, preempting the next threat at every turn. When it's just us three, alone at home, it's easy to forget the outside realm exists. But when faced with the reality that the world continues to turn beyond our vibrantly colored walls, it's all too clear how easy it would be for someone to attempt another takeover. If that happens, so be it. We'll face the fight when it comes, but I'm no longer looking for my next adrenaline rush. I have enough thrills right here.

Out of nowhere, I have the strangest notion. "I love you," I whisper in Tweed's ear. A second presence suddenly presses against my back, Cash's hand slipping into my hair and tugging my head backward.

"You're not seriously dropping the first L-bomb without me involved, are you?" I hear the hint of amusement in his tone. Whereas Tweed is in fully macho, protective mode all the time, Cash is always ready to lighten the mood. He doesn't get hung up on the push and pull of our dynamics; we're all walking unsteady ground here, taking it one day at a time. Besides, Cash doesn't need the repetitive reassurances like Tweed does.

"You know how I feel for you," I drag my fangs over Cash's jaw. "Both of you."

"Yeah, I do," Cash groans as I dip my mouth towards his neck. "But I want you to say it in front of him." Rolling my eyes, I grab a forearm of each twin and rush us through the crowds and stalls. Beyond the field, I keep running until we enter the quaint town where the Hattery sits. Down the side alley, I throw Cash against the wall, snarling with the full length of my fangs.

"I fucking love you." My hand curls around Tweed's throat, tossing him against the brick beside his brother. "As much as I love you. You two are my heart, soul, and spirit. There isn't one of us without the other." Holding them both in place, I let the beat of my heart, now fully in-sync, pulse throughout the alley. We're one being, an entity which only needs one another to thrive.

Two pairs of emerald green eyes begin to glow with love and desire. Their breathing grows erratic, swallowing hard beneath my palms. I shudder at the raw power I'm holding, the bodies of tattooed muscle pinning themselves against the wall without trying to fight me for control. The Tweedles have submitted to my will, and finally accepted the love I'm prepared to give.

Breaking through our moment, a gong rings out, drawing a steady stream of beings toward the town square. I bite my lip, needing to control the desire which refuses to be contained. With an immense amount of willpower, we fall in with the line of vampires and their mates, preferring to mix with a crowd that doesn't despise us.

The town is mostly the same, a mismatch of animals in dresses locking up their shops and glaring my way. To the north, a new building stands tall behind all the rest–a rehabilitation center and blood bank for those 'cuisine challenged.' Only Gryphon would have the idea to make it a whole damn restaurant looking over the river, serving a range of liquid copper delicacies.

"Here ye, here ye!" Hatter awaits in his giant top hat and tails, his year-long beard parted in two big braids tied back on either side. He stands next on a plinth by the water fountain, urging us all closer to the linen-covered statue. "Come witness the unveiling of Wonderlust's hero!

The Shadow Slayer has commissioned a statue to remind us–no one is too small, too insignificant, or too insane to make a difference." Hatter continues to repeat this several times, waiting for a large enough crowd to come close enough. Arabelle is amongst the fray, her throne being carried over.

Hatter catches sight of the Tweedles and I, and flaps his hands to draw us to the front. "Behold, the Shadow Slayer's Hero," he smiles, seemingly only speaking to me. The glint in his eye is unnerving. Gripping the linen, his smile lingers in my direction and my heart flutters. Those gathered begin to count down, giddy with excitement that resonates in my chest. Three, two, one! With a gigantic whoosh, Hatter whips the cloth free of the impressive statue, a ball lodging in my throat as I look upon...

"Humpty Dainty?!" I shriek, my jaw hitting the floor. The twins catch me as the small egghead pushes her way through the crowd, almost knocking me onto my ass. Ignoring the fact her carefully crafted dress is the Diamond replica of Arabelle's, the crown atop her flowing blonde wig nearly poked my eye out. "You've got to be kidding me!" I turn to glare at Tweed and Cash, outraged by their bewildered silence. "She wasn't even there!"

"Oh, thank you! Thank you!" Humpty Dainty cries, accepting the dozens of flowers being thrown at her from a cheering crowd. Through it all, I catch Arabelle's hidden smirk. Oh, that's low, even for her.

"I can't believe it's been a year since we defeated the witch who terrorized our lands!" The crowd cheers again as Humpty Dainty climbs the podium to stand beside the fourteen-foot version of herself in shining marble. There's a sword seethed to her army attire, one leg poised as if she's scaling a mountain. "I only wish my beloved King was here to witness such a glorious moment. Alas, I know he'll be watching on from beyond his early grave." Dainty gives me a pointed look, and those nearby take a step back.

In the twisted tale of events Arabelle has allowed to circulate, we three were Lillianna's thugs; killing off the competition and using my own Allure to lead many men to their deaths. The vampires know different, but no one believes the dead. Cash is first to clear his throat, signaling we should duck out early. I let the twins fall back first, giving Humpty Dainty a hand gesture which symbolizes my fist being shoved up her ass. There's no way in hell the Diamond King agreed to marry that freaking egg. I'd bet my right biker boot he didn't even know she existed.

Somehow, I find the will to exit without causing a scene. Lingering at the back of the crowd, tucked into the shadow of an alley, the Verax hovers in all her gnarly beauty with a huge orange afro atop her hand. I give her a small wave, making a heart shape with my hands. I'm still determined to make her my bestie. On the edge of town, Cash awaits by the two motorcycles we rode in on. Seemed fitting for a trio of outlaws. Tweed pulls a helmet onto my head, and assists me climbing on the back of Cash's bike.

"Drive safe," he warns his brother. Cash's chuckle is drowned out by the roar of the engine catapulting us along the graveled path towards the forest. As we speed across the uneven terrain, I feel my heart beating in rhythm with the thump of the bike beneath me. The wind whips around my large skirt, and I smile behind the visor, relishing the freedom we've been gifted. I wasn't lying when I told Tweed that Arabelle did us a favor. Beyond Red Kingdom, there's no one and nothing, but fresh air and vast land. My home and my Tweedles.

The journey takes longer by bike, but I much prefer it to running, watching the world pass in a blur of motion. Woodlands become coastlines, and onward towards the border of Heart Territory. As the sun begins to set, Cash eases off on the throttle and pulls onto a side road that leads us up a hill. The serenity of the rolling fields soothes me as I snuggle into his back in comfort. We've left the chaos, drama and politics far behind, coming to rest at the top of a large grassy mound with sprawling views of all four kingdoms below us.

Cash cuts off the engine, allowing my feet to hit solid ground before climbing from his bike. There's an old log, carved into a bench only large enough for two bodies. I take my cue, removing the helmet and settling to face the sunset while Cash opts to sit side-saddle to face me.

"Is Tweed joining us?" I raise a brow. Cash takes my hand, letting his thumb travel along the thin white lines of my palm.

"Not this time. We'll meet him at home." Dropping his emerald gaze, I watch Cash intently studying me, tracing the invisible map he's memorized to perfection. Contrary to normal, his presence is calm, pensive. The silence becomes too much so I lean into his body, admiring how perfectly we fit together. Despite coming from different worlds hostile to one another, I could remain snuggled in Cash's hold until the end of time. "There are a few things I wanted to say," Cash swallows thickly. I remain against him, keeping myself out of his line of sight so he can speak freely.

"Tweed has needed you so much this past year, and I'm so thankful for your patience and attentiveness with him. Slowly but surely, I can see my brother coming back. Still a protective, bossy asshole, but the love in him swells every passing day."

"But..." I continue when Cash stalls.

"But I don't want to hold myself back anymore. I don't want to spend my nights in the club, giving the two of you space. You've never once made me feel like a third wheel, but it's only a matter of time. I want to be present for you, in every way possible."

"Cash," I breathe, sitting upright. "I had no idea you were holding back. I thought you wanted to dance."

"I do love it, but not more than you." Cash's eyes fill with an emotion I haven't seen him show so freely before. It hits me hard in the chest. "I love you so fucking much, Malice. I want to spend every moment by your side, making you laugh, seeing you thrive. And in the times where you can't conjure a smile, I want to be the one who brings it back."

I stare at him, stunned and speechless. All this time, I thought it was Cash who needed space to be himself, but it turns out–he was doing it for Tweed. If I hadn't already given him my heart, I'd be throwing it at him now.

"I love you too, Cash," I whisper, resting my forehead against his. "But not because you make me laugh. There's so much more to you than the comedy clown you hide behind." Cash scoffs, a hint of sadness in his tone as he turns his head away.

"Yeah, right."

"I'm serious. I don't love you because you're funny. I love you because you chase away the shadows of my self-doubt, fill me with light when I'm drowning. Tweed's my anchor to sanity, but you're the lifeboat which keeps me afloat in a chaotic sea. You don't hold me down or bind me to one place, you give me the freedom to find my own way and I know, with you," I turn him to face me, "I will never, ever be alone again."

Leaning in to press my lips against his, a kiss which was meant to be gentle erupts into something much fiercer. Our tongues tangle, fangs clashing in a frenzy of passion. Cash's hand tangles in my hair, pulling me closer as the kiss deepens. I moan softly into his mouth, overwhelmed by the intensity of Cash's passion. This isn't like all the other times where he flips me over and makes me see stars. This is something else entirely, filled with love and the desperation to be closer than our bodies can allow.

Pulling me up onto his lap, I wrap my legs around Cash's hips, our arms tangled in a tightened hold as if we never want to let go. Our mouths move together in perfect sync, a dance of desire and longing. He pours every emotion he can't explain into that kiss, his love and devotion for me evident in every touch. Gasping for breath, Cash's hands pause just beneath the net of my skirt.

"I can't fuck you right now without Tweed. We made a deal."

"Oh yeah? What kind of deal?" I smirk, the butterflies in my chest tripling. Standing in one, smooth motion, Cash walks by over to the bike and plants my ass on the back.

“It's our anniversary, Crazy One. A whole year since we became official. No one is sitting with his dick in his hand, watching on tonight.” Cash lowers the helmet over my head, luckily cutting off my girlish giggle. I don't think I've ever made such a noise, but I'm not wholly sure I'm myself right now. My head is light, a little dizzy, and I feel like I might internally combust. Is that what love is?

The ride back to Club Chaos is a race against the vibrations rolling between my legs, doing half of the work of foreplay. I'm fairly certain Cash can scent my arousal, because his hand on the throttle is starting to bend the handlebar.

As the club approaches, Cash vaults from the bike, grabbing me off the end and allowing it to speed into the nearest tree. Apparently, we're ignoring the explosion which follows. Cradled in his arms, he runs the rest of the way, bursting through the front doors while I struggle to push the helmet off my head. It's all for show anyway, since I can't die twice, but I appreciate the sentiment.

"We're going to fuck you senseless," Cash laughs, the sound ringing out as he pries the helmet from my fingers. "You have no idea what madness is yet, Crazy One. You won't be able to remember your own name by morning."

I lick my lips, eagerly accepting the challenge.

Still cradled in Cash's arms, he zooms me up the spiral staircase and into his old apartment. Dust sheets cover the furniture, the light flickering a few times when he turns it on. Placing me on my feet, Cash leads me to the closed bedroom door. I smell burning, enhanced with the sweetness of apples and an undertone of leather. Twisting the handle, I open the door to see what Tweed has been up to in our absence.

The room before me bears no similarity to what used to be here. Deep crimson coats the walls, the wooden floor gleaming under the glow of apple-scented candles and twinkling lights. The bed, lined with plush red satin sheets, holds three sets of manacles. One is attached to the wall behind, while the others are easily ten feet long and hang from the ceiling to hold a leather contraption. My core twists at the sight, a shudder rolling through my spine. Whatever it is, a weird sex swing or mechanism to restrain me, I want in it. Now.

As soon as I step into the room, Tweed is behind me. His arms wrap around my waist, pressing me against him as his lips scatter tiny kisses across my neck, his free hand already tugging at my dress to remove it. His sinful mouth trails upwards, nibbling at my ear while he unties my corset. One strap hangs diagonally on my shoulder, baring one breast for immediate attention. Cash is at the ready, dipping my dress low enough to suck my nipple between his fangs, just firmly enough to make my knees weak. I groan, my senses colliding all too fast.

"Boys," I moan. Tweed delivers a quick, harsh spank to the back of my thigh. "I-I mean, Tweedles. I need a minute to freshen up." I seek for an out to catch my breath. After the anticipation which has been building all day, I want to get a grip and make sure this lasts all night, as Cash promised. Pulling back slightly, they both just stare, faces taut with arousal.

"There's no need, we can wash you. Bathe you, massage you. Whatever is required." Cash grabs the back of my hair, pulling my head back to expose my neck. Tweed matches the movement, whilst edging me towards the bed.

"Offers I will take you both up on, but a girl needs a moment to herself sometimes." I slip out of their hold. "I'll be right back. Feel free to get started without me," I grin devilishly, edging towards the bathroom. The twins follow me hungrily but I hold up one finger, easing the door closed between us. Moving to the basin, I splash cold water on my face. My heart beats erratically in my chest. I've been with the Tweedles in every which way imaginable, but tonight feels different. More intense, after our admissions of love and the care Tweed has taken to set this all up. Our anniversary. Fucking around is easy, safe. This is real relationship shit.

Drying my face on a hand towel, I glance at my reflection. I've allowed Tweed to ink my skin as and when he sees fit. A butterfly in black, white and violet sits upon my neck, matching the patterned artwork Tweed has inked over my chest, along with a certain diamond dagger we all now have on our left arms.

I stroke my fingers over my body, pushing the dress to the floor. Sensing the twins on the other side of the door tugging on their cocks, I smirk at myself, at peace with who I've become. A lethal being craving blood and lust as if the pair go hand in hand. Still batshit crazy, but as someone who has finally found a way to be loved. The word bounces around my head, giving me a dizziness akin to vertigo, causing the mirror to seem like it's rippling. I steady myself on the basin, squeezing my eyes tight and blinking them open. The glass is no longer moving, but it's not my reflection I'm looking at. Well, not really.

An image of myself appears. A huge nest of blonde hair, a blue dress made of paper. Hugging a doll to her chest, she rocks on an inch-thin mattress in a simple room. One I know all too well. I squint, leaning in further.

Suddenly, her head turns to look towards the matching plastic mirror in her cell. Sliding from the bed, she pads over, peering straight back at me. In complete unison, we raise a hand and place them together. Crystal blue eyes meet, locking with uncanny certainty. Around her shoulders, there's a shimmer to suggest a feline is curled around her neck, a tilting smile glinting in the low light.

The breath locks in my lungs, the world around me beginning to crumble and seep away. The mirror separating us vanishes, allowing our fingers to interlock. Tears well in my eyes, spilling over as she refuses to let me go. Opening her mouth, I barely hear the words she says, although it's clear they aren't for me. They're intended for you.

*"So I put it to you, dear reader, where does this story end? Did Malice find her destiny, or was it all pretend?"*

# AFTERWORD

Before you set the lynch mob after me, that ending was a necessity. Malice doesn't do conventional. I sincerely hope you have all enjoyed this chaotic duet as much as I've enjoyed letting my inner crazy loose. I'm sated for now, but no doubt Malice will make her appearances throughout my other works soon enough! I've always had a thing for writing twins and I'm so thrilled I was able to give the Tweedles the glow up they deserved.

Until next time, happy daydreaming!

# ACKNOWLEDGEMENTS

During the course of writing Embrace the Mayhem, I've faced many trials in my personal life. There were times when I thought I wouldn't find the words to finish it. This book is truly a testiment to others around me who continue to boost and support my work on a daily basis. Family, close friends, encouraging indie authors and readers I can't thank enough. I hope Malice's wild ride has done you proud.

**A special thanks to:**

**Jo** for her incredible editing skills.

**Kristina, Lou and Joy** for being my Alphas.

**Megan J Parker-Squiers** for the cover and **Nautilus Visuals** for the illustrations which inspired this duet.

**Lewis Carroll** for the chaotic and limitless world he has opened up for so many imaginations.

**And lastly, my readers**.

It's plain and simple; I'm nothing without the readers who support me! Thank you all for devouring my books, and also becoming my friends. I love getting to know you, seeing your gorgeous book shelves and building connections with so many talented and wonderful people.

# FREE NOVELLA!!

**Wait! Before you close this book, I have a super spicy treat for you!**

Beautiful Delusions is a free novella which is downloadable from my website (www.authormaddisoncole.com). You can expect:

- Reverse harem
- High school setting (of university age)
- New girl on campus
- Foster brothers who like to dominate
- 'Pet' internship to suit their eclectic tastes
- Extra spicy group sessions
- Pierced D
- An introduction to all of Maddison's characters via halluncinations

Sounds like your jam? check out the blurb below and head over to my website to download for FREE now!! Also available in paperback from Amazon.

Blurb:

Reality or Fantasy? Who knows.

Sophia hasn't been lucky in life or love, but this new school will be different. Her anxiety prescription is filled and the library is nearby. That's all this bookworm needs to remain invisible and survive her final semester unseen.However, the Thorn brothers did not get the memo. Claiming her as their 'pet', Sophia is thrown into a world of sex and secrecy. Of dares and doms. But that's the least of her problems.

Without access to her meds, the books Sophia reads to escape begin coming to life around her. Her world is warping, her mind slipping. Battling the delusions and escaping these brothers is a full-time job, and she can forget attending classes. The Thorns have vowed to rule her mind as well as her life, if only their new pet would let them.

# OTHER WORKS

If you're a new reader to Maddison – welcome to the Mole's Burrow!!
Maddison is a married mum of two, and a serial daydreamer. As a huge fan of all romance tropes herself, it was time to pen the stories which consume her mind most hours of the day.
As a child, Maddison was a jet setter and has lived all over the world, only to return to the south east of England, where she is now happily settled.
With a double award in applied arts and art history, Maddison is a creative with a dark passion for feisty females and spicy stories.

Join my Newsletter or on my website:
www.authormaddisoncole.com
Facebook – **Author Maddison Cole**
www.facebook.com/Maddison.cole.314
Facebook readers group - **Cole's Reading Moles**
www.facebook.com/groups/colesreadingmoles
Instagram and TikTok - **@authormaddisoncole**

***Other Works:***

**I Love Candy**

Dark Humor RH - Completed

- Findin' Candy (novella)
- Crushin' Candy
- Smashin' Candy
- Friggin' Candy

**All My Pretty Psychos**

Paranormal RH with ghosts and demons - Completed

- Queen of Crazy
- Kings of Madness
- Hoax: The Untold Story (novella)
- Reign of Chaos

**Bound by Fate**

Fated Mates Shifter Romance

- Moon Bound

**A Deadly Sin**

MMA Fighter BSDM RH - Standalone

- A Night of Pleasure and Wrath

**A Wonderlust Adventure**

A Twisted Menage Retellling

- Descend into Madness
- Embrace the Mayhem

**The War at Waversea**

Basketball College MFM Menage - Completed

- Perfectly Powerless
- Handsomely Heartless
- Beautifully Boundless

**Co-Writes**

- Life Lessons with Emma Luna

www.ingramcontent.com/pod-product-compliance
Lightning Source LLC
Chambersburg PA
CBHW070424170726
48291CB00002B/341
*9781916521032*